THE PROFESSOR AND THE SUICIDE GIRL

A NOVEL BY NICK TOTEM

For Dylan & Mila

'The most beautiful things in the
universe are made of paradoxes.'
—The Doctor

Dear Professor:

I am writing you about a most wonderful discovery, one that will bring about a new understanding of the orders of biological entities to which you have devoted your life. This discovery will herald a new era of effective treatments and bring about the alleviation of pain and suffering for countless millions . . .

I humbly ask you to come by my office at precisely 10 a.m., the fifteenth day of March, whereupon a fresh specimen will be made available to you for further study . . .

With this letter in his hand, the professor of virology mounted the steps to a door, on which were the words: Center for Modern Medicine. The conspicuous gall seized him for a moment. Modern medicine must come from the test tubes and microscopic twirls of DNA being manipulated to yield secrets and thus miracles. Having recently been promoted to assistant professor at a world–famous university, the Institute for

Advanced Science in Los Angeles, he knew something about modern medicine.

At the counter, a lone receptionist raised her tired eyes.

"Yes," her throat buzzed.

"I have an appointment with the doctor," the professor said.

"Have a seat."

He glanced around the waiting room. An arrangement of chairs took up all the space along the old, yellowish walls. There was not a plant or a decorative object in sight, but worst of all, there was a feel of the sixties' decor. On the ceiling, dim white fluorescent lights blinked now and then. In all there were fifteen chairs, all occupied by patients—all of whom were very old. An air of obedience hung over their faces by which he could reckon the state of their mind—delirium, Alzheimer's disease, semi-comatose, or general obtuseness. Doubt suddenly rose in his mind, and he turned back to the receptionist.

"I'm not a patient." He handed her the letter.

"Oh, another one," she said as she looked at the letter, and then she raised her eyes to him with a sort of puzzled disbelief on her face.

"Any problem?" the professor couldn't quite decipher her look.

"No. Please come in."

The door next to the counter clicked open, and he hurried in. Behind him, diseases of all sorts seemed to fill the air, and reflexively his hand closed off his nostrils lest he get infected. He fled into a hallway whose walls were stacked high with boxes of paper and books.

"Doctor, someone is here to see you," the receptionist yelled down the hallway before resuming her place.

Alone in the narrow hallway saturated with a stale odor wafting from the back, the professor dithered. Doubt increased manyfold, and the absurdity of the endeavor struck him. Could this be a twisted hoax? Straight ahead, the hallway seemed far off, appearing as a kind of illusion, an uncertain opacity. He slowly looked back at the door through which he'd just entered. But as he was about to take a step toward the exit, a voice grabbed him from behind.

"Follow me."

The voice startled him so badly that he dropped the letter on the darkened floor. Much farther along the crammed hallway, the professor made out a figure highlighted by a white lab coat and a head of white hair with an intervening face made shadowy by dark eyes behind a pair of glasses. He looked down at the letter on the floor and then back at the white lab coat. Then he stared back at the floor, which must have been blackened by decades of shuffling, dragging, pattering feet, and saw bacteria and diseases everywhere. The dithering intensified. He bent slightly, preparing to pick up the letter and cringing as he did so.

"Follow me," the white lab coat commanded.

"Coming," he uttered meekly and dutifully stepped over the letter.

In silence, he was led along the crammed hallway that became narrower and narrower. Now and then his shoulders scraped against flaps of paper that jutted out from the boxes on both sides. A pale fluorescent bulb blinked every dozen feet or so, and under the dim light the white lab coat appeared to have a brownish tinge, resembling more a butcher's smock. They went on. After a while, the professor realized that the uncertain opacity he'd noticed earlier at the end of the hallway did not mark the end but in fact the beginning of a very long hallway. Unable to see beyond the gray head of the doctor, he felt as if he was descending straight down a precipice. His heart began to palpitate, and he began to breathe rapidly.

"Doctor, how much farther?"

Shhh . . . shhh . . . came the answer, the noise made by the doctor's lab coat scraping against pieces of paper. Now a smell of moldy dust filled the air.

Nausea drummed in his stomach, bubbling up his throat in uncontrollable waves.

"Urrrr . . ." Gas escaped his mouth. "I don't think I can go on."

Just then the doctor stopped abruptly. The professor almost ran into him as the doctor turned around with a snap and said, "Here we are."

To the left side of the hallway there was a clearing that opened up to a tall door. Now that he was close up to the doctor, he could study the doctor's features—white hair; a nose with a slight bony ridge; dark knowing eyes under dark brows exuding a similitude of omniscience; and a strong, slightly pointed chin. A sort of mesmerism projecting from the doctor's eyes through his glasses seemed to reassure and at the same time stoke up the professor's sense of foolish gullibility, so that he felt as if he were being marked for experimentation.

The professor tried to regain his composure and said, "Where are we?"

The doctor didn't answer right away but studied the professor intently. The slightly curly brown hair; intense, startled brown eyes; thick eyebrows; strong chin; angular face; and compressed lips—the professor appeared youthful and seemed to fit an archetypal scholastic type.

"We're here," the doctor said at last and gestured to a tall door at his side.

"How far have we gone?" the professor said.

"Far? Twenty yards."

The professor looked back, and the door through which

he'd entered indeed appeared about twenty yards away. He could have sworn he'd gone a mile.

"Please don a mask." The doctor indicated a box of surgical masks sitting on a stand next to the door.

"Yes, of course." The professor put on a mask.

After putting a surgical mask on himself, the doctor pointed to the door and said, "After you."

Under the dim light, the professor scrutinized the brass door knob, leaning in to bring his eyes closer to it, and he imagined colonies of bacteria happily camping out on the surface. He could smell the gases of bacterial fermentation rising into his nose.

"Interesting, a classic case of nosophobia," the doctor spoke softly, but he was loud enough to be heard.

"All right," the professor muttered. Pressing down hard on that repulsive, nauseating bubbling in his gut that seemed to come whenever he was about to get his hands dirty, the professor clenched the door knob and twisted. No movement. The door seemed glued to its frame. He rattled the knob while his throat emitted a low pitched rumble.

"This is a sterile room. As such it is necessary to maintain a constant positive pressure inside. The pressure is precisely calculated and maintained to be twice the atmospheric pressure," the doctor explained monotonously, his voice warm but with an authoritative distinction. Then he pounded on the door with a closed fist.

The door popped open, and the professor, who had been leaning in toward the door, tumbled into the room against an outward rush of air.

Glaring white light momentarily blinded the professor. Trying to recover his vision and orientation, he stood very still while holding out the hand that had touched the door knob as though it was contaminated.

The professor squinted, and when his eyes were fully adapted to the bright light he beheld an enormous man lying prone on a surgical bed that had been configured into an inverted V shape so that his head and feet were lower than his buttocks. The abundance of the man's face gave him a cheery cherubic quality, but his deep-set eyes also had a peculiar focus and a willful intent. Those eyes looked at the professor's outstretched hand, and the man said somberly, "I am sorry. I'm unable to shake your hand." He had a German accent. A blue sanitary drape covered his body, with the exception of his head, feet, and rump, over which an antibacterial glistened. Next to the surgical bed, a table had also been covered with a blue sanitary drape and that displayed various accoutrements for the impending procedure—large syringe, big bore needles, surgical gloves, scalpel, etc. A strong smell of alcohol and formaldehyde whiffed of sterility to the point of suffocation.

"Hello." The professor stared at the enormous man on the surgical bed.

"Professor, I present to you the nuclear physicist. He's world famous by the way," the doctor said. "Nuclear physicist, this is the professor of virology I spoke to you about."

"It is a pleasure meeting you," the physicist said.

"Likewise. Did you say world famous?" the professor said while still holding out his hand and glancing here and there for a sink, an alcohol swipe, anything to clean his hand with.

"Yes, the nuclear physicist is world famous, I assure you, though you've never heard of him," the doctor said without a hint of sarcasm. He walked to a sink and proceeded to clean his hands.

The professor followed him and waited patiently as the doctor scrubbed his hands. Since he'd been preoccupied with his contaminated hand, only now could the professor truly take in his surroundings, and he was awed by the room's enormity, its dimensions extending many yards distally, and its fabulous configuration of machines, some of which he recognized. There were supersonic centrifuges, super–porous chromatography columns, a heavily magnetized spectroscope, and in the far end a chemical fume hood with the glossy shine of a Rolls-Royce.

"As I informed you in my letter, there is a distinct possibility of discovering a novel human leukemia virus," the doctor's voice boomed above the splashing water. "We're all familiar with the murine leukemia virus, which infects only mice; however, the virus inside the physicist infects human. Our famous nuclear physicist is rather unfortunate to have been infected. When he came to me, he was convinced that an exposure to radiation early in his life had caused his leukemia, but I thought differently."

"How was he diagnosed?" the professor said softly while he continued to inspect the machines.

"The characteristic clumping of the DNA, the dysmorphic shapes of the blood cells," the doctor replied. "Though it can be difficult to tell by looking through the microscope, thus the need for DNA analysis, which of course confirmed the diagnosis."

Glistening under the bright lights, these machines of science seemed to vivisect space itself and rearrange it into a sort of organism, so much so that as the professor gazed, he heard only vaguely what the doctor was saying.

"What's more, I'm convinced that his leukemia was in fact caused by a novel viral agent," the doctor went on, and having finished scrubbing his hands he walked toward the surgical tray and began to dry his hand and to put on gloves. "This is where you come in, professor."

Warm, stale air accumulated behind his mask, and the professor hurriedly scrubbed his hands.

"You will extract this virus. You will sequence its DNA. You will characterize the mechanisms by which it causes human leukemia," the doctor announced. "And you will become famous. Like the rest of them."

The last announcement seemed strange to the professor; perhaps he hadn't heard correctly but he was quite sure that this was something he wanted. "What do you mean?" he asked. His ears honed to the doctor's voice.

"You will be famous . . . as famous as the nuclear physicist here, I assure you, though ordinary people have never heard of him, and never will, because of a certain metaphysical anomaly," the doctor said sternly.

"What metaphysical anomaly? What are you talking about?"

The doctor turned to him. "The slippery nature of the will. You will or you will not, not in the sense of an action in a future time but of an action as according to your design and choice. This is the very crux of this particular metaphysical anomaly." He then turned to the tray of equipment next to the surgical bed.

The juxtaposition of the cluttered, narrow hallway against the state-of-the-art machines inside the lab, and the cogency of the doctor's assertions against the oddity of his statements about fame and metaphysic, suddenly became clear to the professor and made his head buzz. A cold sweat oozed on the back of his neck as the professor with bland eyes stood there, trying to gauge the situation in which sanity could be missing.

"Well?" the doctor snapped. "Aren't you going to put on gloves?"

"Why?" the professor jerked back.

"To help me."

"Can't you do it yourself?"

"No," the doctor said calmly and slowly. "Inside the physicist's hip bone is the virus. A new human leukemia virus. Do you not want it?"

"All right, all right."

While the professor put on the gloves, the doctor positioned himself next to the physicist and began to speak to him. "Now, we've already talked about it. And we've already gone through the steps, haven't we? You need not fear anything. I'm here for you. I've given you Marcaine, a powerful local anesthetic. You won't feel a thing. And more importantly you have to make sure that I can do my job. You see . . ." Here the Doctor's voice became slow and mellifluous. "If you make unnecessary noises then I won't be able to concentrate. I'm sure you understand, don't you?"

"Yah . . . yah," the Physicist said through clenched teeth.

"All set." The doctor's voice resumed a stern authority. "Let's begin. Professor, kindly stand here and hold onto his buttock to steady it. Be careful not to contaminate your gloves. Now below the skin is the iliac crest, a part of the pelvic bone. It has a great deal of bone marrow." The doctor lectured monotonously. "It's one of the places in the human body where white blood cells are manufactured. It is from here that we'll harvest the cancer cells . . . for you to study and for me to cure the physicist."

With his hand over the physicist's fleshy heap of a buttock, the professor was seized by a repulsive fascination of a queer type in which the disgust of touching a stranger's buttock, let alone a man's, was indistinguishable from the onset of a fascinating sensation, a gelatinous warmth he could hardly imagined to be originated from matters. Nitrogen, oxygen, carbon and a plethora of starry combustion waste, thus arranged, had given form to this flesh under his gloved hands.

"Wait. Wait." The nuclear physicist panted loudly. "It hurts. It hurts."

The doctor hollered, "I haven't done anything yet. You must have courage. Courage, man. We're all lost without courage."

"I'm so sorry. Yah, yah. Courage. Go on. Please."

"The procedure I'm about to perform is a bone marrow harvest," the doctor resumed his monotonous lecture. "The patient is positioned in a prone position. Due to his copious size, this position will serve us very well. In leaner patients, they may have to be in a lateral position which would allow us to approach in a superior to inferior fashion . . . " The doctor began to assemble the instruments as he spoke.

Nitrogen, oxygen, carbon, and all the elements from starry combustions eons ago thus arranged—the professor's rumination resumed—constituted human flesh and invited spirit; how wonderful it was that the same starry combustion waste, differently arranged, could become a jelly fish, a rock, or a man.

" . . . Now in this case, it's noteworthy to anticipate the anatomy. First the needle will penetrate the skin in which there are various nerve endings, more specifically pain fibers. Next there is a layer of fat and in this case it will be rather thick. Next the muscles. Then things will get interesting when the needle hits the bone. You see the periosteum is thick and has more pain fibers. But first, the instruments. The needle I'm going to use is a cutting needle."

Then, very swiftly and silently, the doctor thrust a gigantic glass syringe with an equally gigantic needle into the white heap of flesh, and, encountering resistance, pushed hard, grimacing. At last, soft, squishy, red marrow was seen filling up the transparent syringe as the doctor withdrew the plunger. In a quick yank, he extracted the contraption. The doctor placed a thick gauze over the puncture wound.

The physicist groaned.

"Kindly put pressure on the gauze while I process this marrow," the doctor said.

As the doctor went off, the professor fidgeted awkwardly and averted his eyes from the buttocks, and had to fight the fear of germs getting through the gloves onto his hands. Droplets of sweat soaked his mask.

"Thank you, professor," the physicist said, turning his head to look at the professor.

"But of course, you're most welcome. I should thank you instead for letting me have your bone marrow," the professor replied, bending down toward the cheery cherubic face. His voice now resumed its normal clarity.

"No, thank you for agreeing to study my marrow. Perhaps you'll help cure me, yes. It is my great hope. So thank you."

"Very well. You're welcome. Was it painful at all?"

"Nay, not at all. The local anesthetic worked quite well."

"Considering all the noises you made, one would think that you suffered a lot of pain."

"No pain. It was just the idea of it, you see."

"Idea?"

"Ideas scare me," the physicist said. "That's why I try to keep them all in my head and never let them out. One day I will tell you about my ideas for making nuclear bombs, quite revolutionary. But that will have to wait. Right now I cannot help having ideas of pain."

The professor sensed an opportunity to mine information about the clinic, the doctor, and the types of modern medicine being practiced here. He said softly, "So have you been under the care of this doctor for long?"

"Oh, yes. I was most fortunate to find him. He's a most capable doctor. His method is almost miraculous. Miraculous but terrifying, simply terrifying," the physicist said.

"Terrifying? Tell me more," the professor said.

"Yah, the doctor cures diseases of all kinds. Physical and metaphysical kinds. You'll see. You'll see about the metaphysical anomaly. Now that you are here, you will see."

"Metaphysical anomaly," the professor repeated, and he raised his eyes again to the shiny laboratory machines as though to verify his whereabouts and to reassure himself that he hadn't wandered off into a mental asylum.

"My name is Truheckler," the physicist said. "It is awfully nice to meet you."

"Conrad," the professor said hurriedly.

"In time he'll lead you to Minh the Marxist," Truheckler said softly. "Metaphysical nutcase but a most famous Marxist, a legendary revolutionary that the world will never know. His plan won the Vietnam War, almost single–handedly. Now a peddler of chickens. The chickens have wonderful viruses inside them. Yah, in time. But be careful of the doctor, Yah, a metaphysical virtuoso . . . "

"A Marxist . . . a peddler of chickens . . . "

"Minh the Marxist, he will give you chicken viruses to study, yah."

But before the professor could press for more information, footsteps sounded from the back.

The Doctor appeared, holding a cooler. He said, "Here is the specimen. A quick spin through the centrifuge. It'll be a great boon to mankind once the virus is isolated and identified." He handed the cooler to the professor and said, "Long live mankind."

Straightening up, the professor didn't know exactly what to say, so repeated through his face mask, "Long live mankind."

"Yah, long live mankind," the physicist said softly from under the cover.

Nine Months' Gestation

One fine morning nine months later, Conrad N., the professor of virology, was strolling to his laboratory. His steps were light and brisk. He was sending his work to the premier scientific publication today. He would announce to the world the discovery of a novel virus.

Conrad had been laboring almost continuously for nine months, and he had found the work most exhilarating. From Truheckler's bone marrow, Conrad had isolated the virus, which he had named the Human Leukemia Virus. Under the electron microscope, he had seen the shape of the virus, the first human being to do so. From the virus's spherical body, prodigious spikes struck out in all directions. "Dmitri!" Conrad had exclaimed when he first saw it a few months ago, "Come and look at this beauty."

Dmitri, a trusted laboratory assistant, had come running to look at the computer screen. "A true beauty," Dmitri had said in his heavy Russian accent. "You publish and show the world, Professor."

"Yes, soon," Conrad had answered.

And today, he would send out the paper that had taken months to prepare, which would contain the DNA sequence of the virus and its specifications.

Conrad quickened his steps as he neared the building in which his laboratory was located. He smiled to everyone he saw, although everyone he met seemed to be in a grave mood and looked at him strangely. He hopped up the steps and waltzed into his laboratory, one of the biggest on campus. He said good morning to the various students, to the many postdoctoral fellows, but they, too, were acting in a weird way as they kept their heads down. He dismissed their behavior; perhaps they were concentrating on their own work.

He went into his office. It was spacious and bright and had a wide window with a view of the quad below. Often times, Conrad would sit by the window and have a cup of coffee as he meditated on the nature of the viruses and college students alike. Toward one wall, a bookshelf filled with technical books and bound journals rose all the way to the ceiling. An acrid smell of bacterial broth sometimes wafted into his office from the adjoining lab, but he found the smell not entirely disagreeable. On his desk were various papers being worked on, charts of data, notes filled with calculations, and journals in different stages of being read. And as always, there was a bottle of hand sanitizer within reach.

Conrad's fear of bacteria as well as his many phobias had begun at the age of thirteen, at a moment he could mark with the exact hour and minute: his father's funeral. His beloved father had died of complications of appendicitis. The man had suffered abdominal pain for days but had resisted his wife's pleading. "It is just food poisoning," he had said and thought he could cure himself with antibiotics left over from a previous bout of pneumonia. Finally, when the pain had worsened and his abdomen had begun to swell, he conceded defeat and went to the hospital. The doctors operated on him right away, but it was too late. He went into septic shock and died within two days.

At the conclusion of the funeral and before the coffin was closed, Conrad's mother urged him to say goodbye to his father, but he could not come close. All Conrad could see was bacteria everywhere, on his father's face, on the coffin, and even in the air. How he wanted to kiss his father, to hold the hand that had held his, and to whisper into his ear some words of goodbye as he journeyed onto the beyond. But he couldn't. He couldn't budge from where he stood, at a distance, with tears blurring his eyes. It was then that the fear of germ took complete hold of him. At about the same time, his fear that his destiny was not his own to control, that life was capricious and free will might not exist at all, emerged and became unshakable in his mind. Over the years, these uncertain phobias morphed slowly into different types of paranoia, so much so that he didn't own a cell phone or a modern car for fear of being listened to or followed. And he would only use computers when absolutely necessary. Though he knew his phobias were irrational and could frequently subdue them—such as during swimming, which he had been good at in college, or when being intimate with women—he hadn't been able to master them completely. No matter how hard he mustered his will power, he had not been able to cure himself, and because of this failure his phobias at times gripped him so tightly as to incapacitate him. But it was also from the death of his father that he wanted to know all about viruses and bacteria, the unseen that existed along side the concrete world. And so he became a virologist.

On this morning sunlight filtered through the branches outside the window and shone through pleasantly. Conrad sat down at his desk, and without even thinking his hand went for a squirt of antibacterial sanitizer. *I like to study bacteria and viruses, not to get them on me,* he had often said whenever he was asked about his nosophobia.

In front of him was a journal, opened to an article. As his eyes gleaned the title of the article, his thoughts were cut short and his lungs seemed to fail him.

"Hah," he squeaked weakly. He focused on the article. Unconsciously he picked up the journal and brought it close his eyes. "What is this?" he said to himself. "No, this can't." But right there in front of him was an article with the title "The Specifications of a Novel Human Leukemia Virus," and the author was someone whose name he immediately recognized.

"Dmitri!" he screamed for his assistant. "Dmitri. Dmitri."

Almost instantaneously, Dmitri appeared at the door. Under bushy eyebrows, he squinted at Conrad. A mass of graying hair rolled down to his shoulders, and a thick beard reached below his neck. He said, "Yeah, Professor."

"What is the meaning of this?" Conrad's eyes opened wide and glared with a crazed look. His hand shook the journal in the air.

"The chairman published the virus."

"How can that be? It's mine. I took it from Truheckler. I . . . we did all the work. It's not possible."

"He published, Professor."

"He stole it from us." Conrad flung the journal down on his desk. "Nine months of work. And all this time he kept coming over here to ask us about our progress. I had no idea. I never suspected that he would steal it. I told him everything. I shared everything with him. I even gave him a sample. He said he wanted to help. To let me know if he found something I didn't. He said he just wanted to see for himself." Conrad spoke breathlessly, and with each sentence he seemed to realize that he should have known Abe's true intention.

"What we do, Professor?" Dmitri asked timidly.

"I'll make him pay," Conrad howled, grabbed the journal, and marched off.

ABE F. WAS THE CHAIRMAN OF THE MICROBIOLOGY DEPART-
ment and had been for over ten years. In fact, he had been a
member of the committee that had interviewed and hired Conrad seven years ago. His office was in a building adjacent to
Conrad's. It took Conrad only a few minutes to get there. Abe's
laboratory was bigger than Conrad's, and Conrad had to trek
past the glaring eyes of countless students and postdoctoral
fellows to reach Abe's office.

"What is the meaning of this?" Conrad yelled well before he
had reached Abe's door.

Some students, who had been meeting with Abe, scuttled
from the room frantically.

At the door, Conrad trained his eyes on Abe.

"Oh. Hello, Conrad. How are you?" Abe said.

The casual tone of Abe's voice infuriated Conrad.

"You know very well why I'm here. What is the meaning of
this?" He held up the journal.

"May I take a look?" Abe said.

Conrad entered the office and threw the journal at Abe,
who caught it and opened to the correct page as though he
knew exactly where to look.

"You stole my work," Conrad screamed.

"Calm yourself." The calmness in Abe's voice persisted as he
perused the article in front of him. "I don't know what you're
talking about. It's an article about a virus that we've been
working on for all these months. We publish dozens of articles
every year. This is just another one."

"What . . . huh? What are you talking about? You know very
well that's the virus I discovered. That's the virus I gave you.
You're not going to get away with this. You can't do this."

"You just said it, Conrad. You gave me the virus to work

on. It's just that we finished the work before you did. You can't expect us not to publish our results we've worked very hard to get."

"You can't be serious. You're twisting my words. I gave you the virus. No, I allowed you to have a sample because you asked to see it for yourself. I never thought you would do this to me. You know exactly what I mean. Stop twisting my words," Conrad cried. The white of his eyes flashed at Abe.

"But dear Conrad. Why would you give it to me if you didn't want me to work on it? You give a virus to a virologist and expect him to do nothing?"

Abe's voice seemed to grow more and more mocking as he spoke, which caused Conrad to feel a pressure in his neck, choking him. "Ah . . . " he gasped and then breathed heavily for a moment. "I'll bring action against you. You'll see. You'll pay for this." Abruptly he turned around and marched off, trying to control the shaking of his body.

Conrad headed back to his own lab, but as he approached his own building, he stopped and turned his eyes upward to the second floor where his office was. He realized now that it was Dmitri who had placed the journal on his desk. All the work through all those months, through all those years before that, seemed to have been voided by something invisible but real enough, something like the confluence of air currents that could bring down an airplane, or wreck a man's life. There was nothing in his lab anymore. Conrad turned away. He walked unconsciously, and his mind busied itself with remembering and conjuring from its deepest recesses all things he had heard and seen, so as to make sense of it all. A forlornness crept up on his face. His feet performed their perfunctory duty, while his mind chased after something he had heard and found absurd quite some time ago but his life now seemed to depend on. At last he saw a bench, and feeling a tiredness in his legs, he sat down. He was at a bus stop. Unbeknown to him, he had walked across the campus, and then for many miles along Sunset Boulevard, and he had walked for hours because the sun was now at high noon. All at once he was startled to realize his immediate whereabouts but also more profoundly the thing that his mind had been chasing after. "Ah . . . ah . . . that's it," he said to himself. "This is what the doctor had warned me about." Warmth returned to his forlorn face as he looked about expectantly. A couple of people sitting on the bench eyed him suspiciously as though he was one of those mad homeless men who loitered around bus stops. But Conrad didn't seem to care and continued to speak to himself. "A metaphysical anomaly." All his fears suddenly came to him as the metaphysical world appeared more real than the concrete world, and he gasped. Abruptly he jumped and began to run back.

3

Suicide Girl

In the months following the theft of his work, Conrad N. became increasingly despondent. He often took long walks along the beach, contemplating not only the nature of his work but his own free will as if he had no control over his own life. He had sued Abe F. and the university, and in doing so had nearly gone into bankruptcy. The trial had ended in arbitration, more than a year after he had gotten the virus from Truheckler. As far as Conrad was concerned, he had lost the case. As a part of the settlement, he had been given full tenure as a professor, but Abe F. had gotten all the credit for discovering the Human Leukemia Virus and the potential monetary rewards as well.

On this day, as he was walking, he looked out over the ocean. The water was a grayish blue, and surfers bobbed here and there in the water. Just at the water's surface and immediately above that in an aerosolized mist existed a microscopic world the surfers would never discover. But he had a special privilege, a window on this world of microbes, just to observe and sometimes to nudge them here and there, a world whole unto itself whose phylogenic roots extended as far back as any other living things. He could see how the surfers might inhale the microbes through their nostrils, from where the microbes would wind their way into unseen places, into the nasal cavity, sinuses, trachea, and bronchus to rest in the alveoli; there they would multiply—one to two, two to four—until the power of exponentiation would collapse the lungs, making the surfers drown in their own fluid. Then, if that weren't deadly enough, the microbes could very well latch onto to a blood vessel, a vital conduit to the brain, and there by that same power they would multiply again. A meningitis, a murderous headache, and finally a wish for a quick death.

How about a deadly virus, he contemplated again as he had often done in the past few months. A virus capable of bringing death to them all.

He walked to the south, away from the surfers. Along a deserted stretch of the beach, the guard towers were all shuttered. Behind him lay the pier, the long concrete structure that started like a centipede, cut through the sand with longs legs, all the way to the waves. The sun hid behind the monotonous gray dome of the sky, and now and then glowed brightly enough for him to see the movement of thin wisps of clouds. The wind seemed to intensify, and under its power, a pillowy expanse of dust rose at the edge of the sand and unfurled all the way to the boardwalk and beyond. In the distance, banners along the shops fluttered violently. The palms swayed. Dust wrapped the houses with brick–colored roofs in haze.

He quickened his steps, trying to pass beyond an imaginary boundary to an undetermined destination. His nostrils sucked in the fresh, cold, salty air, and once he felt the air pass his throat, he held his breath to let it inflate lungs and crevices unknown. His black, heavy jacket was buttoned up to his neck, around which a scarf had been coiled and tugged tightly. Over his head, he had put on a wool cap, which enveloped it whole, and over his eyes was a pair of dark sunglasses. His fingers, snug and warm inside his pockets, touched the edges of

the notebook, the most important object in his possession—
a manifesto that encompassed all his writings.

He saw pelicans searching for food and running out every
time the waves receded.

Then ahead of him he saw something across his path. A
line cut across the smooth surface of sand, which was otherwise unblemished. Curiosity spurred, he hurried closer, and
as he approached, he beheld footprints in the sand, leading
out to the water. The front parts of the sole had pressed deep
into the compact sand, while the heels barely left any traces.
It was a quick dash into the water, and he turned to scrutinize the waves. In between the six–foot high crests, the
water's surface zigzagged violently to the tempo of a mad
percussionist. And there was no line of footsteps coming out
of the water.

Suddenly, he saw it. The black head bobbed with the
rhythm of the waves, and as the wave crested he could see
the plume of black hair in the water. Here, she must have
entered the water and began drifting with the current farther
along the beach. He gazed at the black head, which at times
was poking above the edge of the wave and then disappearing
in a mist of vapor. The plume of black hair enlaced with white
foam as though it was intent on making its home among the
waves. With increasing wonderment and bewilderment, his
vision was lost in the movement of the black head.

"What a fool to be out there," he muttered. "Pity, she must
have a death wish."

With his head hanging and shaking in disbelief, he continued
his trek. A few steps farther, the reality of this thought, perhaps
being carried by the searing cold wind, finally struck him.

"No, could it be true?" He spun around and trained his eyes
on the black head. The longer he stared, the more substance

the thought seemed to accrue. Yes, who would even think of swimming in this condition? And it made perfect sense; a deserted beach, violent waves, and a quick dash across the sand into the frigid water—there couldn't be better a setting for ending one's life.

A suicide girl. But how could he be sure? He decided to remain still, watching and thinking. How can anyone be sure that their action isn't killing themselves in some ways? How can anyone be sure that at any moment in their short lives their insignificant actions are not suicidal?

He laughed.

Perhaps, he could just study the girl as he would the bacteria in a petri dish—to see what would become of her; if her body would lose its balance as the waves continued their ferocity; if, at any moment now, the waves could pick her up and toss her into the air, pretty feet and all.

If the setting was perfect for a suicide, it was even better for him to watch this tentative act in progress, all with impunity. He scanned the beach; from where he came, the surfers were barely visible, busy riding waves—no other eyes around to implicate.

Soon his eyes became lost in the movement of the black head, the vertical movements dictated by the waves. In its movement, he could trace out a sinusoidal function as the earth revolved through space. How perfect she looked; crest, trough, amplitude, and especially periodicity, recurring forever, suddenly reminded him of recurring flu outbreaks, as timely as the winter solstices to cull the weak. But more than that, he quickly realized, the beauty of the sinusoidal function, generated by a suicidal act, was nothing more than an absurdity. Beauty through death? But . . . but, he deliberated; wouldn't saving one who's wishing for death be equivalent to killing one who's clinging to life?

As he contemplated, the black head continued its stubborn movements, as though inured to the worst that the waves could muster.

If she toppled already, she would spare him indecision; she has floundered long enough.

He must do something. But why? As with the intention to create a deadly virus, just because he could. Or perhaps because there was still an iota of humanity and compassion left in him, which he didn't want to acknowledge. Whatever the reason, he decided to interfere, not so much to save her but to prevent her from killing herself, which to Conrad represented a small but critical difference.

"Hey, hey," he screamed at the black head, but his screams were muted against the booms of the crashing waves. He continued to yell and waved his hands, pacing closer to the water's edge. Perhaps he could race to where the surfers were and beckoned them to do his bidding, but seeing how far out they were, he wouldn't be able to get their attention. Despite any of his ratiocination and abhorrence for the cold water, he knew that the next eventuality demanded a physical act.

He threw off the wool cap and the sunglasses, and sunlight glared in his eyes. A moment ago, the clouds had opened up and the sun now beamed obliquely a bright swath of light along the immediate stretch of the beach, and in the presence of the light, he saw a clear sign, egging him on. The scarf and the heavy coat flew off. Cold seeped through his dress shirt, but he unbuttoned it quickly. He kicked off the shoes and the socks in a couple of movements, efficient and graceful. The pants fell easily enough. Now, down to his boxer shorts, he clenched his teeth as the wind ripped at his skin. "Ahh," he moaned, and remembering the quick dash of the footsteps, he ran into the water.

At thigh deep, the cold numbed his legs. "Argh," he shrieked, but he kept on, moving out toward the egging light. A wave rolled toward him, and the water flowed over his nipples, constricting his chest and numbing his entire body so that he felt his manhood shriveling into a vestigial appendage. Automatically, he panted quick, shallow breaths. Another wave enveloped his head completely. When he emerged on the other side of the wave, salt water dripped over his eyelids, and his vision blurred. The black head appeared farther out; had he misjudged the distance? Underfoot, he lost the sensation of sand, and his arms began to claw. But he was swimming toward the black head.

In the water, time could only be measured by the incoming waves, and he had lost count of its relentlessness. Even though he had been a good swimmer in college, his arms now swung, and his legs kicked, doglike and out of form, because he hated immersing his head under dirty sea water. His heart slammed around inside its cage, as though it was trying to escape a death sentence. Every time his mouth rose above the water, he sucked in air along with some portion of water, and his tongue was bathed in salt. For every forwardly propelled paw, he was pushed back by the wave, but he was making progress; he was out far enough that the water rose into a high wall he must then sink into to emerge on the other side. Once on the calm side of the swell, he searched for the black head but saw nothing human. In the vision of that nothingness, a chill inside him, colder than the water, percolated outward from its hiding place inside his chest, and he panicked. Could he have imagined it all? A mirage? A phantasmal siren was luring him to his death. The clouds opened up farther, and the sunlight, now more intense, shimmered on the water's surface.

Then, as the swell crested and lifted him high, he turned around and his eyes caught the black head some twenty feet away from him, which brought instantaneous relief that he wasn't mad after all. As his perception was transformed while in the water, he had swum out much too far, and now he must change his heading. He pawed vigorously toward her. Every few seconds the water swelled high, carrying him up with it, and passed through, leaving him behind.

Her pale, ashen face barely floated above water, and the black threads of her hair, flowing outward web-like, seemed to truly interlace with the strange substance formerly known to him as water. She appeared suspended effortlessly. A jelly fish in dead water, a dandelion in a permanent breeze, a planet transmigrating on a moonless night. Her outstretched arms barely flapped and her head was propped up well above the water. The dark eyes, slightly elongated, stared sharply at an ephemera that only existed somewhere at the tip of the crested waves.

Now within a few feet of her, this nymphlike apparition, his doubt redoubled. Surely, there was no struggle here, no last–minute regret in the throe of a final breath. He, however, saw in the intensity of her stare a disquiet of transcendence and an otherworldliness.

"Hey, hey . . . Are you . . ." he managed to let out before he was smothered by a wave.

She glanced at him. A brief smile broke out over her purple lips.

Baffled, he came closer. Now, he faced her and he could see behind her the empty beach. As the water swelled, it lifted him first so that as each wave peaked high, he rose above her, and as the crest became the trough, it was she who looked down upon him.

In between hurried breaths, he managed to yell, "Are you all right?"

Her face didn't move. When he was lifted up by the water, the sunlight threw his shadow over her face, which was punctuated by two glazed eyes. In a quick flash, the glaze on her unseeing eyes shattered his assumption and pulled away reality from underneath him. Something awful from her eyes shot askance at him and electrified through his limbs, making them move in confused jerks, and he sank. Under water, he felt the numbing cold in his toes and fingers morphing into an aching pain, a dull tiring pain that he also felt in his limbs. Sinking down farther until his feet touched the sand, he kicked against it, propelling himself up, splashing through the surface, gasping for air.

Through vision blurred by dripping water, he saw her floating as before, unperturbed. He pawed and kicked frantically. But he couldn't move an inch, and the nymphlike figure was still in front of him. Suddenly he felt her arms latching onto his shoulder. With a wave rising high behind him and with resurgent excitement, he tried to move with the wave, to steer them both toward land. But a resistance somehow thwarted his efforts. "Let's go," he screamed, his voice muffled by the water. Another wave rose behind him, and with all his might he pedaled for land. But he felt no landward movement; his only motion was the vertical displacement caused by the wave. He no longer had any doubt, he was being anchored in place as her fingers clawed into his shoulder. With each wave cresting he felt himself being elevated higher, a gesture similar to a mother's holding up her child. During the brief instant when he rose high above her, her eyes squinted at a vision just beyond the edge of his head as though his head, having suddenly gathered incredible mass and thus inescapable gravity, was now capable of diffracting light straight into her soul.

The instant passed. That which elevated him now depressed him toward the trough of the wave; his head went under unexpectedly. He blew bubbles from his nose, trying to push out water. His chest ached for air. Despite his struggle, he couldn't surface, as though the creature was intent on smothering him. Just as fast, the process reversed itself; now he was elevated up high as he had been a moment ago, as light diffracting around his head, as her eyes lost in seeming religiosity. Then back down again to near fluid suffocation, and reversing again, and again. The same periodicity would help him breathe, and he timed his ascendancy to inhale a lungful of air. His arms slowed and his legs fluttered lightly, but he still floated, cocooned in a sinusoidal fluctuation, uncontrollable and yet there was no need for control, being cleansed of his mortal fibers with each douse into the numbing cold.

There were no eyes around to witness how long they were together as such.

Totentanz, the thought sparked in his mind. Phalanges interlocking, radius rubbing against ulna, hollow sockets staring endearingly into one another, bony pelvises colliding—a macabre tango of two skeletons, like a psychic worm, burrowed its way into his mind. And it terrified him. "Let go," he shrieked. "Let go." His limbs, after a brief respite, were now energized enough. He broke free of her clutch and dove with the wave. He glided along the wave's face, and then he was slammed by the collapsing wave. Scraping painfully against the sand, he tumbled about, head turning down and then finally popping up. At the ever changing transition of water into air, he clung to life with half breaths, and his vision was rendered useless. Finally, partly walking whenever his feet touched the sand and partly pawing through liquid turbulence, he stepped upon firmness and thrust himself onto land. On fours now, he crawled the last few feet while the waves slapped him from behind.

His rabid heart, banging against its cage throughout the whole tango, now seemed to escape into his stomach, surfeited with seawater, convulsing painfully. As he crawled a few feet more, his esophagus ejected a curvilinear spray of seawater. Stomach slime streaked down his neck as he stood up. Cold wind whipped against him, and his body trembled in response. The pummeling ache in his limbs and chest and the burning in his esophagus for the moment made him forget the near drowning, or perhaps the rays of the watery reality lost coherence at the demarcation of land and thus could not be perceived by a terrestrial consciousness. In any case, free from recent terror, he took a few steps forward, but then a squeeze of his stomach made him bend over. He got down on all fours and closed his eyes.

A hollow sound echoed in his ears, clogged with seawater. With eyes still closed, he hit the side of his head, trying to clear his ears, but the sound grew louder with each tap. A shadow flickered behind him. He opened his eyes, looked around, and jumped back. The girl stood there. The sunlight glaring behind her hid her face from him, but on the sand he saw a line of footprints leading to the feet themselves.

"What the fuck?" she shrieked. Her hands flaring out like fans flapped along her side as she spoke, "It's like you got a death wish."

"Ahhh," he gasped. He jumped up, wiping stomach slime from his mouth and scanned the beach, searching for his clothes. At a distance away, his clothes lay scattered across the sand. He scuttled toward them, his wet boxer short stuck to his crevices.

"What were you trying to do? Kill yourself?" Her voice chased after him.

Fine sand particles, stirred up by the wind, struck his legs with pointillist pricks and adhered to his wet skin. The cold seemed to have traversed his core, passing through on its way to the opposing surface, and he shook with jerking tremors.

"Did you hear me?" Her voice remained annoyingly loud, and it occurred to him that she was following him.

Was it a suicide? Misgauging his aquatic ability, and her voice drifting with the wind and informing him of his own self-reflexive thoughts, all revolved around his head unresolved.

He picked up his trousers, held them out, and balanced on one leg as he tried to slip the other leg in, but as soon as he lifted one leg, the other foot lost balance, and he fell on the sand. Quickly he jumped up and found half his body covered with sand. Ignoring the sand, he slipped the trousers on. With an iota of self-respect restored, he looked for his shirt.

He heard the shirt flapping in the wind. Holding the shirt with both hands, she offered it to him. He snatched it from her.

"Are you okay?" Her voice, perhaps tenderized by the wind, now sounded melodious and soft. "I didn't mean to yell at you. But you know, you looked like you needed help out there. We could have drowned together. We got all tangled up."

Without buttoning his shirt or hearing her, he turned to find his shoes. The sand had partially buried them and his socks had vanished along with his glasses, scarf, and wool cap. He grabbed the shoes, emptied them of sand, and stuffed his raw feet into them. As he was doing so, he glanced at her figure, which was toned and refined in a black swimming suit. She stood there looking at him, seemingly impervious to the cold. With her right hand she bundled her black hair together, and with a flick of her left hand she squeezed from her hair the last of the seawater, and at last, as though now strictly terrestrial, she assumed solid form. From the pretty feet, her legs elongated into high thighs, curving hips, narrowing into waist, and blossoming fully into delicate shoulders. Without any bit of awkwardness, she went to pick up his black coat and shook it in the air to get rid of the sand.

"Are you okay?" she repeated, approaching him. "I'm Diaphany by the way."

Diaphany, the strangeness of her name, seemed to batter his ears. An anguished sensation urged him to flee, to burrow into the sand if he could, to get away from her voice, a mocking and disguised sincerity.

He yanked the coat from her. Their eyes crossed and opposing images entered the respective retinae. Her slender eyes bent slightly at the narrow tip toward the side of her face and imparted a subtle gentleness. Below the straight nose, the purplish lips were becoming pink, and the raised cheeks were complemented by full lips. Lingering on her for a few seconds, enough time for him to study her, as he put on his coat, he absorbed all he needed. And closing his coat around him, as though redrawing the battle line, he turned away.

"It's you who have a death wish, Miss," he pronounced.

He lifted his chin and walked away. As he trekked slovenly across the beach with sandy particles inside his shoes and clothes chafing against his skin, he mentally recounted her image. He was not mistaken, because he had seen fine lines ran across her wrists, many more marking the pale smooth skin along her arms, where the skin had opened and let out its vital fluid. The scars were like the insignias a soldier would earn after many battles. Deeper scars appeared as dark jagged shapes on the thighs, where without doubt the cuts had gone too deep, twisting and contorting about and speaking of unknowable despair.

"Suicide girl," he muttered as if to comfort himself. "Look at the scars on her. I was right about her."

Then he coughed, inhaled deeply, and coughed again, expelling mucus from deep within his lungs.

With the cough, he turned his attention back to himself and realized that, during his struggle with the waves, he had inhaled microbes through his nostrils, from where they could wind their way into unseen places, multiplying as they went—one to two, two to four.

4

A Hypochondriac

From the beach Conrad ran to his car. The 1975 Mustang swerved out of the parking lot, sped along the street, and screeched to a halt at a stop sign. The engine rumbled with a series of staccato bursts, and the slight scent of seaweeds wafted through the vents. Farther from the beach, along the wide boulevard, all the traffic lights were red. As Conrad waited for the light, his hands tapped on the steering wheel, and he mumbled a repetitive, tongue in cheek murmuring, perhaps an incantation to command the traffic light. The light turned green, he shifted gear and the car jerked forward. After a short block it screeched to a stop a few feet behind another car, and then the tapping and the incantation resumed.

In the minutes since ingesting the microbe–laden seawater, he feared that their number inside his stomach must have doubled. He must halt their progression. In his mind, the route, through the streets, through his front door, down the hallway to his bathroom where the antibiotics were kept, was already measured and drawn out. He wasn't sure what concerned him more—the actual microbes, or the antibiotics disturbing the precarious balance of all his vital organs, the balance that has been maintained by a meticulous schedule of a vegetarian diet, vitamins, regular colonic cleansing, and, most importantly, a state of mind that remained untroubled by adhering strictly to said schedule. The use of antibiotics would destroy the intrinsic microflora that have been coexisting inside his body, and it would also screw up the precarious balance that he had maintained in a Zen–like state. What followed would inevitably be a disastrous tipping of that balance into a multitude of predictable and easily diagnosable ailments that would surely drive him mad with symptoms, real or imagined. He grew queasy with indecision.

He burst through the front door. The modern house, with only two bedrooms and twelve hundred square feet of space, had been rehabilitated with sleek stones covering the front, and low hedges of equisetum. Inside there were straight lines to everything, from the furniture to the walls and ceilings, as though hiding places had been prohibited. Behind the front door, he threw off his clothes, which must be dealt with later. He scrubbed off the sand from his naked body and walked in a straight line so as to limit spreading contamination on the floor. In the bathroom, he stood before a mirror and examined himself. To his relief, there were no injuries. Particles of sand sprinkled his hair.

In the drawer, bottles of vitamins and herbs were neatly arranged. Toward the back of the drawer, he saw a bottle of antibiotics, which he had used some months before, and picked it up. Despite the doctor's warning and his own knowledge of the mechanism of bacterial resistance, he had taken them randomly whenever he felt a certain twitching in his liver, or a heaviness in his chest. A slave to his phobia, he had been unable to resist the compulsion to do so now and then. The situation, however, was wholly different this time, for he had actually ingested dirty ocean water filled with bacteria. If he was to take antibiotics, he must take a ten-day course. He shook the bottle, and from the tablets rattling inside, he estimated the number of tablets remaining, no more than two days left. He ran to the living room, to the telephone on his transparent acrylic desk. He inserted the cord into the phone and quickly dialed the number.

"This is Conrad. Let me talk to the doctor," he said.

"The doctor is busy," a woman said.

"I have an emergency. I have to talk to the doctor right away."

"What's new? You always have an emergency. Hold on."

Classical music came on; a screeching violin assaulted his ears, a tone shifted, and the violin now at a different frequency moaned. Tethered to the base of the phone by a cord, he stood over the desk, holding the receiver, and looked at his naked reflection on the desk's acrylic surface.

"Yes, this is the doctor. What can I do for you?" the doctor's voice came through the receiver.

"Doctor, can you call in a course of antibiotics for me? Please."

"Oh, it's you. Conrad. You were fine when I last saw you. What symptoms do you have?"

"Hah, it's complicated . . . you see . . . earlier at the beach, well, I went in the water." Conrad felt flustered as though he were being quizzed.

"We've been over this before. I can't give you antibiotics just because you feel different, because the weather just changed, because you just came back from a walk on the beach," the doctor shouted. His voice was distinctly commanding, bordering on chastising. "If you want antibiotics, you'll have to come in for an exam. For God's sake, you're a virologist, you should understand the effects of indiscriminate antibiotics usage and bacterial resistance. Why do you want to harm yourself? You should know better. Do you understand?"

"But . . . but," Conrad tried to say a few more words.

"No but," the doctor's voice rang out from the receiver. "You know my policy."

He heard the click of the phone while still trying to speak. He put the phone down.

The air inside the house, only slightly warmer than the air outside, seemed to tighten around his shriveling skin. With head hanging low, he unplugged the phone and scuttled back to the bathroom. Enough time had passed for another doubling of the microbes. He picked up the bottle of antibiotics, and as he was uncapping the bottle, he felt sharp pain digging into his shoulders. Turning his back to the mirror every which way, he saw red marks punctuating his shoulder where the girl had held onto him.

"No," he gasped. He'd been injured. Her sharp nails had punctured his skin during the struggle, though he had felt no pain. The capillaries in his skin had opened, blood had escaped and subsequently clotted, and microbes in the seawater had invaded his circulation, migrating to all of his vital organs. "No," he uttered and thought of running to the phone, calling the doctor again to demand a course of antibiotics.

But then a fear spontaneously inflated squarely in the center of his stomach. He felt himself shaken by an extraordinary tremor, which seemed to diffuse throughout his limbs and rise to his head; his body seemed to be on the verge of fracturing. His fingers caressed the wound, his fingertips moving over the indentations he could barely feel; even so they were marks of battle, an ongoing battle.

He turned on the shower and waited for the water to get warm. He twisted and removed the cap off the antibiotics bottle. In his mind, the struggle with the girl who had clawed him had given way to new battle fields in unseen places, in his gut, his lungs, and his blood, where his white blood cells now wiggled a deadly tango of their own against the bacteria. His white blood cells, which long ago in evolutionary time had themselves been microbes, were now part of him; his mitochondria, for instance, also came from an ancient unicellular organism; how befitting it was for this battle among ancient combatants to conclude as it should, inside of him. At the thought, he felt a fierce sensation of camaraderie with his own white blood cells. Giving in to his phobia, he swallowed a tablet.

He stepped into the warm shower, and the water and steam enveloped him. With a meticulous compulsion, he scrubbed every inch of his body.

When he had finished cleaning himself, he took to the floor and wiped it with bleach. His clothes, which had been shed at the front door, went into the washer, and it was then that he discovered his notebook, the manifesto, was missing.

5

A Reason for Living

At last Diaphany M. saw it. In the numbing cold that deprived her body of all sensation, she saw it in the light curving around the edge of the stranger's head and for a moment felt that all was right. More than a visual perception, it was a sense of place, a recognition of finality, a space unto itself that was exactly what she had been searching for nearly all her life. But could she be sure? How could a traveler on a lifelong journey of an intangible nature be sure of her destination? How would such a traveler know that she had arrived when all she had to guide her was an unflappable intuition, one that had been coarsened by repeated failures and passages through alien land?

The stranger disappeared into the cloud of dust. She was left standing on the beach, looking after him, reliving the experience and wondering what he meant when he told her that she had a death wish and whether he was suicidal for being out in the cold waves in his underwear. She noticed his black sock sticking out of the sand nearby, and, a few feet away, something red. She came up to it and kneeled down to pick it up. It was a notebook with a hard, red cover. Immediately, she turned to look in the direction the stranger had gone and thought of running after him, but it was too late. It must belong to him.

She shouldn't have been so tough on him, but that reaction had always been automatic on her part, her immediate reaction to strangers. She went to search for her beach towel; the sand had nearly covered it. She shook the towel in the wind and wrapped it around her, and walked barefoot to her car.

With the car's windows all shut, the still air inside was warm and comforting. The familiar smell of perfume, a hint of rose, light and sweet, reassured her. A quick, obligatory check of her cellphone showed a text message from her manager reminding her of the work schedule. She drove home.

Her apartment was six miles from the beach, straight down Wilshire Boulevard and a quick right turn. The four story building was over a hundred years old. The bluish façade, with its decorative moldings along the rooftop, columns and balconies dotted with geranium, hid its true age inside. Once past the front door, the wooden floor of the lobby creaked; the wallpapers missing in places showed cracked wooden planks; and the elevator rumbled as it descended. The acrid smell of fresh paint from somewhere in the building saturated the air, and Dia sneezed several times as she ran up the creaky staircase. Inside her apartment on the fourth floor, Dia's costumes were laid out haphazardly over the couch, her wooden Buddha statue presided over a side table, and other disparate objects—figurines, books, vases, dolls—littered the rest of the apartment. She dropped the red notebook carelessly on the coffee table. A window drew direct sunlight into the living room in the morning, and beyond the living room were two bedrooms, one of which belonged to Dia. The door to the other was closed. Dia stopped by the closed door and put her ear to it; the whirring sound of machines vibrated against it, and the occasional thuds informed her of life inside.

"Moiro, do you need anything?" Dia called through the door.

No answer. Then a piece of paper slipped under the door and landed next to Dia's foot. Without picking it up, she read the words written in red ink across it: The body has no need for food.

"Okay. I'm working tonight. There is food in the fridge if your body ever needs it." She headed to the bathroom.

In the shower, the hot jets of water slowly dislodged the frigidity of the ocean from her muscles. As Dia cleaned herself, her fingertips caressed the various scars—on her wrists, along her arms and thighs—the same ones the strange man on the beach had inspected, that represented how futile all her endeavors had been. Nearly all her life, Dia had been searching for a place, a thing, a sensation, or even an idea that would answer questions she could not even formulate. And nothing could quiet her daily yearning. An unflagging instinct, like that which drove the salmon's tireless trek across vast oceans, had been drawing her toward clear water from wherever she came. Now pain from a dull blade awakened under her fingertips as it slid along her skin, and pain from the sharp blade was fleeting and came only after the blood had flowed. The pain had conjured a country of its own, gray rocks over black earth underneath an unchanging cloudless sky of a perpetual dusk, but beyond the barren landscape, a horizon glowed with a silvery contempt, daring all those who sought it. And with the first cut on her forearm with a kitchen knife at the age of ten, she had entered the forbidden country, and with subsequent slashes along her thighs and arms she had traversed well into its hinterland. The coupe de grâce was a slit across the right wrist at sixteen, and as her consciousness slipped away through the severed artery, she beheld the silvery horizon that could only reaffirm what she already knew and, since she did not even know what she sought, could not show her anything new beyond its unchanging silvery light. When she woke up in the hospital, having been discovered by her mother, she remembered how cold and alien it had been at the end of that barren land.

Diaphany got out of the shower. In the living room, she began her stretching routine. Her feet tightened and pushed upward, until finally she was standing on her toes but only for a few seconds. With parted legs firmly anchored on the floor, her upper body twirled above the hip. On the floor, her legs split with a perfect straight cut, and her shoulder leaned to one side and then the other. Then she jumped up and kicked with a straight leg high into the air. She went through all the moves that taken together in a sequence became dances, which a few hours later on the stage of the Caravelle Cabaret Club she would perform in unison with five other girls.

Later that night, under the lurid stage lights, the dances came alive to roaring cheers; the dancers became secretaries, nurses, and stewardesses. Their shirts opened low showing pale, powdered chests, and their short skirts accentuated their long, thin legs, but it was mostly their eyes that drew in and held the audience. Even through the bright lights on her, Diaphany could catch their eyes fixating on her features. Not that she cared; on the contrary, their ogling gave cause to her indifference and made them more contemptible in her eyes, more carnal and stuck tighter to this world from which she longed to flee. She danced, raising her leg in unison with her dance partners. Even Hucks H., a hustler known to all the dancers, was there, checking on her, but she didn't return his stare. During her solo performance, she dangled from a cross bar hanging off the ceiling and tap-danced on the bar, deftly navigating beer bottles and cocktail glasses. The boom of hands clapping and the hoots, screams, and whistles from the audience amplified the music so loudly that the foundation of the building seemed to shake. It was only during these dances, as if insular in a forged space, that a certain peace seemed to quench her disquieting searching.

DURING THE INTERMISSION, JOEL S., HER EX–BOYFRIEND, came into dressing room and went to Dia. Sitting in front of the mirror, she was adjusting her makeup, adding powder and lipstick. Cool air flowed in through the back door with the chatters of the other girls smoking outside.

"Hi, baby," Joel said. "You guys were just great. One of your best dances yet. You know what I mean. You got a lot of chutzpah. Helluva show."

"Hi, Joel," Dia said coolly. "Thanks."

"So, how are you doing, babe?" Joel sat down in a chair a few feet away, crossing his arms. He was dressed in a sleek dark blue suit, his collared shirt open at his neck. He looked intently at Dia, and a labored grin hung on his pointy face as if he was trying to hide a peevish condescension.

Dia recognized that look instantly and could guess why he'd come. "I'm doing great. I couldn't ask for more."

"How long have you been back at work now? A couple of months?"

"What do you want, Joel?"

"Nothing baby girl. I'm just saying. You know what I mean. Just checking in on you. Seeing how you're doing. Don't be difficult, baby, you know I care about you."

"We've been over this a dozen times already."

"I get it. It's not like I don't get it," Joel said, and then reflecting for a moment he added, "Well, but really I don't completely get it, you know what I mean? It was like we were having a blast. Going to New York, Paris, London, show open-ings, movie premieres, parties. Didn't you have good time? It was good, wasn't it? Late night jam sessions, the . . . ah." He put one hand up to cover one nostril and snorted air while squint-ing at Dia. "The stuff we had was good right? And the dancing, you were great. It was like you owned the place. I could tell the other guys were like checking you out. They were jealous of me you know."

"Joel, I was there. You don't have to tell me."

"And the private jets. Going on private jet everywhere, it was like an awesome time wherever we went."

Dia applied mascara to her lashes.

"Then what the hell happened? What went wrong?" Joel said. "It was like you were shopping on Champs–Élysée one day, and then you . . . just dropped out the next day."

"I don't want to talk about this, right now."

"Come on, baby . . . You know I can get any of these girls. Any of them would be happy to have what you had. You know that."

"What's this about?" Dia turned away from the mirror to face him. "Really, Joel. It's because you didn't have the chance to dump me like all the other girls before. Is that it? You have to be the one to dump a girl. Is that what this is all about? You want me back so you can prove to yourself that you're the one in charge?"

"Come on, baby. Give me some credit." Joel's voice trembled. "Believe it or not, I care for you. I've never felt like this about anyone before. It's like I can't explain it, you know what I mean."

"Thanks, Joel." She turned back to the mirror to examine her eyelashes. "But let's just be friends. Okay. And do me a favor and tell Hucks to lay off me. It's like I can't turn around without him stalking me and telling me to go back to you."

"Hucks is all right. He's just keeping an eye out for me, that's all."

A girl came in from the back and smiled brightly at Joel. He nodded and smiled back at her. She sat down in front of a mirror at the other end of the room.

"Enough already."

"Come on, baby." Joel lowered his voice. "I got a premiere in New York I got to go to. I'm hitching a ride on a private jet in a couple of hours. You can come with me. It'd be like before. We'll have a great time. They got some good stuff on the plane. It'll be a blast. What do you say?"

Another girl came in and walked up to the wardrobes.

"If it makes you feel any better, just think of it like you dumped me."

"I just don't understand. I thought you want to be in the movies, right? I was going to hook you up with my friends. You know what I mean. We got this whole Hollywood thing sewn up. We got New York and everything in between sewn up, you know it. You know what I mean. We got everything, so I can hook you up with whatever thing you like. Modeling, movies, Broadway. Why are you stuck in this dump?"

"I don't want to be in the movies. Those girls do. You can ask them."

"I just don't get it, and it's driving me crazy. You know what I mean." Joel leaned back in the chair, and exhaled deeply. "It's like what do you want?"

"I don't know, Joel."

"I may even love you," Joel whispered. "There I said it."

From Dia, a suppressed laugh burst out, and she put her hand to her mouth.

"But we had such a good time, baby." Joel raised his voice a notch. "You know, one day we may even get married. You know,

I can't promise anything but one day. This is it, baby. There is nothing there. Don't look there."

Dia shrugged. It was time for the next act.

AT THREE IN THE MORNING, HER MOST CHERISHED HOUR OF the day, Dia got back to her apartment. All was quiet except the usual low pitched whirring emanating from Moiro's room. In the stillness of the night, the concreteness of matters seemed to swell as though having soaked up nocturnal reality, and she sensed the fullness of the coffee table, the couch, and the disparate items strewn about, and was fully at rest. In the bathroom she washed the powder off her face and chest and wiped the mascara from her eyelashes. She went back to the living room, lay down on the couch, and stretched out. The stillness of the night tempered the searching that daylight agitated so relentlessly, so much so that now her mind could hardly conceive of its destructive energy. She yawned as she savored this quintessence of night. Outside the window, darkness was holding off the sun with the heaviness of time.

She turned on her side and drifted off to sleep. A ready dream was waiting under her eyelids. In her dream, cold waves threw sprays of water over her face as she was suspended like a buoy in the water, and her eyes stared at the break in the clouds from where an intense, golden ray beamed down and haloed the stranger's head. That was where she belonged. But where was it exactly? What was it exactly? Her neck twisted here and there, looking and trying to get in the right angle. Don't kill yourself, she heard her mother yelling behind her. I'm not trying to kill myself, Mother, Dia replied. It amounts to the same thing, with you always in the hospital, her mother screamed back. I've never tried to kill myself, she said, and exasperated she turned around to face her mother and instantly began to sink.

She awoke with a gasp. She hadn't slept for long. The first thing she saw was the notebook lying on the coffee table, and the night seemed to have distilled the dark red color of the notebook into blood. She'd forgotten it. It belonged to that stranger. Now she reached for it. Inside the cover was a name and an address. She opened to a page with dense but neat hand writing. She began to read.

"The Book of Cain

On the morning after the third night since the beginning of his dreaming, Cain, son of Adam . . ."

6

The Book of Cain

On the morning after the third night since the beginning of his dreaming, Cain, son of Adam, woke up to the strange lucidity of that ancient sky and knew that he would dream no more and that his dreams had not been merely dreams but revelations of a future truth. Sheep skin cloths hung heavily on his body. Beneath him, voluble vines had been woven into a sturdy bed and made soft by an abundance of leaves, a bed whose growth and shape he'd coaxed and nurtured for three full moons. He'd made this bed of living vines because often times he would sleep out under the night sky, to be among his vines, corn, wheat, apples, pomegranates, indeed a bewildering variety of crops and fruit trees, but also to be among the wild daisies, roses, and daffodils and the countless plants that could not be eaten but somehow pleased him. Under the open sky and away from the warmth of his wife, he would lie among his plants, talk to them, and on moonless nights look up at the heaven full of old stars and young stars being born every night. And on nights when the moon appeared

with changing shapes he would carefully draw its
shapes on parchments of sheep skin and already
could see a repeating pattern and had an intuition of
its usefulness. Beside these things, he also noted the
dew falling on his skin as he lay in the open field, the
movements of clouds, the directions of the wind, and
the deviations of the sun from its apex. He would
chart all that he'd observed into a grand tapestry and
tried to explain it to Adam and Eve, Abel, Adah, and
Zillah, with such excitement that everyone whispered
about him with puzzlement and prayed for his soul.

Three nights ago, after telling his wife Adah that
he would sleep in the field to study the night sky
again, he had gone out with suppressed excitement,
for he had observed that the shapes and movements
of the moon had been repeating themselves among
the stars and that the patterns of the stars would
mark the peregrination of the moon. Heaven itself
could be predicted. He lay down and looked up at
the light of the crescent moon pushing up from the
horizon. A peaceful patience engulfed Cain. Crickets
chirped a soothing rhythm. The sweet scent of wild
flowers hung densely near the ground, and he felt
the crumpled leaves on his back. Running his fingers
along the vines, he could feel as clearly as he could see
during the day the sinuous twirls of tenacity, and he
was glad.

On this first night, a slithering sound had echoed
from the undergrowth of the wheat field. Cain sat up
and gazed toward where the sound came from, and he
saw dimly that it was the soft undulation of the wheat
stalks moving under a cool breeze. He lay down again

and let his eyes drift across heaven, now lingering over the soft flickering of a newborn star, now studying and remembering the formation of three bright stars that were part of a larger formation. The configuration of all the stars appeared familiar to him, as he remembered them, and with closed eyes he could draw them exactly.

'Heaven can be known,' a voice said suddenly.

Cain jumped up and fell on his knees. It was a movement he did reflexively whenever he heard the voice in his head, a voice that resonated from above and that could only come from the Lord God. But he had never heard the Lord God's voice at night, and this voice came not from behind the sun but from somewhere beneath the earth. He decided that the voice could not be from the Lord God.

'Who art thou?' Cain said.

'Thy descendants shalt know me by many names.' The voice was calm and surfeited with an overflowing warmth that put Cain at ease.

'My descendants, but Adah is not with child,' Cain said.

'In time.'

'What dost thou want with me?'

'Only to give.'

'The Lord God hast given all I shall ever need.'

'To give that which the Lord God giveth not.'

'The Lord giveth what is needed for he is infinite and wise.'

'Infinite he is not,' the voice said most humbly.

Such sacrilege Cain had never heard before and it startled him, and he suddenly realized that he had been conversing with two red eyes piercing out from the undergrowth of the wheat, eyes that seemed too far away and at once right in front of him.

'Do not speak thus for the Lord God shall strike thou down.'

'I shalt be struck down if I speak of untruth,' the voice said boldly and loudly.

The same curious thirst with which he saw and approached everything in the world spurred Cain on. 'Then speak the truth lest thou be struck down by the untruth.'

Redness in the dark flickered brightly and said, 'Thou believe the Lord God is infinite.'

'Yea,' Cain replied firmly.

'Thou believe that earth and water and all its plants and animals exist outside of the Lord God.'

'Yea.'

'That thou are also separate from the Lord God.'

'Yea.'

'Thou art not made of the Lord God.'

'Nay.'

'Because thou exist outside of the Lord God, the Lord God is not infinite?'

Nay, Cain wanted to say. But the enormity of this knowledge, this new knowledge that was strange and wonderful and so different from the knowledge of the dirt upon which plants grew and of the plants themselves, silenced him. He sat and thought, going over again and again what had been said. To be infinite, the Lord God must contain all within him, and yet I am not part of the Lord God, I am Cain, he thought. All his reasoning seemed to be answered and reckoned with, without his ever speaking out loud as the crescent moon rose and descended and as the red eyes waned and vanished with the light of dawn.

The roosters awoke him. A dream, an awful nightmare, that must have been all that he had been through, for if he had actually sat up all night conversing with the red eyes he would have been very tired, but he was not. His body was rested and his mind was alert save for the nagging question his dream had left in him. Does thou not exist outside of the Lord God and is the Lord God thus not infinite? He remembered the question but could not answer it. The sheep's baas echoed from over the hill to the west, and he knew that Abel had followed his advice and taken his sheep to graze on a different hill, to rotate the grazing sites. Now the commotion of baaing and hoofs trotting in the early morning and the smoke rising from his house bade him to go about his usual farm work.

But when night came, this most damning question has not ceased to fester in his mind and had colored his vision of his plants, his crops, and indeed all the world in a shadowy pastel of half–reality so that at times he could not tell if he was himself real and proud or only a part of the Lord God. Being a part of the Lord God should make him joyous but it did not; he should be himself, Cain, the first born of Adam, the farmer, the seeker of knowledge. Most of all, being simply he, separate from all things, even the Lord God. A forlorn, troubled look fell on his face as he ate with Adah that night, and soon after supper he decided to sleep in the field again for a second night."

Wow, wow, the words automatically escaped from Dia's throat when she finished reading. Her hands were gripping the red notebook tightly; her back was straight and stiff, and only now could she feel the strain in her back as though she had been fixed in one position for hours. Perhaps she had gone into a spiritual world and only now resumed physical existence. She felt as if she had been there beside Cain. The red eyes had penetrated her soul, and the voice had done more than tell her these strange things, it had spoken to her yearning. She could smell the ripening grains, feel the vines under her, and even sense Cain's breaths. And the Cain she had just met seemed wise and gentle, so different from the one she had been taught as a child; how could that be?

Outside, the hint of dawn streaked crimson across the sky. She looked back at the notebook, turned the few pages that she'd read. Did it take all those hours to read these few pages? How strange, how strange, she couldn't help repeating. What about the second night? What would Cain find? What glorious knowledge would the red eyes reveal to Cain on the second night? And she saw that there were a few pages about something called the Godevil and a plethora of other thoughts but nothing about the second night.

Then, as though she suddenly remembered something, she flipped to the front of the notebook. Just inside the cover was Conrad's name and address.

7

A Conspiracy of Four

A few days later, Conrad steadied himself against the cold wind that every December swept in from the ocean, as he waited. He had convened a meeting with the doctor, the physicist, and the Marxist. "A new virus," Conrad said under his breath, against the cold December wind that customarily swept in from the ocean. All across the sky heavy clouds extinguished all reminders of the afternoon. Standing near the water's edge with his back to the water, he huddled under the shadow of the pier, waiting restlessly for the others. A black coat wrapped tightly around him as if to mummify him, and came up to his chin. His hollow eyes looked on, beckoning the others to hurry. His hair was whipped by each gust of the wind. A cynical disquiet had twisted his youthful face and his cheerful mouth into an unconscious frown, and his dark eyebrows came together as a corrugated wrinkle.

Since the theft of his work, he had grown closer to the doctor, Truheckler the physicist, and Minh the Marxist, so that by now he was completely in their world, a world beyond the concrete world. He had taken in their stories, submerged himself fully into their shadows, and in the end had now come to an idea of his own quest. He remembered these things as he saw his comrades moving across the sand.

Coming from the boardwalk, Truheckler the physicist was somehow able to advance his six–foot–five frame over the sand, using a cane and perhaps a modified version of Newton's Third Law; his expansive feet cleared a curvilinear pattern over the beach. Next to him, Minh the Marxist moved with the hopping, agile motion of a jackrabbit, hardly leaving behind any traces on the sand. And farther back, the doctor sloshed through the dunes, kicking up plumes of sand with each step.

Conrad led them under the pier, though it seemed unnecessary as the beach in winter was nearly deserted except for the occasional surfers bobbing far out among the waves. They settled behind a cement pillar and faced one another.

"What a place to meet, yah?" Truheckler the physicist said first. "It's better, yah, to meet in a nice restaurant. A nice cup of coffee and some sweets to eat."

"No, this is ideal, Comrades. Very logical, very cunning," Minh the Marxist countered; his sharp, accented voice cut clear against the cold wind. "They will suspect nothing. We are but beach-goers, enjoying a walk on the beach. They have nothing on us. Even if they were to torture us." His skin seemed to drape over the bones of his face and the muscles of his thin neck; his sparse beard was gray; and his eyes pierced with menace as he spoke, perhaps reliving his former days as a spy and a communist revolutionary.

"Stop all this paranoia already," the doctor commanded. "Tell us why you would have us meet here, on this cold deserted beach. And under the pier no less."

"And you made us leave our cellphones. What if I were to have a heart attack?" Truheckler said.

"Is it not plain enough, Comrade?" Minh said. "It is widely known that cellular devices can be used to eavesdrop on the unsuspecting. It's no paranoia, Comrade. I must commend Comrade Professor for his thoughtfulness. Nothing left to chance."

In between gusts of wind, a scent of the sea enveloped them, and Truheckler brought a handkerchief to his rosy nose. Minh sniffed deeply and turned his head askance for a moment, reminiscing about his past. Now that Conrad finally faced them the urgency that had been churning in him all these days and nights leading up to this meeting, the cause of his restlessness, seemed to have exhausted itself; without that urgent energy his logic now floated, baseless and becoming a void, similar to a squirrel chasing its own shadow around a tree. He wanted to announce and proclaim his plan, but instead he thought about how he'd changed so completely since he first walked into the doctor's clinic so many months ago, how he was now in a world shared by few, a world beside the concrete world, in which purposes extended millennia and the unseen was indeed real.

Following on the tails of the wind, a melancholy and a coldness suddenly descended upon them all. And amid the hissing wind that seemed to have come from the far side of the world, no one spoke, and the three avoided Conrad's twittering eyes. For him, they waited. And in their own eyes, an enlightened suffering flickered—something of "I am become death" veiled the physicist's half smiling, awkwardly shy face. Something of revolution and firing squads stirred sadly in the Marxist's averted eyes. And what dust from Adam and Eve and anguished curses at God that had settled on the doctor's shoulders now held his countenance in patient abeyance. It was now Conrad's turn.

"A deadly virus . . . " Conrad began at last.

"What are you saying?" Truheckler said. "You must not let that idea out."

"What is your great plan, Comrade?" Minh said.

"What did you say?" the doctor said. "I don't believe I heard you correctly."

"I have decided to embark on a grand experiment: to create a virus. The most versatile, the most adaptable, the most durable, the newest, a virus unseen thus far by mankind," Conrad's voice burst with such resonance that he could have been channeling the wind for the power of speech. "A human virus to be sure. One capable of destroying all of humanity."

"Nein, nein. Put that idea back," Truheckler's voice screeched. "Put it back inside your head where it will not hurt anyone."

"Hmm, a most ambitious plan indeed," Minh said. "To conquer humanity by using a biological agent is most glorious, most revolutionary. This plan of action can be compared to the Workers' Revolution. We mobilized ourselves, our own body to destroy the corrupt petite bourgeoisie . . ."

"The end of humanity?" the doctor said.

"That's right. Death to all. If I so wish to unleash it." Conrad's eyes beamed. "I'm confident I'm capable of such a feat."

"Of course you are," the doctor said. "But what's your reason, my dear Conrad? What is your real reason? Have you thought it through? Is it because of your recent setback? Perhaps this is but a fierce reaction to the loss you suffered. Your greatest work yet was stolen from you, and that has caused a profound harm, a damage of the psychological type."

"It is because I can. I've thought about it for much too long already. It is a response to this metaphysical anomaly," Conrad said curtly.

"You should reconsider this," the doctor continued as Truheckler and Minh listened intently. Conrad nodded impatiently, with a ready rebuttal. "You have done well for mankind, my dear boy. You isolated a novel Human Leukemia virus that will help countless thousands and far into the future. With your work, I cured the physicist of his disease. And though this world does not know of you and all you have done, just as the world does not know of the physicist's nuclear invention or of the Marxist's exploit, is it not enough that the world beside this concrete world knows? This is all part of the metaphysical anomaly."

"Doctor, you're off the mark," Conrad replied with poise. "That little Human Leukemia virus is an afterthought. Yes, my discovery was stolen from me, but I don't care about that anymore. I'm beyond that. I just want to make a virus that's capable of infecting all human beings. It's simply a challenge, you see."

"This little bourgeois who stole your work, Comrade," Minh said. "If you like, I can send someone to liquidate him."

"A scoundrel. I made the mistake of trusting him. But I'm beyond that now," Conrad said.

"Ah, ah, then a wonderful case for the application of Marxist psychology," Minh said. "What you have realized was the futility of the individual, the alienation of individual striving for material reward. The desire to subjugate humanity is a manifestation of the great need of the individual to be one with mankind, to submerge one's self in the brotherhood of workers. Only through selfless labor can one find true happiness and true self worth."

"Nein, nein. You must not think of it anymore," Truheckler said. "Many have tried before . . . Oppenheimer, Teller, Sakharov . . . even . . . even me. That story I have told you many times."

"I think it runs deeper than psychology, Minh," the doctor said as he adjusted his glasses and nodded, indicating that he understood. "It has entered the realm of metaphysics now." The wind suddenly strengthened and shrieked; in turn, the doctor raised his voice. "I think it's the age old struggle of the will. The free will to be more exact. What parts of our actions are the result of our consciousness."

"The curse of consciousness."

"To know of the free will but never able to prove it. Is that right?" the doctor said.

"Can doing something great prove that one's will is indeed free?" Conrad said.

"It is unprovable because the fabric of matter is unknowable," Truheckler said.

"There is only one thing worth knowing: from each according to his ability, to each according to his need," Minh said. "There is only the will of the Revolution that's worth proving."

"I admit there is something curious about the whole proposition," the doctor said. "The whole question remains unsolvable to this day. How does one decide to do this or that? Psychologists tried and failed to explain our actions, even the Marxist psychologist. Philosophers went in circles. The physiologists reduced our actions to chemical reactions, the evolutionists reached back into the past. All inconclusive and unconvincing. Some say suicide is the ultimate act of free will, while others argue rightfully that suicide is never an expression of freedom but of ultimate bondage."

"Yes, it will be a glorious revolution if it succeeds," Minh said. "I can tell you a story. My own history. The Marxist Revolution was on the march to dominate the world . . ."

"Please, save your story for another time," Conrad said. "Your enterprise had too many variables. Too many unknowns. Too many people to conclude successfully. What I do, I do myself. A mere man. Simply and singly."

"I agree. Too many variables even for physics," Truheckler said. "Though there is great power in the atoms. We came very close to it many times. Ten of thousands of hydrogen bombs were built and are still ready. And yet miracles happen again and again. We came very close, but nothing yet. Perhaps too many variables."

"If I understand the situation properly," the doctor said, "The professor's grand experiment is to create a virus and then to unleash it upon the world, in the process destroying the human world, so as to prove his free will."

"Perhaps, but for now I just want to create a new virus. That's all," Conrad said.

"But my dear Conrad, if you're successful you'll have the power to destroy humanity," the doctor said. "I guess only by doing the incredible, the incomprehensible, the most despicable or the most magnificent deed can one prove one's will is actually free. Don't you see? Anyone in the world can claim to choose to sleep in or get up early, to give alms or not to give alms, anyone in the world can claim to choose marriage or bachelorhood, any idiot can write a book, people can do such things and millions of other things, but all amounts to naught. In doing any of these millions of frivolous things, one can prove one's free will just as surely as the psychologists, the philosophers, the physiologists, the evolutionists, can explain it away."

The doctor waited for the wind to die down and continued, "Your grand experiment shocks the mind, arouses it from complacency, from an existence buried in psychological habits, physiologic tendencies, and even evolutionary handcuffs. That the intention is so grotesque, so barbaric, unthinkable for any thinking being means that one who is contemplating this action must by necessity be fully conscious and truly will his action. One doesn't just decide to destroy humanity because it happens to look like one's mother-in-law."

The doctor went on, "The same intention, the same demiurge has existed throughout human history. The ancient conqueror relentlessly drove his army to make the unknown world known and thereby to dominate it. Or similarly the explorers risked their lives on journeys to discover forbidden lands. The physicist secretly hoped to destroy the world as he studied the atoms; he may have his wish yet. The idealist turned the paupers into kings, whores into saints, and sought to subjugate all men's natural impulses."

"I see," Conrad said.

"Yah," Truheckler said.

"That is the truth, Comrade. A Marxist is an idealist," Minh said.

"Gentlemen, this is an old story, as old as humanity itself, and buried deep in its psyche. It's mythical. Let me explain. We must go back to the mythical Cain. According to our sacred text, Adam was the first man created, but Cain was the first man to truly demonstrate free will. In a way Adam was tricked into eating the fruit of knowledge. But only for Cain did the condition necessary for true willing exist. You see, after killing Abel, which was undoubtedly due to an unknown motive, Cain now found himself in a most unique situation. Here was a flawed, insignificant creature in God's eye, and yet he was the only one who could have destroyed God's greatest creation. How?" The doctor paused as though to give his listeners a chance to prepare themselves. "Death to all. After all, Cain was already a murderer, you see, Cain could have easily killed Adam and Eve, and finished off his other remaining siblings—Adah, and Zillah. If he had performed this horrendous deed, he'd have perpetrated the greatest free act of will in the universe, he'd have stymied God's will by destroying God's greatest creations, usurped divine power not by forgiving but by abolishing the original sin. At last he did not; instead he went off, burdened further by his guilt. I sometimes imagine that he suffered from regret more than guilt. So your quest is just another iteration in humanity's long quest."

"Ah, you expressed it well, doctor. I never considered this problem in such a mythical context, but I had a vision such as you described, doctor. A vision about the mythical Cain. I even wrote it down in my notebook," Conrad said, missing his lost notebook. "Perhaps the grand experiment may prove it one way or another. In doing so . . . I thought I would call it . . . my personal Godevil."

"Your Godevil?" the doctor asked.

"I can think of no other word to describe it," Conrad said, remembering how he'd written down his vision of it, described it so eloquently in his notebook. "If one considers one's free will to be an internal process, then there must be a force existing externally that seeks to thwart one's free will. Whether this force is conscious or a coincidence of mere randomness, I hoped to bring to light with my experiment."

"An external force that reigns over everything, you say," the doctor mused. "Could it be God that tries to stop you? Or perhaps the Devil that goads you on? Or an internecine partnership of both? A Godevil? Hmm, sounds about right."

Then they said no more, each remaining with his own thoughts, their eyes elsewhere. And among them, an awareness and therefore a sort of complicity hung in the air, and there was no question of whether they would help him as there was as much certainty in each of their stories as in Conrad's.

"I pledge myself to your struggle, Comrade," Minh the Marxist said at last. "I have given you all my chickens to study. You informed me that you had successes and extracted many viruses from these chickens, so it was all good. But there is one last chicken that I am afraid I cannot give you. The Black Chicken of Sa Pa."

"Sa Pa?" Conrad said.

"The most beautiful place in the world," Minh said. "At least for me since I can never see it again."

"All my resources are at your disposal," Truheckler said.

"I will help you until my last breath," the doctor said. "Though I fear the riddle is difficult. Will you succeed? Will you or won't you release the virus? Is there a free will? Anyway we proceed. I'm afraid we all have the mark of Cain."

"It is settled then," Conrad said. "I will call it the Cain virus."

Daily Bread and Other Drudgery

"The manifesto . . . " the professor lectured to the students' flaccid, drowsy faces.

Under the white fluorescent light, the auditorium resembled a frigid hospital ward. The students were scattered throughout the room, and Conrad seemed to be only minimally aware of them. He already knew their faces by heart, four young men and two young women, all bland and disheveled. The women were slightly androgynous, and the men without question frustrated; they were all undergraduates, wanting to be medical doctors. Before the theft of his research, Conrad's classes were always filled with eager faces, and his lectures earned him a reputation of being hip and cutting-edge. Those days had long passed.

He brought his right hand to the wool scarf tightly wound around his neck. Ever since the incident at the beach, a week ago, a fever had been recurring with no particular order, alternating with a slight chill, but he hadn't yet been able to verify this fluctuation of temperature inside his body. The thermometer had been stubbornly constant at 98°F. When he was not on the lookout for the emergence of bodily aberrations, he bemoaned the loss of his notebook, and he had gone back to the beach and combed it over many times, searching for it.

"The manifesto . . . " he said again, as he stood next to the blackboard, holding a piece of chalk in his left hand.

This time several of the students' foreheads wrinkled, their heads perked up, directing their ears toward him, and their eyes narrowed.

"Professor, did you say the 'manifesto'? Like the communist manifesto?" Benjamin B. sitting near the front said. "I didn't know that a virus could be a Marxist."

Giggling rippled through the auditorium.

"The manifestation," he corrected himself loudly. "The manifestation of the phenotypes goes through different stages. Different genes must be expressed in a precise sequence. From these genes, protein products come into being. These proteins, having various structures, are assembled as though they are Lego pieces, only there is no one there to put them together. They have to come together through thermodynamically allowable reactions, meaning that it is more energetically efficient for these structures to come together." He spoke intentionally fast, his back to the students, and his hand swiftly moved over the blackboard drawing the configuration of viral parts. Now he turned to the students and was pleased to see the effect on their faces: an acute state of confusion. He turned back to the blackboard and continued in the same fashion, goaded on by the sound of frantic scribbling into notebooks behind him. "I'm sure you've been told that there is no free lunch. Well, the same principle applies to our dear virus. The thermodynamic cascade must run from high to low, as is well known by the law of entropy. So where do the viral components get the energy from? You might want to take this down for the exam," he said, knowing that saying so always sent the students into a panic. A smile formed on his lips.

"Where?" he said, turning around to face his students, keen to see their panic. Perhaps this was the real lesson.

"Evolution?" Benjamin a superficially clever boy, who seemed to have an answer for everything, offered. He waited for his verdict.

"Evolution. Interesting," the professor said. "That's the catch-all answer in biology, isn't it? Evolution is an indisputable observation that can account for certain biological processes. Evolution certainly can't explain the asteroid, if the theory was correct, that wiped out the dinosaurs. Or why the dinosaurs came before the primates. Why not the other way around? Evolution can't explain why matter became conscious or why there is even matter. The world would have been fine with just bacteria, or our friendly viruses."

Sitting alone on the right of the auditorium, Heather moved her hand, and Conrad waited a few seconds for her, but at last she remained silent. As with any good professor, he had formulated a mental dossier on each of his students, and Heather was a good and shy student.

"Are you saying theory of evolution is wrong?" Benjamin said.

"Absolutely not. Evolution is what you get after the facts. But you must go farther, beyond evolution." He turned back to the blackboard. He drew a line and marked it off into segments. "Now, this is the DNA sequence of our virus. Each segment corresponds to a protein product."

"Maybe that's the way it is," a clear voice projected assuredly across the auditorium.

The voice, which he didn't recognize, belonged to a woman. And what kind of gibberish was this, this was advanced viral genetics, and this answer would never do. He turned around, and his pupils constricted, focusing on his students' faces, as he surveyed the auditorium.

"Why not, right? I mean why can't whatchamacallit, the thingy. The things you were talking about. You know. Why can't they just be the way they are?"

Laughter erupted.

The seats in the auditorium were arranged with an ascending elevation. He hadn't noticed her sitting high up in the back row. The woman's black hair hung straight like threads to her shoulder, smooth and thick, reflecting the white fluorescent light off its velvety shine, and a thin rim of mascara outlined large and sharp eyes. Her pale face was powdered, accentuating the rouged lips. As he saw her, his body jerked back. Something about her appearance startled him—her unique beauty, or a faint but unmistakable familiarity.

"I'm sorry," he projected his voice toward her. "I've not seen you here before. Are you auditing this class?"

"Auditing," she said. "What . . . do I look like the IRS?"

More laughter broke out.

"Auditing is not allowed in my course," he said. "But never mind that now. Let's get back to the viral DNA."

"I'm just, you know, saying. And don't be mad, I'm not attacking you or anything."

He ignored her and turned back to the chalkboard.

The lecture now proceeded much too slowly. In between remembering the notes on the virus and drawing the viral structures on the blackboard, he intuitively felt her presence and at times a burning sensation, as though her eyes were cauterizing the back of his neck, so much so that his scarf and black jacket became stifling, which made him fling them off. The black jacket crumpled into a heap, and without the notebook in its pocket, it seemed no longer to possess the same substance.

In her lips, eyes, and nose, an elegant unity existed, summing up an uncommon façade.

"You might want to take this down for the exam," he said now and then, but kept his face to the black board. Somehow he was reluctant to turn around and risk her gaze. His joints suddenly seemed to creak and his movements felt labored. He sensed her eyes on him, scrutinizing him from behind, and in his stomach a gaseous bubbling expanded uncomfortably. Who was this creature among the bland faces of his students?

The remaining minutes became uncomfortable, but at last he had exhausted the material. He took a deep breath and swallowed reflexively before turning around. Timidly raising his eyes, he peeked in her direction. She was gone.

THE NEXT DAY, HE SPENT ALL DAY IN HIS LABORATORY. THE whole of the laboratory consisted of a single twenty–by–twenty foot room with an office attached. Along the walls, work benches separated the cabinets on the upper half from drawers on the lower. A jumble of the usual laboratory equipment—flasks of various types, Bunsen burners, centrifuges, beakers, shakers, magnetic spinners, pH meters, petri dishes, etc—had once been placed in their positions under careful design for maximum efficiency, but now that ergonomic efficiency had been long lost, they were scattered haphazardly drifting to their final resting places over time. Acetone hung in the air, mingling with a foul odor of bacterial broth, and into this air Conrad wandered and his nose took in the smell without fully acknowledging it. Bitterness seemed to reside permanently around his lab and surround him as soon as he entered it.

If Abe F. hadn't stolen his virus, the discovery of which had heralded a new understanding of diseases that hitherto have falsely been attributed to non–viral causes—dementia, certain Alzheimer's, some types of heart attacks, and leukemia—he would have had everything—international recognition, wealth, and enough work to sustain him the rest of his life. His old laboratory had been ten times more spacious and had had two dozens students, post–doctoral fellows, technicians, and it had always been teeming with activities and meetings and producing scientific papers so fast as if they were coming off a conveyor belt. Though it had been an enormous laboratory by any measure, Conrad had run it with exactitude and efficiency, like a science onto itself, and that seemed to extend to his personal life as well. After the loss of the virus, he lost funding and had to move to a smaller laboratory.

"Professor," Dmitri R. called to him in a heavy Russian accent. "Work with rabies virus going very well."

Despite the downsizing, the budget cut, the loss of funding and students, Dmitri had stubbornly remained as the last technician, perhaps his very body had metamorphosed into an apparition condemned to wander among the flasks, the beakers, and the microbes. Though his eyes were large, they were barely visible under thick, bushy eyebrows. His thick Russian hair, already graying, partially hid his bony face and strong jaw.

"Rabies virus," Conrad said. "What are we doing with the rabies virus? What can we possibly learn about rabies virus that's not known already?"

"Professor, don't remember?" His lips extended outward awkwardly as he pronounced the words. "We trying to see factors that could trigger viral activation."

"Rabies virus?" he uttered. "Dmitri, my trusted friend, tell me. How have I stooped so low?"

"Professor. We discussed already. Sure way to get funding from NIH," Dmitri chastised him. "Don't remember? Rabies infects brain so rabies pays. The only way to keep the centrifuges spinning around here."

"Right. Right you are, Dmitri. I remember that I entrusted the entire lab to you. Do as you wish. But keep it open long enough for me." Something in the musty, acrid, sulfur-filled air must have overwhelmed him with nostalgia. "My trusted friend. You have always stood by me through good time and bad times. Do you remember how it was before? We were on the cutting edge of research. If I had listened to you and published what I had when I had it and not waited until . . . Damn the perfectionist in me."

"No use crying over stolen research. I did work that Abe stole."

"Yes, you're right, my friend. But don't worry, I have gotten beyond all that. I'm up to something much bigger," Conrad lowered his voice.

"You let me know of something big?" Dmitri growled.

"Carry on, my friend. There is only you now. You must keep the lab open. Long enough for me anyway. I leave it all to you now, I've moved onto another world." He turned toward his office but stopped, as if remembering something vital, and said, "Dmitri, are you keeping those viral samples safe?"

"But of course, professor," Dmitri replied. "I guard them with my life. What are they for?"

"Never mind that now. Back to the rabies for you."

As Dmitri turned back to his bench, he hesitated: "Professor, you might be interest to know."

"What?"

"Maybe unpleasant to tell you," Dmitri said.

"Spit it out, Dmitri. How can things possibly be anymore unpleasant around here? Just look at us. Stooping down to rabies."

"Rumor is Abe got new virus. From South America. Very high mutation rate."

"Rumor? Really Dmitri? I don't deal with rumors." Though Conrad knew that a virus with a high rate of mutation was exactly what he was looking for to construct the Cain Virus.

FINALLY, SITTING DOWN AT HIS DESK, WHICH WAS CROWDED with countless stacks of journals, articles, books, and a dusty computer, he pushed away some papers to clear a space in front of him and put down a few sheets of white paper. Bookshelves filled with more books, bound journals, and notebooks from all his experiments lined the four walls. Secluded in this cloister of knowledge, he sensed an easy flow collecting his thoughts into words, long tracts of words bridging his mind and the world. He began to write:

> In order to create a multifunctional, multifarious virus
> that is capable of infecting a big, genetically diverse popu-
> lation, one must use that which is already given by nature.
> One must keep everything simple. One must be able to
> facilitate the production of this virus using naturally avail-
> able materials. One must be able to go anywhere and use
> available natural materials to facilitate the production of
> this virus. It is important to emphasize that this process is
> one of "facilitation" and not one of "creation." If one were
> to try to create such a viral agent with a high infectivity
> and a high kill rate, one would surely fail. To create such
> an entity would be a monumental task beyond the ability
> of the best microbiologist. If one were to attempt such a
> creation, where would one begin, how would one account
> for the immensity of genetic variability in the human pop-
> ulation? Very soon one would find oneself groping in the
> dark and finally back to where one started from, trying to

mimic nature again. Bear in mind that these viruses, by their very nature and process of evolution, would come together one day as they inevitably would. Therefore, "facilitation" would only expedite natural processes that are meant to occur anyway.

Now, since creation is no longer an option, only facilitation remains. To facilitate, one must identify that which already exists in nature and combine its specific characters with other viruses with other distinct characters to achieve unity and novelty . . .

Friday morning saw heavy mist floating in the air, taking the forms of surreal monsters behind the backs of students racing to classrooms and wafting through open doors only to dissipate in the warm air inside. About the sleepless starring eyes of the students a void seemed imprinted into their dermises, half crazed façades. Conrad's students scattered about the auditorium and took their seats. Beside them, they placed stacks of books and notebooks, ready for the final exam.

"Everyone is here," Conrad said. He rubbed his hands together with glee as he observed his students. "You have three hours for the exam. I want to remind everyone of my policy of no electronic devices of any types. If you're caught with one, you will be expelled from the room, and your exam will be voided. Any questions before we start?"

Silence.

"I am going to hand out the exams. Please leave them face down until I tell you to start," Conrad said and began to walk around the auditorium. The pile of papers was still hot from the printer. He waited, watching the clock. "Eight o'clock. Please begin and good luck."

Heads being scratched, eyelids squeezing tight for a brief moment, hands turning over the textbooks only to give up midway, heavy sighs reverberating, lips miming sibilant words—Conrad noticed all this as he surveyed the students. In between acoustic dissonance a profound silence seemed to sting the ears. But what was that noise? Against the silence the door suddenly screeched, and the noise sheared through air. They all looked up. A figure came halfway through. Smooth, black hair framed a pale face, slightly elongated eyes rimmed by dark mascara, and red lips. The same creature, how dared she? He raced to the door.

"Yes," Conrad said through his teeth. "Can I help you?"

"Professor, may I talk to you?" she said softly as she stood outside the door. Inside her blue jacket a white, collared shirt was unbuttoned below the neck, a short black skirt reached beyond her thigh. With high heels her thin calves tightened.

"Make an appointment with my office. This is the final exam and you're disturbing the students."

"I'm sorry." She looked at the students who promptly returned to their problems. She whispered, "I know it sounds weird, but do you mind if we talk for few minutes?"

"Please leave," Conrad said

Before he could close the door she spoke rapidly. "I'm sorry about the interruption, but do you mind if we talk now?"

"Who are you and what do you want?" Conrad blurted out; his throat felt constricted by the thumping of his heart. He went outside and closed the door behind him.

"You don't remember, do you?"

"Remember what? You're disturbing the students."

"You don't remember," she exclaimed.

In the empty hallway, their voices echoed loudly.

"I'm sorry, I don't know you." A sense of danger crept along his spine and up to his neck, and he turned for the door. His mind spun with an intangible fear.

"What's your goddamn problem?" she shouted.

"Keep your voice down." He turned back to face her. "How dare you talk to me like that?"

"Hah, you're unbelievable, you know." Her voice screeched. "You're welcome."

"Are you a student here? I'll have you expelled." He reached out for the door knob.

With a quick hop, her high heels tapping against the hard floor, she intercepted him.

"You know you're so unbelievably ungrateful," she said.

"For what?" He smelled her perfume, light and sweet. And the fullness of her eyelids sprouting curved, delicate little lashes caught his eyes.

"For saving your life."

His face dropped. The beach, the waves, the mad pawing toward shore—reality suddenly reconstituted around her face; yes, it was she. Her makeup had transformed her face so much that only now could he recognize her.

"So you remember," she said.

"Ah, ah . . . " He muttered. A spasm took hold of his larynx, and he couldn't breathe or speak.

Instantly they seemed to be transported back to the beach by a dark force to pick up again exactly where they had left off.

The intensity of his indignation finally overcame the paralysis of his larynx, and he countered, "You didn't save me. I wasn't the one who was trying to kill myself."

"Then what were you doing in your, you know, underwear out there? Going for a walk?"

"If you must know," Conrad said, "I was trying to save you."

"Trying to save me?" she snorted. "What? Are you crazy?"

Even in her denial, a scattered admission and recognition of truth coalesced around a single point on her face, and he seized on it immediately; through this point he could pry away the hardened veneer one morsel at a time. He grabbed her hand and held it up, twisting it to expose her wrist and the undersurface of her arm. He said, "You don't think I noticed when I saw you on the beach. These scars on your wrists, arms, and thighs. You are the one who has been trying to kill yourself. Not me."

She yanked her hand away violently, and said, "I don't care what you say, Mr. Know-It-All-Professor. I wasn't trying to kill myself that day."

"But you certainly didn't save me. And now if you would excuse me," he said as he took a hand sanitizer from his pocket and squirted it on his hand.

She didn't budge. Both her hands went up. "Look. We got, you know, we got off to a bad start. Let's just shake hands and start over."

"Get out of my way."

"I have your notebook," she said mockingly.

"How?" he gasped.

"You dropped it at the beach."

"You must give it back to me." His voice suddenly softened.

"Meet me tomorrow. Noon at the Chestnut Café. Do you know where that is?"

He nodded and beheld her shape vanishing as she turned and hurried along the hallway, her handbag hanging from her shoulder, as if late for a business meeting.

Deeper Than Scars

The morning was locked under a fog when Conrad peeked outside. Still riled up by the encounter with the suicide girl the day before, he was unable to read or write, so he loitered about his study, now and then looking out the window at the milky atmosphere. It had been another night of staring into dark corners and vents along the ceiling, and his hyper-vigilant ears had tried to pick up the slightest murmurs from the house, the fleeting movements along the floor of an unknown assailant. Though he knew full well that any attacks would come not always in the shape of a burly, hard fisted criminal but sometimes from a suicide girl. Ah there, he was thinking about her again; however diffused and peripatetic his thoughts were, they always gravitated back to those eyes, the perfumed breath, and the pointed nails that had dug into his shoulders. His thought increased his paranoia so much that he was fearful of meeting the girl. What if she were to do him harm? How would he protect himself?

Then he envisioned a plan, and he got into his car. A cocksackie virus, he hollered inside his car; a virus whose infectivity and pathogenesis had been modified by him would have a ninety percent chance of giving her meningitis. This would be his defense against her, just in case she turned out to be evil. A heathen cackle reverberated inside the car and he stepped down on the gas, sending the car screeching along the open road. Only a few minutes later he was navigating through the cluttered space of his laboratory and there in the corner he found the liquid nitrogen storage that contained all the viruses he had modified over the years.

At nearly twelve o'clock, when the sun had burned off the fog to reveal a bright blue sky, Conrad sauntered toward the Chestnut Café. At once his stomach tightened and his mind flittered about in a state of suppressed nervousness. The frozen vial with the viral particles had been melting in his right pocket, and he felt a cold dampness there, but he must leave it there, letting the warmth of his body melt the ice and release the viruses which would buzz about like microscopic bees and do the one thing they could do best: infect. A quick flip of the plastic cap would spill the liquid onto his hand, and then that hand would reach out to shake hers. He could see it clearly: the greeting of death. The average person would touch her face thousand of times a day, so surely the chance of the viruses finding their way into her nose or mouth was assured. What about himself? Of course he had been immunized long ago; after each viral creation, the first thing he had done had been to immunize himself.

From the street, he searched the café through the window; customers now filled nearly all the seats. Then he saw her face. The girl in a simple blue dress and a white sweater was sitting at a table by the glass wall, looking into the street; on the table were a cup of coffee and a yellow handbag. All his life Conrad had never known a girl of such beauty, not that she was necessarily the most beautiful girl in the world, but without question she was the most sublime in his world. Sharp nose, slightly elongated eyes that looked about expectantly, and lips tight as from shyness blended into a gentle quaintness as she sat cross-legged with chin resting on palm. Ah, so she actually came. He felt a strange regret as his hand went into his pocket to touch the vial with the ice inside nearly completely melted. As he observed her, that strange regret surged and he felt it as strongly as when he, as a child, had dropped a piece of chocolate in the street but couldn't get himself to pick it up and eat it because of his fear of getting sick. He suddenly realized how forceful his paranoia had been to cause him to bring the vial of cocksackie virus; he couldn't possibly harm her.

An involuntary compulsion planted his feet where he stood and he continued to observe her, enjoying an odd predatory pleasure that ended suddenly when the girl raised her eyes and caught his. She lifted a tentative hand to wave at him, to beckon him inside.

Inside, the smell of coffee and the roaring of a blender engulfed the air. The customers' ears were plugged with earphones and eyes fixed on the computer screens. Loud noises pervaded—the rumbling of coffee machine, swishing of blenders, clanking of cups filled in with the rhythm of an indistinguishable music blaring from overhead speakers.

"Hi," the girl said and smiled at him as though she has known him all her life and whatever row had transpired between them was now as distant as an insignificant spat between dear friends.

"Hello," he murmured, seeing how her cheerfulness could mask a deviousness.

"Please sit down."

"What is this all about?" He sat down across from her with his back to the window which made him uncomfortable. He folded his arms across his chest.

"Would you like something to drink?" she said.

"No." His head leaned slightly forward so that he glared at her from under his brows.

"Ah . . . hmm. I just want to talk. You know how we met at the beach. I'm sorry, you know, I wasn't as friendly," she muttered. Her hand went up to her smooth hair and she ran her fingers through it.

"Are you serious? Where is my notebook?" His head suddenly felt clear.

"You'll get it," she said. How was she to let him know that reading his little notebook has changed her life, that there was now a bond between them? If only she could make him feel what she felt.

"Give me the notebook now."

His voice was loud enough that nearby customers lifted their eyes from their computer screens and stared. From behind the counter, the barista gazed at the girl through his big, square eyeglasses, and in that gaze Conrad detected envy, an easily discernible, rotten sentiment. At the next table a man had taken his eyes off his computer and was now glancing at the girl from the corner of his eye. Conrad had seen and envied other men with beautiful women before, but he had never imagined that one day he himself would become an object of envy. Only if they knew the whole story, there would only be jeers.

From her handbag she pulled out the red notebook.

"Ah," Conrad gasped and reached for the notebook.

She yanked the note book out of his reach. "You dropped it at the beach. You can have it back if you promise to talk to me first."

"That's private. Give it to me," he growled.

"I want an hour."

"Okay. Okay."

Her hand holding the notebook moved forward and he snatched it. His hands palpated the red leather covers and he opened it, flipping through one page after another, as though he was examining a once–lost child for hidden injuries.

"Don't worry. It's all there the way I found it." She smiled.

But he wasn't hearing her as he continued to look through the notebook.

When he finally looked at her, he was startled to see her head lowered to the table's edge as she raised her eyes, showing the white of her eyeballs, to stare not exactly at him but at something just beyond his head.

"What are you doing?" His voice was shrill and strained. "Why are you looking at my hair?"

"Just a minute. Stay still," she said. Her head moved sideways as if to place herself at the right angle, to focus on light from an ether world that would curve around the unseen gravity of his head straight into her soul.

"What are you doing?" he lowered his voice.

"Never mind." She sat up.

"All right one hour." He looked at his watch. "What do you want to talk about?"

"I don't know. Maybe we can talk about your notebook."

"My notebook. You read my notebook?"

"Yeah, I'm sorry. But I was really moved by it"

"Don't you understand it's private?"

"I didn't steal it from you," she protested loudly. She leaned forward and her fingers, those same fingers that had brought chaos to his life, fanned out and gesticulated puzzling messages.

"Still, you don't have the right to go through it."

"Oh, yeah, so you're telling me that you know if you were in my shoes, you wouldn't read it at all. You wouldn't take a little peek inside? Is that what you're saying?"

"Of course I wouldn't. I would just return it to its owner and that's it."

"I don't believe you. You talk like you're not human."

"All right, just forget about it. All right." He looked at his watch again.

"Just hear me out." Her voice was soft. "I really felt what you wrote."

"You're joking?"

"No, really. I really felt it. I felt like I was there, next to Cain. Like it was something I was looking for all along, like the red eyes were talking to me."

What she said puzzled him, and, taken aback, he looked around the café and saw that the other customers were no longer drawn into the computers; their eyes leered at him and in their eyes there was an intense curiosity. Perhaps they thought they were witnessing a lovers' quarrel.

The girl, too, followed his eyes and said, "Let's get out of here. Let's take a walk."

Conrad stood up and followed her outside.

"Do you have a cellphone?" he asked her as they exited the café. He placed the notebook with care into the coat's left pocket.

"Yes, my number is . . . "

"No, I don't want your number," he interrupted her. "Why do I want your number? I want you to take the battery out of your cellphone."

"What?"

"I want you to remove the battery from your cellphone."

"Why? You're kidding, right?"

He leaned toward her and whispered, "They can listen to you. That's the only way I'll talk."

"Who?" she uttered, but remembering something she had heard on the news she corrected herself, "Oh, yes. You mean the NSA. I've heard about these spying things."

He put his finger to his lips and mimed the words, "Your phone."

She opened her purse and dug through a jumble of personal things: scraps of receipts, a make-up compact, a check book, various tubes of lipstick, mascara. At the bottom where the phone had sunk, she felt it and pulled it out. Her fingernail dug into the side of the phone, popped out the back cover, and dislodged the battery, and then she carelessly dropped the disjointed parts of the cellphone back into her purse.

"Yes, all of them," Conrad resumed in his low, cocksure voice. "They're all interconnected. You understand?"

"I got it. You mean this Godevil, the thing you wrote about in the notebook."

"Yes, all parts of it."

She turned to him. In heels, her eyes were slightly higher than his and she looked down at him. "I'm Dia," she said and extended her hand.

He took her hand and even for only a second he felt the bones and sinews of her hand, strong and steady. Then, without the slightest sense of impropriety, he took out the antibacterial sanitizer and doused his hand.

"Dia? I haven't heard that name before," he said as he rubbed his hands together.

"Diaphany. It's short for Diaphany." She stared at his hands.

"I see. I'm Conrad."

"I know. I saw your name and address inside the notebook. That's how I found you." She smiled.

They were walking now. Dia followed Conrad as he yielded to his habit, walking along Wilshire Boulevard, following a familiar path toward his laboratory.

"I really like what you wrote," she said.

"You're not a student at the university."

"No."

"What do you do?"

"I dance. At least for now."

"Dance? Where?"

"Cabaret."

"What exactly is a cabaret dancer? Tell me more." He continued to glean details from her body—the fine scars on her wrists and arms, the strong muscular figure revealed by the simple, snug blue dress, the well–formed feet whose lovely shape he remembered seeing in the sand.

"Well, I dance on stage with five other dancers, sometimes more. We wear different costumes, like, a secretary, a nurse, a flight attendant, even a nun. Kinda like acting out a skit to music."

Diaphany's words drifted through the air, somehow finding a place in the sunshine, enclosing them both in a privacy afforded by constant movement. They trekked along the wide boulevard, oblivious of the sound of traffic, and at times came together through a narrowness on the pavement and at other times gave way to one another.

"Interesting. What about your scars? How did you come to cut yourself?"

"It's a long story. It began when I was really young." There was no hesitation or embarrassment in her cool, steady voice as she divulged the details of her childhood: She was raised by her mother in a Las Vegas suburb, and though she had a middle–class life and all its comfort, from her earliest memory she had always felt but couldn't articulate a sensation of being beside herself, beside the physical realm most people accepted without question, as though a remembrance or a vestige of another dimensional reality was still attached to her at birth. Bearing that vestigial existence, her childhood was marred by tantrums, uncontrollable crying spells. As she got older, she endured visits to various doctors, surgery to remove her tonsils and adenoids, and even trials of medication for hyperactivity disorder. Nothing worked. One day at the age of ten, she fell during a bike ride and scraped her knee badly, but instead of crying she marveled at her bleeding knee, reeling with sharp pain and her mind experienced as if for the first time an immediate realness.

"I remembered it so clearly," she went on. "It was the beginning, from then on I was always trying to find it again." She lifted her arm to display the scars. "After that I didn't have any more tantrums. All I wanted was to be by myself. Well one day my mother found me doing it. Cutting myself. She was beyond shocked. She nearly went nuts. And after that I saw a bunch of shrinks. They thought I was abused or molested by someone. Even got hospitalized a couple of times."

"Are you still cutting yourself?" He looked at her and wondered why anyone could be like that and go and tell all to a stranger.

"I cut myself more and more. After I slit my wrist and nearly died. I guess I came as close . . . I don't know. It just wasn't there. It was just not what I looked for. You know what I mean?"

"I understand."

"So I tried other things. You name it, I tried it. Like sky diving, bungee jumping, meditation, yoga."

"Is that what you were doing at the beach?"

"Yeah."

"It's very personal."

She stopped and looked him in the eyes and without awkwardness said, "Well, I read your diary and it's personal. I guess it's only fair if you know my personal things too."

"No, that's not right. First of all, it's not a diary, it's a manifesto."

"A what?"

"A manifesto. Secondly, it's private but not personal. It's a manifesto and a historical document, a record of a long running struggle. One day when it's complete, it will be made public for everyone to see."

"Okay, whatever, but the point is we're both looking for the same thing."

"I'm sorry. I can't see how that is."

"Trust me. I read every page. Nice hand writing by the way. We're looking for the same thing."

Conrad's lips pursed, his forehead wrinkled, and his eyes strained toward her, studying and wondering if she was trying to draw him into a cult of some sort.

They resumed walking. On one side, shop fronts, offices, restaurants, and tall buildings sped by, mirrored by the unending flow of cars on the streets. Above them the sun moved across the sky and the clouds drifted against the sun. Heading along Wilshire Boulevard, passing under the freeway, and turning left toward the fashionable Westwood district, they were locked in a mutual pull between the fields of their eyes. Soon they were climbing up the long steps to the university's quad.

"This Godevil you wrote about," she inquired. "How do you say it, it's not exactly of this world. It's like a spirit. It's from somewhere else. Isn't that right?"

"I assure you it's very much of this world. It's the cause of all untold suffering. It makes a mockery of our consciousness, our free will," he said, finding it odd to be discussing matters mostly important to himself with someone whom he considered to be unbalanced. The vial of viruses in his pocket flashed through his mind again.

"That's not how I felt when I read your notebook," she persisted. "You know, it's hard for me to explain. I'm here but I tried to find something that's not here. Do I make sense?"

"I understand. The Godevil, like so many other things, is not perceivable by our senses but our intellect can find it, make it manifest itself, bring it to its knees so to speak. But it's here all around us, not somewhere else."

"I know. I know. But . . . Ah, I guess that must be it because I never wanted to kill myself. Yeah, that's what I was thinking about. I never wanted to leave this world, I'm here but I want to find something that's not in it. Do I make sense?" A wave of elation lifted Dia as she finished the sentence. Never in her life had she talked like this with anyone, delved into the thing that she hid from everyone lest they think she was crazy. Now here was another person listening to her words, a mind that comprehended them and a creed that meshed with her thoughts.

"Perfectly. Then we're in partial agreement." Conrad wanted to bring the encounter to an end. He found the conversation tedious and frankly unflattering, unlike the long discussions he had with the doctor, the physicist, or the Marxist, men who had real experiences with monumental historical events, in whom insights and nuances abounded, conversations from which he would come away with a flood of ideas to fill his notebook.

They were now at the cafeteria that served the university's south science campus. Tall research buildings cast long shadows. Dia sat down at a table and before Conrad could sit down, she said, "Don't move."

"Excuse me?"

"Stay exactly where you are for a second."

"Why?"

"Shhh, just stay still, won't you?"

Just like before, the winter's sunlight broke through the clouds, scraped the edge of a building's rooftop, and bent around his head; in that purest of light her essence transmigrated across vast distances carrying her to a familiar place that existed beyond the earthly dimension.

An utter amazement was about to burst through his vocal cords when sudden recognition triggered a chill that washed down from his head and struck in him a cold realization that he had seen it all before. Yes, it was the same look he'd seen on the waves. What insanity was this? Her face set an unmoving trance as his eyes squinted to stare at her in disbelief. He wanted to run away, but something was holding him back. Her fingers clenched tightly around the edge of his coat. Taking a half step, he tried to pull away but couldn't budge. Somehow the trance must have infused her with paranormal strength. Inhaling deeply, he grabbed the edge of his coat just above her fingers and bent his body down to gather leverage for the spring away from her; but as he did so his head moved and she too moved with him as if two heavenly spheres were locked together in a . . . Totentanz. His mind murmured the word and he realized he had the same thought on the waves. Now in his mind the movement that consisted of his body springing up and running away from her and leaving her as an after-image on his retinae forever had already occurred, but he stood there still and was rooted by a curious fascination. Under the beam of sunlight, his head cast a shadow across her eyes and at this juncture of light and shadow he looked at the minute folds of her blue irises and beyond that, into her depth, trying to see what she was seeing. Perfect stillness now enveloped her face which seemed to be derived from and destined for a mold already existing in his mind. Her red lips coiled with ready kisses and darts. And her eyes that pulled him into despair and exuded transcendence like an infant whose innocent gaze could see the face of infinity.

How beautiful she was.

Finally restored to herself again, she looked at him in front of her. In the light bending around his head, she had traveled somewhere or had been given something she knew not what, and, upon awakening, she attained a state of contentment like lying on soft grass on sunny days, all by herself and yet not alone, all the moments condensed into a timeless present, beholding all at once, and with all the energy being spent and instantly refueled without yearning or regret.

"Sit down," she said softly.

Her voice startled him. So it was over, then? He slouched down into a chair next to her. How much time were they together in that eerie choreograph? He couldn't tell. Feeling as if he had committed a perverted act, his eyes flitted around the nearly empty quad and saw a student walking away in the distance. So no one could have seen them together except for the unknown eyes behind the countless glassy windows dotting the research buildings around them. Perhaps the beady eyes of Abe F. had witnessed the whole thing, his nose smearing against the glass window because he couldn't get close enough. Conrad jumped up.

"Let's walk." Conrad began walking without waiting for Dia.

"Hey, what's the matter? Wait." She ran after him, still giddy with contentment.

"Nothing. I just want to walk."

"Okay. Your lab is in that building right? The same one as

the lecture hall?" she said, trying to make conversation as mental clarity returned to her.

"Yes, it's on the third floor."

"It's okay if you don't like being around there. Sometimes people don't want to be around their workplace all the time," she said.

He glanced at her, sensing a connivance under the frivolous talk, and yet a curious fascination still over-powered his reason and caution.

They strolled to North campus, passing the physics buildings, and finally came onto another open quad, much grander and bordered by the main university library to the south and Celine Hall with its two tall towers on the opposite side.

"So tell me about yourself," she said. "I mean you know a lot about me now. It's only fair."

"There is nothing to tell and I don't know everything about you."

"Come on. Don't be like that. I mean I told you everything."

"There is nothing to tell."

"All right. Just start with your birth place."

"Pasadena. I grew up there. I went to college there and later became a professor here. My life is quite conventional."

"Oh yeah, that's not what I heard. I heard your work got stolen. You could have gotten rich and famous. There was a big scandal," she said excitedly.

He stopped and looked at her straight on. "Who have you been talking to?"

"Don't be upset. I Googled you. It's not like it's a big secret or anything."

"Why do you want to know? Who sent you?" he demanded, unable to control his paranoia.

"What do you mean? Nobody sent me. Don't be so paranoid. Nobody sent me. I'm not from the NSA, FBI or any of the goon squads. Jeez, relax."

"I'm sorry. I didn't mean to imply that you're with any of them."

They resumed walking into the shadow of the library where the air was noticeably cooler on their faces. A faint, earthen odor rose from the ground.

"Well, it's true, and yes it was a scandal. The whole campus knows about it. Lawyers were involved. I could have handled it better," he conceded.

"Ah, lawyers. I hate lawyers. Even I know to avoid them," she said loudly, and then seeing him smile awkwardly stopped herself. "I'm sorry. Please go on."

"There was a lawsuit. A lot of documents, evidence, and so on. It was very expensive as well," he was almost whispering. "In the end there was an arbitration. He admitted no fault and I got tenured. I was only an assistant professor before."

"So he got away with it? Fucking bastard. Why did you let him get away with it? It was your work."

"Not everyone believed me."

"I believe you. You know something like that happened before. The . . . hmm . . . HIV. Yeah, that's right I read about it. A guy claimed he discovered HIV when he didn't."

"Yes, it happens sometimes in academia."

"So, then what happened?"

"It was too late, you see, the work was already published. The university administration didn't want to expose one of its tenured professors as a thief. They reaped the benefits regardless of who made discovery. So in the end I ran out of money and so I settled."

"What was it anyway? What did you discover?"

"A novel virus. One that caused some cancers of the hematopoietic system. It has a short sequence of DNA. The structures were marvelously simple and so energetically efficient. It was a beauty. It was there all the time until I discovered it."

"I'm sorry. I really am. What's a hemato . . . poietic system anyway? Is that right, a hematopoietic system?"

"It's the blood system that's made up of white blood cells, red blood cells, clotting factors among other types of cells. Anyhow I'm beyond all that now."

"So what are you working on now? It's really great. You got right up. You must teach me more sometimes about all that stuff. I like to learn. It sounds really interesting. "

"No, no. It's not like that. I'm beyond trying to publish any-thing," he glanced at her.

"No," she lamented. "You should continue with your work. I mean you still have a lot to offer, right? You can still find other things."

"Hmm," he muttered.

There was a condescension under his breath that jabbed at her and was mutually recognized as he saw in her eyes a diffi-dence that had not been there a moment ago.

"I'm serious. You know I may not know much about your work, but I know something about people. It's like they always have a way of surprising you. They always have a way of coming back, doing better things, making themselves better. They're like springs, springing back to do better for themselves. Like a friend of mine, Cecilia, she was into speeds and coke for a long time but you know she just got clean, just like that. Went to rehab and has stayed clean ever since. Got a job. She is one of the best dancers in our group. And I can tell you stuff about me."

He said nothing and smiled and his silence pronounced a judgment more devastating than anything she'd known before, cut deeply, and induced a hurt that was clearly visible by the fleeting twitch of her suddenly waxen face, the slight tighten-ing of her lips, and down-cast glance. He perceived it clearly.

"You shouldn't underestimate me," she said.

He contemplated her words as they echoed without meaning through the cool air.

"You know, I don't know how or when but I'll help you," she persisted. The twinkle in her eyes flickered into something brutal.

"Like, this one time my friend's house was in foreclosure and the bank kept sending her papers. And you know what I did . . . "

"You seem to talk a lot without saying much," he said.

Her lips were still open in mid–sentence but words no longer came out and her whole being seemed to vanish with the words.

At last, with a triumphant resolution that he had just put an end to it, he put his hands into his pocket and was on the verge of bidding her goodbye forever when he felt liquid against his fingers. Suddenly remembering the vial of viruses and realizing that the cap had accidentally popped open during the walk, he jumped back in panic. He had to get away right now unless he wanted to end her or anyone else with whom he might come into contact. The liquid could soak through his coat and become aerosolized, or by accident he could touch her hand and thus infect her. Taking a few automatic steps backward, he blurted out, "I have to go. Goodbye." Fully turned around now, he ran along the same path to his laboratory where he could decontaminate himself.

10

Mysticism Renewed

What Conrad said hurt her with a deep, impalpable vagueness, disturbing Dia's sense of being the same way an earthquake can shake loose each stone of a building's foundation so that the building, though still standing, is now considered unsafe. At first, she had only been stunned that he had run away like that; after all they had been talking, hadn't they? She had told him about her life—no, more than that; she had relived dark moments of her life with him and that had required a boldness, a sacrifice, and even a recklessness, for who knew where it could lead, what daring it could open to her again. Retracing her way back, desultory steps led her through Westwood, with its shops and restaurants full of people, to the Chestnut Café. The sun was much lower now in the winter sky and the unending roar of traffic engulfed the air, but she saw and heard none of that. Her senses had taken notice of nothing at all except for the world inside her mind, and only as she approached the Chestnut Café did she smell the putrid smell of shame, hear the crumbling of her own self, and feel her body shaking like a cornered rabbit. She had to stop and lean against the wall.

She looked upward to the sky and let out a scream. Son of a bitch, she screamed again in her head, but, despite all the cursing that impalpable vagueness now coalesced sharply and lanced straight through her as though through so much frivolity. "Talk a lot without saying much," she mumbled. She noticed a sudden coldness in her hands and feet in the same way too much blood loss had made her feel just before she passed out in the bathtub years ago. The car was nearby and she ran to it, got inside, and sat quietly, almost daydreaming, having all the time and yet no fixed destination. Time went by, cars passed on the road, people sauntered along the pavement, clouds drifted overhead, and the sun became redder as it approached the horizon. Then she reached inside her handbag and got out her cellphone. The cell–phone was dark. "Son of a bitch made me take out the battery," she screamed and then giggled with a long, crazed, uncontrollable throaty roar. Hmm, out of breath at last she stopped giggling.

She steered the Ford Coupe from the curb. Now meandering, now encroaching on two lanes, the car sped along haltingly, and with each pause, loud honking blasted from behind her, but she was disturbed only slightly because the honking sounded muffled, unable to pierce through a depressive bubble that surrounded her. Sunlight, too, seemed blunted and the sky appeared to be getting darker much too soon. The freeway entrance coming into view just ahead, she pressed hard on the gas pedal. Traffic on a Saturday afternoon was moving smoothly and she was hemmed in by rows of speeding cars on both sides, the yellow flicker of headlights behind and red taillights ahead drawing her into a place unknown. All was in a blurry motion, distorted by the tears pooling in her eyes.

At first a drop of tear spilled over the edge, leading the way and moistening a path, and then drops and drops all came flowing, following down her cheek, smearing her mascara, joining with the tears that escaped through the tear ducts and were dripping from her nose, finally getting caught between her lips. Reflexively she tasted the tears, a hint of salt as though the best of her was being expelled. She hadn't cried for so long. She hadn't cried when she cut her thighs, nor in the hospital when the pain in her wrists had been too intense to bear, nor as her mother held her and wailed as if she was already dead, nor when she overheard the psychiatrist telling her mother of the diagnosis: Self-mutilation Syndrome. When was the last time she had cried? It must have been ten years ago, but she couldn't remember why. The reason she was crying now was plain enough.

The 405 Freeway led south to Long Beach, where she worked, and an instinct, an unconscious desire, or perhaps a memory lodged deep in her bones drew her that way. Safe inside the car and enclosed further in the low rumbling of the engine, outside cars moving more or less at the same speed and the yellow and red lights always being there, Dia was being transported along, all the while the images and sounds of the encounter with Conrad were replayed and re-experienced only with hollowness and regret.

The sign for the 710 Freeway startled her. How fast, it seemed just a few minutes and already here was Long Beach. Taking the 710 Freeway south, her mind now refocused on the present and she looked at the dashboard's clock. It was 5:08, and though the winter sky was getting dark, it was too early for work. The dancers usually didn't appear on stage until ten o'clock. Farther along the 710 Freeway would take her to downtown Long Beach, to the Caravelle Cabaret Club, but she took the next familiar exit and headed east. At variable stretches of the street, a few streetlights threw yellowish cones of light on decrepit, old Chevrolets, Oldsmobiles, and Fords with dusty windows. At the periphery of the cones of light Dia saw darkened houses and windows with iron bars and shoes hanging from electric wires, hung there by drug dealers. Then farther on, in front of an apartment complex, she pulled over and parked in the street. She felt in her handbag for a can of mace and a 0.38 caliber revolver and put both within reach. Then she pulled down the vanity mirror and examined her face. Her eyes were swollen, the smeared mascara ran down her cheeks, and her lips were pale and flaccid. She blotted out the smeared mascara, retouched her lips, and powdered her cheeks, but nothing could get rid of the inflamed blood vessels webbing the white of her eyes. At last, clutching her handbag tightly, she went to the apartment's gate, stepping over ubiquitous scraps of paper and plastic bags, and rang the bell.

"Who is it?" Martha W. said through the intercom. She was also a cabaret dancer, who had recently moved to Los Angeles from the midwest.

"It's me. Dia. Let me in," Dia said.

"Dia, what are you doing here?"

The door buzzed. Dia pushed it open and went into a narrow courtyard and then up the stairs.

The door creaked open and Martha, wearing a pink bathrobe pulled snuggly up to her chin, greeted Dia. As soon as Dia stepped into the warm light of the apartment, Martha asked, "Dia, what's the matter?"

There was no use trying to hide, and, feeling the pressure pushing under her eyelids from crying, she didn't answer, sat down on a couch next to the door, crossed her legs, and folded her arms, trying her damnedest to suppress another teardrop.

"Honey, what's the matter? Did something bad happen?" Martha said in her usual soft, whispering voice, a tad high-pitched, accented with a Midwestern earnestness and a touch of naïveté. She sat down next to Dia. Her face was plain, slightly rounded, and littered with tiny freckles and her hair was still wet from a shower, and yet the tenderness of such plainness seized Dia. The round, earnest eyes waited for Dia, and the full lips tensed in anticipation.

"It's nothing. Don't worry about it."

"Oh my God, like your eyes are swollen and red. It's not nothing," Martha said, now reaching out and holding Dia's hand. "Honey, you can tell me. Do you want, like, ice or cucumber for your eyes? There's plenty of time to get the swelling to go down before the show. It's, like, all red and swollen."

"No, I'm fine."

"I'll get it anyway." Martha went into the kitchen.

From the couch, Dia could see everything in the kitchen, the cabinet's doors hanging crookedly from broken hinges, the stove, the wooden stirring spoons sticking out of the sink, and the old refrigerator into which Martha was bending and searching for cucumbers.

"Is it your mother again?" Martha said.

"No," Dia protested. "Do you think I'd cry over my mother?"

"Then what? You're, like, crying so it must be serious."

Dia slipped her feet out of her heels and stretched her legs on the coffee table crowded with cups and plates, tabloid magazines, a hair curler, and various bottles of makeup. In the living room, dirty clothes spilled from a laundry basket while others clumped together on the worn-out carpet. Various shoes were scattered about. Dia smelled the staleness of sweat, of dirty clothes, of pot smoke, and the residual odor of grilled cheese in the air. In the smell as in the cluttered living room that Dia knew well a familiar comfort and a homeliness beckoned her to a reality whose shades and shadows had been delineated with clarity so that nothing further could be known, where there could never be any danger of hurt or tears.

Martha came back from the kitchen holding a ziplock bag with a few pieces of ice and said, "I'm sorry I don't have any cucumber. It's weird, you know. I thought, like, I bought a whole bag."

"Marty, I'm fine. Don't worry."

Martha sat down next to her, put the ice bag on the coffee table, and looked at Dia. "Well, what is it then? It's like you're driving me crazy," she said.

Dia didn't answer.

Martha now grabbed her by the shoulders and turned her to look straight into her eyes. "So it's a guy. A guy who made you cry. You got to tell me. Everything."

Dia sank back farther into the couch, pushing her back against an old, lumpy pillow.

Beyond her conscious will, the intuition of the reality she'd shared with Conrad, so different from Martha and her little apartment, seeped back and scratched and reopened the little wound as Dia tightened further, her arms folding across her chest, squeezed her shoulders, and looked at an empty space in front of her where now hung that intuition. "Yeah, it's a guy," Dia spoke softly as if only to herself. "But it's not what you think."

"I knew it," Martha exclaimed, and then looked at Dia and saw the unchanging forward gaze. "Oh, I'm sorry. Tell me."

"It's this guy I met. But it's not what you think."

"Oh my God, what is he like? Is he hot? He must be to make you cry. Did you catch him, like, screwing around?"

"No, Marty. It's not like that," Dia continued speaking softly and thinking but without letting thoughts escape into words, words that would surely sound strange and foreign to Martha should they be vocalized.

Then Martha grabbed her arm and looked at Dia's eyes.

"You know. Guys are tricky but . . . but, like, they can be handled. You know with a little here and there . . . even tough guys."

Dia sat up and turned to Martha. "Marty, what are you saying? What tough guys? Are you hooked up with Hucks?"

"Dia, relax. Why are you so worked up? And what have you got against Hucks anyway?"

"Marty, tell me you haven't gotten yourself hooked up with Hucks."

"He's not, like, bad or anything. You know. He's kinda fun," Martha said and shrugged.

Now, it was Dia who took Martha's shoulders and turned Martha toward her; it was Dia who now studied Martha's soft cheeks, still full from youth, and saw what she had always seen since the first day she met Martha, but now with astonishment and anguish, the gall of youthful innocence that had compelled Martha to abandon home and honey for Hollywood land. "No, Marty. You don't know what you're getting yourself into. He's a really bad guy."

"We're just having fun, Dia."

"What kind of fun?" Dia said sharply. "Are you doing coke with him?"

"It's nothing. It's, like, once or twice. And we were at a party."

"A Hollywood party? He took you to one of those?"

"Yeah, it was awesome. It was like nothing I'd ever seen. The food was great, the wine, the champagne. Everything was so . . . classy. Oh my God, you wouldn't believe . . ."

"Did he try to pimp you out?" Dia said curtly, interrupting Martha.

"Gosh, no. Dia. He introduced me to some people he knows. They were, like, his friends. That's all."

"He's a pimp, Marty. He tried to pimp me out to the Hollywood crowd. It's the same with all the girls at the club. You haven't been here long enough to know, Marty. You should stop right now," Dia said, breathless. "What did he promise you?"

"Nothing."

"Did he promise you he'll get you into the movies? Did he tell you he's got friends in the movies business? Oh my God, Marty. Don't listen to him. He's a pimp and he pushes coke for them. That's all. He's been telling the same lies to all the girls. Oh my God, Marty. He got you, too."

"Stop it. He hasn't tried to pimp me to anyone."

"Promise me you won't see him again. It's trouble, Marty."

"Look who's talking," Martha snapped. "You're , like, crying over a guy."

"Marty. Promise me."

"All right. All right," Martha said and exhaled.

Unconvinced, Dia sank back into the couch and thought quietly to herself that she must try again later for both their sakes, for seeing Martha being ravaged would hurt her in equal measure.

Martha remained quiet for a moment and finally said, "I'm going to get ready." She got up and went into her bedroom. Once inside the bedroom, as if having crossed back into a familiar cheerfulness, Martha's voice, slightly high-pitched, sprang out again. "You know, Dia . . . maybe we can try like something new . . . a new dance . . . I have been going to the gym . . . You know the stage . . . It's like . . . Are you hungry? . . . I'm sorry I like forgot to buy groceries . . . "

"I'm not hungry. Don't worry"

"Do you want to like call for pizza? . . . Let's hang out here . . . for a couple of hours . . . you can give me a ride . . . like I hate driving . . . maybe watch a movie . . . there is like . . . it's like a really good movie . . . he . . . she . . . like . . . a mystery . . . "

Words spoken with little heed bounced off the little walls

of the little hallway leading from the little bedroom. No longer listening, with arms crossing and squeezing tightly across her chest and with her legs off the coffee table and knees bent, Dia withdrew herself into the couch and seemingly tried to find a little place in that little apartment so as to escape. From a fecund profundity the spawning of words droned on as if coming from a natural and organic process, being part of but only accessory to something inherent and essential, like the sloughing skin of a snake shedding. Suddenly Dia could behold it all as meaningless, having lived it all her life. Startled from sudden knowing, she jumped up, and now dizzy, swaying and suffocating, she struggled to regain balance and bearing. "I . . . ahhh . . . I got to go." Her voice was barely above a whisper, trying to overcome the words still droning along the little hallway.

"Marty," she hollered at last. "I got to go."

Martha rushed out. Her face was fully made up, lips rouged, and eyes outlined by black mascara.

"What? Why? Why?" Martha pleaded.

"Thanks but I got to go."

"No, honey, stay. We'll call for pizza." A layer of powder covered the freckles on Martha's cheeks where once shined youth and innocence.

Uncontrollably, Dia put the back of her hand on Martha's cheek. "Take care of yourself."

"Honey, you are, like, scaring me. Dia. Stay here, we can go to the club together."

"No, I got to go."

"Dia, I'm, like, worried about you."

"Don't worry. I'm okay."

"Are you going to the club later?"

"No. Tell Hank I'm not working tonight."

"Why?"

Dia went to the door and opened it, but Martha grabbed her arm and held her back.

"Stay here for a while. You know you shouldn't . . . like you got you know."

"I got to go."

"Don't Dia. I'm worried. . . you know, like you got like your history you know. You're not going to do anything crazy, are you? Stay here with me, Dia."

"Don't worry." Dia stepped out of the little apartment, breaking free into the darkness of night.

From knowing she must go and remembering drove her on and forced her through the darkened path, through the gate into the street. Martha's voice lingered behind her, sweetly worrying and already regretting all the possibilities. After the gate, Dia emerged into farther darkness, onto the front lawn with patches of wilted, brown grass and scraps of discarded papers, plastic bags, and litters, all under the jaundiced light shining down from light poles high above. But now instead of illuminating, the jaundiced light thickened the air and turned putrescence all under it.

Now she was driving along a boulevard running through the middle of downtown Long Beach. At the first red light when the car stopped Dia felt cold sweat against her back. A red light cut her short, and somewhere beyond green lights and white fluorescent lights of distant shops were receding into a nebulous background, except for words on lit billboards, on storefronts, on signs of myriad shapes. Daichi Sushi, 24 Hours Gym, Midnight Coffee, Injury Law Center, New Age Yoga.

A heat now hovered about her head, and she panted shallow breaths and felt a compulsion for air and stepped on the gas as hard and fast as she could as soon as the light turned green. The car flew along. Lights passed, words passed. Going very fast, still Dia felt that compulsive heat. And she kept her foot down on the gas. She saw ahead the freeway entrance and above that a darkened, lonely winter sky, the only place to where she now wanted to go.

Once on the freeway, the car reached ninety miles an hour but here too words on the lighted billboards came shearing through her eyes and reaching deep into her mind, but here these words left no mark among a multitude of similitudes. Something deeper her mind had felt had barely scraped her with a dull hurt, the same type of hurt one of her cuts left after many days of healing—not as glorious as a blood-gushing cut, but a dull, aching hurt that had in it far more wisdom, all the time tugging and aching, existing. What did he say? she tried to remember. "Talk a lot without saying much." He did say that. But that wasn't all; there was something else before that. A car honked behind her as she had unknowingly slowed down and now she steered the car to the right, the slower lane. Already she saw the Wilshire exit and pulled off the freeway. In the same direction from which she had come only a couple of hours ago she turned left and headed back as if a part of her insisted upon returning, upon confronting an existential dilemma and righting an affront. The Chestnut Café came into view, and she pulled over, sat in the car without turning off the engine, and observed the table where they had sat earlier.

From within the café yellow lights glowed, warm and comforting. Inside the car she sat as cars whooshed outside, and she waited for memory to drag itself into light, for that morsel of knowledge tittering on a darkened cliff in her mind to fall into consciousness, into remembering and knowing.

Abruptly she turned from the curb and drove toward the ocean.

The same prickly heat now alternated with a sweating chill and hovered over a vacuity that was Dia, a vacuity where a self had once resided with confidence and poise.

Recognizable storefronts and promenades labeled by recognizable words came into view but in her mind seemed to vacate into chimera, floating by under the streetlights. She pulled over and parked in the street. She got out and walked along, her feet light, almost as light as air, slightly staggering. Around here she must stay for now, following an instinct and seeming to believe that sanity lay within the boundary of these streets. Ahead of her was Third Street Promenade where she had sauntered about on countless nights, nights long gone and no doubt happier, when there had only been the excitement of shopping and where now beckoned glamorous, bright store windows displaying expensive dresses and sleek high heels. She walked on, heedless. Hollowness hid behind everything, everything appeared frivolous. Only words seemed to remain, on storefronts, on signs, describing things, telling her things and of things, but coming truly from that fecund profundity and merely passing through her mind. She knew that now.

That profundity where the words comes from, she was thinking again, resembles that thing she'd read in the red notebook that belonged to Conrad. He called it the Godevil. It was a terrible thing, but why?

What terrible machination could come from this Godevil that Conrad N. had described and evoked such fierce opposition, she couldn't possibly fathom but sensed a sameness between this Godevil and this profundity where all her words, words through thoughts and words through actions had come from.

The thin blue dress had lost its freshness and now clung to her body like an unkempt rag. The night air percolated through her white sweater chilling her shoulder. Her feet, still light and on the verge of tipping over, performed automatic movements as if chained to the earth itself, having taken her to the end of the promenade. Dia looked up, surprised to see a bookstore and to realize she had already walked the entire block.

Through the bookstore's windows illuminated brightly by white fluorescent lights, words pullulated densely inside, teeming here and there with an insectile gravitation, simmering into odd shapes, perhaps a sign, perhaps a daring, visible only to those recently defiled by knowledge. As such, Dia could see it and was amazed that she could see it. A word took flight from the teeming mass, its wings buzzing fuzzily like a beetle, and flew directly in front of Dia, just on the other side of the glass. It tracked her gaze, following her irises wherever she looked as if it had a consciousness, as if it wanted most of all to let her know it was alive.

"Huh," she muttered. What was happening to her? A hallucination?

Her head felt light, dizzy. Nudging herself sideways toward the door, she saw the solitary word on the other side of the window follow her. Through the doors, being pulled in as if falling into a sibilant susurration, Dia was instantly submerged into a strange symphony. Suddenly loosened from between the covers' clutches, black inky words in the millions took to the air noisily, and upon seeing them Dia gasped, stood frozen, and darted her eyes every which way, trying to subtract hallucination from reality. From the shelves choked with books about business, finance, technology, cooking, psychology and on and on, words that had been arranged into sentences that then had become paragraphs and in turn pages now took flight into the air, obviating any meaning from their previous arrangement as if their only purpose was to take flight.

Dia could not tell how long she was caught in her daze, but at last she caught the stares of other people in the bookstore, their puzzled ogling and surreptitious glance. Hurriedly she moved forward and stepped on the ascending escalator. Couldn't these people see the words swarming around? The escalator delivered her to the second floor. It must be only her.

On the second floor, swarming words were waiting for her. As soon as she stepped off the escalator, they surrounded her in full embrace without quite touching her. Sibilant shuffling hissed in her ears and the smell of paper and ink seized her nose. Dia crinkled her nose, and the inhaled odor going straight to her head reminded her of childhood's books and reading comfortably in bed. Her heart was thumping strongly now. Her hands jerked abruptly and felt their sharp edges, as they swirled to avoid her. More words joined in as she moved, almost gliding, along the aisles; her feet were tireless and light. Lost in wonder, she tried to decipher the meaning of these words fluttering about, of their leaving their places behind and the supposed meanings in books, of their abandoning that very purpose for which they had been conjured. There must be something true and lasting among this frivolousness.

"Miss, can I help you?"

The question halted her. Amazed by a human voice, Dia looked to where it came from. At the other end of the aisle, a woman with graying hair, a wizened face and tired eyes, stared at Dia.

"Is there something specific you're looking for?" the woman said and approached Dia.

"Hmm," was all that Dia could manage. A mellifluous volubility, a reservoir of words overflowing its brim, and much more that had formerly been at the throe of her throat, ready to be projected forth instantaneously and profusely, now stagnated helplessly.

"Can I help you find something?"

"I am looking for . . . " Dia said. She pronounced the words as deliberately as if she were learning how to speak.

The woman waited patiently for her.

"Something about meaning, truth," Dia said, surprising herself.

"You mean philosophy. It's in the next aisle," the woman replied. She led Dia one aisle over. "Here," the woman said, "these books are arranged in alphabetical order under authors' names."

"Thank you." Dia wanted to ask the woman if she too could see the inky words buzzing about, but her fear was too strong. Instead she smiled.

"You're welcome. Let me know if you need more help." The woman walked away.

Dia turned to the books, which were packed tightly together, and pulled one out. The thick volume was by an unknown author, and the moment she opened it, the words scrambled into the air, joining the millions of others already hovering about her. Immediately she closed the book and stuck it back into its slot. With the next book, she tried to read the words before they could unglue themselves from the page, but as soon as she opened the book, the words jumped off the page faster than her eyes could glean their meaning, leaving behind an unblemished white page as if no ink had ever touched it. And the same with the next one, and the next one, until, furious and hopeless, she opened a book only to slam it shut, crushing the inky words in mid flight, and she heard painful squeaks from the pages. Somehow alleviating her frustration at once palpitating and smothering, their squeaks sheared through the overpowering sibilant hissing all around her. With another book and another slam, she heard a different squeak, this time more tonal, lower pitched.

But of course, they were all different, different words would cry differently. Her excitement grew as her frustration ebbed. She pulled out another thick volume with a blue cover and steadied it between her upturned palms, readying for quick actions. She let the book fall open from the middle and brought her palms together as hard as she could. The book slammed shut with a boom, nothing else. There were no squeals, no modulation or gradation of extinguishing life, or crushing of wingbeats, only the inanimate boom of paper colliding. "Ugh," escaped from her throat. So they wised up. She shoved the book back into its slot and grabbed another one at a distance away. She opened it and an inky swarm of words rushed upward, scraping past her face. Another "Ugh" escaped. She turned back to the blue book now, the one whose words had not taken flight.

Slowly, Dia retrieved the book from its place as if keen on not disturbing the words inside. Why, why was this one different? She put it close to her ear to listen for the restless whirring wingbeats readying for flight but heard nothing. The thick volume felt heavy in her hands and her fingers caressed its sharp edges; on the blue cover the elderly author stared out, straight ahead, balding and serene. Her heart now fluttered and she opened the book lightly. Falling open at a random page, the book showed itself to Dia, letting her see its words, one after another, lining up into beautiful sentences, row after row like soldiers at attention. Why weren't these words flying off? What was holding them here?

Precisely because the words remained still on the white page as if bravely manning the trenches, their order streamed through her eyes, leaving their marks on her consciousness.

Word after word that had been laid down by the author, cloistered in his study under candlelight, precise and determinate, had remained so for the ages. Seizing her eyes, the ordered stream whizzed with fluvial swiftness into her mind, effortless and almost without control, so much so that she dared not even blink, until a rawness in her eyes forced her to.

Somehow she sensed a meaning, and though she could not compare the exact text, a sameness clearly emerged, a sameness between this book and the red notebook of Conrad N.

Gripped by a paroxysm of joy, she pressed the blue book to her chest, went down the escalator as in one smooth glide, and paid for the blue book while enduring the scrutiny of the cashier, a young man who perhaps wondered why such a beautiful girl was purchasing such a book and if she could really read and understand it. Then she drove home on Wilshire Boulevard under the phantasmal streetlights, lights that seemed oppressed under the sky's darkness. Then she scaled the stairs to her apartment, dashed through the living room into which the low murmurs of electronics and machines from Moiro's room percolated, and finally lay in bed, partly leaning against the headboard with the blue book still clinging fast to her chest. Now lying in bed under a bright light, she had only a fuzzy notion of how she had gotten home like so many an afterthought.

With the same paroxysm of joy residing roundly on her chest, at once delirious and lucid, Dia perused the blue book and was drawn in. The text submersed her, doused her, and dragged her into its propositions and explications to arrive at apparent conclusion. Now focusing with intensity on the words, now slipping to a half sleep in which the stream of words whirred on ceaselessly, she read one thing, understood something else, and sensed a different thing altogether. It could not be said that she understood the text with the same claim of a pedagogical philosopher. What was transpiring in her mind, far more peculiar, was a wink the author, balding and serene, had sent across the ages, perhaps to a kindred spirit. Abruptly she jerked awake and cried out with joy, and holding the blue book fast to her chest she turned onto her side, suddenly overcome with an overwhelming obsession that she should find Conrad again, if only to find the connection between Conrad's thoughts and the blue book.

11

Of Things Small and Smaller

After a week of final examinations the students had left for winter break. Their absence had transformed the campus, draining it of puerile angst and frustration, into a mere assemblage of enormous concrete structures. A cold breeze blew among the darkened buildings and lecture halls and sometimes shook the trees' branches, whose rustling leaves Conrad could now hear. It was his favorite time of the year. He had taught the obligatory genetics class and was free for the rest of the year to follow his own plans. In his customary black coat he climbed the stairs toward his laboratory with the sturdy steps of a devout pilgrim, and he thought of the finality of his plan and how to bring about its conclusion. In the liquid nitrogen storage in his laboratory were many viruses with distinct characteristics, and yet he knew they were not enough.

"Good morning, professor," Dmitri said.

As Conrad walked through the narrow path in the laboratory, he sensed the bearded Dmitri somewhere behind the flasks and Bunsen burners, seemingly as ubiquitous as the rancid smell of bacterial broth.

"Good morning, good Dmitri," Conrad said without actually seeing him.

"A good harvest of rabies this morning , professor."

In his office, Conrad took out his red notebook and began to write:

The qualities of the perfect virus are 1)high infectivity rate, 2)short incubation time 3)ability to survive outside of a host for a long time 4)high mutation rate 5) high resistance to natural immunity.

Here, Conrad closed his notebook, leaned back in his chair, and fell into thinking. The first three requirements he had achieved for sometime now; he had isolated these viruses and spliced their DNA together, and yet he hadn't made any more progress. The next characteristic, high mutation rate, could be found in a rumor. A rumor? Conrad laughed.

"Dmitri," Conrad yelled. "Come here now."

"Yes, professor." Dmitri materialized at the door.

" Tell me about this new virus what's his name has gotten a hold of, from South America."

"The bastard Abe F.?"

"Yes, yes."

"New virus. Amazon virus. High mutation rate. From a virologist in South America. Could be more grant money. But only a rumor."

"Get it for me."

"Get what, professor?"

"This virus of course."

"Professor is ridiculous. No. Pray tell how I get virus from a rumor?"

"I don't know, Dmitri. You know your way around these buildings. You must know some of his lab technicians. Figure out a way to get it for me."

"It's theft, professor." Dmitri furrowed his furry eyebrows at Conrad.

"Well, yes it's theft, but it doesn't matter anyway because he'll never know it." Conrad pointed to the chair across from him. Dmitri came into the office and deposited himself heavily into the chair. Now Conrad's voice was just above a whisper. "Listen, Dmitri. I want this virus for my own purpose. I'll never publish any of it so he'll never know. No one will ever know. Well, except you and me."

Dmitri sensed he had the upper hand and he grimaced. "Professor, you behaving strange lately. Working on secret experiments but you don't want to publish. What you want Abe's new virus for, if you not going to publish?"

"I'm working on something but I can't tell you just yet. Be patient my friend."

"And all those viruses you keeping in liquid nitrogen. What you will do with them?"

"Dmitri, let's not digress. Please get me the new virus. A high rate of mutation is just what I need."

"Absolutely no."

"Please, be reasonable. I'm sure you can sneak off a tiny vial of that new virus if you put your mind to it. They won't even miss it."

"Absolutely no, professor. He calls security moment I come near his lab. Absolutely no."

"All right. Off you go. Back to rabies for you." Conrad growled.

Dmitri got up with a jerk, sending the chair skidding backward, and left the room, grunting like an angry bear.

Exasperated, Conrad leaned back in the chair and thought that there must be another way to get a sample of this new virus. He got up, plugged in the desktop computer that had been dormant for months, and began to search the Internet and the scientific archives for any publications about new South American viruses. The computer whizzed silently as pages after pages of information, scientific articles, images of scientists as well as totally unrelated junk, popular cultural gossip, and gratuitous advertisements popped up on the screen. At last, he narrowed his search down to two virologists, one at Buenos Aires University and another at the University of Chile, and emailed them both, inquiring about their work and whether they had any knowledge of a virus with a high rate of mutation.

When he finished, he turned off the computer and yanked the cord from the wall socket. Wanting to stand up, or perhaps to sit still, instead his body oscillated with a strange anxiety, as indecisiveness assaulted him and propelled him out of his chair. He took a few steps but turned around and ended up twirling around in the office. Arms crossing, hand now stroking his chin, now combing through his hair, he mumbled to himself, "What to do, what to do."

No further progress can be made to achieve the ultimate virus until he could get a hold of the last two types of viruses, and the red notebook, the manifesto, was being written as well as it could be. "What else, what else?" he mumbled, looking up at the ceiling. With the anxious sensation that something was still incomplete, he left the lab, leaving behind Dmitri's grumbles and grunts reverberating among the glasswares and the bubbling, boiling solutions.

Outside the building, the sun had risen high, and the campus appeared bright and cheerful. He sat down on a bench nearby and tried to tease apart the thread his sudden anxiety had wound itself into. He concentrated. After a while, like a great unction, slippery and soothing, his thoughts insinuated and teased apart the anxiety, laying it bare and revealing its innards. The thread of anxiety began to wiggle and show itself retracing into an extraordinary reality outside and separate from matters, into a void itself not a void at all but a world unto itself with unseen mechanistic and quantum laws; in short, his thoughts now gravitated back to the Godevil.

Yes, that was it, the source of his anxiety, sitting there with the sun warming the top of his head. He would defeat this Godevil by creating the Cain virus. He would force its existence into the world. It was just a matter of time, of getting the last two viruses. What about the casualties, the collateral damage?

He took out his notebook and wrote:

From the beginning of time, the Godevil has given rise to life, then countless lives, and then finally countless sentient lives that respectively existed at first in a 'Brownian existence', then burgeoned forth with a vast variegation, and finally filled every terrestrial crevice with sentience only to finally loop back with a paradoxical recidivism to 'Brownian existence' once again. With controversy and without dwelling too much on definition, the earliest life could be said to consist of viruses that continue to exist with 'Brownian existence' or an existence exemplified by such motion, in other words by basic thermodynamic principles. The reigning principle of these viruses continues to this day to be one of recycling; proteins, lipids, and nucleic acids coming together, existing for a while, then breaking apart ad infinitum, characterizing 'Brownian existence', in the process accumulating changes and thus giving rise to novel forms. Now, considering sentient lives, since these sentient lives, currently in the billions, have looped back into 'Brownian existence', it can be argued that any destruction of the current sentient lives is merely analogous to the recycling of viruses, and if so the process lacks any repercussion. Yet, the crux of the matter is pivoted around the necessity of a Grand Rule, one that subsumes all lives and even the Godevil itself. With the necessity of this rule, the difficulty becomes one of justifying the destruction of sentient lives, difficult but doable; however, without such a necessity, there remains only meaningless Brownian motion in the whole universe.

What is this Grand Rule?

He heard someone calling and shut the notebook.

"Professor. Professor," someone called.

He turned and saw Heather approaching. Already an impression of her flailing gait and of her timid legs preceded her. A diffidence marred her smile as she stood at a distance from him, and her hands moved about as if one hand was trying to hide behind the other.

Conrad beheld her image, and what he had just written in the manifesto somehow dovetailed perfectly around her, this sentient creature living a 'Brownian existence', buzzing about in a droplet of water.

"I'm sorry, professor. I hope you don't mind but I was just wondering if you graded the final exam," Heather said.

Conrad was struck by her hairband upon which a plastic rose appeared bright red in the sunlight, imparting to her face a childish innocence.

"I'm sorry to bother you, professor," Heather repeated. "But you know I'm applying to medical school. It's really hard to get in and I'm really nervous. You know, if I got a good grade from your course, it will help me a lot."

So much hope was entwined with so much timorous expectation, yet neither yielded to reality.

"Do you have our final grades? They're not posted yet."

Conrad awakened from his thoughts. "The grades will be posted soon. Tomorrow or the next day at the latest," he said and remembered all their grades and that the highest grade in the class was a B.

Heather's hands appeared to dance around one another even faster, as if playing hide and seek. The trembling and twitching of her hands migrated to her face. She said, "Do you mind if I ask you about my grade?"

Conrad remained silent and looked at her timid face twitching in the sunlight without actually seeing her; instead he saw a sentient creature like billions of other creatures on this planet, could comprehend her motives and desires, and even empathized with the activities of her 'Brownian existence'. That was the crux of things. Her existence, as well as that of the universe, was governed by a grand rule. Could he deconstruct her like many a virus, discard her existence, or dismiss her sentience even if it was bounded within this insignificant Brownian motion?

"Professor. Professor." Heather insisted. She now stared at him.

"Oh. Yes," he muttered. "Your grade. Must you know it now?"

"If it's not too much trouble. Since I'm here already." The trembling of her face seemed to have migrated to her whole body.

"All right then. Let me see," he said. He looked at her and seemed to be remembering. "Your grade is . . . " He remembered clearly that Benjamin got a B- and Heather a C. "You grade is . . . an A."

"A," she shrieked. Her hands flew up in front of her face. "Oh my God. Thank you. Thank you."

"Why not? If it will help with medical school."

"Thank you. Thank you," she said, gasping now, and her body twittered where she stood, perhaps not knowing if she should try to shake his hand or hug him, but finally she waved and ran away.

He opened his notebook and wrote:

Like any rule, time is a mental attribute. Perhaps by examining time first, this Grand Rule can be better understood. First only matter exists in the universe; matter that accrues and accumulates into stars, that moves about and collides, that explodes and radiates, but everything transpires in space and everywhere is as good as anywhere else. With the emergence of a mind, more specifically consciousness and memory, time comes into existence. A mind can behold the present, anticipate the future, and remember the past, and thus can evoke time. Time in turn reigns over space and matter, or, in short, the universe. Space is now locked in the linear prison of time, every millimeter is accounted for, every atom has a past and a future.

Likewise, a mind can behold dilemmas, anticipate consequences, and remember decisions, and thus can evoke rules. Without rules, living things exist as pure matter, actions are anonymous like the collision of unknown asteroids into distant stars, every action is as good as any other action in the infinite universe. Regret, guilt, suffering, and, by contrast, their opposites can not exist.

Like time, a Grand Rule emerged with the emergence of the mind and the battle against Good and Evil is waged first and foremost by the mind and within the realm of mind; therefore, the Grand Rule itself must be reconciled first, in other words the mind itself must first be strong, consistent, and at peace. To reconcile with itself, the mind must answer the question: Is the destruction of sentient life justified in any battles?

Minds that have not reconciled this question and yet can destroy sentient life are defective and should be considered as pure matter, like a stone, or one of the lowest animals.

"Professor," someone called him.

"No, not again," Conrad grumbled through his teeth. "I can't even get a moment to myself. I should have posted the grades already. Maybe I should give them all A's, then they'll leave me alone."

He turned toward the voice and upon seeing the person he almost leapt from his seat. A sudden panic seized him and he gasped, uncertain if he should flee. But it was too late. Diaphany came up to the bench and sat down. A morose shadow residing deep around her eyes, sending out tentacles, seemed to negate sunlight, but in spite of the shadow a spark in her eyes cut through sharp and real as she looked at Conrad, whose face hung in the sunlight aghast and motionless.

"Professor, I understand now," she said.

"You?"

Somehow, her slow, elaborate words alarmed him and he tried to see past the shadows encircling her eyes to ascertain her sanity.

"I understand now."

"What are you doing here? What do you want with me? Why are you still harassing me?" he said quietly as if he didn't want to be overheard by anyone else around. He looked quickly about, but they were alone.

"Don't worry. I don't have my cellphone with me," she said calmly. "Anyway, I read a philosophical work from 1818 about the will."

"The will?" he asked as if he was being drawn into the conversation beyond his control.

"Yes, the will is similar to what you described as the Godevil in your manifesto," she said, churning out slow, elaborate words, each heavy with sleeplessness, each an effect of meditation and brooding. "According to this book, everything is a manifestation of the will. Pain and pleasure, happiness and suffering are different fingers of the same hand. Though I don't think I understand it completely, you have to admit it's similar to what you wrote."

"I'm familiar with that work. Without question it's a great work. Schopenhauer called it the will, some called it the life force, others the vital substance. The good Descartes called it . . . "

"Really, professor?" Dia interjected. "So many people have thought of the same thing . . . It's wonderful . . .Really it is . . . Also strange don't you think? That so many people have thought of the same thing. I couldn't believe that there are books like this. It seems like this is what I've looked for all my life." From her purse, she took out the blue book and holding it tightly and gingerly bringing it forward she showed it to him. "I know I don't think I understand everything . . . or even a big part of it. But it just feels like that, it just feels right . . . You know what I mean . . . It feels like that's the way it should be . . . "

Deliberately avoiding her fingers, he took the blue book, looked at the picture of the balding author on the front cover, and handed it back to her.

"It must be the truth. It explains so many things . . . and it was so weird. When I discovered this book I was having a hallucination, I saw words flying all around me. It must be fate."

Her slow, elaborate words not only dissolved the pointed probe he had sent to ascertain her sanity but also, incredibly, conspired to make him an accomplice, pulled him away and threw him back so that his own words confronted him, and reflected against him his own sanity. Her words seemed to push him away, making him scrutinize her closely now, and only now he noticed her dress glowing a baptismal white under the sun.

"There is no fate, only the Godevil. Anyhow, explication is just one step. An important step but nevertheless only an initial step. You see a great theory must be verified by experimentation. One must carry out an experiment just as great as the theory to prove that the theory is correct," Conrad said.

"But what experiment are you doing?" she pronounced her words timidly and deliberately.

"As you said earlier, things are like fingers of the same hand. So the question is how does one finger knows the other fingers? Or how does one prove that the Godevil pervades everything?"

"How? What experiment can this possibly be?"

"I have devised such an experiment . . . " he said but caught himself and halted.

"I will help you. You must let me help you."

Something was amiss in her words, something that was there the last time he spoke to her that had been frivolous; now only an earnestness remained. Was she pretending, faking it as women often do?

"I have some good friends who have studied this problem. In fact they have lived through it. I can arrange for you to meet Truheckler, a physicist. He can make things much clearer than I can," Conrad mused.

"Who is he? Are you guys in a cult or something?"

"Absolutely not. We're free thinkers. We worship no religion and, most certainly, we worship no one."

"All right. But I'm serious about helping you."

"There is something . . ." he said as he raised his eyes toward the building in front of him, where in a freezer in Abe's lab the Amazon virus was stored. "There is something you can do to help with the experiment."

"Anything."

"Anything?"

"Anything."

12

One Small Trick for a Woman

From afar Diaphany M. watched as the man approached, carrying a heavy leather bag, his back hunching slightly, his belly bulging, his head sitting tightly over his shoulder as if lacking an intervening neck. When he was close enough, she could see instantly that Conrad's description of Abe F. jibed perfectly with the man.

Rolls of flesh bunched up on the cheeks, over the jaw, under the chin, and over the forehead, burying Abe's beady eyes under the bushy eyebrows. The large nose with flanking, curving nostrils sat squarely in the middle of his face. Just below the nose, glabrous, pendulous lips were stretched thin by a permanent grin, which no doubt had been transformed by age from a sycophantic to a condescending one. A thin crop of graying hair clung to his oval, pointed head. His age appeared more or less approaching sixty. Finally, a dark bronze colored his face, a color that must have been due to some bad bile flowing beneath the skin.

The late afternoon sky threw down layers of cold air. An occasional breeze made Dia colder, as she only wore a white dress shirt that opened down to her chest, its long, crisp collar accentuating her neck. Her dark blue silk skirt stopped short before her knees, making her shapely legs look longer than usual; her calves tensed as her heels rose over black stilettos. She had been waiting there for over an hour, looking out for Abe, and as she saw him from afar, she began to walk toward him. The cold air and waning light seemed to imbue her pale façade with a wispy, feminine fragility and made her lips appear redder.

"Excuse me," Dia said when she was close enough. Already she saw how his eyes had caught onto her. "Can you tell me how to get to Celine Hall?"

"Oh, why of course." His grin deepened, and he turned to face the same direction as Dia. His voice had a tinge of a nasal New York accent. "Go straight ahead until you get to that brick building there. Then turn left."

She shifted her purse onto her shoulder and car keys into her left hand.

"What does it look like?" she said, purposely bathing him in her perfumed breath.

He turned to her. His flanking nostrils widened, inhaling the perfume, and the grin deepened even more. "It's a brick building with two tall towers. You can't miss it."

"Thank you so much." She smiled at him. Her hands now grappled with the car keys and she let them drop.

"Oh, allow me." He put down his heavy leather bag and leaned down to pick up the keys. Then the stubby fingers held up the keys toward her, the grinning face tried its hardest to force the taut folds of cheeks into a smile, and the beady eyes still lurching deep could not be seen.

"Thank you my dear. You're such a gentleman," Dia said softly, taking the keys from him, and gave his stubby fingers a gentle squeeze. Still smiling, she resumed walking.

"I'm Abe by the way."

She turned around, still close enough to extend her hand. "Diaphany. Nice to meet you."

"Diaphany," he murmured as they shook hand, and he inched up to her. "What a wonderful name."

"Abe is a nice name too." She touched him lightly on the shoulder.

"You must be on your way to see the concert."

"Concert? Yes."

"I hear they're putting on Wagner . . . I'd love to go but I'm always busy, you see, I run a microbiology laboratory here . . . In fact I'm the chairman of the department. . . As a matter of fact, it's really convenient for me to go. My office is that building over there . . . Wagner, wonderful music, what more can you say about it . . . You're a music lover, I see." Abe let his eyes wander toward her chest, but dared not linger too long.

"Poor dear, you should make time for great music. You say you're the chairman of the department? I adore clever men." She took hold of his arm and pulled him closer. "You must tell me all about your work. So fascinating, microbiology, is it?"

"If you are fascinated, I'm at your service. Anything you'd like to know."

"I would love that, but another time. I must go now. Bye." She let go of his arm abruptly, waved her fingers in front of her face to bid goodbye, and walked away at a brisk pace. Abe's voice clamored after her, inquiring and protesting, but she kept going.

TWO DAYS LATER DIA WAITED AT THE SAME PLACE, STALKING Abe.

This time, she chose sophistication and modesty over overt seduction. Besides the cold air had nearly made her sick the last time. Now a black jacket with a high collar fit her snuggly, white pants made her look tall and elegant, complemented by the obligatory red high heels.

"Hello," Abe hollered, almost running as he saw her from afar.

Dia pretended not to hear him and kept going until she couldn't ignore him anymore.

"Hello. Diaphany, right?" He intercepted her. "Hello."

"Oh, hello." Dia feigned surprise by opening her eyes wide, staring at him, wrinkling her forehead as if she wasn't sure he was talking to her.

"It's Abe. We met a couple of days ago," he blurted out.

"Oh, hello. Yes, yes."

"Are you going to Celine Hall again?"

"Where?"

"Celine Hall?" he repeated, a little surprised.

"Oh, yes. I am."

"How was the music last time?"

"I don't know. I didn't go there for the music."

"I thought you were going there for Wagner . . . I once went there for a play . . . I can't remember exactly which . . . but it was wonderful."

"Oh, yes. It must be great in Celine Hall." Dia smiled.

Abe had been inching closer to her all this time. Dia noticed this and she showed him all smiles.

"You said . . . hm . . . you wanted to know more about micro-biology. I'm the chairman of the department. I don't know if you remember."

"Of course I remember now." Her voice purred. She reached out for his bicep and took hold of it. "Yes, you must tell me all about it."

"Where should we begin?"

"We begin another time. I'm sorry but I must go."

His hand grabbed hold of her arm and the grin on his face seemed to have lost its confidence. "How will I see you? Please give me your phone number. How do I contact you?"

"Why of course Abe." His name flowed mellifluously from her lips as if she'd been saying it all her life.

He fumbled in his pocket for his cellphone, and his hands shook noticeably as he entered her number.

"Call me my dear," she said.

"Absolutely. I will." Abe stood still looking after her, anticipating a future filled with pleasure.

HE CALLED HER THE VERY NEXT DAY AND SPOKE TO HER FOR five minutes but could not set up a date because she refused all his requests. He called her again in the afternoon and again at night when his wife was in the shower but got only the voice mail. In the following days, he fought with himself and struggled with the compulsion to call her again, and such struggles only inflamed and inflated his urges.

Oppressed by his urges, he couldn't help imagining the taste of Dia's skin, how he might position her, how tightly he would grip her, so much so that in the middle of the night he turned to his wife. In the big, sturdy bed, his wife always slept a couple of feet from him and through the years, they had never been bothered by the other's movements. "Sleep time is for sleeping," his wife had often screeched during rare episodes when he was besieged by a strong urge. Now, lust for Dia propelled Abe to move closer to his wife, groping underneath the blanket. He felt her night gown over her thigh and took hold of it, pulling it up slowly. Her snoring marked the silence of the bedroom at regular intervals. The nightgown was now up above her waist. His heart beat fast, and excitement overwhelmed any reservation as he began to slip his hand into her underwear. Her body, heavy from multiple pregnancies and rich food, jerked suddenly. "Heh, what's this craziness?" She hit him with short slaps. "Sleep time is for sleeping." She turned her back to him, speaking under her breath, "What's gotten into you? Sleep time is for sleeping."

THREE DAYS LATER, DIA AGREED TO MEET ABE AT A COFFEE shop, one of those chains that sat on every street corner. The vacant look of one who has been looking for something too much, yearning for something too much and yet not finding anything, something that was external to his own reality, now occupied solidly around the hollows of Abe's eyes as he shifted his body restlessly while waiting for Dia. She could see what a mess he was the moment she stepped into the coffee shop. She wondered if it had anything to do with her, but she felt sorry for him all the same.

"Diaphany," he called; his voice was a bit too loud for the coffee shop. The grin on his face expanded into an obscene smile, a rare showing of his yellow, pointed teeth.

"Good morning my dear." Dia smiled as she approached. They shook hands.

"Thanks for coming. It's hard to get a meeting with you. But I'm glad you're here."

"Yes, I'm always busy," she lied. She hadn't been back to work at all and all her time had been spent trying to understand the blue book. And since she had agreed to help Conrad, she had been mulling over his instruction and suggestion of how she should go about stealing a sample of the Amazon virus from Abe's laboratory.

"Anyhow, it's not important. What's important is that you're here. You must tell me about yourself."

"Oh, Abe. My dear. You must tell me about your work and yourself. You're such a clever man. I'm so interested in what you do."

Even deep within his beady eyes, Dia saw a sparkle; his face perked up.

"Well where do I begin? Perhaps you would be interested in a little history first. It ties in with microbiology and why it's fascinating," Abe said. After so many days of pining after her, he felt an irresistible compunction to tell her all the minutia of his life, or perhaps it was a conscious trick on his part to ingratiate himself to her. So he told her of his boyhood in Brooklyn where he and his brothers had grown up, being good, studious, and clever boys. In fact, he was so clever that his father had chosen him to study religion. He obeyed his father and studied religion because his religion told him to obey his father and he couldn't figure out what else to do. So he studied religiously, he could recite passages of the holy book from memory, he could extract obscure meanings from the holy book that had made his mother cry and his father nod approvingly. Each holy day, he had trekked with solid steps from his apartment to the temple, carrying the holy book under his arm, feeling divinity weighing heavily over his skull, as constant as snow, rain, hail or even the occasional thunder storm. First the neighbors had complimented him, and then they elevated him as an example of virtues with which to chew out their own children. Soon, the neighboring kids mocked him and bullied him. And finally his divinity became certain and unassailable when he himself bore no grudge against his neighbors, adults and kids alike, for worshipping and persecuting him at the same time. And though he didn't tell Dia, he remembered how holy his faith in himself had become that he had stopped masturbating, which for a teenager was a verifiable miracle.

One day his father got sick, and this suddenly changed Abe's life forever.

"He had come home from a bathhouse. He went there twice a week." Abe glanced at Dia now and then as to gauge the effect on her face.

For her part, Dia obligingly held his bicep as if pumping up his masculinity and squeezed it at the timely mention of holiness, persecution, and sickness.

"No, was he very sick?" she purred.

"You wouldn't believe. He must have gotten it from the bathhouse. Only God knows what he did there, but he must have gotten it from there," Abe said.

Abe continued with his story. He told Dia how drool oozed from the corners of his father's hollow mouth and the corners of his blood–red eyes, so much that it caked up his beard. Fever made him fling off the blanket only to pull it over his body again a few seconds later. During lucid moments he cursed his wife and warned her not to take him to the hospital, as though he feared the real diagnosis. Throughout the ordeal he kept mumbling, reciting something inside his hollow mouth. Even during sleep, which was sporadic and brief, these gargling utterances continued. After three days like that, his father appeared to be coming out of it.

"Then he asked for me. His religious son."

"You must have been a really good son. You must have comforted him." Dia looked at him sadly.

"Oh, let me tell you." In the midst of the story, he didn't forget to put his hand with the utmost casualness on her shoulder and let it trail down along her back.

No matter how much his family begged, coerced, reasoned, or cajoled him, Abe would not go near his father. 'Heh, what's this craziness?' they had said. 'But he's your father. The man who raised you and loved you and is so proud of you. You can't even go and comfort him. Are you possessed?' They appealed to his holiness, but he wouldn't budge. He couldn't explain to them why any more than he could explain the sensation of his own divinity. Beyond his understanding, something was keeping him away. Finally, his siblings, his uncles, even his mother, descended on him with slaps and kicks and had to drag him into the bedroom. They threw him down next to the bed, and as he got up he caught his father's eyes. By the movement of his father's mouth, Abe knew what his father had been mumbling all this time; it was a prayer. The sick man ignoring his own sickness and suffering had been asking for divine salvation all this time, and finally, upon seeing his son, he seemed to behold the scale against which his sin would be measured, the final confirmation of whether his prayer had been answered. That night he died unexpectedly.

"Oh, no. I'm sorry to hear that." Dia squealed with an exaggerated horror. "You must have been really sad."

"Yes, everyone was."

Abe now remembered clearly the days after his father's death, that he'd lost his faith as if it had served its one time purpose. As suddenly as it had come, he was shocked to be free of it but was even more amazed that he'd stopped masturbating. To make up for it, he had then committed himself to a rigorous schedule of jerking off at least three times a day. He would lock himself up in the bathroom so often that his mother thought he was grieving. "Ha, ha," Abe laughed quietly to himself as he remembered how he had walked around for weeks with a pale face and a painful groin. There was no way that he could ever tell Dia what he had done with himself.

"What's so funny?" Dia asked.

"It's not important. Nothing." He resumed a solemn demeanor.

"So did his death inspire you to study microbiology?"

"Not exactly. I lost all interest in religion and I wanted to be a doctor. I studied very hard. I got into an Ivy League College, then medical school. I was in the third year of medical school when I dropped out. I changed my mind. I went to graduate school instead and here I am."

"That's interesting. Why did you change your mind?"

"I found out that I couldn't handle people," Abe lied. The truth was that his brief stint with an asexual existence had caused a paradoxical yearning for the opposite sex, and all he could think of doing was to be a gynecologist, to be as close as he could to as many women as possible, for all his life. *My holy son, a women's doctor*, his mother shrieked when she found out. *A vagina doctor*, his siblings piled on. That was the end of it.

"You're so smart," she said. "I'd love to see your laboratory. It must be so sophisticated."

"Why of course. It'd be my pleasure to show you any time you like."

Dia knew she had him.

13

To Steal from a Thief

The plan was simple enough. Conrad had drawn it out, accounting for each minute and giving extra time for unanticipated interferences. Though coming onto the campus and going into the lecture halls, as Diaphany had done when she entered Conrad's lecture, was relatively easy, entry into the laboratories was much, much more difficult, especially at night. There were various security measures that had to be overcome. After going over various alternative schemes, they had finally agreed on one.

So the very next Sunday night, Dia arranged to meet Abe. His laboratory was on the fourth floor of the research building that was located diagonally to Conrad's.

"Diaphany," Abe called to her as she approached the building.

"Yes," she answered, looking around.

Abe came into the light. A misty dew was descending from the clouds. He hugged her, inhaling her light, sweet perfume, and even kissed her on the cheek.

"I wish you'd allowed me to take you out to dinner first."

"I'm sorry. I was so busy," she said, but the truth was that she had been at home, sitting nervously on the couch and trying to see how the scenario might play out and how far she was prepared to sacrifice for the cause. Several times, she had decided to renege and never to see Conrad again; after all she didn't owe him anything and he couldn't do anything to her, but in the end it seemed precisely because she was free to do as she wished that she came.

"What's important is that you're here now."

"Oh, did you remember to turn off all the cameras like I asked? There are cameras everywhere these days. We don't want to be caught . . . compromised. Maybe even end up on YouTube. Just in case."

"Yes, I did. You're right. We don't want to end up on YouTube. All right then. Let me give you a grand tour. My lab is quite large. The largest on campus." Abe put his badge against the electronic sensor. The locking mechanism of the heavy door buzzed open. "Please come in. We should use the stairs, we can't be too careful. It's on the fourth floor. I have five graduate students, three postdoctoral fellows, countless students and technicians, over fifteen grants. We've received grants from the government, from the NIH, from the pharmaceutical companies. You name it. It's basically money to do research."

They mounted the stairs until they reached a door that opened into a hallway with doors on both sides. Abe used his badge to open the doors and turned on the light.

"This is the main lab. This is where we do cutting-edged research."

White fluorescent lights from above filtered through the flasks, the beakers, and the sundry glassware stacked high on shelves, illuminated centrifuges, the Bunsen burner, the magnetic spinners on work benches, and finally shone on the spotless floor. Nothing was out of place. It seemed to Dia like a perfect place, though she had never been in a laboratory before. She glanced at her watch to note the time.

"Wow, everything here is so high tech," she said, feeling

truly awed, and because she had never been to Conrad's lab, she wondered if his was of similar magnitude. A faint smell of disinfectant reached her nose as her fingers ran over the smooth surface of the work bench.

"It is." Abe moved close behind her. "We study viruses and bacteria here. We dissect them piece by piece, look at all the components that make up a particular virus, try to understand why it's dangerous to human beings. Do you know that a virus is just a prepackaged set of instructions? It needs a bacteria or a cellular organism to reproduce. We want to study them so one day we may prevent an outbreak that can kill millions of people. Like the flu outbreak in 1918."

Abe beamed with superiority as he led her along.

Dia suddenly stopped and looked Abe in the eyes. "But my dear, I don't understand this alarm about viruses. They have always been with us and we have done well enough. Don't you think? There are many more of us than ever."

"That's true. But the next outbreak can cause massive devastation. Imagine even a five percent death rate, that's hundreds of millions of people. We must be on constant vigilance. And we're superior to them, so I have no doubt we'll win."

"Superior? If we're really superior, we shouldn't be afraid, right?" Dia remembered what she had read in the blue book. "I mean we can't compare ourselves to them because they don't have a mind. I mean if our bodies are made of truly superior stuff, then there is no need to be so alarmed right?"

"Hmm, I never thought about it that way." Abe drew closer to her. "I find you incredibly attractive. I've never known anyone like you, so interested in my work."

Dia broke away. "Show me your latest work."

"Let's go to my office." Abe's whole body trembled, ready to burst from uncontrollable excitement.

"Sure," Dia agreed, and as a queasiness spun in her stomach, she thought to herself that she mustn't debate her decision yet again.

ACCORDING TO THE PLAN, CONRAD WAS TO FOLLOW THEM into the building. From behind a tree at a distance, Conrad felt a chill descending over his head as he watched the whole scene. He saw Abe sitting in the dark, then Dia appearing, and them entering the building. And he waited. After a few minutes, he saw lights turning on in Abe's fourth-floor lab. He was to give Dia fifteen minutes after seeing the lights go on in Abe's lab, then proceed to the freezer and there he should be able to get a sample of the Amazon virus while Dia kept Abe occupied in his office.

There was no other way; all his inquiries to South American researchers had been rebuffed.

As the seconds ticked on, a nervous energy built up in his stomach. His heart seemed to abandon its regular beat. His legs began to carry him forward. Conrad could see the heavy door and the red light on the electronic lock, and even more clearly he could foresee himself entering through the door, going up the stairs, and sneaking into Abe's lab. And he needed only one vial. Just a few more steps, he would be at the door. But he heard someone behind him.

"Excuse me," a male voice called out from behind him, paralyzing him. "Excuse me," demanded a gruff voice. From behind, a flashlight beamed at Conrad's head. The jostling sound of shoes approached. "Can I help you?"

Conrad turned around and was blinded by the flashlight shining directly in his eyes.

"Do you have any ID?" the voice demanded.

"I work here. I'm a professor here," Conrad said meekly and brought up his hand to shield his eyes from the light.

"I need to see your ID."

"All right." Conrad pulled his badge from his pocket and handed it to the man.

The bright flashlight now moved away from Conrad's face as the man inspected the badge and then shone back on his face, alternating between the two as he compared them.

Once the light was off his face, Conrad could see the man was a campus police officer.

"Where are you going at this hour?" the man said.

"To my lab."

"You're working at this hour?"

"Yes, some experiments can last for hours or days."

"Is that so?"

"Yes. That is so."

"Experiments lasting for days?"

In an instant and in the policeman's belittling voice, Conrad recognized an ulterior force thwarting him, using these sentient creatures to frustrate him. He had no more time; it had been much too long already. Conrad said, "Listen you. I'm a tenured professor here. I'm going to my lab to do important work and unless you let me go this very instant I will take it up with your superior. I want your name and badge number."

"I'm sorry, professor," the policeman said and handed back the badge. "I was making sure you're not a terrorist."

"Terrorist? That's a brilliant excuse."

Conrad snatched his badge and, turning away from the door that he was so close to, marched away in the direction of his own lab, leaving the guard looking on with confusion, flustered and mute, not daring to question why Conrad was walking to another building.

In a couple of minutes Conrad was running up the stair to his own lab. The air stagnated in his throat, making him breathe fast and shallow, and his thumping heart might just stop at any moment. To his amazement, the door to his lab was open and all the lights were on. He rushed inside. There was no more time, it was too late, his head buzzed with the image of Dia wrestling down Abe to keep him occupied.

"Professor," someone called him.

The word startled Conrad and he thought he'd gone mad.

From the corner of the lab, Dmitri, in his customary stained white lab coat, stared at him. "Professor, what you do here? At this time? You should be home, no?"

"Dmitri, Dmitri," Conrad gasped and rushed toward him. "You have to help me. I don't care what you said before. I demand that you help me right now, this second. There is no more time. There is no more time. Do you understand?" He seized the collar of Dmitri's lab coat and pulled his face close.

"Slow down professor. What you blubbering about?"

"Dmitri, shut up and listen. Listen for one second. You have to go over to Abe's lab and get a vial of the Amazon virus. You must do it right now. Time is running out."

"You mad . . . "

"Shut up and listen. I'm not mad. I have someone inside there right now, keeping Abe busy. There is no one else there, just him and he is busy. All the doors are open. All you have to do is to go in and get a vial."

"Someone see me. I'm deported."

"There is no one around, you stubborn Russian," Conrad growled and groveled at the same time. "You must do this for me now. There is no more time. I was going but I lost my nerve. I can't do it anymore."

"They have camera."

"They've already been turned off. Go now. I'll give you anything. But go now."

"Easy professor. I go. I go for you."

"Thank you. Thank you. Go. Go."

"I go."

"Oh, one more thing." Conrad recovered a little calmness. "There is a guard out there."

"What?"

"A guard. He stopped me, so be careful."

"Oh, a goon. I understand. I am used to goons. I was young in Soviet Union. I am used to goons. Don't worry."

"Now go. Go. No more time. Oh wait and what are you doing here at this hour?"

"I work on rabies virus, remember. Rabies make people crazy so rabies pay," Dmitri said as he ran out of the lab.

MEANWHILE, DIA HAD HER OWN PROBLEM.

An odor, part stale and musty, part old and decaying, hit her as Abe let her into his office and turned on the light, revealing a desk stacked high with journals and papers. Shelves full of books were against the back wall. A leather couch pushed against a wall covered with framed diplomas, certificates, and plaques. The fourth wall was made of glass through which she could see the lights down below in the quad and the faint outlines of buildings nearby.

"Please have a seat," Abe said.

"Thank you." Dia sat down on the couch. She glanced at her watch again; about six minutes had passed.

Abe came close, stumbling and trembling, and flopped down on the couch. "Heh, heh, so how do you like my lab so far?"

"I'm sorry, Abe. Could I trouble you for something to drink?"

"Where are my manners? Of course, I'll be right back." Abe jumped up and left the room.

Dia looked at her watch again and tried to estimate. Six minutes had passed; in another nine minutes Conrad should be entering the building, making his way up to the fourth floor, entering the lab, and, hopefully, he would be able to find a vial of the Amazon virus. From the moment the light went on in Abe's lab, Dia was supposed to keep Abe busy for about thirty minutes.

Abe came back in and handed Dia a cold bottle of water.

"Thank you so much, Abe."

Abe sat down next to her.

"Let's not be too formal. I don't say this often. As a matter of fact I've never said this to anyone before. I feel like I know you already. Even though we've just met. I know you must get this all the time since you're beautiful. Let's be honest. I want to be honest. I think you're also very intelligent and I don't want you to think I take you lightly, because I don't and I would never take you lightly. I want to get to know you and for you to know me and not just my work since you seem very interested in my work, which is fine. I mean it's great that you're interested in my work. That shows how intelligent you are, like I said. I already knew that. You know what I mean. I want you to get to know me, not just my work. You know what I mean, me as a man."

Dia sat cross-legged and cross-armed, still wearing her coat and hoping that she could leave before having to take it off. In Abe's breath, she could detect the tangy smell of Listerine. She took a sip of the water and she watched him closely, following his movements, anticipating a strike, much like a snake charmer.

"What do you think? Tell me what you think. I want to know what you feel. Am I right? Diaphany, we can have a great time together. I'd do anything for you. You know I would. Hmm." Abe breathed hard, and suddenly with pendulous lips protruding he lunged at Dia. His hands wrapped around her.

She jerked away and thrust her shoulder toward him, only to feel his face nuzzling against her hair and neck. She pushed him away. "Take it easy, Abe. I'm not that kind of girl. I thought you were going to explain your work to me. What you do here, that's all."

"Please, please. You're so incredibly beautiful."

Her shoulder and then her hands pushing against him, she tried to keep his face away from hers, but his frenzy was too much for her. It was tricky to keep him excited and occupied without giving away too much.

Lost in himself now, the heat, the frenzy shooting through his fingers, Abe floundered, his hands reaching to feel as much as he could feel; his nose inhaled against her hair, as if taking in the stuff of life.

In a flash, Dia poured the bottle of water over his shirt.

"Aaaaahhh," Abe cried.

"I'm sorry. I'm so clumsy."

"That's all right. It's just water. I'll be fine." Abe got up. "I'll just dry myself off."

"No, no. I'm sorry." Dia knew that she must keep him from going outside at any cost. "Sit down here. Why don't you take off your shirt? Yeah. Please stay here and, you know, take off your clothes. I'll make it up to you." She softened her voice into a sultry whisper. "I promise."

"All right." Abe sat down.

"Why don't take off your clothes?"

"Everything?"

"Yeah, everything. I'll just go to the bathroom to freshen up. I'll be right back."

Backing out, Dia smiled at him. She closed the door, and as soon as she turned around, she nearly toppled as she saw the bearded Dmitri tiptoeing from the staircase. The bearlike Dmitri kept moving and brought a finger across his bearded lips. Dia glared at him and she followed him into the lab. Dmitri stopped in front of the freezer.

"Who are you?" Dia whispered.

"Professor sent me," Dmitri whispered without looking back as he opened the freezer.

"Conrad?"

"Yes." Dmitri pulled out frozen metal containers and started to open them.

"How do you know I work with the professor?"

"I know everyone here. I don't know you. Professor told he has someone. That must be you."

"How much time do you need?" Dia continued to whisper.

"Ten minutes, maybe."

"I'll go back and keep him busy. But hurry."

Dia went back to the office and stood outside the door listening. She heard nothing. The queasiness in her stomach had crept up her esophagus and began to expand at the back of her mouth. She opened the door; to her amazement, the light had been turned off. She entered. White light from the quad below shined obliquely along the wall and was enough for Dia to see the naked abdomen bulging on the couch.

"Diaphany, baby. I'm here. Come and give me some love. Come on baby. I'm so hot for you."

Dia approached the bulging abdomen. The rest of Abe seemed sunk into the darkness with the couch, and the moment her hand touched his bulging belly, he uttered an exuberant groan, "Ohhh." She had to turn her head aside to avoid laughing. The bulging belly was round and smooth, like that of a pregnant woman about to deliver an abnormally overgrown, diabetic baby. Her fingers dangling like the feet of a spider went north over his round, bursting chest, and pinched his nipples.

"Oh baby, baby." His hands grabbed at her jacket frantically, trying to pull it off and being unable to do so, they squeezed anything within reach.

"Abe, relax." Dia pushed his hands away. "Stay still and let me take care of you."

"Okay, okay. Baby. I'm sorry. I'm just too excited."

"All right. You don't want to be too excited. Just take it easy and enjoy yourself," Dia said, while thinking about the minutes that had passed. She tried to look at her watch but there was not enough light to see the watch's small face. Resigned to keeping Abe occupied, she had no choice but to continue. Caressing, slithering, her fingers set his skin tingling and erupting with goosebumps, all pushing up and channeling the pressure toward a dampness in his groin. Then abruptly her sharp nails dug into the tense skin surface, knowingly cutting him short and setting him up for more. After a while, though, his body stirred and Dia knew she could no longer delay.

From the bulging belly, her fingers descended toward his manhood. The moment she touched, a loud groan shook the room. She yanked her hands away.

"Oh hohoho," Abe moaned. "I'm sorry." He blew out a long breath, deflating. His voice became slow and mellow. "I'm sorry. I didn't mean to . . . so fast. It's important to me to take care of the woman too."

"Let me get some paper towels." Dia quickly left the room.

"Give me a few minutes. I can do it again. It's just that . . . "

As Dia went out and closed the door behind her, she saw

Dmitri, holding a vial, eyes wide and white, without doubt having heard the room-shaking groan, tiptoeing toward the stairs. Silently, Dia followed him, also on tiptoe.

14

Secrets in Hollywood land

WITH THE SUCCESSFUL ACQUISITION OF THE AMAZON VIRUS, Dia had proven herself very useful, and more unexpectedly Dmitri had become an unwitting accomplice who was now just as guilty as Conrad and, if necessary, vulnerable to intimidation if not outright blackmail. Not that Conrad would ever think himself capable of such thing, but to accomplish his mission he must allow himself such freedom. He was pleased with the most auspicious turn of events, but he still couldn't quite ascertain if Dia would ultimately thwart his entire experiment or help him.

Anyhow, there was only one more thing to do and that was to seize the opportunity and educate Dia, to cement her commitment, to let her develop an unbreakable empathy toward his quest and a deeper understanding of the theoretical aspects and the history of the struggle. In other words, to brainwash her, though Conrad didn't like that vulgar term. He preferred the term *indoctrination*, and to achieve this, he thought it best to have Dia meet Truheckler first and Minh later so that Dia could see that there were others, who shared his belief. He wrote Truheckler a letter detailing the full history with Dia, to arrange a meeting.

One sunny day, a week later, he picked her up in his 1975

Mustang and drove her to Truheckler's house. Conrad was so intent on thinking about how Dia should be brainwashed that he seemed oblivious to her presence.

Uncomfortable with the silence, Dia asked him, "Do you like classic cars? This car is great."

"Of course not. It's just a vehicle," Conrad answered and resumed his forward stare.

"It must be worth a lot. You should sell it and get a modern car if you don't care about classic cars."

"You don't understand," he said slowly. "The reason I drive this car is because it's an old car. It has no electronics, so they can't track or know what you're doing, where you're going. The same reason I don't have a cellphone. By the way, you didn't bring your cellphone, correct?"

"Of course not."

"Do you know that the size of the Herpes virus is to a balloon as the size of a balloon is to the Earth?" Conrad said suddenly, as he thought that he should prime her for the conversation with Truheckler.

"Wow, really? That's amazing."

"There are other viruses much smaller. The parvoviruses are much smaller. Viruses can have DNA or RNA inside them. The Herpes virus is one that inserts its DNA into its hosts, once it's inside you it stays for as long as you live. Unlike other viruses that only pass through. There are viruses that can stay dormant in the earth for thousands of years before waking up and becoming infectious again. Some infect only the brain, others the immune system like the HIV. Still others infect other organs like the saliva glands."

"Mumps," Dia said excitedly.

"Exactly," Conrad replied and went on to regale her with tales of the microscopic world.

Truheckler's house was in fact a mansion; it sat on several acres of land in North Hollywood and was called the Grind Mansion; its name was probably due to its lurid history, rumored to have had been the go-to place for fantastic sexual escapades for movies stars in the sixties. Through the winding streets which were lined on both sides by majestic trees and opulent estates, they finally came to a gate. Conrad drove up next to the intercom and dialed the security code.

The driveway curved around an enormous arching entrance and then led to the guest house and servants' quarter. Conrad stopped the car at the entrance to the main building before a court yard paved with smooth stones around a fountain, now dry. The three wings of the main building, built in the style of a French château, had twenty-four rooms and divided into three wings and enclosed within its embrace an atmosphere that was stagnant and foreboding. Conrad jumped from the car and rushed toward the door, which had been left unlocked, barely hearing Dia's gush of wonderment: "Wow, your friend lives here all by himself? It's enormous."

Conrad led Dia into the main hall. Wood dyed to burgundy had been laid to make the floor, carved into elegant handrails for the staircase leading to the second floor, made into the tall doors that lined the hallway, and used to decorate the columns rising up to the high ceiling. A sofa and several arm chairs were spaced around a coffee table holding a vase of tulips, still fresh. Against the walls and in the corners, strange and convoluted sculptures stood, and from them, imagined faces seemed to leer.

"It's gigantic," Dia said. "It's beautiful. Where is everyone?"

"Please have a seat. He'll come soon. He lives here with a butler and a cook. That's all," Conrad said and hollered to the back. "Truheckler, I'm here."

They both sat down.

An odor of old wood and old books occupied the air, but there was also a fruity aroma, strong and sweet, wafting toward them from somewhere in the back. From tall windows sunlight shone through, reflecting off dust particles that took flight as they sat down.

"Ha, my boy. Conrad," Truheckler called out from the back. His cane thumped loudly against the wooden floor as his enormous body lumbered toward them.

They both rose and waited for Truheckler. Conrad shook his hand. Dia tried to shake his hand, but Truheckler embraced her and kissed her on the cheek.

"Walter, bring them drinks and fruits," Truheckler called to the back and then turned to Dia. "You will like the strawberries. They have a wonderful, strong aroma. And peaches as well. Do you smell them? You have to inhale, take in the aroma."

"I like your accent." Dia noted the chesty ring of a German accent, one that had been softened by the many years in America.

Walter brought out a silver tray with bottles of Perrier, three cups of coffee, and strawberries, peaches, and apricots, all in ziplock bags.

"Please, try the fruits. You'll see they're wonderful. The aroma, sniff the aroma first. You see I age them in plastic bags to trap the aroma, like trapping the soul of a dying man. Go on. Try it."

Dia picked up a bag of strawberries and opened it, and the concentrated smell of strawberries surrounded her. She took one to her mouth and it tasted like tangy nectar.

"Hmm, hmm," Truheckler laughed softly. "You see, my dear. Wonderful, isn't it?"

"So sweet. The smell is wonderful, truly wonderful. Very good strawberries. Won't you have some?" Dia said.

"I'm afraid my body won't tolerate it. You see, I have severe diabetes among many other ailments. Walter and I work very hard just to keep my body in balance. I only want the smell, the memory as I remember it, when I was young, when I could smell and taste them. Now the smell brings back my youth. You see, my dear?"

"Truheckler, please. Enough about your fruits," Conrad said. He had been watching them closely and seemed to have run out of patience.

Truheckler leaned back, his body overwhelming the chair. "Yah, my boy. I read your letter," he said as he turned to Conrad and winked. He turned back to Dia, "Diaphany, my dear. What a wonderful name. Conrad tells me you have proven indispensable in his experimentation. You must understand what he is trying to do. His logic, so to speak."

"Sort of. I think I feel it to be right more than I know it to be right. Do I make sense?"

"Perfectly. Truth is meant to be experienced. Perfectly."

From her purse, she took out the blue book and handed it to Truheckler. "Do you know this book?"

"My dear. How can I not? We all know it. It's the closest description of the being, the life force, the vital substance."

"He called it the will."

"Yah, it's just as good. And the doctor called it the Godevil, which is also true in many senses. So you see, my dear, many people throughout the ages have come face to face with it, to the same realization."

Truheckler saw Conrad starring at him and nodding to urge him on. He acknowledged with a faint nod and continued, "You see, my dear, when I was a young man, I too did my part. My expertise was in nuclear physics, so that's what I did. Let me tell you, it was . . ."

"It was during the coldest, most paranoid period of the Cold War. The year was 1969, and the Soviet Union had just crushed the Czechs' revolution the year before. The Cuban missile standoff, which had occurred a few years before, was still fresh in my mind. The atmosphere at the nuclear laboratory in New Mexico where I worked as a junior scientist was one of suspicion and fear. My job was to work on a team to develop and test nuclear weapons. I had been working there for five years and yet I never knew whom I was talking to. I could never trust my colleagues. But I sensed an opportunity in the world. I was ready to commit all my ability to advance our cause. I had heard of Klaus, who many years before had passed secret information to the Soviet Union. Though to this day, I don't know if he had any understanding of our struggle. I'm sure even if he did not know about the grand scheme, he must have had some intuition for him to do what he did. As for me, I had no knowledge of these grand schemes in the world that men since time immemorial have attempted to bring to light, at least men who knew. It all started with the storied Cain, you see. I did not know what I know now, but I had the intuition that nuclear knowledge should be spread across the globe to . . . one day.

Well, anyhow, I was a young man then, full of health and life. I don't remember so many things so clearly any more, but this is something I can never forget. It was spring in New Mexico, when it was not quite so hot yet and all the flowers were smiling. I loved the flowers. Around the house where I lived, I had camellias, lilacs, nasturtium, even wild poppies, and of course roses. Such eclectic aromas, every morning I came out of the house to breath them in. But at last it was time to leave. That spring I left for Los Angeles for a two-weeks vacation. But the real reason was to deliver nuclear secrets to the Chinese. Hahaha.

There was a man by the name of Li Bai. A Taiwanese scientist. I had met him for only a few minutes at a scientific conference. We happened to be standing next to each other in the coffee line. I knew at that time that the Chinese were working to perfect the hydrogen bomb. They had help from the Soviet Union but if I could give them what I knew, it would certainly help them along. So I told Li Bai that it was a shame for nations not to cooperate. That was all I said and that was enough. A week later, as I was having a meal at my favorite Chinese restaurant in town, where I often went for dinner, the waiter placed a hand written note next to my Kung Pao chicken. It said 'Hello' and under that was the name Li Bai. The same waiter made a round of the restaurant, picking up some empty dishes, and on his way back to the kitchen promptly passed by my table where he quickly removed the note.

That restaurant became my contact point. That waiter was my handler. Li Bai must have informed the Chinese that I was an easy recruit and he was right. I was eager to give information, but for months I gave him nothing. Every time he confronted me, I simply told him to wait.

Then in the spring of 1969, I was ready. I had made arrangements with the laboratory director and requested two weeks of vacation. My destination, Los Angeles, or more precisely Hollywood, was filed on the necessary papers with them. You see, I had fallen in love with the movies and Hollywood, the idea of it. It was a place that supported another world, a dream world. Up to that point I'd lived in America for five years, and, even so, I'd never been to Hollywood, so the excitement of going to Hollywood together with the fear and anxiety of delivering nuclear secrets to the Chinese was truly overwhelming. My nerves were on fire.

I had packed a simple suitcase. My car was full of gas and sat waiting for me outside my house. I was looking forward to enjoying a long drive to Hollywood when a knock shook the front door. I held my breath when I heard it. Maybe it was a sales–man; back then packs of them roamed the city, selling everything from vacuum cleaners to plastic containers to shoe polish, and I thought if I could stay still long enough, they would go away. But the knocks kept on pounding right through me. I went to open the door, and two men dressed in black suits were standing there. By their look, I thought they were selling coffins, or life insurance. I was about to shoo them away when they stared at me in a very strange way.

'Mr. Truheckler,' the older man said.

How did he know my name? Immediately it occurred to me that this was serious. Sure enough, the man said, 'We're from the FBI. I'm agent Holder. Can we come in?' Then he just entered without waiting for my reply.

The older man was balding, and I never shook his hand, but I could see that his hands were large and hard. His face was also large and hard. But the younger man who was standing behind him had a glaze over his face, a kind of psychotic glaze; he said not a word but I knew he was the dangerous one. Terrified, I couldn't breathe right. My poor heart was nearly wrecked. I don't think anyone can possibly understand my panic. Could they possibly know my method? But I had to remain calm. I had to. They couldn't possibly know my method. Nobody could.

I had to show that I was not shaken, so I asked them for identification, which surprised them. The old man put his badge up near my face.

Once inside the house, the young man went looking through everything—the drawers, behind the TV, behind the mirror, the bookshelves. He tapped on the wall for hidden compartments.

'Where are you going?' Holder said.

'To Hollywood. For a vacation,' I said.

'You like movies,' he said.

'Yah, very much.'

'You're a German?'

'You knew that already. It's all in my file.'

'What part of Germany?'

'Dresden.'

'You like Chinese food.'

'Yah, very much.'

You see, then it became clear to me what they were doing. They weren't really looking for stolen secrets, they were trying to scare me. I knew they had searched my house many times while I was at work. Sometimes a pencil was misplaced, a cup off its mark by half an inch, or a book pushed in too far. And I'd seen the black car always sitting there, down the street from the Chinese restaurant where I met my handler, or down my street, watching my house late at night. Even at work, they had people watching me to see if I'd taken any documents. Of course they found nothing. They must have decided to scare me just in case I had any idea. The technology was too important to risk allowing any chance of it escaping. So it didn't surprise me when they went rifling through my suitcase. But what the young man with the psychotic face did next shocked me; he took out a pocket–knife and began to cut the lining of my suitcase.

'Stop. You're destroying my suitcase,' I protested. My protest only made him more crazed, and after a couple of minutes, my brand new suitcase was a completely shredded.

Holder who was watching with amusement now said, 'How are you going to Hollywood?'

'I'm driving,' I said before I could stop myself.

'Give me the key.'

I handed him the key, and they went outside to the car. They opened all the doors. To my horror . . . I don't want to remember . . . to my horror the psychotic young man went to the leather seats with the knife. It was a new car, hardly six months old.

I couldn't take it anymore. I said, 'This is against the laws. I will file complaints against you.'

'We are the law,' Holder told me and laughed. 'You're not driving today.'

All I could do was watch them; I had no rights, I wasn't even a citizen yet, but after all these years of living here, I know now that being a citizen wouldn't have made any difference anyway. They could have shot me right then and there, and they could have gotten away with it.

When they were done, Holder said, 'We'll need to take your car in for further inspection. Can we offer you a ride to the bus station?'

'No. I will take a taxi.' I went inside.

'Wait a minute.' A voice followed me inside the house.

I turned around. The young man with the psychotic face was right behind me. He said, 'I have to search you.'

I knew the routine; I put out my arms and waited as he groped and felt every inch. I must admit that it was the most wretched humiliation I had ever felt in my life. But you must know this intimately every time you go the airport these days.

When the young man finished, he said, 'Where are you staying in Hollywood?'

The question threatened to disturb my whole plan, but I told him without delay the name of the hotel which he recorded in a little black note book.

They probably thought they had scared me enough, and they were right. They didn't have to say much, their actions were all too convincing. Oh even to this day, knocks on doors terrify me so. But though frightened as I'd never been before, I was more determined than ever to bring my mission to completion.

The next memory of that adventure is Hollywood. Like a child waking up to find wonderland, I couldn't have been more ecstatic. The hotel was right off Hollywood Boulevard, and the first thing I did was wander the streets where beautiful women in short skirts were walking along with me. I could see in their eyes the hope of one day becoming famous. The air had a faint scent of the ocean, which was not so far away; even gasoline exhaust had its own distinct tolerable smell here. The sidewalk had a certain concentrated mystique with the names of movie stars right under my feet. And the Pantages Theater was majestic; it did not disappoint. For lunch, I followed the advice of a newspaper boy and went to the Hungry Tiger Restaurant, hoping to see some famous movie stars; luck was with me because I thought I saw Elvis sitting in the far corner of the restaurant with a roast beef sandwich.

By the late afternoon, I could barely drag myself back to the hotel. My sore feet and tired legs nearly stopped obeying me. Though I'd enjoyed Hollywood thoroughly, a sense of being followed irked me now and then. But when I got back to my room, the real world startled me with a cold shock. I saw on my table pencils and papers laid out on my table just as I had instructed my handler. You see, they could never prevent me from sharing what I know, for they could never imagine my method. I had it all in my head; my memory was just as good as any camera. I sat down at the table, took up the pencils, and began to draw, nearly a hundred diagrams in all, fully annotated, with precise measurements and units, all that I had seen during my years at work.

The very next morning, the diagrams went out with the dirty sheet and towels. The Chinese chambermaid was only too happy to clean my room. Needless to say, I never went back to work; my excuse was that the FBI had threatened me and violated my rights. Under such harassment, I no longer felt safe working in the nuclear laboratory. Since they could never know my methods, and nothing was missing from the laboratory, they didn't persist in harassing me. They watched over me for awhile as I made Hollywood my permanent home.

I gave the Chinese everything I knew, and I never asked for money. Not once. But they knew honor, something altogether missing now–a–days, so when China opened up its country for business, I was welcomed as a businessman. I have more money now than I could ever spend. Everything you see here came from that."

"You have a photographic memory," Dia uttered with amazement. "Was that how you could remember every single detail?"

"Yah, my dear. That's correct," Truheckler replied, beaming with pride. "With my help, the Chinese were able to build the hydrogen bomb in record time. They were the country that had the fastest time going from a uranium bomb to a hydrogen bomb. I gave them much more than information. I gave them my own innovative design. Then I gave it to the Pakistanis, the Iranians, the North Koreans. Yah, it was all for a purpose."

Conrad was content to sit quietly in the background and observe the change in Dia, the facial expressions that revealed wonderment and awe as she traversed deeper and deeper into their world.

"But the knowledge you gave away could destroy life on earth." Dia wrinkled her face with confusion. "I don't understand your motive if not money."

"I didn't fully either at that time. But it must . . . must simply be the same demiurge that drove the countless others, all the way back to Cain. But none has succeeded."

"Conrad is pursuing the same thing." She glanced back at Conrad.

"It must be . . . So the Chinese rewarded me with business deals and now I'm quite rich," he said as though trying to change the subject.

"It must be good to be rich."

"Yah, my dear. This mansion you see here. And many more buildings downtown. All over Hollywood. Yah. If you ever need money, my dear, please come to me. Yah. Do promise."

"Haha." Dia laughed with delight. "Sure, I promise. That's an easy one to make."

"Do promise, also, that you will help Conrad again. Yah."

"Yes," Dia said hesitantly.

And the conversion of Diaphany was well on its way.

Love Endangers

A part of Conrad, or of any man, that is sensual but has been blunted and buried by life's familiarity, by years of banality he can't decipher anymore, is no doubt aroused by a novel femininity and all the imagining it inspires. If that part of him, or of any man, that he had allowed to wither, suddenly comes back to life, he will need time to know it again, to discern what it requires in order to nurture it, for with its revival a strange pleasure begins to simmer. And as that part of him simmers brighter, to his amazement he recognizes its unyielding demands and wild tempestuousness, but most of all he is shocked to discover it as no less than life itself, and by contrast his recent life has been no less antithetical and decaying if not already dead.

Since involving Diaphany in the struggle, Conrad began to feel these things. And it would be wrong to think that Conrad had planned for what would happen next because he did not. He merely became alive again and reacted reflexively to the steps of a macabre entanglement that had begun in the waves and seemed to be never ending. It would also be wrong to think that Conrad was insensitive to physical attraction because he was not; in fact, he had to concentrate his efforts to ignore any emergence of desire for Dia. For all he knew, she was just another soul like the few others before, like him, Truheckler the physicist, or Minh the Marxist, all trying to find answers. Though he saw no further use for her after the theft of the Amazon virus, he couldn't resist her persistent insinuation into his life beyond simple camaraderie of a common yearning. She would call and ask to meet for coffee to discuss the nature of the will and the Blue Book which she continued to read and to try to decipher. "The way I understand it . . ." Conrad would begin to answer her each time. Outside the wintry sky rotated away from light and grew gloomier; inside the Chestnut Café, they sat under the warm glow of light across from each other, each receiving the soft vocal undulations of the other, their eyes, too, conjoining in dialogue. But often a spark emanating from a carnal depth would interrupt the penetration of their eyes and stir up an awkward moment as they both recognized it for what it was. Then one day, Diaphany took a seat next to him as they talked and gazed at the traffic outside.

"It's strange," Diaphany said.

"What is?" Conrad asked.

"I notice that you keep using hand sanitizer. You're a virologist and you're afraid of bugs."

"I'm a bit of a hypochondriac, the doctor has told me often enough."

"No kidding? What else are you afraid of?"

"Nyctophobia. Fear of the dark."

"What else?"

Fear of being watched, fear of being listened to, he told her; the greatest fear, however, remained unspoken, it was the fear of merely being a finger of an invisible hand.

Then they walked along the streets, still talking, and sometimes along the beach, in complete silence, as though listening for messages from the sea.

ONE DAY CONRAD LOOKED TO HIS LEFT AND SAW DIA'S PALE and beautiful face, eager as they waited for the orchestra. Rustling and voices deluged the grand Celine Hall as her eyes traced the columns that rose to the high ceiling with its intricate mosaic. In the bright lights, the teeming audience filed into their seats. A wisp of her perfume, now familiar to him, hung still in the space between them. How it happened, how it came to be that she was now sitting next to him in the concert hall where he had always gone by himself, the only time when he truly listened to music, he couldn't figure out, but it had been spreading so slowly like the roots of a great tree and thus escaped detection until too late.

Then abruptly the discordant noises of tuning instruments ceased and a silence exploded with applause as the conductor came on stage and bowed. The diva followed. An under current beneath the diva's voluminous purple gown appeared to lift her aloft. She glided across the stage and curtsied. The diva smiled brightly; the smile hid for the moment the vacuity and dissipation of age the powdered face and the rouged lips could not hide. Immediately, a melody expanded whimsically and resonated to the farthest corner of the concert hall as if to lay the ground for her voice, slightly trembling, racing out to accompany the music.

Conrad closed his eyes now and then and allowed the music to infuse him and to become memory, so that it might come alive for him in the following days. "Oh, Conrad," he thought he heard a voice whisper, interspersed among the exaggerated words of the aria. Glancing at Dia now, he saw her lips quivering and her arms tucked close to her chest. The aria ended to loud applause, and another one began, a love song, this one more somber. "It's so beautiful Conrad," he thought he heard, but this time he knew he'd heard for real, for Dia grabbed his arm and pulled herself close to him. "I never knew music could be this beautiful." He only nodded. And so Bellini, Delibes, Verdi, Saint-Saëns, Faure, Dvôrák, each was relived one by one through the decades of the diva's long career. Through the diva's gestures and the tensing and convulsing of her face against the vacuity of age, a spectacle against sadness that was punctuated by moments of triumph and of realization of as much in the diva's eyes looking away from her audience now and then. In the end the 'Song to the Moon' was invoked in the diva's stirring voice. Mournful sounds rushing from the diva's tensed, craning neck, she poured out all her being, dared herself to reach beyond to heaven itself, and, nearing the end of the song, just as she was about to subjugate all the trembling souls before her, nearly tearing apart the terrestrial confine of the concert hall, the voice slipped, missing that height, that great magnitude. The diva's face betrayed the briefest anguish, but immediately thereafter her art, the mournful expression, resumed. Conrad heard her voice slip and saw her anguish; how tragically perfect it was. It was perfect, and as the song ended, he flung himself up to applaud.

Nearing midnight, when the sky powdered the air with a frigid mist, they left the concert with the teeming mass of people hurrying to their cars. All along the crowded aisle, through the reception area where the chattering voices were deafening, and finally down the stone steps into a quad in front of Celine Hall, Dia clung to Conrad, but constantly felt herself being watched. At last she turned to look back and caught a glimpse of a round face and beady eyes that had haunted her. In the crowd, Abe F. was watching them.

"I will cure your fear," Diaphany said a few days later when they were in the car.

"What fear is that?" Conrad said.

"All your fears."

They were on their way to the Caravelle Cabaret Club. Conrad had picked her up in the old Mustang and the engine was roaring loudly along the 710 Freeway, heading south toward Long Beach.

Dia had gone to back to work for a few days. Somehow she had gotten the idea, which had very quickly become a determination, that Conrad must come to see her dance, as though her recent immersion in his life required reciprocation. So without much deliberation, Conrad had agreed.

It was nearly ten o'clock when they arrived. The darkened atmosphere of the club seemed further oppressed by red lights along the ceiling. The odor of beer was accompanied by the smell of freshly cooked French fries, and the scattering light reflecting off the disco ball seemed to stir the air along with the eighties background music. Diaphany left Conrad at the bar and disappeared into the dressing room. He ordered a cognac and waited for the show, listening to the music from his youth.

"Hey, this your first time here?" someone said loudly to Conrad.

Conrad turned; a man had just jumped on the stool next to him. Something about this man appeared odd to Conrad; his ears were protruding, his eyes were disarming, his hair tightly curled on his scalp, and his dark complexion was darkened further by the low lights of the club. The man wore a blue suit and a burgundy shirt without a tie, and around his neck was a gold chain with an ornate medallion.

"Pardon me?" Conrad replied.

"Pardon me. Pardon me eh," the man repeated. "You're not from around here, are you?"

Conrad didn't quite understand what the man was getting at. "What can I do for you?" Conrad said.

"What you can do for me? What you can do for me is be nice." The man grinned. "Heh, heh, I'm sorry. I'm just messing with you, man. How about I buy you a beer?"

"That won't be necessary. I already have a drink."

"That won't be necessary," the man repeated. "Heh, heh. You're not from around here. That's cool. Cool."

Conrad sensed hostility in the man's belittling tone and turned away to look toward the stage.

"You know what, man. Check this out," the man leaned toward Conrad and recited in a hypnotic voice: "Some writers have so confounded society with government, as to leave little or no distinction between them; whereas they are not only different, but have different origins. Society is produced by our wants, and government by our wickedness; the former promotes our happiness positively by uniting our affections, the latter negatively by restraining our vices. The one encourages intercourse, the other creates distinctions. The first is a patron, the last a punisher."

In the voice and beneath the words that were full of common sense, a strange quality, a delectable sugar for the primitive part of the mind, seemed to cling to Conrad's consciousness. Even though the man's vocal emphasis seemed somewhat misplaced on the wrong syllables when he spoke, the voice sounded soothing and like that of a preacher's, almost messianic.

"How about this? Right, check this out, man. Hmm, hmm." The man cleared his throat. "Four score and seven years ago our fathers brought forth on this continent, a new nation, conceived in Liberty, and dedicated to the proposition that all men are created equal. Now we are engaged in a great civil war, testing whether that nation, or any nation so conceived and so dedicated, can long endure. We are met on a great battle-field of that war. We have come to dedicate a portion of that field, as a final resting place for those who here gave their lives that that nation might live. It is altogether fitting and proper that we should do this."

"That's quite interesting," Conrad said.

"So I got your attention huh. I can recite stuff, huh, any stuff as good as any politician. Man, in another life I, uh, could have been a very good one. Maybe a president. Better than a lot of folks. Man, huh, I know some of them folks, congress-men personally."

"You have a gift then."

"Yup, an oratory gift, so they tell me. Folks say I can pull lightning out of the sky. I can mesmerize them, put a spell over them, man. Huh, so what's your gig, man?"

"I'm sorry. What do you mean?"

"What do I mean? Your gig, your jibe, your angle, man. Man, what do you do?"

"Oh, I understand. I'm a professor."

"Hah, a professor. That's, huh, impressive man. Impressive. I'll drink to that," the man raised his beer bottle.

Conrad also raised his glass.

"So professor hah, I'm Hucks," the man said.

Suddenly all the lights went off and the low murmuring background music quieted down, and after a few seconds punctuated only by the low voices of the customers waiting and the clanking of beer bottles, the music began again. This time, the music boomed loudly, loud enough to vibrate the beer bottles rhythmically. Then bright lights burst out on the stage and shone on five girls standing in formation, in their tiny shorts and tight shirts, slowly lifting and tapping their toes to the music.

Through the hooting, the guttural howling, the loud whistling, Conrad stared at Diaphany. Under the glare of the spotlight, he beheld her as though for the first time, her face serious and removed, her pale skin with scars hidden by makeup, and the gestures of the dance he now felt intimately. Her perfume was still strong in his mind, her warmth next to him still felt, her whispers still heard, and yet he saw her a few feet away inhabiting an altogether different world, new and exciting.

"Those are my girls, man," Hucks howled in Conrad's ear. "That's Marty. Isn't she great? There's Gisele, Gisele, my girl. Check her out. Wow. Look at that kick. Yup. And Dia. What more can you say, right?"

No longer listening to the man, Conrad gleaned all he could from the girls dancing, and all he could he devoured. It seemed strange to be baring her flesh for strangers like that, and yet an uncommon dignity, a fearless indifference imbued all her movements, which were enthralling, teasing, daring all those who watched her. The songs marked out the dances, the catchy tunes changed with the costumes, from flight attendant to secretary to nun, and the routines somehow evoked the sentiments exactly, carrying the audience away, always conjuring a sultry yearning just below the surface. As Conrad watched her, a distant yearning came, closer and closer, until he regretted all the moments he had had with her that he'd somehow let go. How graceful she was; she was delicate, yet vibrant, unflappable. What could this beautiful girl possibly want from him? She said she'd cure him of his fears, but he was afraid now, afraid to think, to measure these thoughts by the yardstick of logic to see where they'd inevitably end, perhaps in loneliness.

When the show stopped for the intermission, the song

still softly lingering, the conjuring was indeed complete. The tentative sense of first infatuation, like the fleeting wisp of a perfume at once intoxicating and forbidding, that he'd perceived but had never had the power to consummate was wrenched violently from the depth of his memory and thrust upon him. It was during his senior year in high school and her name was Alicia. Oh, how beautiful she was, full of innocence and seduction, a budding womanhood, a coy look from her that had perturbed him all day, Conrad remembered. But all he had been able to do was to look at her from afar, all he could do was to see and become sick from her image, nothing else. Yet in that oppressed sickness, that yearning made infinitely worse by the impotence of inaction, a cherished pleasure would peak in his mind now and then during the most feverish hours when in his imagination he could touch her. The wretched pleasure of that infatuation now subsumed him as he waited for Dia, made his skin burn with anticipation, and neutered his mind that had busied itself with his quest.

"Those are all my girls," Hucks shouted. "You know what I mean, man. Well, do you?"

Conrad nodded absentmindedly.

"That's right, as long as you know it. You really like that hah. That's some show, right? Those my girls, man. You listening to me?"

Conrad didn't answer. In his mind, the lingering music inflated further the cocoon of nostalgia, and his heart palpitated for the real thing of blood and flesh that could make real everything, that could rectify all the opportunities that had been ignored and suppressed, that were now suddenly transformed into regrets.

"So what you like, man. You like girls, right? I can see that," Hucks leaned toward Conrad. "You like to party too, don't you?

With a lot of girls. Uh, I can get you to party with lots of beautiful, and I mean beautiful girls, right?"

Puzzled, Conrad looked at Hucks, trying to understand.

"Leave him the fuck alone," Dia shouted. Conrad had been so enthralled in looking at the stage, he hadn't noticed her approaching.

"Oh, Dia," Conrad uttered.

"Leave him the fuck alone, Hucks," Dia shouted. "He has nothing to say to you. You don't talk to him."

"Chill, baby, take it easy. We got no problem here. Me and the professor here are just talking. Being nice," Hucks said.

"You don't talk to him, Hucks." Dia turned to Conrad. "Let's go. We're leaving."

Dia grabbed Conrad's hand and pulled him off the stool. She led him toward the back, through the dressing room, where the other girls glared at them and where she snatched up her purse, and they went out the back door and into the back alley.

"Hold on there, baby." Hucks followed behind them. "Baby, don't get mad. We can all be good friends, right? Tell her, professor. We can all party. Come on, baby."

"Don't fucking call me baby." Dia suddenly spun around and shouted at him.

In the alley, a single bulb from high above the wall cast a faint yellow light on them. As though the claws of nostalgia still clung tightly around him, Conrad seemed detached from the commotion around him; he gazed upon Dia in her nurse's uniform, pristinely white, with a short skirt, high heels and gossamer stockings, and found himself still engrossed by her red lips, still mesmerized by the magic of it all.

"Come on, baby. Don't fight it. You end up where you belong. With or without me."

"With or without you? You, too. Same bullshit as Joel," Dia said.

She grabbed Conrad's hand and pulled along down the dark alley. Conrad took a couple of steps but felt Hucks's hand around his arm, holding him back.

"I ain't done with you. You done when I say you're done," Hucks said.

As Conrad felt Hucks's hand, he jumped back violently, afraid of being contaminated, and freed himself. Suddenly he realized the insult of it all, of Hucks's behavior as though he was invisible, and felt a fierce anger rising.

"I'd appreciate it if you'd leave us alone," Conrad said.

Hucks looked at him and grinned. "Leave you alone," Hucks shrieked as he came up to Conrad. "Leave you alone, man. All I've been trying to do is to show you folks a good time. To hook you up. And this is the gratitude I get."

"Let's go." Dia pulled Conrad along.

A sudden punch shot into Conrad's gut and seemed to burst into his lung; he fell to ground and struggled to breathe. Then he felt the sharp pain in his stomach and heard Dia's frantic screaming.

"I told you, didn't I? Motherfucker, I ain't done until I say I'm done." Hucks hunched down over Conrad, ready to hit again. Conrad squeezed his eyes tight and waited for the blows.

A shot exploded in the darkness. Conrad looked up; as though the magic of the night had resumed, he couldn't quite believe what he saw. Dia was leveling a pistol at Hucks, both of her hands holding the pistol steadily.

"I'll fucking kill you if you hit him again. Look in my eyes, you fucking pimp, am I bluffing?"

"Wow, wow. Take it easy, baby. I know you serious." Hucks stood up.

Conrad got on his feet and moved behind Dia. They walked backward and then started to run.

"You can't run from me," Hucks howled after them.

THINGS TRANSPIRED SO FAST THAT CONRAD BECAME FULLY aware of driving, of his stomach still aching, of his heart throbbing, only when the Mustang entered the freeway.

"I'm so sorry, Conrad," Dia said. "Are you okay? How do you feel?"

"I'll be all right," Conrad said, breathing fast and pressing down hard on the gas.

"Slow down. You're going too fast."

"Okay." He lifted his foot.

"I'm sorry. I had no idea he'd attack you."

"Thank you for helping me. I didn't know you carry a gun."

"It's for protection. It's a mean neighborhood, and I always leave work late."

"Who is he?" His mind seemed to slow down and his reason returned.

"Hucks? He's a freaking drug dealer. A pimp. He pushes drugs to the Hollywood crowd. He recruits girls from the club and pimps them."

"How so?"

"Well, there are lot of young girls from all over country who come here to get into showbiz and, you know, they'll listen to anything. And Hucks, he peddles hope and change. He hooks them onto drugs and promises, takes them to fancy parties for these rich Hollywood guys."

"Did you experience that yourself?"

"Yes . . . " she said hesitantly. "Yes, he brought me to a party. And when I realized why I was there, I got out of there. You wouldn't believe. A bunch of bald men, tan, very tan. Short and fat. And rich, very rich. Haha, it was a nightmare."

"I understand. Does he own the club?"

"No, but he's got Hank in his pocket. Hank owns the club."

The car was heading north now. Outside, the air was cold, and across the freeway hung a light fog into which the light beam from the car cut relentlessly. As the car sped along, it seemed to deliver them into safety and to revive for Conrad the magic of nostalgia and adolescent seduction. He glanced at her, her red lips, her eyes that squinted when a strong emotion seized her. And that wretched pleasure from his youth, his secretive infatuation, now came back to him, but this time was made sweet and real by her sitting next to him.

"I'm sorry," Dia said after a few minutes. "I shouldn't have shouted at Hucks. I think that set him off. The man is psychotic."

"Why were you so angry?"

"I was talking to Marty. You know the girl dancing next to me. Anyway, Hucks got her. He's taking her to a party, one of those Hollywood parties . . . She's a really nice girl. Young and innocent. He targets them young and innocent. That's how he could peddle hope and change and get them hooked. Let's just forget it."

"You danced well together. Everyone. You were really exceptional."

"Yeah, you're not just saying that?"

"Of course not. You're an artist. You evoked the mood exactly. You became the dance. It was truly transcendent."

"Yeah. No kidding? Thank you. No one has ever said that to me before." Dia looked at him and smiled.

"I'd love to see you dance again."

"No, I can't go back there again after what I did. I'll find some other work."

"Don't worry about him. I'll get rid of him for you."

"Don't be silly. What are you going to do? Please don't lower yourself to a pimp's level. If I had wanted a man like that I'd have gotten one." She stopped abruptly as if she'd shown too much of herself.

"Don't worry," Conrad said softly.

EXCITEMENT FOMENTED BY A BRUSH WITH DANGER NOW SO completely engulfed Conrad that he found himself parking in the street when they arrived, climbing the stairs to Dia's apartment, and finally settling down on the couch. He couldn't remember if he'd heard her asking him to come in or if he was acting out of his own desire.

At midnight now, when the sky above them looked out toward the vastness of darkness, the amber warmth of the apartment had an otherworldly flavor, the concentrated molasses of sexual intoxication laced with excitement from their recent escape. As he waited for Dia, heard her voice saying different things, and saw in the corner of his eye her figure moving about in the kitchen, he could almost step out of his body, which throbbed with a growing intensity from his groin to his neck. From somewhere her perfume traversed through still air, picked up along the way the scent of a female lair, primitive and overpowering, and drifted to his nose. Now crossing, now uncrossing his legs, he twitched about on the couch, and he looked at the coffee table, the itinerant pieces of clothing, the old posters of ballet dancers on the wall, but without really seeing anything. The fear of bacteria, of being contaminated in this messy apartment, rose in him, but he suppressed it, pushed it down until he only thought about her.

"How do you feel now?" Dia brought him a cup of tea.

"I'm fine. Thank you," he answered. The meekness of his voice surprised him. "Do you live here by yourself?"

"No, I have a room mate. But don't worry, she won't bother us. She's always in her room." Dia looked at Moiro's door, which was closed. A bright light shone through the opening under the door. "I have never even met her."

"What? That's incredible."

"It works out just fine. When I was looking for a room, I answered an ad through the Internet. We emailed back and forth. Then she left the key under the mat, and I moved in."

"That's unbelievable. Is that how it's done these days?"

"I think so." She went to Moiro's door, knocked on it. "My friend is visiting. His name is Conrad. He says hi."

From under the door, Conrad could see a shadow of someone moving about, and a piece of paper was slipped out under the door. Dia picked it up and showed it to Conrad. It read, "Hi, I'm Moiro."

"See, she's fine with us."

"What does she do in there?" Conrad asked.

"I don't know exactly, but I think she does something on the Internet. One of those virtual reality games. She plays games and earns money, a lot of money. I think she even has a virtual family, having a husband, raising children on the Internet."

"I see," Conrad said. Somehow here everything seemed possible and if he was told that there was a beastly savage behind that closed door, he'd believe it too. He'd believe anything she said.

Dia came to him, holding the piece of paper, and stood over him. She stood still. Her eyes, steady and clear, absorbed reality and him, met his eyes, saw no incongruity or awkwardness but only a wonderment. The stillness of the night arrested her, and in the night's unseen ripples, an interminable duration was interjected as if they had been together through countless nights, discovered in each other all their quirks so that words were now extraneous. In the silence, the paper fell from her hand. Silently she lifted her foot from the high heel; her leg, sheathed still in its white stocking, moved sinuously along his leg and up his chest, and with her arms extended and her body balanced, her pointed toe caressed his neck while he sat immobile, incredulous, his mind empty of all thoughts and fears. Now her toe touched his lips. Reflexively, he jerked back slightly, awakened by an ingrained fear, fear of bacteria, of sickness. But the toe advanced. It touched his lips again. With a slight thrust, it penetrated. Nosophobia be damned.

She looked down at him and felt his lips enclosing and imbibing, his soft tongue around her toe, his hands firm around her calf. Now he pressed his lips to her calf and kissed, and his teeth sank into the flimsy stocking as if his desire had exceeded all physicality. Now her fingers slithered through his hair and she grabbed him, pulled him in.

His body racing through the night met hers, at times in confusion clashed against hers, at times in selfish disregard took her so completely as to push away her gentle caresses to satiate a singular desire. She, too, held him but curbed his ferocity with feminine accommodation, and at times she hissed as if an intensity unbearably pleasurable overflowed the boundaries of her mind. Suddenly he pushed her away, he stared at her, but then slowly in his eyes incredulity yielded and he dove in again, feeling against his cheek her softest part.

In the depth of night she slept. Next to her, he lay and kept vigil on the low murmuring sound coming in from the outside. Of his work on the viruses, of this night that seemed like an end for all the preparation he'd accumulated throughout his life, his mind struggled to tabulate. Incredulity swept over him again and he found himself immersed in an adolescent reverie; he touched her lightly now and then. She had threatened to shoot Hucks to protect him, and he marveled at how no one had done anything close to that for him before. As the sky began to lighten, he fell asleep. Dreamless, he slept until he felt her pulling him over her. It was midmorning. She took him in and clung tightly to him while her eyes were lost in the sunlight beaming through the bedroom window, bending over his head. The morning sky brightened into noon. They smiled at each other and giggled as they ate a lunch Dia hastily prepared. Cloistered in the apartment as though in another world, they moved about. By the window looking down the street, seeing the cars passing was like seeing clouds moving across the sky. By the afternoon, they had collapsed in exhaustion. Detached, vanishing from the world, and wordless, they knew only each other.

16

Love Warps

A catharsis of the senses, a renewal of mental perception, as if being displaced forward a few paces through space and a few seconds through time, recurred to Conrad with an increasing frequency whenever he was with Dia. Quite the opposite of déjà vu, everything remained as he'd left a few moments before; they appeared as he remembered, only a new perception was layered upon his memory but was in no way attached to that memory, sitting above it, sliding effortlessly, leaving in him a sensation of being dropped into existence for the first time. And on this occasion when coming back to the bar where he'd left Dia, this sensation overcame him; he stood afar to peek at her as though through a portal, sitting cross-legged on the bar stool, holding a glass of white wine marked by her lipstick, her dark hair confluent with her black dress, accentuating her pale skin, drawing the eyes of men around her. Awkward in his gray suit, he came up to the bar and sat on the bar stool next to her. She smiled at him, and clarity shone on her face.

"You'll love this place," Dia picked up the conversation again. "The food is so delicious."

A waiter came and led them to a table by a window that looked out over the night traffic. On the center of the table, a candle was burning inside a glass jar, barely adding any light to the dim restaurant, whose ambience was shifted by hand-held devices scintillating with their whitish glow. Above the low murmuring roar of voices, the clanking of dishes, the scraping of chairs on the marble floor, clear words now and then rose high and sharp, enough to be distinguishable. The smell of wine and Dia's perfume pulled at his nose, pulled away his thought of why he was here with her, of the demarcation between predator and prey, and issued forth a pleasant buzz he had gone too far in surrendering to.

"I saw a book. You wouldn't believe the title . . . How to Talk to God." Dia laughed. "There are hundreds of these how-to books."

Conrad laughed too, forgetting the thread of the conversation and what he'd just said.

"I'm sorry." Dia turned her eyes away. "I know you explained the Godevil to me. But I still don't completely understand. Tell me if I understand it correctly. What about the second night?"

"I had a vision of Cain again."

"Really. The second night?"

"The second night."

"Will you let me read it?"

"Of course, darling."

The black dress held her body tightly, stopped at the shoulder, and let free the arms that appeared flawless under the dim light. His eyes could not discern the smooth scars on her arms or wrists. With great privilege his eyes ran over the skin of her shoulder, along the side of her neck, up toward her delicate jawline to her soft earlobe, or down the open cut of her dress and then back up where her eyes caught his and she smiled. An immediacy, a sense of finality one can often see in the eyes of young children who have yet to learn abstraction, overcame him when her eyes came back to his again. What was this she inquired about, everything suddenly seemed strange to him, and he would never know if she asked to know, or if it was because of him that she asked. Secretly, he hoped he would never know the real reason she asked. She no longer looked beyond him even when they held each other in the passion of the moment; instead everything about her converged on here, wherever they happened to be.

The waiter brought out plates of food, the appetizers, the main courses. They ate slowly because they were hindered by questions and answers, which were alternatively and confusedly expressed and examined, not really knowing one from another.

"Did you find what you need with the Amazon virus?" she asked.

"Yes, thank you. Exactly what I need," Conrad said. "How did you manage to distract Abe?"

"Oh, you don't want know." She put her fingers up and tapped them together in succession. The tiny candle flame seemed to shine triumphant in her eyes; then she put her hands down and looked away. "Don't think about it. It's just one of those things a woman must sometimes deal with."

"I won't then."

"So you're done? You have everything you need." She looked up at him again. "I still don't understand. What's this grand experiment?"

"Not quite done yet. I still need one more piece of the puzzle. One more virus."

"Can I help?"

He wanted to kill the thought right away, but it was too late. Why not? When the time came.

Leaving behind the restaurant with its bustling air and its tastes of food layered with rich aromas that they didn't even seem to register, they broke out into the cold air descending off tall buildings and washing over empty pavement. The wine seemed to give her head a delicious buoyancy in the cold air, and she clung to him to steady herself on her high heels. In the cold air and on the deserted pavement was the complicit understanding that this place was as good as elsewhere, that they needed no others, no distraction, save her giggles, unexplained and spontaneous, echoing off the buildings. She said many things without sounding frivolous. "My mother taught me all about fashion and postures. She used to say that a lady is measured by a ruler from your ankle to the back of your head. You have to live like that ruler is always behind you. This is the only body you'll ever have, she would say. That's how I have my posture." He laughed and told her that it was true and how she had a wonderful posture. "I miss my mother," Dia said suddenly as one, who had finally found happiness, thought of those closest to her. "She raised me by herself. She was a cocktail waitress at the Flamingo Hotel. She served drinks at the VIP tables for rich businessmen, hedge fund managers, and hardcore gamblers. She dated many of these men. She had me with one of them. I have never met my father." Dia held on to his arm as they walked, until they had to turn, and walked on again. "You know, my mother had always tried to cure me of cutting. She even had a rabbi, a Kabbalist, a practitioner of white magic. He did his little ritual, but I chased him away. And she never tried again."

Ferocity of passion dribbles into a quiet gentleness as the new is not lost but renewed. Conrad sensed this as he drove home. They sat quietly in the car, and between them, doubt usually accompanied by wonder was vanishing. That this was good seemed to dovetail so well with his varied states, whether it was catching a glimpse of her lips pressing together in a half smile, or smelling her perfume, or when the pheromonal intoxication peaked in his head during passion resurgent. Lights in the house were turned on, shoes kicked off, clothes shed, as though the lever needed to keep themselves apart in public was suddenly crushed and into each other their bodies collapsed, searching, palpating, bent on discovering something new in something already known but flagging fast. To escape the coldness under the sheet they pulled close together, seeking, amid giggles and moans. Then the room was quiet, and he could hear the movements she made in the bathroom, he laid back and saw abandonment in the ceiling.

"Dia," he whispered when she jumped back into bed.

"Yeah," she replied with a sleepy voice.

"Do I please you?"

"Hah." She sat up and held his face between her palms. "Ohhh. You mean do I come?"

He nodded.

"Of course."

He stayed silent.

"Next time, put your hand under my breast. You'll feel my heart, and you can tell by the way it beats."

What she said seemed to move him to something inexplicable, and he turned to her, took hold of her arm in his hands. "I want to know what you feel." With one hand, he twisted her wrist to turn her palm up, and with the other he ran his fingers over the fine scars.

"What do you mean?"

"What it feels like when you cut yourself?"

"No, no. But why?"

"I want to know."

"It's just pain, nothing else."

"Not just pain. To feel what you felt."

She giggled. "You're a weird one. You really want to know what I felt? No one ever asked to know that before. Well, they were curious and wanted me to tell them, but they wanted to know it all safe in their skin. No one ever asked to actually feel."

He looked at her, undeterred.

"Okay, we'll do it." She jumped off the bed and fetched her handbag from the nightstand. After a quick rummage through the handbag, she took out a switchblade. "I'll be right back." She withdrew into the bathroom. A moment later she came back, holding the switchblade on a folded towel, and placed them in front of him. "I washed the blade."

Conrad picked up the switchblade. It felt cold and spanned his palm to the tip of his extended thumb. Patterns of gold leaves were etched into the handle, which was made of white stone. He opened it, and the blade sprung out with a click; it was shiny, silvery, and glistening and reflecting light, and the cutting edge was vanishingly thin.

"It's a special blade. At least for me. Are you sure you want to do this?"

"Yes." Conrad put his arm over the towel, and with his hand shaking handed the switchblade to Dia. His face grimaced, and through his slightly open lips, she could see his clenching teeth.

"No, darling," she said gently. "You have to do it yourself. If I do it for you, it's not the same."

His left hand shook more as he moved the blade back over his right arm.

"It's very sharp," Dia said calmly. "All you want to do is to move very slightly over the skin. Don't press down. The blade will do its job. Remember, don't press down, or you'll cut right into the muscles."

His hand shook visibly as if trying to shake off the command, itself a conflicted battle of a singular will against terror, self-preservation, and anticipated pain, but the hand advanced, and already his head seemed to be floating in pain. That the edge of the sharp blade caused a bewilderment of a sensation he'd never known before enthralled him and steadied his hand so that he kept on pulling the blade across his forearm, while his eyes glared at the skin opening into another world that let the blood out, pooling and dripping.

"Stop," Dia said sharply. Her hand grabbed his and lifted the blade away from his arm. She took the blade away, closed it, and wrapped the towel around his arm. "That's enough." She squeezed his arm and sat looking at him. His eyes were still glaring, his face flushed, his mouth open and panting. "Was it painful?"

He sat still, recovering.

"I'm sorry I shouldn't have let you."

"Of course it was painful," he said at last. "But the actual cutting itself only added reality to the anticipation. You see, the anticipation of the pain, the anxiety itself was the hard part. The pain was already in my mind and the cutting only made it real. But there was something else, a part of me, inside me but also separate, that I had to subdue. You were right, I had to do it. I had to subdue it, that me. A sort of self–reflection, only I saw something I'd never seen before, something I'd never felt before when the skin opened. It's a different world, Dia."

As though his words could very well have been spoken by her, she jumped on him, and kissed him.

Pleasure that had formerly been so distinct and carnal, like taking a drug that deluged and then retreated, leaving pockets of emptiness, now assumed a manifold of flavors and a multitude of aspects, leeching out the unknown from behind his face. The cold from the night outside advanced and insinuated itself into the bedroom's air as Dia buried her face in the soft pillows, while her mind contemplated Conrad's face, now motionless in deep sleep. Different from all the others that she'd known and she had not been above wanting the usual things, the good looking jock, the sultry type that seduced so well, and even Joel with his wealth and glamour. At the end of those little affairs as she liked to think of them, she had surprised her lovers by her abrupt departure, but to her the affairs were no more than the little scars on her thighs. Behind Conrad's face was a beautiful place. But there was also fear she now felt, not knowing whether it was the fear of losing this, or of no longer searching.

On the nightstand next to the bed was the red notebook, and Dia reached for it. She began to read: *The Book of Cain, the Second Night.*

17

The Book of Cain, the Second Night

On the second night, the sky shimmering bright with stars and the crescent moon pushing up from the horizon, the crickets chirping, the aroma of blossoming flowers wafting through the air, and the sundry nocturnal creatures—all disappeared from Cain's perceptions as he sat cross legged, waiting.

'Where art thou, giver of truth?' Cain called out.

'Doth thou answer the question?' the red eyes emerged from a pair of flying fireflies as the voice answered.

'Yea.'

'Then thou doest exist, whole and separate from the Lord God.'

'Yea. Give me other knowledge.'

'Know thyself first.'

'Yea.' Cain's heart thumped strongly.

'Man is a trinity of three. Body, soul, and will . . .' the voice began and it became Cain's voice, speaking inside his head. And Cain saw himself outside his body, looking over it as it began to levitate, and opened up under the command of the voice. 'First, man is as the animals. Here is man's brain, where reside his thoughts. It is more magnificent than all the animals' . . .' Wonderment and fear burst through Cain as he saw his own skull yield to the voice and come apart, and the brain's convolution began to unwind and its parts dissociate from one another. Though it had been very dark when he first sat down, he could now see even the minutest blood vessels traversing the surface of the brain, the slight change of color in the brain matter and in the delineation of arteries and veins. '. . . Tis where man's thoughts occur. Therefore, taketh care to protect thy head at all times, or else thy mortal life itself is in danger.' Partly imparting knowledge and partly consoling with a warm, tender melody, the voice showed Cain his whole body from head to toe and, to his great surprise, how similar his body was to that of the sheep he had often butchered. 'Behold thy body. Life from dust. Tis the first miracle.'

Miracle, a word Cain had not heard before, but he understood it and felt within it awe and a strangeness of discovery.

Then, in reverse, the dismantling warped into a furious conjoining of parts, and the body settled down into its original sitting position until Cain rose and inspected his hands with a sense of self–awareness.

The voice rose again in earnest: 'Thy soul . . . thy soul. Thy immortal soul. To be condemned but never to be destroyed. Oh, how bright, how luminous its silvery radiance, its light never to be found in the world of the flesh. From before the light it came and it will be till the end of time giving spirit to matters.

It doth glow brighter in sufferance and perseverance and love and hate since hate is nothing but love suffered. Thy soul the loveliest thing in all the universe. Immortal beyond thy flesh becoming dust. 'Tis the second miracle.' Silvery radiance emanating from the voice deluged his vision and immersed Cain in a coolness that was immeasurably purer and brighter than a thousand full moons, and yet there was no heat as he often felt under the sun. Immortality condensed and made knowable in the silvery light, he comprehended for the first time. Cain as a singular awareness floated without time.

'Thy will, the last of the trinity complete. Sharper than the flaming sword and as constant. Under thy soul's command thy will reigns over thy body and indeed shapes all the world of the flesh. Thy will is thy own, separate and whole, even from the Lord God, though God is almighty. 'Tis the third miracle.'

At last he understood the trinity in terms so inexpressible that it was more akin to knowing and feeling than understanding, and he was glad.

'Much gratitude to thee,' Cain uttered. 'By what title shall I call thee?'

'I am the Bearer of Light, the Giver of Knowledge, the Punisher of Evil,' the voice pronounced. 'Thou shall fear me not so long as thy soul is pure.'

With that Cain jerked awake, and the crowing of the roosters drew dawn's rays from the horizon. He rose from the voluble vines, and though it had been only one night, he gazed across the landscape and saw a new world. His fields of crops and his orchards of fruit trees that he had so cherished now seemed to him a trifle. He felt his mind had aged ten thousand moons. And that he had not dreamed but had seen the truth was beyond all doubt. But to what purpose did the Lord God create the heaven and earth and man? Cain thought and felt no pang of guilt in thinking so. He hurried off to see his father.

No one except for his father, Adam, could possibly understand Cain, the origin of his drive, his unfathomable thirst to know alike the grass within his reach and the stars in heaven itself. Adam had told Cain and Abel of the Garden of Eden and the fruit of knowledge, but what knowledge did the fruit of knowledge bring? Was it the same as what Cain had seen the night before?

'Father, Adam, my father,' Cain called out as he ran up the hill where, as was Adam's matutinal routine, he stood staring toward the east, searching.

Adam turned from the gleaming red light of dawn and smiled, wiping away from his face traces of reminiscence and regret. 'Cain, my first born. Praise the Lord God for a new day,' Adam said.

'Praise the Lord God.' Cain was breathless as he came up to Adam.

'What troubles thee, my son?' Adam asked as he instantly saw in Cain's eyes his habitual willfulness, exaggerated by fright.

'Blessed father, tell me of knowledge.' Cain unconsciously grabbed his father's arm. 'Forgive me father, but pray tell what thou knew after thou partook of the forbidden fruit.'

With Cain's question, Adam realized that, whereas he had merely tasted knowledge, it was through Cain's flesh that the forbidden fruit was embodied and its enigma would now become manifest. 'Myself, my son,' Adam said sadly. 'I knew myself.'

'Then what, father? What other knowledge hast it given thou?'

'Shame, regret.' Adam put a hand on Cain's shoulder. 'But love also, love made greater by uncertainty, by hardship, by knowledge of myself, greater than the magnificence of the garden.'

'But father.' Cain's eyes fixed on his father's. 'But what of the knowledge of heaven and earth, and the purpose whereof the Lord God created them?'

'Question not the Lord God, my son. For he works in mysterious ways. His purpose shall never be known,' Adam said sternly.

With that, Cain knew he would not gain further knowledge from his father, so he bid his father a blessed day, and wandered off into the wheat fields. For the rest of the day, he did no work but was buffeted by hidden purpose everywhere he looked, be it the sun, the earth, the plants, the insects or the birds in the sky.

As the third night approached, a moroseness seemed to seep under his brows and he wanted to go to the field as soon as the last light faded, even without dinner. Adah, who had been watching his restlessness for the last two days said at last, 'My husband, what troubles thee? Crops are plentiful, fruit is abundant. The Lord God has blessed us in all our needs. Thou need not worry.'

'The Lord God giveth to our bodies but not to our souls.'

'Speak ill not of the Lord, husband, I pray thee.' Adah's voice trembled sweetly.

'Yea, I shall go the field again tonight.'

'Do as thou must, husband, for thou art the wisest of all of us. Then be content and come back to me.'

Anxiety brimmed in Cain as he waited for the third night.

18

A Decider Decides

One morning a few days later, a man came to Conrad's laboratory.

Everything about the man seemed contrived. Dressed in a black suit with a blue tie, he looked to be in his early sixties. His wizened cheeks, accompanied by a slightly curved nose and flaring nostrils, were pink from sunburn, and his thin mouth became a dark, round hole when he spoke. His grayish blond hair adhered neatly to his scalp. His narrow eyes darted about, searching, exuding obsequiousness, sly conniving, and pure indifference.

When Dmitri called out for Conrad, he was shaken from a happy daydream, in which he and Dia were together. He wanted to ignore Dimitri, but the urgency in Dimitri's voice couldn't be dismissed any longer. He came out from his office.

"Professor, this man has questions," Dmitri said.

In the narrow walkway of the laboratory, the stranger appeared to be familiarizing himself with the various pieces of equipment. The man picked up a flask, sniffed with his flaring nostrils, and dropped it with a clank, while with squinting eyes he observed the startled look on Dmitri's face. He pushed the glassware about as though searching for evidence. Effortlessly, his chest puffed up, like an ape's display of dominance.

"Who are you? What do you want?" Conrad demanded.

The man raised his eyes and puckered his lips as if annoyed. He took a few steps toward Conrad, his chest still inflated.

"I am Agent Weed," he said with a Texan accent and nodded. "I'm from the Home and Country Department."

"Home and Country Department? I've never heard of it," Conrad said.

"No? If you haven't, you'll get to know it real good, real soon," Weed nodded, grinning.

There was a strange spark in Weed's eyes so that Conrad couldn't be sure where the man was looking at.

"What can I do for you?" Conrad asked sternly.

"You're the professor. Ain't you? You can answer my questions as honestly as you can. That's what ya can do," Weed said. "Heck, it doesn't matter none. Ya see, I know everything anyway, or will know everything by the time I conclude this investigation."

"What is it that you want?"

"Your superior. A certain professor Abe F." Weed took out a cellphone and tapped at it successively. "He filed a formal complaint with the Home and Country Department . . . alleging that you stole a virus from his laboratory."

Conrad struggled to keep from laughing at the drawn out words exaggerated by the agent's Texan accent.

"He's not my superior and I don't know what you're referring to."

"So you don't know huh? You can play the fool if ya want, see, but I got to warn ya that the charge against ya is mighty serious. That charge would label you as a domestic terrorissst."

"Domestic terrorist. That's brilliant. How do you people come up with these things? Do you have psychologists and propagandists working for you?"

"Don't change the subject. Believe you me that I know everything or I will know, so help me God, by the end of this investigation," Weed shouted, and his face reddened.

Suddenly, Conrad realized that this could be not just a serious problem for him but also a chance for him to gain more information. Conrad's face broke into a forced smile.

"I'm sorry," Conrad said softly. "I didn't mean to upset you. Please come into my office. I'll answer any questions you have."

Agent Weed snickered, his shoulder bobbed up and down, and he squinted even more. "That's the right thing to do. Smart of ya."

Conrad led him into the office and offered him a seat. As Weed sat down, he unbuttoned his jacket and opened it wide to show the butt of a pistol at his side.

Immediately, Conrad goaded him on, "I know that you are very well connected. You must have direct access to all the information companies."

"Well, it's classified, ya see, but I can tell you unequi . . . un..e.. qui..vocably, that the Home and Country Department . . . of which I'm a field agent . . . we work closely with folks, lot of folks, you name it, CIA, FBI, TSA, AAA, AA, ACLU, NSA, NCAA, NFL, NBA, NAACP, NASA, TWA . . . wait," Weed said breathlessly, spelling out each letter with emphasis. "Is that right? . . . Yeah . . . We work with the IRS, IRA, DEA, AOA, AOAA, ADD, ADHD, ATF, . . . FDA, FAA, FUU . . . What we got? How many is that? I'm going out of order now. But the great thang is . . . is all the informations flowing. It's all about information and communication . . . we got it all tied together at the hubs . . . the Internet companies folks are heck part of us . . . what you got . . ."

"Internet providers and computer makers?"

"You got it . . . them folks make computers. Ya see, very handy to have spy chips embedded in them." Weed began to snicker loudly with his shoulders bobbing up and down, eyes squinting. "The folks at the phone companies, you bet ya, we know everything."

"I suspected as much," Conrad uttered.

"So, you seem like a smart fellow. Heck, what I'm saying, you're smart. You're a professor, hehe. Why don't you co..operate with me. I quaranteed that something good will come out of this for you. How's that? That sounds good?"

"If you guarantee, then absolutely, I will cooperate with you in any way I can." Conrad realized that Weed was up to the typical carrot and stick approach.

"Great. So what's this about a virus? Abe F. said you stole a virus from his lab."

"No, I don't know anything about that. Why would I steal a virus from him?"

"Maybe because he stole one from you. I know all about your history. Professor, it's ya chance to come clean."

"Yes, he did steal from me. He published my work. But I can assure you that I'm not working with any viruses that he's working on. What is this virus?"

"Amazon virus." Weed read from his phone. "I got everything in here. He claimed that the Amazon virus was sent to him from a South American university. He stored two vials in the freezer. Two weeks ago, he was told by the technician one was gone."

"Interesting." Conrad tried to maintain an unchanging face, while at the same time he felt sweat breaking out across his back.

"Yeah, it's the darnedest thang too. He's so damn set on you. He's so damn set on the fact that you stole his virus. Well, I don't like a wild goose chase, especially after going through the court case between you and him. This whole thang can be just one big ruckus, ya know, a friendly altercation shall we say, among colleges, the smarty pants, you folks, ya know what I mean. Like I said, I don't much like wild goose chases and I got important cases to work on, I got folks depending on me, but you know, Abe, the man is obsessed. He pulled all sorts of strings with his people, and you know how much power them folks got. I got a call from my boss, who got a call from a congressman and from a senator. So here I'm trying to find out if acts of terrorisssm in fact occurred. And I know you ain't no terrorissst but you could be. It all depends, ya know what I mean?"

"I am . . . not following you. What does it depend on? You mean evidence."

"Evidence. Heck no. It all depends on whether you and I get along. Ya catch my drift?"

"But what about the law, due process, gathering evidence, innocent until proven guilty?" Conrad protested.

"You must watch a lot of TV, huh?" Weed growled. "Listen here. I tell ya like ya a friend. So it all depends on how we . . . get along. Understand? Now if you want evidences and laws, I'm good at that too. Listen here, I can declare you a terrorissst, who possesses a WMD, so under NDAA and the Patriot Act I can put ya in Guano Bay and no buddy will ever hear from ya again. No lawyer, no trial. Heck, we can waterboard ya if we like. Indefinitely."

"What's WMD?"

"Why? Weapons of Mass Destruction, of course. Just like Saddam Hussein. He got a good old-fashioned hanging. Too bad it wasn't done in Texsas."

"Yes, I remember something on the news a while ago." Conrad's eyes narrowed on Weed attentively. "What about NDAA?"

"National Defense Authorization Act. See, I don't blame

ya for not knowing. Not many folks outside law enforcement would know anything about it. But make no mistake that ya don't want to tick me off. Ya see, ya don't want to go there."

"Of course not, I don't want to go there wherever that is." The sweat collected around the nape of Conrad's neck and along his spine.

"Supreme. So we got ourselves a good understanding, that's how ya cooperate." Weed's Texan accent seemed to be drawing out more and his eyes squinting even tighter probed Conrad's reaction. "See, Abe's sure that ya masterminded the whole thing. But he ain't got no evidence. He's still set on ya like I said. He testified under oath that a certain person by the name of . . . Dia . . ."

A chill blanched Conrad's face and swept to his fingers.

"Dia . . . phany," Weed read from his cellphone and then turned his squinting eyes to Conrad. "Some folks got strange names . . . Abe testified under oath that this here person seduced him, tricked him into taking her to his laboratory. And while he was distracted, she stole the virus from his freezer. And he got no evidence being that she fooled him into turning off all the surveillance cameras. That's a mighty big mistake for any security setup, I always say, you got to have cameras, lot of cameras, to catch the terrorisssst as they sneak in . . . or out."

"Is that so?" Conrad said, barely above a whisper.

"Yup sirree, that is so. Now I ask ya. Do ya know this person Diaphany?"

Conrad saw the trap clearly and that it was a test to see if Weed had full control over him.

"Yes. She came to my class one day. She said she was interested in virology. That was all."

"You've had no contact with her since?" Weed asked and

shifted his body heavily; the butt of the pistol along his side stuck out, as though Weed wanted to remind Conrad of its presence.

Weighing the options very quickly, Conrad answered, "No. Why would I? I thought she was a student." His heart smashed against the inside of his chest as he awaited Weed's judgment.

"You don't say. Abe testified that he saw you and this Dia . . . fanny together at the concert."

"That's absolute nonsense. I always go to concerts by myself. Where is the evidence? He could have taken a picture of us with his cellphone."

"You got a point. But then, I don't need no evidance. Make no mistake. I'm the decider. Don't ya forget that?" Weed said.

"I understand. You're the decider. You decide."

"Now, see ya here." Weed tapped on his cellphone several times and a female voice emanated from the phone.

A voice was somewhat muffled, but Conrad recognized it instantly. The recording was of Dia talking to another woman; in the conversation, he heard giggling, sighs, and exasperated screams. Weed brought the cellphone close to his ear, listened intently while his eyes drifted from side to side as though an intense pressure was building up inside his small head and awaiting release. His face broke out into a smile, then he laughed loudly, not only his shoulders but his whole body bobbing up and down.

"Hehe, ya hear that, professor? Hmm, hmm. Hell downright ticklish. I know everything or will know everything."

"Yes, I understand. How powerful the system, you, you all are."

"So ya say ya don't know this gal. Hmm. Did she steal something from ya too? Ya lost something, too."

"No, I haven't lost anything."

With an abrupt movement, Weed put the cellphone away. He said, "Well, that's enough for now." He stood up. "I'm going to leave ya folks . . . so ya can practice your love . . . for viruses . . . and bugs . . . and them critters."

Weed buttoned his jacket and turned his back to Conrad, and stood still for a moment as if to instill suspense and fear into his target. Finally he turned back and said, "Ya know what? This here place is not as nice as Abe's. I can help ya with that. I'm sure ya folks can do more with more funding, more money, more equipment. Am I right? Ya know what, we can use your skills. The DOD has a biological warfare division. They can sure as heck use someone like you."

"Pardon me but what's DOD?"

"Department of Defense. Unlimited funding, how's that sound to ya? Provided ya must make them lethal bugs for us. Make them lethal, that's how I like them."

"We can always use more funding."

"Great, I'll make some calls and get back to ya. Well, I'm off now. But you can rest assured that I'll get to the bottom of this here mess. I'll go and have a chat with this gal Diaphany. She's as good as in Guano Bay."

"Do you know where she is?" Conrad asked timidly.

"Heck yah, I know everything. Til' we meet again, partner, we'll be on the same team soon enough."

CONRAD WATCHED AS WEED LEFT. IMMOBILE IN HIS CHAIR, HIS arms and legs flaccid as if paralyzed, he looked on without seeing. He knew he must alert Dia, but the buffoonish Texan oppressed him, and precisely to the same degree that the Texan was such a bumbling, inarticulate buffoon that his threats were visceral, damning and real. Far above the threat of imprisonment and torture, the sudden realization of his help-lessness, of the inevitability of defeat in this fight, a fight that had barely begun, depressed Conrad. Now his head swirled with dizzying force and nausea made worse by acronyms of all the governmental agencies flying before his eyes.

"Professor." Dmitri's roar shook Conrad. Only now did Conrad see Dmitri standing before him. "Professor. Must warn the lady."

Conrad looked at Dmitri without understanding.

"Professor," Dmitri roared again. "Must warn the lady now. Call her."

"No, no." Conrad jumped up from his seat. "No, no. They'll know if we call."

He rushed past Dmitri and headed for the freezer.

"What you do, professor?" Dmitri said and followed him.

At the freezer, Conrad pulled out a metallic container and rummaged through an assortment of plastic containers within which were frozen liquids holding different viruses. Then Conrad turned to Dmitri and put his mouth next to Dmitri's ear, feeling the beard on his cheek; he whispered, "Listen carefully, Dmitri. They're on to us. We have to hide all these viruses."

"But where, professor?" Dmitri whispered in return as they stood enveloped by the freezer's cold mist.

"At my comrade's house. His name is Truheckler."

"Your comrade?"

"Yes. Go to him and tell him you work for me. You can trust him."

"Maybe we get lawyer. Better, no? Lawyer to fight govern-ment man."

"No, Dmitri. No lawyer can help us. Man's laws don't exist anymore. We must play along now." Conrad seemed to finally realize what he must do. "And no electronics, computers, or cellphones. They can track you."

"No worry, professor. I have no electronics. I used old motorcycle," Dmitri said.

"Good, good." Conrad ran out the door.

OUTSIDE, THE SKY WAS FILLED WITH GRAYISH CLOUDS, AND A cold wind blew against Conrad's face as he ran to the parking lot. What he must do from now on he knew as well as he would ever know, and he knew his fate was already determined, himself already a cog churning in a machine that was nebulous and all-pervasive and unforgiving. Because of his knowledge and skills as a virologist—the Texan had insinuated as much—he would be spared but assimilated into this machine. He revved the engine and the old Mustang's tires squealed as it jumped into the street. Dia's apartment was not very far away, perhaps five miles farther along Wilshire. Each stop, each red light roiled him up so much that he could almost have turned the car onto the sidewalk and sped headlong toward her. He must get to Dia before the Texan, he must protect her from the Texan's grasp. I'm the decider—the Texan's words resounded in Conrad's mind and left no doubt of their truth. There were no laws anymore, no recourse for the likes of him or Dia. That realization penetrated deep into Conrad's consciousness. How strange, too, were the contortions of fate, the chance meeting with Dia, whom he had distrusted and thought of as an agent provocateur, the one person whom he would now willingly sacrifice himself for.

When he arrived, he parked at a distance away and walked briskly to Dia's apartment, all the while watching the street for signs of Weed. At last in front of the building he ran up to the intercom and buzzed Dia's apartment. The intercom rang and rang. No answer. While it rang with a low pitched buzz, Conrad scanned the street. Jerking with fierce violence, his heart transmitted this violence into the palms of his hands so that they shook uncontrollably. On his back the sweat triggered by the earlier scare with Weed never quit and trickled down his spine, and chills rolled over him in waves. He buzzed the intercom for the third time. He took a few steps away. Abruptly the intercom stopped. Something was different this time; it hadn't rung long enough. Conrad turned back to it and listened.

"Yes?" a tentative female voice whispered.

"Hello, hello," Conrad shouted and rushed to the speaker. "Yes?"

"Is Dia . . . I need to speak to Dia," Conrad said breathlessly.

"She is not here," the voice came through, coldly.

"Are you Moiro? This is Conrad. Do you know where she is?"

"No."

"I need to leave a message for her. Please let me in."

"I will write the message for you. Tell me what you want to tell her."

"Okay, Okay . . . Please write carefully," Conrad gasped and then took a deep breath. "You're in danger. Go to Truheckler's place right away. Signed Conrad."

"Anything else?" the voice asked.

The steady, monotonous voice somehow gave him the impression that he was speaking to the intercom itself and not a real person on the other end. Conrad said, "Can you read the message back to me?"

"You're in danger. Go to Truheckler's place right away. Signed Conrad," the voice said.

"All right. Okay. Thank you, Moiro."

The intercom's clicking off left him floating, as if unmoored from reality, half unfinished, and Conrad fidgeted next to the cars parked on the street and looked at one end of the street and then the other. He suddenly realized that Weed, if he were to come now, would see him. He took off running, and at a short distance away, he stopped at a big tree, a magnolia, whose girth could hide him. Next to the tree, he stood still and studied the street with the feigned demeanor of someone without fear or anxiety waiting for someone else also without fear and anxiety. At length he leaned against the tree and felt against his back its sharp bark he had never felt before; he turned around and his fingers touched lightly the scaly barks at first and then explored the crevices, and finally his palms pressed against the uneven sharpness. Even as a child when he frolicked in the backyard among the Japanese maples, the palm trees, the fig and apple trees, he had always kept them at a gaze's distance, only close enough for distinguishing their features. Now his hands learned something else altogether, he pushed against the tree's immobility and felt a thread of a spiderweb, and he picked apart a piece of bark and smelled it. And he seemed to have no aversion to the bacteria that he knew were there. Perhaps she had cured him. From an apartment's window nearby, he saw someone watching him, someone who probably knew nothing of the tree but probably thought him crazy for trying to know it, and so he walked away aiming for the next big tree along the street.

"Conrad."

He looked up and saw Dia coming toward him, carrying two paper bags of groceries. He ran to her; her smile changed into a frown as she saw his face.

"What's the matter?" Dia asked.

"Come with me right now," Conrad whispered. He looked past her, up and down the street very quickly. Several cars were speeding by.

"What's wrong?"

"I have to get you away from here this instant. No time to elaborate. Let's go," he whispered again, grabbed her by the arm, and dragged her, running toward his car.

Dia dumped the bags of groceries into the back and the Mustang screeched as it swerved away. In the rearview mirror, a black bulky sedan surged up and stopped abruptly in front of Dia's apartment.

"Your phone?" Conrad's mouth mimed the words. He turned the car at the first stop sign.

"You can talk. I don't have it."

"I'm so sorry, Dia. I never meant to get you into trouble," Conrad said mournfully. "It was never my intention to get you involved. In fact, when I first met you I thought you were sent to sabotage me. It's all my fault. I'm sorry . . ."

"Stop. You're not making any sense, Conrad. What are you talking about? What kind of trouble?"

"A government agent came to my lab this morning. Home and Country Department."

"Home and Country? It sounds like a tabloid."

"Please, Dia, it's serious. He threatened to put me. . . and you into Guantánamo Bay. Abe F. filed a complaint. He had his people go to the very top."

Conrad veered toward the freeway entrance.

"You mean this guy will arrest us, make charges, take us to court, things like that? Why are we running? We can get a lawyer and fight them."

"No, Dia. He can take us straight to Guantánamo Bay. All he has to do is to label us domestic terrorists."

"Really? This is America. How can they do that?"

"They control everything," Conrad said. Glancing at her now and then, he saw in her face the feisty, carefree spirit replaced by furrowed forehead, squinting eyes, tightened lips. "One more thing. He had a recording of you."

"What do you mean, recording?"

"He had a recording of you talking to your girlfriend."

"What do you mean?" she shouted.

The car swerved as Conrad jerked, startled.

"Please Dia. I'm truly sorry. Don't be so angry. He must have recorded your conversation through your cellphone."

"So he was on his way to arrest me," Dia said softly now, perhaps resigned.

"I think so. But we're good now." Conrad knew he was lying and that they were still in danger, but he must reassure her.

As if suddenly awakened, Dia turned her eyes to the road. "Where are we going?"

"I have to hide you. I thought about Truheckler, but Dmitri should be there already. You'll have to stay with Minh, another comrade of mine. He'll keep you safe until it's all over."

"That's okay, Conrad," she said. Her hand clasped his tightly. "We'll go underground together. They'll never find us."

"I'm sorry I disrupted your life . . . "

"Disrupted my life? I've never been more alive. That searching and yearning, I'm done with that." She was surprised at how easily she could tell him her deepest thoughts.

"Don't worry about anything. I'll take care of everything. When I'm done, no one will fear them again."

"What are you saying, Conrad?" She turned to look at him straight on. "What are you going to do? Aren't you talking about the Godevil? That's philosophy right? Just like the stuff I was talking about. The stuff beyond this world. This Weed guy is a person. What are you going to do?"

19

Rice Chicken

Too sparse was the apartment, and the sparsity was reflected in Minh's thin face, aged beyond reckoning, furrowed with deep lines, hollowed behind the temples and under the eyes, which still appeared sharp and dark. A thin beard extended from his upper lip to well beyond his chin and over his sinewy neck.

A square table squatted close to the dark, wooden floor, and flat pillows were positioned along all its sides. A single Chrysanthemum arched limply to its side, held up in a tall, narrow vase in the center of the table; next to the vase sat a teapot and two cups. Beside the table, there were no other pieces of furniture. In the air was the leftover smell of cigarette and burned incense.

Up high on the wall, Diaphany saw a lone wooden platform attached to the wall with wooden hinges, which must have a shrine, and on the platform, leaning against the wall, was a black–and–white picture in which she could discern obliquely the face of a person.

"You must excuse the bourgeois sentimentality," Minh said as he followed Dia's gaze. His accent was heavy, his voice slow and serene. "Ah, it's Vietnamese tradition to worship our ancestors. A shrine for my father. I light incense for him on the day he passed. Without the company of other comrades, one becomes lax in one's discipline, one lowers one's guard against superstition, one no longer practices self–criticism."

He picked up the teapot and filled the cups.

"That's . . . hmm . . . very thoughtful. And thank you, Minh, for letting me stay, putting up with me. I'm sorry Conrad just dropped me off like that," Dia said. Unaccustomed to sitting on the floor, she shifted her weight awkwardly on the flat pillow. At the mention of Conrad she wished again that he could stay with her, perhaps just the two of them here, secluded and isolated from the world outside; nothing could be more pleasurable.

Opposite her, Minh sat unmoving, with his legs crossed, in the lotus position.

"Of course, Comrade. It is assumed. Ah, you are welcome to stay as long as your situation requires. Please have a cup of tea," he said.

"Well, thank you anyway." She brought the cup to her lips and smelled the scent of jasmine.

Late afternoon sunlight from the windows struck the walls, which were all bare and painted a deep green.

"I will get all you need. Just tell me the size of your clothes. You are in the heart of Little Saigon. You can get everything here." He sipped the tea.

"Thank you, Minh."

"Please dispense with formality. The success of your struggle is my only reward."

"How did you meet? I mean, how did Conrad meet you?" Dia asked.

"You mean how is it that Conrad would know someone like me?" Minh said and paused to consider. "The doctor got us together. Or perhaps it was fate, or my faith in the struggle. The doctor, I hope you will never meet him. It's for your own good. The doctor got us together because Conrad is a virologist and I sell chickens. Viruses hide and wait in the chickens."

"This must be the same doctor that got Conrad and Truheckler together."

"Yes, the very same. Truheckler the nuclear physicist. They renewed my faith in the struggle. It became clear to me. Conrad's struggle is but an extension of Truheckler's, an extension of my struggle."

"You mean the struggle against the Godevil." Dia perked up and leaned forward. "Please explain to me, Minh, this Godevil that Conrad wrote about. What do you mean it's an extension of your struggle?"

"Yes, that's what he called it. Others have it by other names. Will, life force, vital substance, earth spirit, the unseen . . . yes, I'm happy to explain to you as much as my knowledge will allow. You must also be curious to know my story. How a Marxist came to be in this country, the home of capitalism. But first I have to prepare for you, my guest, a special feast. Forgive me, but it's my tradition again, you see. I will prepare for you a free range chicken. It is fresh. My chickens are never frozen. It has lived its life very happily on a farm. It will be cooked in a special broth until it is tender, but not over-cooked. I will carve it just before you eat. I will cook a special rice in this broth that the chicken will have been boiled in until the rice is just cooked but not over-cooked. I will shred the chicken meat and rub it in green onion, white onion, garlic, black pepper. I will prepare a special fish sauce with crushed ginger and red chili paste. I will cook for you the best chicken dish ever."

Gesturing expressively, at times chopping, at times slicing with his hands, Minh described the cooking with the hands that Dia had not noticed until now, and now that she saw them, she was surprised that she did not notice them sooner.

Thick cords of sinews wove with thin veins of blood vessels, all extended into protuberances that were his fingers ending with brownish beds of fingernails, all bounded tightly by dark skin. Multifarious scars covered his hands, and as Minh noticed Dia's gaze, he hid them under the table, bowed slightly to her and withdrew to the kitchen.

Only a few feet away and still in full view of Dia, Minh scuttled about in the kitchen as though he were cooking in a far-away hideout in the jungle. Metal scraping as knives were sharpened, the thudding of a wooden cutting board, and the soft soughing hum of Minh's voice saying different things, all came to Dia as from a strange world. Soon the smell of the boiling chicken, so familiar to Dia and yet now so puzzlingly exotic, wafted toward her, and her nose struggled to pick out one scent among the others.

The chicken was indeed the best Dia had ever tasted and the rice had a rich aroma that lingered on her tongue. At first Minh went about serving her, but at last he, too, sat down and ate. The sun set as they ate. Rice pudding, chilled over ice, was offered for dessert, and its sweetness complemented the after taste of the pungent, salty fish sauce.

"This is the most delicious chicken I've ever had. Thank you, Minh." Dia sipped the jasmine tea.

"You are welcome."

"Now please tell me how it is that a Marxist came to be in the home of capitalism."

"A sorry turn of events, Comrade."

He lit a cigarette and took a deep drag, and blew circles of smoke toward the ceiling. His eyes were lost in the vanishing smoke and his voice rose. "Let me tell you how I came to be here . . ."

"I WAS THIRTY-FIVE YEARS OLD IN APRIL 1968. THE AMERICAN war in Vietnam was still churning, grinding, and demanding more young men from both sides than ever. Just a few months before, the Tet Offensive had been a disaster. Thousands of my comrades died. Young men, old men, and women of all ages willingly attacked Ben Tre, Vung Tau, Hue the Imperial City, and even Saigon, only to be butchered. It was sad enough to see their surviving relatives mourn for them; as a founding member of the National Liberation Front who formulated parts of the plan, I found it excruciating to shoulder responsibility for their death, but most of all, the thought that their deaths were in vain was unbearable. Though the official directive came directly from the politburo in Hanoi, it was I who gave the idea for that directive. I couldn't control the guilt that was rising in me by the day. Hopelessness and futility in an ever darkening sea of death, I could see only that.

By day, I was a respectable banker, the manager of Commerce Bank of Vietnam, but when night came, I was my true self, a Viet Cong in South Vietnam. At night, I met with my contacts in back alleys, in restaurants, in cafés—the locations were always changing—to deliver to them information about American and South Vietnamese military movements that in turn had been given to me by my spies.

Though the Tet Offensive was at that time a devastating military defeat, it would later achieve an equally devastating effect on the psyche of the American people, which was far more significant in attaining the ultimate victory, though at that time I could not quite see that. None of us could. The military defeat of our movement had become my own personal defeat. Brooding led to moroseness which bred only darkness, and I stayed in the darkness a long time, losing the desire for tasty food, for my wife's touch. Even in this all consuming darkness, I acted normally by day, fake smiles and laughter preceded my handshakes during business dealing, but after work I wandered into strange places in Saigon, sat alone at distant cafés, and observed people bustling about earning a living, corrupt policemen plying their trade, and an endless convoy of military trucks carrying fresh young faces to their deaths in the jungle.

When I emerged from the darkness, I emerged not into light, but merely altered. As though transformed by the slow burn of hatred, I became more determined than ever to see the triumph of Marxism over capitalism, not just in Vietnam but in the entire world, to witness an idea originated by a mere man, to partake in a hard and long struggle to implement that idea, and to witness the ultimate triumph of that idea over the human species. Whatever the cost. The testimony of man's will demands nothing less.

To prove to myself that I had the conviction and the will, I imposed upon myself a most unusual task.

I decided on Nam, whom I had known for many years. He was three years older and more intelligent than I. He came from a much wealthier family that owned a vast rubber plantation in Cu Chi. We had attended the same French high school and I then followed him to Paris to study. He had been kind to me and helped me acclimate to Paris. Within my first week of being in Paris, all Vietnamese students were invited to a meeting with Ho Chi Minh, who was in Paris to negotiate with the French government for independence. I was deeply impressed with Ho Chi Minh, his ardor for freedom, his charm and nationalism. Nam, however, was not moved at all; he distrusted Marxism. Marxism, as Nam saw it, was unnatural as it sought to abolish class, social and capital structures, or everything that Nam had grown up with, had enjoyed, and would fight to preserve. Ho Chi Minh, Nam was convinced, had paraded nationalism to hide his true adherence to Marxism.

When we had finished with our studies, I graduated with a law degree from the Paris University and became an ardent Marxist, while he got a degree in economics and wanted to continue his family business. Upon returning to Saigon, I contacted Nam again and kept up with him socially so that I could extract useful information from him. Several times, I managed to have my people survey the topography of his vast rubber plantation in Cu Chi in order to dig a vast system of tunnels. They were later known as the famed Cu Chi tunnels.

On that fateful night in June, when I decided to carry out my task, it had been raining. It was the rain season in Vietnam, and it had been torrential at first, but by evening, droplets from low–lying clouds had settled into a persistent drizzle, one that could wither the will of any man and bid him to seek the warmth and comfort of his family, to forget the woes of the outside world for awhile. I, however, was burning with rage, more determined than ever as I took a rickshaw to Nam's house at the center of Saigon.

After the servant accompanied me from the gate to the front door of the house, Nam came out and greeted me warmly.

'Minh, what are you doing out in the rain like this?' Nam shook my hand. 'Have you eaten yet? Let's have dinner together. Kim is picking up Cuong. They will be coming home any moment now.'

Kim was his wife and Cuong, his fourteen year old son, and of course I knew where they were.

'Eating a little is all right,' I said. In my stomach there was no hunger, only anxiety brewing and fear growing, fear that I might not have the courage to see this through.

'We haven't seen each other for a long time. You have been

healthy, I trust?' Nam led me down a long hallway perfumed faintly with incense, to his private study, where he usually received his closest friends.

'I'm fine,' I answered somberly. Though I was doing my best to hide my intentions until the right moment, I was finding it difficult to fake joviality.

'What about your wife and daughter? They are well, I trust?'

'They are well. And Kim and Cuong, are they well?'

'Yes, Cuong is doing very well. I am hoping to send him to America for schooling. Kim is afraid he's too young. I'm afraid she spoils him too much,' he said and laughed softly.

In his study, books lined the spacious shelves along the wall, and throughout the room, various antique vases, gold statues of Buddha, and diverse antiquities were on display, as if his study were the wing of a museum. Calligraphy, paintings, and drawings hung on the walls; a rendering of Confucius's teaching in black ink caught my eye. Raindrops tapped against the windows. We sat on soft pillows on the floor, which was lined with planks of precious wood that had been brought down from the highlands. Between us sat a low, square table with the most delicate carvings of dragons and phoenixes along its sides. It was only when we finally sat down on the soft pillow that I felt the sharp, awkward bulge of the pistol against my back; I hadn't thought about it from the moment I bid farewell to my wife and young daughter, during the walk in the rain, or on the bumpy rickshaw ride. Without doubt, the pistol had been collected from a dead American soldier in the jungle and passed through the hands of various Viet Cong soldiers to finally arrive into mine. Now I also remembered the hand-written note in my pocket.

A servant entered with a tray of tea and proceeded to pour both of us a cup. The strong aroma of jasmine tea took me back to the countless times when Nam and I met to discuss politics and philosophy, and when I used to gauge his political leanings and even to proselytize to him my left-leaning politics. As we drank the tea, I could see in his eyes that the jasmine aroma evoked similar nostalgia. But he was no longer the young man I remembered; a life of abundance and luxury hung on his rounded face, heavy jowls seemed to flow into his neck, and as he sat, his paunch mounted roundly before him.

'Your business is going well, I trust.' Nam saw me looking somewhere beyond, detached. In truth, I was having second thoughts, things could be still undone, and my plan abandoned.

'Yes, as normal,' I turned to him.

'Did it disturb your business much?' he asked.

I knew right away that the 'it' referred to the failed Tet Offensive, since the whole of Saigon continued to talk about it as if the city was afraid to forget it. 'Yes, it did. But things are getting back to normal.'

'The Viet Cong had real gall to do something like that, don't you agree?' he burst out. Though he was following the same habit of engaging me in heated political debates in private, he had always been a shrewd businessman in public, never showing his hand, always a diplomat with his money interests at heart.

'They did,' I said softly. It seemed that I no longer had the desire to debate him on this matter. My mind was still too busy contemplating whether I could carry out the plan when the time came.

'The scale of the attack was remarkable. From Hue all the way to Saigon, can you believe it? But they failed miserably. Thousands died. I, myself, saw many of the dead bodies.'

'They died for their beliefs.' My meek voice seemed to spur him on.

'What beliefs? How can you say that? Communism. No private property. From each man according to his own ability, to each man according to his need. So much dialectical baloney. It's against human nature. It's against Vietnamese nature. The heaven is above and the earth is below. There will always be a hierarchy, the privileged and the poor. That's nature. I said so when we met Ho Chi Minh in Paris, and I say so to you now. Nothing has changed.'

I remained silent, refilled our teacups, and sniffed the aroma as I listened to him.

'I bet you anything that the lowly Viet Cong soldiers have no comprehension of what dialectic materialism is, or Marxism, or proletariat, or bourgeois. All they know is that they're Vietnamese and the Vietnamese have evolved to fight foreigners. They're nationalistic. Their nationalism is being used, hijacked by Marxism, Leninism. That's it. I bet you anything the Viet Cong still worship their ancestors, light incense and burn offerings for them. So you see, they live and fight as Viet Cong but they still believe in a natural hierarchy, in heaven, in spirit . . . Only people like Ho Chi Minh can comprehend what Phenomenology and Dialectic Materialism is, or Marxist ideology, but these people aren't the ones who fight and die. . . again proving my point of an unbreakable hierarchy in nature. What's more, these Communists think they're so smart and pure but they're not smart enough to know how wrong the whole ideology is,' he spouted exhaustively. He picked up his teacup and sipped from it. Deep under his eyebrows, his eyes had been watching me, surely trying to discern the true reason for my visit.

Of course what he said was true, I could not argue otherwise. But it didn't sting me as it should, as it without doubt would have in an earlier time, perhaps before the Tet Offensive, when my belief in and understanding of Marxism versus capitalism had been more conventional, in economical terms, in terms of capital allocation, means of production, equality, and class struggle, or in whatever terminology the theorists cared to come up with.

'You believe in heaven and spirit then,' I said sharply, which seemed to jolt Nam. 'You believe in a natural hierarchy as you say, an order where you were conveniently born into the top.'

'Oh, Minh. You came from a Buddhist family and a wealthy one as well. You should know that it's karma. Whatever good I did in the last life awarded me with a good life now.'

'You believe in honoring your parents, your ancestors?' I persisted.

'Yes, of course, it's obvious. I honor and thank them for all they've done for me.' He smiled as if condescending to naïveté.

'And your child. What would you do for him?'

'I will sacrifice for my son, of course. I will give him everything I have.'

'Can you prove it, any of it, spirit, heaven?' I said somberly. 'That any of it exists.'

'You can't prove something like that.' He snickered. 'You just believe.'

'I think you can.' Then, I saw clearly how my assumption had been correct after all, how the struggle at least for me had transmuted into the antithetical opposition not of Marxism versus capitalism, but between man and something much bigger.

'Enough. Enough already,' Nam said, perhaps sensing my solemn manner. 'I only speak about these things because you've always liked debating them.'

The door to the study slid open and servants brought in trays of food and drink, too much for just the two of us. They lay down bird nest soup, barbecued beef in betel leaves, goat grilled with lemon grass, steamed watercress, a boiling hotpot of oysters, tofu, and Chinese mushroom, and, of course, jasmine rice. The bird nests came from high cliffs in caves where swiftlet birds built their nests to breed. They were rumored to be an aphrodisiac; the soup was Nam's favorite dish. Of course, I never cared for such decadence.

Just then the phone rang.

I glanced at my watch; it was nearly seven o'clock. The time had come. Nam, holding the chopsticks, was about to invite me to eat when the phone rang. He excused himself, got up, and went to the corner of the room where a black phone was buzzing with a loud, clanking noise. As the fragrance of the food rose, I couldn't help remembering the happiness of my childhood, when I had followed the same fragrance to a boisterous family dinner. I reached behind me and grabbed the pistol.

'Alo,' he spoke into the phone and held still to listen. He looked puzzled. 'What? What are you saying?' Then he seemed frozen in place, squeezing the phone receiver to his ear, listening intently. 'Are you serious? What do you want?' A pallor descended over his face, aghast, as if his former face, tanned and satiated, had been but a paper veneer. 'Son. Are you all right? Did they hurt you? I'll get you home. Don't cry.' Then he said, 'Honey, don't worry. I'll get you both home. I'll pay whatever they want.'

The old Colt pistol felt worn and used, though in all its killing days I doubted that it would ever see another more gruesome. I brought the pistol forward and hid it under my thigh as I sat on the pillow. Now I watched him, and my eyes ran over the white numbers on the phone's dial in descending order as though counting down.

Ghostly white, Nam turned to me. He was beyond terror stricken. 'They kidnapped Kim and Cuong.'

As he saw my pistol, his legs must have lost their strength and he stumbled forward. I raised the pistol and aimed at him.

'Sit down,' I commanded.

'What is this? What are you doing? Is this a joke?'

'Sit down.'

He obeyed my voice, now stern and cold. He flopped down on the pillow across from me.

'What are you doing? They kidnapped Kim and Cuong,' he said.

'I know.'

Somehow, his countenance didn't alter at this revelation. Perhaps his intelligent brain had figured out as much upon seeing the pistol, or his highly calibrated mind had already calculated the odds and seen the angle from which his situation could be extricated. Did he think that since I had been his friend I could be used, reasoned with, or lured into acquiescence?

'You're a Viet Cong,' he said softly, somehow resigned. 'What do you want, Minh? Tell me what you want.'

I could tell in his voice that the years of our friendship had vanished. I had betrayed the loyalty of friendship, which was considered sacred in our culture.

'Before I tell you what I want, I want to tell you the situation. My comrades have your wife and son. If they don't hear from me by dawn, they will execute them both. Do you understand?'

'I understand.'

'I will tell you what I want, but first I want you to know that I didn't take this lightly. But it could not be helped. I chose you because you are a petty bourgeois, a collaborator. You have gotten much richer by doing business with the American and the corrupt Vietnamese government. You claimed to know nature, you claimed to know Vietnamese culture, you claimed that Vietnamese have evolved to fight foreigners; if so you should know that by siding with the American you'll have no choice but to fight and kill us, so it's you who go against nature. You live in luxury while our comrades die in the jungle. Half of them died in the jungle from diseases and hunger and never saw any fighting. You continue to spout your belief in the natural order, in heaven and earth, while you shield yourself from hardship, while we're more than ready to die for our struggle,' I said. As if in one breath, I poured out sentences that had been formulated over the years. It was, it would appear, my turn at the lectern.

'Just tell me what you want. I can get it for you.' He seemed unable to remain silent. 'Gold, food, medicines, supplies, even weapons. I can get anything for you. Please let them go.'

'Silence. You were chosen because you must be made an example of. You will be a warning to all of Saigon and to the collaborators.'

'Are you going to kill me? If you want to kill me, let's get it over with, but let my family go.'

A finality in his voice came through clearly and his face had become a dark bronze mask, bloated with sorrow, one which I had never seen before. I knew his emotions were taking over and he was no longer thinking.

'I told you I didn't take this lightly. You must think I'm a coward, that I used our friendship to ambush you. But I value loyalty just as much as you,' I said. The moment had come, my hand holding the gun trembled. I had formulated this plan with cold precision, I had rehearsed it in my mind with flair and bravery, and all was topped off with a dash of high drama, but now at this dreaded moment the dark permanency of my plan seemed to seize my breath.

Then with a flick of the wrist, the pistol was reversed, and with my hand now holding the pistol's butt forward, I extended it to him.

In a flash, he grabbed the gun and aimed it at me. His hand shook so wildly that I was afraid he might shoot me by accident.

'I'm not a coward. I could have shot you and no one would ever know the truth,' I said. I was strangely relieved, I had just passed my own test. 'I give you a choice. You can shoot me or . . .'

'What? What are you saying? Are you crazy?'

'I give you a choice,' I repeated solemnly. 'You can shoot me. But if you do, you'll never see your wife or son again. If my comrades don't hear from me by dawn, you can fish their bodies out of the Bach Dang River.'

Holding the gun too tightly, his hand jerked from side to side.

'Or you can kill yourself,' I continued. 'And your wife and son will be home by dawn.'

'I just want my family back,' he said.

'In my pocket is a note in my handwriting, a signed confession that I've been a Viet Cong for many years, that I came here to kill you. Regardless, with your money and position you will no doubt have no problem with killing me.'

'Then why the confession.'

'Because my death would serve to remind Saigon that any of us could be a Viet Cong. Either death would serve our purpose,' I said coldly.

For this game to end, the scale weighing too many intangibles must finally tip—the intangibles of human mind, love, belief, sacrifice.

A knock on the door startled us. A servant was checking to see if we needed anything. The knock suddenly reminded us of the food in front of us, uneaten and now cold.

'We don't need anything,' Nam screamed toward the door. He turned to me. 'There is a third option. You can let my family go and I'll let you leave.'

I chuckled and said, 'Do you think you can make me call my comrades off by dawn?' I added, 'Only one of us will leave this room.'

I realized that he was thinking again, perhaps more talk would somehow weaken my resolve.

Sure enough Nam said, 'Why are you doing this? This is barbaric. We've known each other for so many years. You're one of my best friends. I helped you when you came to Paris. I helped whenever you asked me. We are like family. Whatever problem you have with me please leave my family out of it. Why hurt the innocent? I beg you. Please let us live. You, me, my family. You can't take back death.'

'I've already bid farewell to my family. If I live, I'm heading into the jungle. You see it's as fair as I know how to make it. My family will also be hurt.'

'There must be another way.' His usually raucous voice was barely audible. He raised the pistol to my face and aimed it steadily, while his nostrils flared and sucked in sharp, short breaths.

'So your talk of spirit and heaven and karma, all just talk.'

To tell the truth, my resolve was beginning to fray. Having emerged from my darkest hours, I had concocted a most cruel game. Slowly, I began to look beyond the barrel of the pistol and saw his pitiful face, saw him who only a short while ago had been my friend and happy. Perhaps I could let his family go and still disappear into the jungle. Still, I had gained something, I had passed my own test.

His face suddenly grimaced, his lips tightened, and his eyes squinted into two dark points. One shot exploded toward me. The noise jabbed at my ears which started to ring with a high-pitched drilling sound.

'Call them off now,' Nam muttered through clenched teeth.

I closed my eyes and remained still.

Another shot exploded.

I felt nothing, I was still alive. Slowly, I opened my eyes and saw him laugh, his laughter hysterically filling the air and dancing to the zigzagged motion of the gun. Then all at once I saw a bright glint on his face, then the gun went to his temple and exploded. It happened much too fast. I jumped up and ran for the door.

At the gate, I told the guard that there had been an accident and that his help was needed. Under the same, unchanging drizzle, I disappeared into the street, heading in the direction of the countryside and eventually toward the Cambodian border, stopping only once to make a phone call."

Outside, the night, fully descended and firm in its grip over matter, had something in it that made the story too real. Not so much that the night conjured the past into the present, rather it took Diaphany and threw her wholly into that distant time, mind and senses, and made familiar and real a land that was far and exotic. The deep green of the walls, as if suddenly alive like the vegetation of a tropical jungle, seemed to close in on them, but was held off by the single, yellow light in that apartment. Not even realizing that she had jerked back reflexively, her mouth gapped open, and eyes glared.

"Even now I see so well, each small thing," Minh continued even as he saw her reaction. "Each movement. The body convulsing before relinquishing. Like a chicken as I break its neck. Each time the same. I see Nam's body each time I have a chicken in my hands."

A sudden nausea rose in her stomach, and Dia held her breath to keep it in check. She looked at his sinewy hands, hands that had prepared the chicken she found so delicious but that her body now wanted to expel. She swallowed several times and said meekly, "Then what happened?"

"I went into the jungle. I became a Minister of Justice. I fought along with my comrades. I saw many of them suffer and die. But we won the war."

"What happened to your wife and daughter?"

"They died during a B-52 bombing raid. Ah, they were on their way into the jungle to visit me. They were caught in a shower of bombs. I never saw their bodies."

Dia swallowed several times again, held her breath, and tried to squeeze the air down into her stomach. She remained silent.

Minh studied her, seemed to understand, and saw in her silence a capitulation and a long distance she had already traversed, far beyond return. Behind his beard he smiled. He continued, "After we won the war, there was jubilation. That was understandable. But for me, the battle was just beginning. I wanted nothing less than total victory over the entire human species. I was eager to see the Marxist fire begin to burn in other places. Indonesia, Malaysia, Thailand, even Japan, Australia. But it was not to be. The leadership changed. All they wanted was land, houses, gold, possessions, women. They became corrupt and they puffed up their chests like the very capitalists they had fought."

"So I left. I fled with the common people. The boat people. Ah, they saw clearly. They saw the hypocrisy. So here I am. A peddler of chickens. A Marxist in a capitalist country, but I find things in this country are becoming familiar to me, very familiar to an old Marxist."

"What about the Godevil?" Dia uttered.

"Ah, the Godevil. Conrad named it such. It is quite appropriate. It turned out that all our struggles, though very different from one another's, though they sometimes appear in opposition to one another, have one thing in common. Ah, you see, man has tried to impose his will over life. And life came from this thing. It is very clear. But do not pay it too much heed. It will undo you. Now, I must tell you one more thing. Very important. It will save Conrad."

But not yet, her mind screamed for him to hold on, but her mouth would not make a sound; what does it mean when all life came from it; how does man impose his will; by man, he must mean all men and not a single man.

"The Black Chicken of Sa Pa," Minh pronounced slowly as if to give Dia time to take it in.

What chicken? She stared at his mouth so as to wipe out her confusion, to make his words understandable.

"This will save Conrad." Minh observed her closely. "Allow me to explain how. You are puzzled. Be patient, Comrade. After I explain you will understand . . . As you know, from Truheckler's blood Conrad isolated a virus. It was to be his great achievement. But it was stolen. Since then, his work has gone into decline. You can see for yourself how he has turned away from his work, how he has turned away from, how do you say, cutting edge research. It is pitiful he is working on the old rabies. Yes, you look surprised because you don't know him as well as I do. I know him well, I have supplied him with chickens. He isolated viruses from these chickens. But now he is more concerned with the Godevil, the realm of philosophy don't you think, just like that blue book you read. You stole the Amazon virus from Abe. But what for? Conrad will never be able to publish it. And what did it get him? The government on his back and yours . . . A grand experiment he said to you? To bring out the Godevil. More philosophy, don't you agree? Good for the mind, but the body must live, too. It must live in the world. I see you agree."

Minh went on, "Your love for him is real. I can tell. I observe you very closely. I see your eyes shine like an owl's . . . Ah, your eyes shine bright when you hear his name. That is why you must save him."

"How?" Dia asked finally.

"Ah, the Black Chicken of Sa Pa. It is a small fowl. It has little meat. Unremarkable in every way. The feather is mostly black with a little white here and there. Hardly any red, or orange. You have to look very close to see the different colors. From the heads of the cocks of this species, a crest droops with a strange pity. The hens are even less remarkable. But the bird is fierce and strong. It roams the hillsides of Sa Pa. Ah, but when you pluck away its feather, its true nature is revealed, its skin is black. No one knows for what purpose. Why such blackness under the feathers?"

"How will it save Conrad? I don't understand."

"Ah, it carries a special virus in its thighbone. Only the local medicine men know about it. It will give Conrad another chance. As a professor, he must publish. With a new virus, he will have funds, another chance to be like before." Minh raised his brows as he spoke.

"Where is Sa Pa, anyway?"

"It is in the highlands of Vietnam."

"Vietnam? How do you think I can possibly get that black chicken?"

"You must go there, of course, Comrade."

"You can't expect me to go there. I don't even know where it is. How am I supposed to go into the hills and get it?" Dia spoke quickly.

"Ah, but I have contacts, of course. Some of my subordinates are still there. You will not need to do anything. Just go there and someone will take care of you. Everything. You will leave with the chicken."

"Why can't you get them to send it? Your subordinates? Or deliver it here."

"It is not possible. Otherwise I would have helped your beloved Conrad long ago. The chicken must be alive, but even so, one can not send it through the mail even if one could manage to get it past the post office. As for my subordinates, they're Marxists like me; the Vietnamese Red Capitalists will not let them leave."

"I don't know anything about going to Vietnam," Dia said softly as if to herself. A scarlet hue infused her face, and she felt a heat rising to the top of her head and realized she was blushing but was not sure if it was from shame.

Though his face didn't change, Minh too noticed the blush.

"Comrade, please sleep on it. You need not make a decision right now. The strength of a struggle comes from the willingness of each revolutionary." He smiled firmly behind his beard. "Now, I will run to the store to get you a few clothes and essential items."

HE MUST HAVE SEEN HER SCARS. TO THE WOODEN FLOOR HER body must yield if she was to fall asleep. She had slept on hard floors before but none seemed harder than this, and a dull ache came on soon after her body lay still on the hard floor, making her change position. He must have seen my scars but didn't seem curious. Strange everyone else had been curious before. Maybe he didn't want to make her uncomfortable, or maybe he'd seen them and figured out a lot more. That was why he said what he said. The deep green walls of the bedroom absorbed the light from cars passing outside; they absorbed, too, any hints of the world outside so that the light moving across the walls seemed to flicker like the dying of a midnight flame, somewhere in a far–away jungle. The bedroom's walls were bare but from their bareness something extended, hovered over her during the intervals of darkness.

Godevil was what? He said man wants to impose his will on the Godevil but that was just philosophy. What people think about in their heads or write about in books is just that, but you must live, the body must live, that's right. But she had been going after something in her head too, nobody knew about it, and all this cutting, all the scars on her body, they all came from this thing in her head. She wished Conrad was here. Missing his being there with her— that must be it—now caused in her a void she recognized with an eerie familiarity. It was a high, a simple happiness, a weird common contentment just to be around him. Outside the door, there was silence; Minh must be sleeping. Midnight must have passed long ago. Minh, the shrewd son-of-a-bitch knew exactly where to pull, he must have seen her scars and figured out everything. What? Was there ever any doubt? Minh, you didn't need to be so shrewd because it didn't matter. A car rumbled loudly outside the window. As Dia turned on her side, the thought still streamed through her mind. I'll go. I'll go anywhere.

20

Punisher of Evil

Meanwhile, Conrad had been busy. But even during the most frantic moments of running to and fro, of sorting out the vials of viruses to be hidden, of calling to Dmitri or reprimanding him, in his mind Conrad saw Dia, and she lived, breathed, smiled, and sometimes looked over his head at the sunlight with an unusual intensity. He tried not to, but now and then when he forgot his own discipline and allowed himself to remember her perfume, it seized him in a paroxysm of intoxication. The few days being cloistered in her apartment, hearing the low pitched murmuring from Moiro's machine, breathing in the air suffused with stillness, had formed a different world in which he had been immersed so willingly as to forget his own purpose, and now he suffered a strange deprivation as if withdrawing from a heroin addiction. To the workbench or the freezer and back again, he would repeat the same action over and over, unknowing and unseeing, until Dmitri bristled at him and told him to get a grip on himself. Startled, Conrad howled and barked back at Dmitri some incomprehensible commands. Oh, but what had he done to her? The fear seized him in the midst of holding a few frozen tubes of engineered viruses. He had embroiled her in a deadly business; Weed was now looking for her, and so by extension all the elaborate and nuanced machination of Weed's world was after her. She was safe for now. No one would know to look for her at Minh's. A coldness bit into his palm and his hand withdrew abruptly, letting the frozen tubes fall to the ground.

Dmitri picked them up and grinned at him.

"Professor, you mad or you in love?" Dmitri said. "Wise man once said, love is madness."

"Get back to work you wise Russian. You must get all these tubes packed away." Conrad turned toward his office. He must also dispose of all his notes, all traces of the engineered viruses.

"Well, well, well, what we have here?" a voice boomed from the door, startling Conrad.

His chest puffed up in a shining blue suit and a yellow tie, Weed stood at the doorway with his arms extended. "You folks moving? Hehehe." He swaggered in, sniffing the stench of the bacterial broth, laughing, and his body shook up and down as he laughed.

"No, no. We're only tidying up," Conrad answered.

"Good, good. What was I thinking? Where would you go anyway, right? We know everything. You folks can run but you can't hide." Weed sauntered in and stood in front of Conrad in the narrow hallway. "You lied to me."

"Please come into my office. Let's talk about it, please."

Weed moved with assured steps, and Conrad followed behind.

"You lied to me." Weed's voice drawled out triumphantly. With his chin extending, he waited for a response with half-closed eyes.

"What did I lie to you about?" Conrad asked softly.

"I have witnesses who will testify under oath that you and a certain Dia . . . Diaphany were together. Why did you lie to me?"

"Yes, I did. You see . . . I did see her one time as I told you. But that was it. That time when these people . . . Who are these people anyway, who will testify under oath?"

"Heh, a mister Hucks. The nicest black man you'll ever meet. Fun loving. Knows how to party. Goes with the flow. Woowee. Let me tell ya about the gals he has."

There was no denying it now, Conrad said, "Oh yes. I did see her that one time, and that was the last time."

"You take me for a fool? You stated that this woman only came to your class. And you never saw her again after that. Now what you have me believe is more hogwash. Ya'll have me believe ya said something different from what ya said. Is that it?"

"No, no. That was not what I said. I remembered telling you that I did see her one time and that was it," Conrad said. Droplets of sweat began to collect on his forehead.

"Hogwash. But it don't matter none. I'm the decider . . ."

"Yes, yes, you are. I don't mean to interrupt, but please excuse me for one second. I have to make sure my technician is doing the right thing. I'll be right back." Without waiting for an answer he leaped from his chair and ran out of the office.

Conrad came to Dmitri, who was loitering not very far away and pretending to clean a work bench while listening. He grabbed him by the arm and pulled him toward the freezer; he whispered into Dmitri's ear, "Get me the West Nile virus."

"Wild type or engineered?" Dmitri replied with an uncharacteristic complicity that made Conrad turn to look at him.

"Engineered. Thaw and bring it to me right away," Conrad grumbled in a hushed voice.

"Yes, professor, but please let Dmitri get away before you open vial. Promise."

"Yes, yes. Right away."

Conrad raced back to his office and flopped down on his chair. A bright smile came across his face, contrasting with his morbid demeanor a moment ago so starkly that Weed squinted suspiciously.

"I apologize for the interruption, but you were saying?" Conrad spoke as calmly as he could.

"You're done, as far as I see. I have enough evidence to bring charges. I hereby charge you with terrorisssm," Weed pronounced and puckered his lips. "A short stop to Guano Bay for you."

"You can't be serious. Even if I was seen with her one time, that doesn't make me a terrorist. You must be joking."

"Shhhhaaa . . . hehehe, got ya. Hehehe," Weed laughed. "Nah, I wasn't going to charge you with terrorissssm. Heck no, I wasn't going to charge ya because ya went out with that woman one time. If I wanted to charge you, I can do that anytime even without any evidence. Heck, I'm the decider; don't you forget that. Hehehehe. I ain't going to charge ya because it's ya lucky day, buster. See here, it seems somebody high up know ya. And they like your work, see. They want ya to be a part of the team."

"I don't understand. You mean you have superiors? I thought you were the decider. Who are these people?" Conrad tried hard to buy time for Dmitri, as he looked past Weed into the laboratory where Dmitri was taking out tray after tray from the freezer.

"Don't you mind them now. I got bosses, and they got bosses, and them bosses got more bosses, and those folksy bosses got more bosses. They're them folks at the top whose names I can't even mention. Wouldn't be good to my health, if you know what I mean. All ya got to know is . . . they like your work from before. Before ya stopped publishing. They want ya on the team."

"What do they want me to do?"

In the background, Dmitri's burly shape bounced around like a ping pong ball, and suddenly there came a loud crash.

Exasperated beyond control, Conrad tried hard to keep eye contact with Weed.

"What in hell's name is going in there?" Weed turned to look at Dmitri.

"Never mind him. He's just rearranging things. Please go on."

Weed turned toward Conrad slowly. "See, they want you. They know about Abe's stealing from you. They still believe you got your stuff. They'll give as much funding as you like. I imagine they'll want ya to make these critters, bugs and all, into some sort of biological weapons for the military. Heck, what do I know? Anyhow, welcome to the team, partner." He extended his hand to Conrad, who shook it, while feigning a smile.

Either the stench of the bacterial broth or the crashing noise must be getting to his nerves, because Weed suddenly got up and began to leave.

"Well, I'll leave you folks to ya tidying up here." Weed took a few steps. He halted and turned around. "Ya better not fool me again. Now get this. Ya fooled me once, shame on me. Ya fooled me twice, ya can't fool me again." With that, he nodded triumphantly and headed for the door.

"Please stay a little longer." Conrad hurried to Weed while wiping his hand, the one that had shaken Weed's hand, behind his back. "Please tell me more. Will someone contact me? For the funding." Behind Weed, he saw Dmitri still fumbling through tube after tube, scattered over the counter, and bringing them one by one up to his eyes to inspect the minute writing on them.

"No worry, partner. There'll be plenty of time for that. Heck, ya folks will be seeing more of me soon enough. But make no mistake, I'll catch that dame. Mister Hucks said she's one hell of a girl for a little fuun. I'll do just that before sending her off to Guano Bay," Weed said and headed toward the door. "I'm off now." With that, he swaggered down the hallway and disappeared from sight.

Finding himself overwhelmed with uncontrollable jitters and helplessness, Conrad stood frozen in place, at the door, feeling Weed's threat and Dia's fate entwining and confounding him and swirling in his head.

"Professor, I have virus," Dmitri's voice shook him free. He was holding a tube with the clear liquid inside still frozen.

Conrad turned to him. "You bumbling klutz. That was really quick of you. I could really use it just now."

"Professor being sarcastic, no."

Conrad glared at Dmitri. He snatched the tube of virus from Dmitri's hand and ran out the door. He ran fast and descended the stairs in quick hops. Once outside, he caught a glimpse of Weed's swaggering, confident strut vanishing into the parking garage. Conrad sped toward him. Once there, he felt his chest thumping and tried to catch deep breaths, at the same time scanning around at all the cars. Too late. Weed probably reached his car already, but Conrad must end this shuffling buffoon if it was the last thing he did. Conrad ran to his car. In a minute the old Mustang jumped from the parking garage, swerving and screeching into the street. At the stop sign a hundred yards away, Conrad saw a black Crown Victoria. That was the car; he strained to see the license plate. The black, hulking car with all its windows tinted couldn't be anything else but a governmental vehicle, so he followed at a distance. Through Westwood Boulevard and right on Wilshire Boulevard, Conrad managed to keep up. Now he slowed down, afraid that Weed would see him, now he sped up to keep the car in sight. At all times his heart beat faster and faster and his eyes appeared startled and erratic, like those of a wild animal that's just been captured.

"No, no," Conrad yelled as he saw the Crown Victoria entering the freeway, going south. He honked and managed to cut into the long line of tightly packed cars that were rolling slowly onto the on–ramp. By the time he got onto the freeway, he could no longer see the Crown Victoria. It was early afternoon and the traffic was moving fast. No matter, if he could go fast enough, he'd surely catch up. The old Mustang rumbled loudly and flew along the freeway, a rumble Conrad took as acquiescence and encouragement, for the old Mustang had been steadfast and faithful. Weaving along the freeway, avoiding one car, cutting right in front of another car only to leave behind its loud honking a second later, Conrad raced heedlessly. Then there it was, up ahead, the black, bulky Crown Victoria, and inside was Weed, oblivious of his own imminent judgment and summary execution. All Conrad had to do was to follow Weed and at the opportune time pour the tube of viruses onto the car's door handle, which would later infect Weed, without a doubt. Fierce and proud, new mixtures of emotions flashed through his mind, but they flashed too real, red and blue, and he even saw them in the rearview mirror: the flashing of a police cruiser. No, Conrad gasped. As he slowed down, the Crown Victoria fled and disappeared around a bend in the freeway.

Conrad pulled over on the side of the freeway and sat, morosely waiting for the policeman. The policeman approached the car slowly and finally tapped on the window on the passenger side. Conrad had to lean over to roll down the window. He looked up at the policeman, who was slightly obese, with a flopping abdomen and a rotund face and cheeks pink from sunburn. Static chirps came from the radio that was clipped to his shirt, and his right hand rested on his gun.

"Sir, do you know why I pulled you over?" the policeman asked.

"Pray tell," Conrad answered.

"Are you aware that you were going over ninety miles per hour?" the policeman said.

"No, I am not."

"Why are you in such a hurry?" he said, looking Conrad over.

"I am not." Conrad tried to compose himself, to erase the expression on his face, which he realized must have appeared excited and half-crazed from pursuing Weed.

"What's that you got in your hand?"

"What?" Conrad looked at his hand. Only now did he see the tube that he had been holding while he was steering the car, and he had forgotten about it. Half of the tube had melted, and a piece of ice could be seen floating in the tube. "Oh, this. It's nothing."

"Is that a drug?"

"Drug? Of course not, not technically," Conrad muttered.

"Please step outside the vehicle," the policeman hollered through the window and stepped back. His hand resting on the gun flipped the top of the holster to expose the gun's butt.

Seeing how the policeman was ready for shooting, Conrad yelled back, "Right away. Right away." He stepped outside and braced himself against his car as traffic sped by on the freeway, and the air turbulence behind them battered his face. Once he got on the same side as the policeman, the policeman commanded, "Go to the front of the car and put your hands on the hood."

Conrad obeyed, went to the front of the car, and put his hands on the hood. Still holding onto the tube of West Nile virus, he remembered that he had engineered this virus to be highly infectious and to have exactly thirty replications, which meant that it could infect at most ten people before burning itself out. He stood and caught the eyes of passersby ogling him from the comfort of their cars. Meanwhile the policeman began to search his car.

Seeing the policeman's rummaging through the old Mustang, Conrad regained his composure and said loudly through the noise of the traffic, "Don't you have to ask for my permission to go through my car?"

The policeman yelled back, "Heck, no."

Of course, the Mustang was completely empty. Finally, the policeman walked up to Conrad; his face seemed convulsed with anger at failing to find anything. His eyes suddenly fixated on the tube and seeing how Conrad was holding onto it tightly, his face perked up with curiosity, as if he could still win a prize.

"Don't you have to have a warrant to search my car?" Conrad asked as the policeman with his hand still resting on the gun approached.

"No, I don't. I'm just following the laws."

"That law isn't just, is it? I always assume that you have to have a warrant to search private property."

"Listen, I'm just following the law. What's in that tube?" the policeman said and studied Conrad.

"Nothing."

"You said it's technically not a drug, what do you mean by that?"

"It's not a drug in the common sense, in the sense that you would usually understand what a drug is. You see, I'm not completely ignorant about the term *drug*, the way laymen use it. It usually refers to addictive substances such as cocaine, heroin, and what not," Conrad said and realized the more he talked the more interested the policeman seemed.

"You don't say," the policeman said, his eyes beaming. "Open it."

"Are you sure?"

"Open it, now," the policeman screamed.

"Right away." Conrad unscrewed the plastic cap and held it out to the policeman.

The policeman put it to his nose and sniffed.

So, this was just bad luck for the policeman. Conrad observed the policeman. "You won't be able to smell anything," Conrad said as though giving him the final nudge.

The policeman put one finger into the fluid and brought it to his tongue, tasting it, smacking his lips. After a moment of not being able to taste anything, he said, "All right you can get back in the car." He then proceeded to write out a speeding ticket.

A few minutes later, Conrad pulled back into traffic and drove south, with the traffic ticket in the passenger seat, and he still held onto the tube of viruses, now completely melted.

THE POLICEMAN WAS COLLATERAL DAMAGE. POOR, POOR policeman was just doing his job. Conrad decided to push this incident out of his mind. Other urgencies now crowded his head. High in the sky, the sun was hidden by passing clouds. Going south on the 710, Conrad soon exited and drove to the Caravelle Club. If Weed couldn't find Dia at her apartment, he must come to the club again, since he had already joined up with Hucks, Conrad reasoned. He saw no one by the entrance to the club, only a few pedestrians were making their way leisurely along the street. The shops, selling clothes, electronics, and furniture, had their doors open but were bereft of shoppers.

He drove around into the alley where Hucks had assaulted him and saw the back door to the club. He parked, put the tube of virus in his pocket, sanitized his hands, and finally got out of the car, observing and making mental notes on the layout of the alley, the club, the surrounding streets, and the parking lot. His plan was to wait for Weed, and when Weed came, he would pour the viruses on the door handle of his car. That would be the end of Weed just as it would be for the poor policeman. Farther along the street he found a bar and went inside, where he ordered a cognac. In six hours the club would open and he'd have to wait.

The cognac went down smooth and strong. The alcohol rose up behind his eyes, and after a while its calming effects perfused his body. He asked for another. Inside the darkened bar, a bartender served him another glass with a stare. To assuage the bartender's judgmental look, Conrad put down a few dollars more for tips.

Waiting made existing essential, something he had long intuited, like the flowing of water or the varied manifestation of a happening. One sees the beginning, or the happening in midway, but to know its purpose, one must wait. First from thoughts he conceived of it, then he willed a plan, and finally he waited. For the doubling time of the virus, for each virus to become two and two four and so on until, they turned the brain of the poor policeman into mush, Conrad would have to wait. Now he would wait for Weed to come and put an end to him, and wait yet longer for another Weed to come along, for surely another Weed would come along and an interminable line of Weed clones must be waiting in the deep state, lining up in the wing to appear and to gladly assume the role and the benefits. It seemed another Weed clone had been waiting all along.

Hemming him in suddenly, an oppressive fog hung at the base of his brain, which he could barely will to work, and the fog rose thickly to the top of his head. He avoided the eyes of the bartender and asked for another cognac. The vapor of the alcohol loosened the fog somewhat to let his mind churn, and Conrad realized that there was indeed an unanswered question: Did he violate the grand rule? With an incredible ease he had put an end to the poor policeman, and he would not hesitate to end Weed as well. But these men were the manifestations of an opaque process, he contended with himself, and so they were legitimate targets. Yes, yes, he mumbled to himself and saw the bartender leering at him. What about Dia? What had he done to her? What about the entire world when the time came to release the Cain virus? He couldn't get himself to follow to a logical end.

By the time he left the bar, a dark gray had descended outside. He had to stand by the door for a while to get his eyes adjusted to the early dusk. How many drinks did I have? he wondered but could not remember. He felt his heart beating vigorously, radiating up his neck, pounding the inside of his head, and blurring his eyes. A wave of nausea swept up his esophagus. His face felt bloated and hot. Taking one unsteady step after another, he made his way back to the club. The Caravelle sign was still dark and the door closed. Down the alley toward the back door of the club, Conrad staggered; after a few step he bent over and his stomach seemed to hurtle through his mouth. Raw gastric juice soured his mouth, and a foul smell hung over his coat where the vomitus landed. With a few more steps, he had to sit down, lean against a wall, and then lie down. He had to put his head down for just a second.

With the sun well beyond the horizon, the sky had not only become dark but seemed to have never existed at all. In the alley, a weak yellow light high upon the wall suddenly came on so that passersby could now see the asphalt, beaten and worn, with deep potholes and running trenches. A scraping noise, a thudding of footsteps, stirred Conrad and he looked up to see an approaching shape. A man was swaggering toward the back door of the Caravelle Club; his pointed alligator boots scraped against the loose gravel. Conrad's hands and feet moved about and automatically felt the ground, and he realized that he must have passed out. Before Conrad could get up, the man was standing over him and nudging him lightly with the tip of his boot.

"Yo, bum. Getta move along. Yo bum, ya can't stay here," the man said loudly.

The moment Conrad looked up at the man, an instant and mutual recognition flashed between them. Terror shot through Conrad but it was too late.

"Hoohoo. What we got here, folks? Must be my lucky day." Hucks squatted over Conrad. His round eyes, the tight curls of his hair, the large protruding ears, and the lips seemed exaggerated, as he hovered menacingly over Conrad.

Conrad got up on hands and knees and tried to crawl away, but Hucks grabbed him by the collar of his coat.

"Whoopee, professor. Must be coming by to look for Dia, heh? Man, you stink. What's that smell? You been drinking, lying in the alley like a bum," Hucks exhaled forcefully.

Though he was fully conscious now, a severe pain pulsed inside Conrad's skull, and his thoughts dragged on, fragmented and incoherent even though the goal was clear: he must get away.

Hucks stood up, lifted Conrad up with him, and pinned him against the wall. "You stole my girl. This here is for stealing my girl." He punched Conrad in the stomach.

Pain shot from Conrad's stomach into his chest.

"She's not your girl." The words came out defiant and sharp, and Conrad was surprised he had said them.

"What you say?" Hucks punched him again. "I can do this here all night long."

Conrad had tightened his abdomen so the pain was not as bad the second time, but his mind still blanked out and he closed his eyes. Nausea swelled in his stomach.

Now Hucks slapped him on the face as though to make him open his eyes, to make his victim concentrate, to make him witness his own punishment. "Stay with me here. Look at me."

"Wait, wait," Conrad pleaded as his hands grabbed and tried to push away Hucks's arms. Pain seemed to have succeeded in pulling his mind together, and different scenarios came to him. "You don't want to beat me up. I work with Agent Weed. He told me about you. He's my partner."

"Weed. You fucking with me. You ain't his partner."

"Not in the strict sense of being a partner. But I've joined their organization. I'll be making biological weapons for them. So you don't want to hurt me. You'll get in trouble," Conrad blurted out.

"You ain't fooling me," Hucks said and was about to punch Conrad again when a jet of gas from Conrad's stomach escaped onto Hucks's face. "Argh, yo that stinks man. How am I supposed to whop ya ass when yo keep stinking my face." Hucks's fist suddenly came up against Conrad's rib cage. "That's for stinking my face."

"Please, please. Wait," Conrad squeaked after the pain subsided. "Please, I can't breathe. You don't want to kill me."

"Yo, yo know what. You right. I don't want to kill ya," Hucks said. A sharp slap flew across Conrad's face. With ecstasy in his eyes and as he slapped Conrad, he poured out his oratory gift,

"If there is anyone out there who still doubts that America is a place where all things are possible; who still wonders if the dream of our founders is alive in our time; who still questions the power of our democracy, tonight is your answer."

From some deep place inside him, an anger flared, and Conrad squeezed a tight fist and hit Hucks's his face.

As though Hucks barely noticed the hit on his face, he hooked Conrad in the spleen. "Yeah, that's right. I like that yo. I like when my bitch fights back. Yo, bitch, hit me again." He heaved heavily and a strange excitement beamed through his eyes, squinting narrow and fierce. Then a flurry of slight, sharp slaps landed on Conrad's face. Then Hucks looked up with a messianic glaze in his eyes and raised his voice to the darkened sky, "And tonight, I think about all that she's seen through-out her century in America—the heartache and the hope; the struggle and the progress; the times we were told that we can't, and the people who pressed on with that American creed: Yes we can." His eyes beaming menace now, Hucks glared at Con-rad and slapped him while saying "Yes we can," with each slap.

A loud burp exploded from Conrad's stomach, bitterness filled his mouth, and a foul gas enveloped Hucks and halted him for a second as he turned his face away.

"Huh, yo that really stinks, yo," Hucks said stomping his feet.

In the extra moment of delay, as though Conrad's mind finally recognized the severity of the danger, it reached deep within itself to find a way out and it found that way deep, deep in his pocket. That was it, the tube of viruses was in his coat pocket, and his hand went into the pocket.

"You ain't fooling me, fool. Weed coming by to party later. And he's bringing someone you know, professor Abe, just like ya. Make no mistake. I'll be sure to check it out with him." Hucks lowered his eyes to Conrad as though he was preparing for the knockout. As his face was inches from Conrad and he was starring into Conrad's eyes, taunting him, he hadn't noticed that Conrad had taken the tube of viruses from his pocket and uncapped it.

In a blitz Conrad splashed the tube onto Hucks's face. The liquid got into Hucks's eyes, nose, and mouth; he jumped back rubbing his eyes.

Free at last, he was free at last, Conrad ran toward the street.

"Waz this shit?" Hucks's screaming boomed through the alley as Conrad ran away. "I ain't done. I'm coming for you. I'm going whoop you good."

21

Late for Redemption

Despite the pain promulgating throughout his body, as if connecting and amplifying from different points of origin, a sense of triumph surged through his aching head. The numbing pain from his knuckles where he hit Hucks's stone of a face, the deep ache from his spleen, and the lacerating jabs along his ribs as he breathed, seemed to fuse and throb into the swelling of his face. He tried to sit very still. He was driving south now, and the farther he left Hucks behind, the more gratifyingly this triumph jelled, and the clearer his conception became about how it would end. In the next few days, Hucks would be in the intensive care, possibly dead, and if not dead, then maimed; his brain would never be the same again. That still left Weed roaming about, hunting for Dia. He must negotiate with Weed. He must convince Weed, bribe him if necessary, or even confess to the theft of the Amazon virus, or go to Weed's boss, anything to get Weed to leave Dia alone. In exchange, Conrad himself would be a cog in their machinery; he would make biological weapons for them, engineer nasty viruses that could kill as easily and selectively as the drones. Until . . . until he could unleash the Cain virus.

The thought was suddenly interrupted by the immediacy

of Dia, her face, her being that his mind and senses had taken stock of, had seemingly teased apart its minutest contours and incorporated into his own by an involuntary reflex. Her face, he would see again in a few moments. Her breath, he would hear next to his ears. He stepped on the gas; the old Mustang sped through the night.

Little Saigon was off the freeway, and soon the old Mustang passed Minh's chicken shop. Conrad saw the familiar sign: *Fresh Free Range Chicken*. He turned into a street and parked. Standing outside the car, he took off his coat, and poured disinfectant on his hands and rubbed it on his face. He stood beside the car, bearing the sting from the disinfectant, and waited for the fumes to evaporate. Finally he ran up the stairs to Minh's apartment and banged on the door.

A shadow moved past the window. The door opened, and Minh stood before Conrad.

"Comrade, welcome. Please come in," Minh extended his hand.

"Hello, Minh. Don't come too close to me. It's not safe. I just spilled a vial of virus." Conrad stepped in.

"You're hurt."

"I'm fine." He looked about. The dank smell of cigarette smoke floated in the air, tempered by a pungent incense.

"Ice will help with the swelling," Minh said.

"Never mind that. Where's Dia? I need to have a few words with her."

"But you must have ice before it's too swollen," Minh insisted and turned toward the kitchen without waiting. "Who did this to you, Comrade?" Minh continued to talk as he opened the freezer and took out a tray of ice.

"A regular thug."

"Do you need my help? I can make arrangement for the

application of force if it's required. You know during my time, our struggle often required force. Sometimes, in very regrettable circumstances, we did away with innocents." Minh came back to Conrad with a ziplock bag of ice cubes. "But it's your struggle now. It's up to you, Comrade."

"No need, Minh. I took care of the problem." Conrad realized that Dia was not in the apartment. "Where did she go?"

"Ah, about that, Comrade. She went on an errand."

The bag of ice was cold and awkward in his hand, and Conrad pressed it to his face.

"When will she be back?" Conrad asked. Cold droplets of water dripped down his neck.

"I'm not sure."

"What do you mean you're not sure? Where did she go?" He looked at Minh. "I'll just wait for her here." He sat down on the hard floor.

"It's not advisable to wait, Comrade. She won't be back until much later."

"Why is that? Where did she go?"

"She went on an errand."

Conrad turned and stared at the Marxist, dropped the bag of ice to floor, and stood up. "Tell me where she went," he said slowly through clenched teeth.

"She went on an errand, one that will help your cause. To use a religious reference, resurrect your career."

"No more evasion, Minh. Where?" Conrad screamed.

"To Sa Pa."

"Sa Pa?"

"Sa Pa is in the highland of Vietnam, at the border with China. To get the Black Chicken. I'm certain we've discussed this."

"I know where it is. But why? What have you done?" Conrad grabbed Minh by the shoulders.

"I thought you'd be happy. This is what we discussed. The Black Chicken harbors a virus in its marrow, in the thighbone. A novel virus that is exactly what you need."

Conrad let go of Minh's shoulders, his arms flopped to his sides, and, turning away from Minh, he began to convulse with short shaking bursts that radiated down the length of his body. He braced himself, as he knew what awaited Dia on the other side of the planet.

Minh noticed the change in Conrad's countenance, and said, "How was I to know, Comrade? You see you brought to me a girl with scars on her arms, her wrists. What else was I to make of her? Naturally I took her to be a street urchin, a damaged creature, a mule to bring back the virus. To be used for our cause. I thought you brought her to me for our purpose. Perhaps it's an old habit from my days in the revolution . . . A damaged creature who would fall easily for my tale, and sure enough she took it all in . . . she agreed to go to Sa Pa quite willingly."

He had brought her here to save her from Weed, only to deliver her to Minh. He was already down halfway the stairs when he heard Minh's calling after him. "You must sacrifice love for the revolution . . . "

22

Death and Other Possibilities

The possibility of death was pronounced from the front of the airplane by a flight attendant who directed all the passengers to pay close attention to video screens in front of them. The beautiful stewardesses on the screen instructed the passengers on an emergency protocol, while displaying nice, bright smiles in which keen eyes could discern a hint of *schadenfreude*, for there must inevitably be a mishap during the lifetime of this instructional video, such as an inevitable disappearance into a fallow field somewhere, leaving behind nothing but scraps, or smashing into a building and leaving behind absolutely nothing at all. So the whitish glow of the video in front of each passenger exuded an irresistible, iridescent, unnatural light, at once embalming and soothing as the rumble of the airplane peaked, as the earth fell away from them. The flight to Hanoi departed right on time.

Dia held her breath and recounted all that had happened in the last twenty–four hours, that had passed so quickly. Minh had had a fake passport made for her within a few hours, and he had specifically forbidden her from contacting Conrad.

Nausea wormed up her throat as she tabulated these things mentally. Then closing her eyes and withdrawing into the seat, she felt the vibration of the engines gently shaking the chair, transmitting its implied terror into her core. Around her, there was nothing on the faces of all the other passengers but bemused boredom, which was no doubt bred by familiarity and the inveterate belief that nothing could ever go wrong. Slowly, Dia exhaled, and the gas exchange in her lungs resumed with a tentative caution. She had contracted the fear of flying during her brief affair with Joel. Despite the glamour of the frequent shuttling back and forth between Los Angeles and New York for movie openings, and New York and the many capitals in Europe for fashion shows, the fear metastasized and morphed into something that only now could she understand clearly and retrospectively as a rejection physically born by her own body. Like ingesting the wrong types of food to which her body would later develop anaphylaxis, the glamor she had experienced with Joel had begun to rattle apart the strong force her soul depended on for cohesion. She hadn't flown since breaking up with Joel, until now, until the choice to do so came along and presented itself with such clarity that she had not so much decided as simply known she had to. Strange as it seemed, her body somehow sensed that she would go to the other side of the known world for Conrad. Amid the uncontrollable anxiety that the buoyancy of flight induced and that she had to suppress, a cold realization sheared itself into her mind, that was logical and tractable in as much as her decision to go seemed purely intuitive and subsequently not really a decision at all. Had she really decided to go, or had the circumstances, the unseen hand, the manifestation of this so-called Godevil, effectively cut off all other avenues save this?

Just last night, Minh's murderous tale had thrust her into an unknown jungle, a place far weirder than those places her acts of self-mutilation could ever take her to, no less bleak or inhumane. Now she was on her way to that very place, and amid the ghostly glow of the screens upon which all the other passengers seemed fixated, she drifted into a somnolent flight, at times jerking awake like a migratory bird on its long flight across the Pacific Ocean.

After a brief layover in Seoul, Dia disembarked to find a modern airport in Hanoi. The trek through customs was quite easy, as the customs agents, all wearing green uniforms with a single red star on their chests, spoke English. Finally entering into the waiting area, Dia saw her name on a hand–written sign held up by an old man. His gaunt face shone with a stubborn longevity, his hair was white but combed neatly, and his dark eyes were partially hidden under bushy brows. With a questioning curiosity, he studied her briefly, asked her if she had luggage, and beckoned her to follow him. They walked silently toward the car amid the noise of traffic, the overpowering smell of diesel exhaust, and the thin haze of dust. In a long sleeved, white cotton shirt and jeans, Dia clutched her bag as she followed the man, who wore a faded collared blue shirt tucked inside black dress pants.

"Welcome, Comrade. My name is Tuan," the old man said once they were inside the car.

"I'm Dia," she said but at once realized that he already knew that. "Thank you for meeting me."

"It is my duty, Comrade, yes. I am sorry I didn't greet you properly in there. I did not want suspicion. Secret police, yes."

"Oh right. I understand. Secret police. Your English is very good by the way."

"Thank you, Comrade. I translated for the Americans during the war. In Saigon, yes. You know Saigon. I was able to gather information. But now I am a tour guide. It is good for me. I am still useful from time to time."

The car began to roll slowly and merged into traffic. The old Toyota rode onto the highway, and the engine shrieked loudly as it accelerated to avoid the big trucks behind it. Above the morning sky was filled with gray, low-lying clouds. On both sides of the highway, long and narrow buildings of various heights crowded together, and on the rooftop, cylindrical water containers and satellite disks pointed to the sky.

"Your first time in Hanoi? You must be tired. Jet lag, yes?"

"Yes." Dia felt a tiring pull on the back of her head. "Yes, I do feel sleepy."

"I will get you a bed. You can rest. Sleep. Train to Sa Pa leaves tonight at nine."

"How far is Sa Pa?"

"Sa Pa is in highland. Train gets there tomorrow morning."

Dia said nothing more and looked out over the city as the highway rose high above the ground. She felt a hollowness permeating and at once squeezing inside her. She thought of Conrad; she hadn't spoken to him since he'd dropped her off at Minh's. What is he doing now? She wondered. How she wished they could be here together as a couple, conventional and ordinary, visiting an exotic Asian destination.

In the rearview mirror Tuan saw her gaze over the city and said, "There were cherry trees here during the war. Cherry trees everywhere, as far as the horizon. They blossomed pink in the spring. But now only houses everywhere."

Tuan commented about this or that, falling into the role of a tour guide. His voice bearing a flow of monotones, a low serenity as though hugging the very earth, a surrender through despair, and yet a fierce resistance awaiting, struck Dia deeply.

Then they exited the highway and entered the city. On narrow streets, an endless stream of motorcycles cackled a staccato of rumbles and puffs. Everywhere looked like everywhere else, people straddling motorcycles, singly or doubly, and sometimes two or three children sandwiched in between adults. Beyond the streets were shops of all imaginable sorts—clothing stores, restaurants, cafés, fruit and vegetable markets, beauty salons, as though even in this bustling chaos beauty and vanity would not be forsaken.

"It is not what you expect, yes." Tuan saw how Dia seemed lost looking out at the streets. "Most Americans still see bomb craters, rubbles, collapsed buildings. But cities and people are like trees, they will grow back. Some are beautiful like the cherry trees, some are like weeds."

Dia burst out laughing. "Yes, some are like weeds."

The car went on, its engine purring weakly as though it were a sick animal. It meandered through the city and finally pulled up at the Metropol Hotel, where porters in tan uniforms came up to the car and nodded to Tuan.

"We are here." Tuan nodded back to the porters. "Metropol is the best hotel in Hanoi. Comrade Minh gave instruction. You will find it pleasant here."

"Thank you, Tuan," she said, saying his name gingerly. "When will the train leave?"

"I will come back for you at seven o'clock tonight, right here."

Tuan opened the door for her. Dia got out and raised her eyes to the façade of the hotel painted in chalk white. The wall was broken by rows of tall French windows, wooden doors that flung outward, and trimmings and decorative moldings higher up. She counted four floors. Inside, young girls in traditional *ao dai* greeted her. Their round, flickering eyes followed her, as if intent on discovering in her a cure for an unspoken curiosity. Inside, the décor spoke of meticulous handiwork and innovative designs, and colorful vases of intricate patterns drew her eyes here and there. She looked up to find fine moldings on the ceiling that was defined and enhanced rather than limited by the walls. The hotel's opulence harkened back to the French colonial era and solidified in Dia the sense of otherworldliness and timelessness Minh had indelibly sparked with his tale. A light perfume, exotic and sweet as though from a flower that only blossomed at midnight in the jungle, stirred in the air around her as she moved. Her fingertips touched the sandy texture of the wallpapers as she walked down the hallway to her room. The pleasant giggling from children playing some-where around the pool pursued her. From sleeplessness and an insuppressible buzz of enchantment fomented by embark-ing alone on a most uncertain quest in a faraway land, she sensed her surrounding not so much as actually being there but rather as having her consciousness transmigrated as she had once experienced when too much blood had escaped from her wrists. Only, this time a warm glow of hope and tender-ness engulfed her.

Once inside the room, she fell on the firm bed and put her face on the velvety, soft pillow. She saw through the half–opened curtains bright noon light. Sleep came over her in increments as her mind held onto old perceptions, a pecu-liar state of standing still and morphing into nothingness as though her consciousness had fled to the very edge of exis-tence beyond which there could be no other world, only a dream world.

A peculiar dreamlike state, unfurling from drowsiness due to jet lag shrouded over everything, hung like a miasma before her eyes, and abolished any transition from dream to wakeful-ness so that she could remember things passing but not know if any of them was real. Anxious and hyper-vigilant, in this state when she was awake, her mind teetered on a precipice of awareness, her vision raced to the object she wished to see and hovered over it as if seeing for the first time. Her mind contemplated familiar things in slowed-down truncated segments of time in between very fast quickening of which she had almost no memory. In this state, a chair was no longer a chair, but a magnificent invention of weight distribution and displacement, designed for a biped creature tall and narrow so that the creature might distribute its weight whenever it was weary, and save for this creature, no other animals could find the chair useful—not the monkey whose legs would only dangle, not the hippopotamus who would squash it, and certainly not the tiger who would only paw at it. Hopscotching in this anxious wakefulness from object to object, scene to scene, while marveling in a new, iridescent light old, familiar things, would finally give way to sleep, a sleep so deep and so tightly entwined in dreams a new reality would take hold.

Dia had fallen into such entwinement of a dream. Lost among a teeming crowd of strangers, amid a flurry of foreign words, she wandered about, moved about the people, searching for someone. Where is this place, this place that has nothing, not ground underfoot, not sky overhead, not even an object in sight, only people, everywhere people? What was she searching for? Search was what she must do. Edging through the crowd, she bumped into and waded against a horde of people. Everywhere she turned she seemed to brush against someone else. A child, she suddenly knew, but why? Whose child? Who is the child? Pushing her way about, she felt exhaustion and exasperation brimming in the very air, but still she must follow this singular command. Then she caught a glimpse of it dodging about among people. It was a chicken, not a child; yes, relieved at last, she remembered that she was here to get the Black Chicken, not a child. But the after-thought of a child now left a misshapen longing. She bent down and scuttled after the chicken as it fled. Then the people all around her rattled, slowly at first, then jumping together in unison to a loud banging.

If increments of sleep came over her, then a deluge of consciousness shook her awake. She jumped off the bed. She had merely lied on top of the bed and the beddings remained undisturbed. A second later, she became aware of the room. From her hand bag, she took out her makeup kit and toothbrush. She had brought one set of clothing and a jacket. As she took inventory of the bag, her hands missed the familiar feel of the pistol, the can of mace, and the switchblade, that had been her constant companions; their absence now spurred a precarious forlornness and an eerie foreboding of being outwitted. Was Minh playing her, setting her up for something bad; was she just a pawn? She wondered. But the difference between this journey and the many quests she had undertaken with the sharp blades, running over her skin with so much masterful precision, cutting only deep enough, letting the blood flow and the pain seize her mind, was only in kind. In the end there seemed to be no difference at all. After a quick refreshing shower, she left the hotel. The few hours of sleep had cleared her mind.

23

Night Train to Sa Pa

The train to Sa Pa chugged into the night. As the metal wheels thumped and scraped on the tracks and chains rattled with the occasional jumps, the compartment swayed and churned. Sometimes everything buoyed up and down like a boat. And outside the window, a few lights flitted by, like fireflies in the darkened landscape.

"We have this compartment. No one else," Tuan said to Dia as she sat on the edge of the bed. "I bought four tickets for us. No one else here with us. We have privacy. Minh instructed me."

"That's very thoughtful. Thank you, Tuan," Dia said.

The compartment was lit by a white fluorescent light and had two beds and two bunk beds on top, enough room for four passengers. A wooden table sat by the window. A stale smell of cigarettes seemed locked in the stagnant air. Tuan closed the curtains, leaned against the head of the bed, and closed his eyes.

"May I ask you a question?" Dia asked. At last a question seemed to enter her mind, solidifying from its ethereal haze Minh had so successfully conjured.

Tuan opened his eyes and looked at her, "Yes, please ask."

"Why are you doing this?"

"For same reason you do it, yes," Tuan replied instantly.

"No, no. I do this for a very personal reason. It's not the same reason you do it. It can't be. I do this to give a man a chance to advance his career."

"For this man you care very much."

"I do."

"You take on dangers to help this man. I see."

"What danger? What are you talking about?"

Sitting under the bunk bed, Tuan's face was cast in shadow, and even so Dia could discern a change in his expression, a slight widening of his eyes as she questioned him.

"Danger in any journey, yes." Tuan smiled obliquely. "For example, this train can crash, yes. Or on your way back, your plane can crash, yes. But I pray you have no danger."

"Why do you pray? Aren't you a Marxist?"

"You're observant. A figure of speech, yes. Marxism is not practiced here anymore, no comrade to criticize, no self-criticism, one makes errors in speech and deed."

Minh had said the same thing, Dia remembered.

"What reason do you have to do this?" Dia willed herself back and silently chastised herself for such an easy digression. "And don't tell me it's for the same reason, because it's not."

"The same reason I explain to you. I'm a Marxist. I follow orders from Minh. He is my big brother, big comrade, you understand, yes. He thinks about theory and he instructs me on practice. He tells me to take American woman to Sa Pa. I take you to Sa Pa. I will deliver you to right people. So your reason must be the same, yes. My reason the same as Minh."

Dia exhaled. She scooted herself onto the bed and leaned back into the shadows. Perhaps Tuan lacked the language skills to explain himself properly. She said, "That doesn't make any sense. I'm not a Marxist. I'm not doing this because of Marxist ideology."

"I will try to explain better, yes," Tuan said. "When I was

a child, I lived in a village in the central highland. There was a big coral tree at the edge of the village. Tall and grand, it had thorny spines along its trunk. No one paid it any attention. Until one day the songs of birds were heard from high in the tree. I saw a nest and colorful birds. I wanted to catch one or get the eggs and hatch them. Colorful birds can sell for a lot of money, yes. I tried to climb the tree. I used pads on my hands and feet but I could not get up high. I could not get near. Just then a wandering monk came by. Maybe he was drawn by the songs of the birds. I could never tell."

The train jumped suddenly, and from underneath the compartment chains rattled. Tuan waited until the regular chugging of the train resumed.

"The old monk looked me up and down. Then he looked the tree up and down. And instantly I got the idea to build a ladder, yes. I worked for days. I cut bamboo. I made a ladder twelve meters long. I was happy. Colorful birds can sell for a lot of money. I put the ladder against the tree. I climbed up. It was easy. I got up on a big branch. I reached out for the nest. At the tip of my fingers. I felt the eggs . . . Ah, a wind blew. A strange wind from somewhere and my foot slipped. I fell but I caught the big trunk. I held on tight. I slipped down to earth. I survived but the thorns cut through my arms, yes."

Here Tuan rolled up his sleeves to show Dia rows of scars along both of his arms. He continued, "It was much pain. Later, there was rumor in the village that a monk was meditating on the coral tree. The birds were singing their songs for him. There was rumor that the monk could see the length of the river from up there. You understand now, yes."

"It's a nice story Tuan. But I don't see how it relates to us." Dia realized that Tuan was employing the same trick as Minh, drawing her in and distracting her with his tale.

"My purpose was the same as the old monk's, yes. I did not get idea to make ladder until he came. It made no difference if I got birds, or eggs, or I fell down. Only I made the ladder. Purpose was same as the monk. You understand. He climbed up high to meditate. He saw things as they were, the real things."

"That doesn't make any sense to me. You made the ladder because you wanted to get the birds."

"Things in life are like that. Dead ends. The old monk saw the real things. Sometimes, sometimes I think that ladder was the only thing I was born to do, yes." His eyes seemed to lose focus, and a remembrance of the past seemed to take complete hold of him. "Marxism was foreign for me. A foreign poison I foolishly took into our heart. Now I wander like a lost soul, or like Minh, an exile. No enlightenment. No forgiveness. All too late, yes."

Someone knocked on the door. Tuan got up and opened it. A young conductor peeked in and let his eyes linger on Dia. Tuan gave him the tickets. He took the tickets, looked over the cabin with a puzzled look on his face, punched them with a perfunctory motion, shrugged, and went on.

"The train arrives at six in the morning. We should rest," Tuan said.

The rhythmic swaying and rattling of the train rose and ebbed like water at rising tide, and like a rising tide, the rhythm inundated relentlessly and muted Dia's senses, finally extinguishing any inkling of the Marxist's deception, which she could see in Tuan's story and wanted to confront him, but she was afraid of offending him, so she remained silent. She pulled the curtain to look outside the window and saw a few lights, whizzing by in the darkness, and, above those, the empty sky full of stars. Perhaps from the vision unfolding before her, a sense of unspeakable loneliness of the great universe dripping down over the land sipped through her eyes and soaked into her consciousness. She jumped back aghast and for the first time realized that she was beyond turning back. She was going through this darkness imbued with the loneliness of universe. The quest to bring back the Black Chicken from Sa Pa that had been so clear cut now suddenly became ambiguous, and she felt a jolt of panic. No turning back now, a moment later she chastised herself for doubting. She lay back into the bed and closed her eyes. In her mind, still very alert and racing about here and there, a foreign vista comprising of unknown land and sky opened and expanded toward vast opacity at its periphery. The land itself was made of undifferentiated soil and strange living things, and above that the infinite, starry sky untethered. A sensation she had felt many times before during her episodes of self inflictions, now seemed to suspend and balance the atmosphere itself and the night train racing through a strange land upon a precarious fulcrum, pitting an anxious forlornness on one side against an excited will on the other. The whole scene was devoid of logics. A nebulous quality suffused everything so that it seemed to Dia the night train might levitate into the air at any moment were it not anchored to the ground by a force of opposite polarity on the other side of earth. As if alone and floating in the heaves and sways of the cabin, she sensed the night train chugging upward to the highlands on serrated tracks, much like climbing a very long ladder.

THE TRAIN ARRIVED IN SA PA WITH EARLY LIGHT. DIA HAD slipped into sleep a couple of hours ago and now awoke as Tuan stood over her, calling her name. Foreign words crackled from loud speakers along the narrow hallway, interrupted at times by the hissing of statics.

"We are here," Tuan said as Dia stirred. "We must go."

Outside, a heavy, cold fog enveloped them as if compensating for the thinness of the mountain air and carried within its wake an earthen smell. Dia put on a jacket and zipped it all the way up to her neck.

"Follow me. I have a car." Tuan led her through a crowd, passing by some taxi drivers on the lookout for passengers.

They walked off to a side street and came to an old gray Toyota parked under a tree. A man was standing a few feet away and watched them. He nodded to Tuan as they got in and drove off.

"Where are we going now?" Dia asked.

"To the mountain, yes. This is downtown. We go the mountain."

"It's really cold here." Dia breathed the cold air inside the car.

"It snows sometimes, in the winter. It will warm when the sun gets higher," Tuan said. He drove with the steady manner of a tour guide. "There, the border with China." He pointed to the form in the distance. Through the dense fog, Dia saw a tall square arch with enormous Chinese characters on top. The red flag was limp in the still air, hiding the yellow stars within its folds.

SHAPES OF SA PA, IF ANY SUCH GEOMETRIC CONFIGURATION could ever be said to characterize a place, rushed in through the sparse openings among the trees lining the winding road. Beyond the trees, hill tops reached high here and there. Into the slopes of these hills, the curving terraces of rice fields had been cut as if by a race of giants, everywhere the same precise terraces repeating, forming a staircase to a place hidden in the clouds. Vertical lines met perfectly horizontal planes, right angles formed, and from the perspective as seen against an empty horizon, these perfect steps along the mountainside seemed to evoke a place so surreal that logics had permitted physical transformation from childlike playfulness, in which it seemed that the longer one looked, the less likely one was to return. Far away in the distance, visible only through a deep valley and made hazy by a fog in the early light, straight horizontal lines along a slope of a tall mountain solidified the impression that all the slopes of all the hills and mountains in Sa Pa were embroidered with such terraces. Likewise, the sensation of something ethereal, light, and fine, seemed to prohibit even the thought of a world left behind. The surreal panorama rushed into one's eyes, and it would seem that here one's eyes could not only see the landscape traversing into the valley and rising into the high mountain but seize at its very seam and take it in thread by thread, as if the landscape had been made anew for each person.

Dia took it in greedily. "Stop the car," she told Tuan. As the car pulled over to the side of the road, she jumped out and went to the trees. Beyond the tree line, the hill side dropped off steeply into a valley below. Here Dia could see the landscape unobstructed. In the cold air moistened by the fog, an earthen smell now mingled with a scent of an unfamiliar foliage. Lost in the air as if drifting high, Dia felt herself taking flight into the atmosphere. She stared and was mesmerized for a long time until she could almost leap and spread her arms. At last, noticing a few corrugated tin roofs of houses here and there and realizing that here too there were people, she stepped back and held onto a tree beside her, her heart thumping. The crows of a rooster echoed up from the valley below. Behind her, cars roared by and whipped up turbulent air.

"No rice grows in winter, yes." Tuan came up to her. "In

summer, rice fields are beautiful. Green then golden, when the rice becomes ripe, yes. You come back in summer. I will be your tour guide."

"Yes, Tuan." Dia felt herself blush as though she was caught in an indecent act. Could she have leaped into the air? She felt embarrassed that Tuan might think the same, for he must have noticed the scars on her arms and thought her suicidal. "That would be very nice," she added and got back in the car.

Now and then Dia saw women walking along the side of the road, wearing black dresses or clothes of varied colors, having their heads always bound in scarves, sometimes holding the hands of children. In their diminutive statures and steady, leisurely strides, their feet seemed to confirm the ground with an unflinching assuredness.

"Who are they?" Dia asked, pointing to the women.

"The natives, yes. The Hmong, the Dzai, and many others ethnicities. They have their own languages. Different dresses. You see the ones in black dress and black headscarf. They are the Hmongs. The ones with red headscarves are the Dzai."

"Yes, I see," Dia murmured.

AFTER A FEW HOURS OF REST IN THE HOTEL, THEY SET OUT IN the afternoon. He started to drive the moment Dia got in. The wooden façade of the Victoria Hotel disappeared around a bend, then the street through town wound around a central circle with a grand monument in the center. Busy with peddlers of too many things with too many colors for Dia to fully discern, the street led into the mountain, and then became a narrow, gravel road lined with trees on both sides. After an hour of hard jostling, the car pulled off the side of the road, high up the side of a hill.

"We must walk, yes. Down into the valley." Tuan got out of the car with a cooler in hand. "This will keep thigh bones alive."

"But Minh said that the chicken has to be alive," Dia said.

"Custom officers will not let you pass with a live chicken, not possible."

"I remembered pretty clearly that Minh said you will help me get a live chicken."

"It's not possible Comrade. You will bring the thigh bone, just as good. Beside the virus is found only in the thigh bone. We must adapt if the revolution is to succeed, yes."

"All right. I guess I don't have any choice. Who am I going to see?" Dia remembered that Minh had also said the same thing.

"A woman. She gives you thigh bones of black chicken to bring back." Tuan hurried forward as though to avoid further interrogation. The cooler dangled from his hand.

The dirt road led downward for a few hundred yards and then curved back on itself, each time descending deeper into the valley. Trailing behind, Dia smelled the earthen scent of dust being kicked up into the fresh air as Tuan walked in front of her. Soon she walked by the terrace rice fields, saw the dark brown soil lying fallow in the winter, and followed the terraces with her eyes all the way up to the side of the mountain. If the sky were divided into four quadrants, the sun had by then traversed through three, but the sunlight was still bright, warm, gentle. Dia saw Tuan looking back now and then, and he seemed to slow enough to settle into an even pace with her. Once in a while, some foreign words echoed from somewhere below, perhaps a woman calling for her child, and sometimes childish laughter could be heard. By the side of the road, as Dia came up to a lone, wooden house sitting amid the vast emptiness of terraced rice fields, a young girl came out, holding on to a crooked wooden fence. With a diminutive, straight figure garbed in a black dress, a pristine face with small eyes, her black hair partially wrapped in a black scarf, she cracked a smile for Dia and showed her white teeth. Dia waved at the girl. Something incredibly hopeful about the girl struck her, and her feet paced steadily, marking this place in her memory, leaving behind the young girl.

Already exhausted when they reached the house, Dia still had to wait in front of the house while Tuan went inside. The house was small, its front no more than four yards wide. Planks of wood making up the wall separated the inside from some shrubs and a grove of bamboo outside. A hen and a few chicks were clucking and mingling among the bamboos. The ground where she stood appeared smooth and hard and extended into the house. A vat of black dye was by the door. A slanted bamboo pole leaned against the corrugated tin roof of the house, and some sheets of dyed black clothes were hanging on the bamboo. A whiff of incense and smoke, strong and prickly, seemed to demarcate the air at the entrance to the house, and beyond it, she could hear foreign words being exchanged inside.

"Please come in," Tuan called Dia from inside the house. Though he was only a few feet away, he seemed strangely blended into a vacillating darkness, as if the objects behind him and the air itself were intent on absorbing him, so that Dia could hardly make him out.

Dia stepped over a wooden plank marking the entrance to the house, bowing her head as she entered the darkened interior. The smell of incense and burning wood engulfed her. To the left, she saw a stove on the ground, consisting of three bricks upon which a pot with some sort of stew was boiling. Nearby, a few clay bowls lay on the ground. From the burning wood, bright flames undulated against the side of the pot, throwing up black smoke. Three short wooden chairs were placed in front of the stove.

"Please sit down." Tuan pointed to a chair.

Dia sat down and, since the chair was so low, found herself in a squatting position. She said, "Where is the woman?"

"She is catching the chicken, yes."

Now Dia heard the squawking of chickens and erratic wings flapping through the back door, then footsteps stamping on hard ground, accompanied by a deep vocal mumbling.

A moment later, an old woman tottered through the back door with a gaping gait. Her black dress covered from her neck to the ground, a black scarf wound around her head. In one hand she held a chicken by its feet and the other a knife. From her deeply wizened face, her sharp eyes exuded an impervious look, without seeing anything in particular. Dia stood up and bowed to her slightly, but the woman didn't seem to notice. The woman continued mumbling, perhaps a sort of incantation, then spoke to Tuan.

"She said you must help, yes," Tuan said.

"Help her, how?" Dia said.

The old woman squatted down on a chair in front of the stove and seemed to beckon Dia to do the same. Dia sat down. They were now two feet away from one another. The chicken flapped its wing vigorously but couldn't get loose from the woman's firm grasp and finally settled into turning its beak here and there, clucking softly, looking about. The old woman laid the knife on the ground and put the chicken's feet under her left foot and its wings under her right foot. She picked up a clay bowl, waved it in the air, and from her throat, the continuous guttural mumbling now reverberated as a loud incantation. After swirling through the air three times, the clay bowl landed in Dia's hands. The old woman's right hand now grabbed the chicken's head and stretched its neck; her left hand picked up the pointed knife that appeared black save for the metallic shine at the sharp edge. Using her thumb and the sharp edge of the knife, the old woman began to pluck the feathers along the chicken's neck.

Indeed the chicken's skin was different, as much black as deeply bluish, as if a bilious venom had concentrated just under the skin. Dia knew what was going to happen next, she had seen it before. Now she held onto the clay bowl, slippery between her sweating palms. The Black Chicken of Sa Pa, this creature that in her mind had morphed into a mythical totem, clucked weakly under the old woman's firm grasp. Its colored skin seized Dia's fixation, tantalized her with proof that all her dreamlike journeys, even ones suffered by deep cuts, were in fact real. Unconsciously, Dia slowly turned her head away, and her eyes squinted and she knew that the moment was near. Amid the quickening flicks of the old woman's wrist set to the rhythm of her throaty incantation, flimsy wisps of feathers floating in the air blended with the curling smoke rising from the stove. The old woman's hand moved too quickly; the sight of the slit across the chicken's neck entered Dia's mind before she could shut her eyes. In complete darkness behind her eyelids, a warm wetness suddenly flooded her nostrils, suffocating her. She threw down the bowl and wiped her face furiously. She felt calloused hands rubbing her face, while the old woman's voice roared in her ears. Warm liquid inundated her and as soon as she opened her eyes, it blinded her. She shrieked, jumped up from the chair the moment she realized what was happening. She ran out the door. Bringing the sleeves of her jacket to her face, she wiped vigorously, and finally opening her eyes and in the waning sunlight, she screamed as she saw the vivid redness of blood on her sleeves.

"Old Hmong ritual, yes," Tuan said from a distant behind her. "The medicine woman put a spell to protect you. Don't worry."

"What was that Tuan? What was she doing to me?" Dia said loudly and squinted at him with eyes that were smeared with blood. She continued to wipe the blood off her face.

"A spell to protect you, yes. Nothing more."

"She splashed me with blood. Look," Dia shrieked.

"Go around the side of house to back. You can wash," Tuan said while he kept his distance.

"All right," Dia shouted and made her way to the side of the house where there was an earthen jug filled with water. She splashed cold water on her face.

"Yes, just as good. I'll get the thigh bones. You go to the car now. Stay on the road, you won't get lost," Tuan hollered after her as he went inside the house.

THE SUN HAD RETREATED BEHIND A MOUNTAIN BY THE TIME Dia reached the car. A misty gray seized the sky and enveloped the valley. From its depths wispy, columns of smoke rose from the solitary houses scattered here and there and dissipated into the empty grayness. Inside the car, Dia took off her jacket and tossed it aside. Soon, the stagnant air inside the car was saturated with the smell of blood, a pungent rawness mixed with a twang of acidity, but she felt none of the shocked revulsion that often rose up at the base of her skull when she encountered a whiff of her own blood. Specks of blood had congealed in the crevices of her hands and she felt a jelly-like stickiness in her hair. The old woman had splashed her with the Black Chicken's blood. Was the old woman trying to cast a protective spell, or curse her? Dia could not possibly know. Nor could she fathom the old Marxist's polite manner, a sort of kindness a propagandist might display toward his will-less victim as she's convinced to become a slave. The more she tried to unwind things, the more dizzying everything around her became, seemingly scintillating with a pseudoreality piqued with nausea. She sat and waited. Her eyes drifted over the vastness of the valley, the grayness of the sky that was emptying into a tentative darkness. Perhaps it was only in this fading light, the shimmering dusk, that its truth could be known, and in the distance of emptiness between her and those houses far below, a forlornness screamed toward her as fast as her eyes could absorb and struck her with a sudden violent sadness. Tears swelled up in her eyes. In this vast valley opening up into the empty sky and outside of those houses with warm hearths, there seemed to be only madness.

24

Madness In The City

Night had gathered substance. A substance with parts unknown had assumed space itself and stirred to the energy of life flowing to the smallest crevice of the earth so as to transmit the lightest animate vibration. Under the sun, light rendered this substance transparent as air, but the thick of night revealed its true form. Now, sitting in his bedroom in the early evening, Conrad could for the first time sense it and wave his hands about, and he saw the night rippling through the open window, crossing the alley, making its way along the road, and engulfing all the lives in its wake.

He hopped off the bed, made for the door, and exited the house. Gravity pulled him down hill toward Wilshire Boulevard.

Night lights from streetlights high above, or cars passing by, or shop windows, revealed the night's substance in its languid sensibility, its unflappable stillness that stripped bare everything. Perhaps from habit, he turned north and passed a long stretch of street that ran along a cemetery. His shadow distorted with the headlights passing by. Beyond the cemetery, life returned in the shops.

As he walked aimlessly, a forlorn sadness consumed him completely.

His mind turned to Diaphany now. Long fingers leading to thin hands, dark hair framing a shapely face, pale skin becoming paler in the cold air, these images of her unfolded one after another, aided by her perfume persisting still in his memory to become a feminine fragility he must somehow protect. These images of her have been interlacing themselves as if from their own volition into his being, yielding at times while at other times taking over completely, pummeling him relentlessly so that his normal affects fell away piece by piece. All he wanted to do was to provide for all her needs, to bring her coffee, to make her breakfast while he hadn't made breakfast for himself for ages, to do anything for her. At last he realized that all he wanted was to be near her. But he could not, she was far away, incommunicado; there was no way to know where she was, or to even warn her. He had sent her there as surely as if he had asked her himself. And he knew what awaited her there.

Sunset Boulevard led him toward the heart of Tinsel Town. Restaurants offering flavors from the world over, shops brandishing the latest insipid fashion, and numerous bars and coffee shops, seemed to draw in a steady flow of tourists. Unceasing engines rumbling and bright glaring headlights flowed in a disjointed concatenation, like a nocturnal centipede pulsing along in the night. Boisterous laughter burst out; a scream peaked and faded away; a heckle undulated in the night substance. So too the bright headlights, the jaundiced streetlights, the dim yellowish glows from inside the bars, simmered and shifted from lit surfaces to dark pockets, all in the constancy of change. Lifting his eyes, Conrad observed these people, following the noises and the lights that had inevitably led to them, to their actions, which they seemed to perform reflexively. They appeared to him as though he had been transported here from a nether world.

With cold objectivity he had inspected people as he tried to formulate a grand rule which would allow him to experiment on them. He had always felt a natural distance from them, but conversely he knew they would see him just as alien, as inscrutable and weird. What would they think of the Cain virus? If they ever found out, they would instantly lock him up in a nuthouse. He seemed to know these people around him, their motives, the little causal things ensuing from one after another that defined their actions, the course of their lives. The gulf that once separated him from them somehow shrunk to nothingness; he became each and every one of them, as though he was transmigrating from one phenomenon to the next and to all simultaneously.

Conrad suddenly regained his former attitude, cold and objective; the moment of pining after Dia had burned itself out. He remembered the beginning, of the beach where his fierce will dared to challenge fate, and then of Dia's earnest face and the sincerity in her eyes as she listened to Truheckler and took everything in wholly. She was an ever-ready tool to be used for his scheme. How easily she absorbed all he had said, so much so that her partaking, her collusion in the grand scheme to create the Cain virus seemed to exceed even his own fervor, and at times even stoked him on, as if she had been born for this purpose, as if all her searching and self-mutilation were but a prelude to this. If so then it was right to send her there, to the other side of the earth, to fetch the Black Chicken of Sa Pa. She should bring it back to him then to compensate for the pain he had suffered because of her; Hucks's stony face and his callous fists appeared to him, inflaming his still swollen face and making him angry. "Damn it all," he said out loud. I had turned her away with contempt and condescension, but she kept coming, so she deserves it, whatever is happening to her in Sa Pa. He mumbled to himself and made gestures in the air as though conversing with an invisible interlocutor who walked beside him. Anger expanded inside him and filled him with a throbbing heat, but most of all it replaced the forlorn sadness, and thus gave him a transient reprieve.

He felt anger's fire liberating and enlivening him; an energy radiated from his bones and propelled him forward. Yes, she should serve her purpose and bring back the Black Chicken. It harbors a novel virus in its marrow, and with it I will make Cain. I will unleash it. It's my choice.

Then he saw something far ahead. A velvety blackness reflecting the white fluorescent light vacillated, long threads of hair hung to the shoulder, and even at a distance, the shape of the head and the figure clicked in Conrad's mind. He found himself running after the figure, knowing that it could not possibly be Dia, and yet still running. Could it be her? Dia, he wanted to yell out. The woman was walking along side a few other people, men and women, and they were talking, laughing. When he was within a dozen feet of them, he slowed down and followed behind them. This is madness, a part of his mind screamed, and yet another part of him believed that that woman was Dia. He walked behind them; he must see her face and know for sure. The group turned into a restaurant, and as they turned he saw the woman's face, the hooked nose, the pendulous lip, and the thick jowl. He turned away and ran down Sunset. A chill filled his chest where the fire of anger had burned just moments ago. "I'm going mad," he said out loud. "What is happening to me? I'm mad."

A frigidity, as much from the cold air now descending over him as from his innards, insinuated itself into his head. Everywhere he looked, he glimpsed the same black hair swaying under the streetlights, the same fragile shoulder, and with these images the memory of her delicate perfume flooded his nose. But always the face was turned away from him, so cruel it seemed, as if on purpose to drive him insane, leaving him ambivalent and standing on the sidewalk, gazing through the windows of bars and restaurants at some unknown women, telling himself that it must be her while knowing otherwise. The bright headlight of an oncoming car for the moment showed him his reflection in the window's glass as he stood watching the diners inside, and he saw in the reflection a stranger, the defeated, pathetic visage of a man he could not recognize but also could not refuse. Suddenly he set off running; he ran back to where he had come from, aiming for the solitude of his bedroom.

He ran fast until his chest hurt from heaving, and when he could not run anymore, he concentrated on the pain. Retracing the path home, at last he saw the old Mustang in the driveway, but now instead of entering the house he stood by the car and uttered a faint cry. An idea made him cry, an idea came suddenly, and it imposed on him absolute power; from the moment he conceived it, he recognized not only its overpowering madness but the futility of resistance. He got in the car and started to drive. *Dia must be home now*—that was the idea. This was madness. He turned onto Wilshire Boulevard. She must be in her apartment. How could she just agree to go to Sa Pa? How could anyone? And for what? To get a Black Chicken, he burst out laughing. He turned onto her street. Everything was quiet. He saw a cold mist flowing underneath the illumination of the streetlights, the deserted street, the dark windows punctuating the night air. He checked his watch and was startled that midnight had long passed. He parked and walked up to the front door of the apartment. Standing by the intercom, he fell into lingering in a finite space for which the intercom became a portal for escape, or for further fraying of the self, or for a validation that his reality has been morphed irreversibly. He checked his watch several times and saw the second hand ticking, and thus time still encompassed him and his dilemma. The tip of his finger finally touched the dial pad. He heard the intercom buzz.

"Hello." In the night, Moiro's voice, fuzzed by electric static, came through the speaker loudly.

"Hello," Conrad spoke as he put his face next to the intercom. "Hello . . . I'm sorry . . ."

"Yes, what do you want?"

"I'm sorry to disturb you. I realize it's late . . ."

"Yes, what do you want?"

"Please let me speak to Dia."

"She's not here."

"Please, I need to speak to her. Will you check her room? Please check her room."

"She's not here. She would answer the phone if she were here. I answer the phone when she doesn't answer."

"Oh . . . right. Thank you. I'm sorry to disturb you . . ."

The intercom clicked off. Silence resumed. In the depth of night, Moiro's voice, that lone human voice sounded inexorably sweet and echoed in the depth of his chaos; he heard pity in her indifferent voice and somehow by hearing it alone, instead of surrendering to madness his mind reconstituted and regained a portion of his former self. Moiro, you strange creature, you raise your children, you nag your husband, you make a living, all on the Internet, Conrad thought as he walked back to the car. Am I somehow like you?

NOTHING ILLUMINATES THE SOLITUDE OF MAN BETTER THAN the amalgamation of lights in Los Angeles—the orderly streetlights, the pale florescent of distant office towers, the yellow hue from countless bedrooms' windows, the red pointed lights on top of skyscrapers, the traffic lights still blinking for a deserted street—all being engineered to be together as if seeking solace from a primordial wilderness. From Dia's apartment, Conrad drove without aim.

At last he pulled into a parking lot, parked under a tree, and turned off the engine. The old Mustang had wandered through the midnight city to end up here where the familiar building became a haven. He waited. Pain seethed in the pit of his stomach radiating outward, and as he drifted into sleep, abstracting from reality and the physical world, it remained, simply transmigrated across the dimension of consciousness as if the pain has taken on neural matter to become his very brain.

Dawn slowly dimmed the city lights, and the horizon's reddish light became brighter and gentler as the sun rose.

The noise from a car woke him up. He opened his eyes and saw the old doctor walking with a lopsided gait toward the door, weighed down with a heavy bag. Conrad jumped from the car and called out to him, "Doctor, doctor."

With a key in hand, the doctor, who was immune to all surprises, stopped his hand in mid-air and stood there without turning around. When Conrad came up to him, the doctor turned and looked at him with a stillness of morning. A silence that was sustained by quiet acknowledgment held them there voiceless, as each tried to reckon the state of the other. No one could tell how long they stood there in silence until all that could be known by human deduction was known.

The doctor unlocked the door, entered, and held the door for Conrad. "Fortuitous then. Please come in. I'm finishing some charts but you look like you should come in."

Through the waiting room and then the hallway crowded with boxes, they entered into the doctor's office, a cluttered space hemmed in by walls of books, journals, and diplomas. On the desk were a computer, a pile of charts, a corded phone, a clock with a transparent case through which the gears could be seen turning, and various mementos of his life that seemed to collaborate with the clock in equaled measures.

The doctor sat down lightly behind the desk and bade Conrad to take a seat on the other side.

"Something is wrong with me, doctor," Conrad said weakly.

The doctor's eyeglasses seemed to magnify the blackness of his irises as they narrowed on Conrad. Then with the same voice that had often taken up words his dying patients could no longer utter, that had fed into their ears and their minds a wisp of comfort, the doctor began.

"I can see it on your face, Conrad." the doctor's voice was warm and steady. "Hollowness under your eyes, in your cheeks. Your eyes flickering about like you're looking for something. Your hair is a disheveled mess. Lips parched and cracked. You have been bashed in the storm and thrown into the barren desert. Hate and bliss alternate in your soul, hate because bliss won't last, and hate itself is just as tenuous. You feel lost, though all your possessions are intact, still in your routine. You walk about and look about but see nothing. Some nagging questions would surface in your mind and you answer yourself, talk to yourself. And finally, you have multi-sensory hallucinations brought on by a sort of withdrawal that craves a former physiologic state."

Unconsciously, Conrad had been nodding to the doctor's prognostication. "Is it schizophrenia, doctor?" he asked.

"No. It's worse," the doctor said. An impish smile pricked his cheeks. "Love."

"Ugh . . . Be serious man," Conrad howled, and as soon as the words left his mouth, he saw the truth of the doctor's diagnosis, and, if it was in any way questionable, it was because he himself had never known such state of existence. That the platitude of it had been thrown around, commercialized, advertised with nauseating frequencies, now struck him with a cathartic ferocity. Oh, how he had never known before, and what he had known of childish infatuation during his younger years had been as brittle as the wings of moths. Lost in his own rumination, he barely heard the doctor's droning voice.

"Minh told me all about her. A suicide girl. Her skin marked by scars, some of them very deep, but still a lovely girl. Nature can't be helped. Minh thinks she's disposable. He sent her to Sa Pa, or rather she wanted to go there. For the Black Chicken. She wanted to help you, to resurrect your career. But she doesn't know, does she? She doesn't know the danger, does she? After all if she brings back the virus, both your career and so much more importantly your quest to create the Cain virus will approach success. Cain will have his day."

Conrad remained silent, his eyes vacant and lost.

"Didn't you bring her to Minh to send her to Sa Pa?" the doctor asked.

"I don't know anymore what I knew." His voice had a hushed tone. "I didn't think it out. I didn't tell Minh in so many words. I didn't plan it so. It's possible."

"Love sinks into you, but you know it suddenly."

"It can't be. I'm not one . . ."

"Not just you. She."

Over the scar on his right forearm where Dia's switchblade had sliced, his left fingers automatically reached to feel the slightly raised skin under which he'd seen the other world. Conrad remained silent.

"Believe me, I know all about it. Yours is just a variation. Thousands of patients, thousands of deaths, over the years I have seen it all. I smell the decomposition of their innards escaping through the stench in their breath. An obscene sulfurous effluvium given off by venery, sloth, rapacity, hidden deep in the contours of their guts. I see the worries in their eyes, those feigning eyes, as they hang onto to this life for however much longer just to be able to hang on. For what purpose, while the body is reduced, divested of all, without choice, so in the end only the tortured spirit must confront it all, all alone by itself. I see regrets, despairs, helplessness wedged deep into the finely corrugated skin of their faces that have changed beyond all remembrance. I see their souls in their ears, a faint reflection off the tympanum but you must be very sudden and quiet, otherwise it withdraws through the eustachian tube. But what they hear they ignore. And the eyes feign. So how can the heart live?" the doctor said. His eyes had been downcast, but he now raised them to Conrad. "I love them. All of them."

"Then why do you help me?" Conrad said. "You must know what I plan to do."

"Of course I know, Conrad," the doctor said. With his head slightly downturned and thus eyes upturned, looking through the bushy brows and the glasses, rolls of gray hair partially hiding his forehead, the doctor then reflected: "We're beyond the priest and the dying man. At least we know it. You call it the Godevil while I know it by another name; at least we know it. Has it consciousness as we conceive it to be, or is what we believe we know, created actually by our pettiness? But your experiment is beyond boldness where true faith heals. Anyhow, for every bet there must be two sides, all the shysters in the world know this. Hence they never bet but always take their commission, a slice on the sly. By the wayside they stand and gawk, the comfortable cowards. But you and me, we go all in, don't we? Up or down. All our scruples on the table and let the dice roll."

"That doesn't make any sense," Conrad said. A quickness of the mind, a spurt of logic, seemed to return to him. "If you love them, then why do you help me? You can imagine the end, can't you?"

"But I must help you as hard as I believe. Like an asymptote, only one that will never breach the infinite line."

"You don't think I'll succeed."

"I help you while believing you won't succeed."

"A paradox then."

"The most beautiful things in the universe are made of paradoxes," the doctor said. His eyes gleamed brightly.

"I'll unravel the paradox."

"Only at the end of the universe."

"You don't have to worry about your faith," Conrad said, suddenly remembering Agent Weed. "I'm afraid I've already lost. A government agent came for me. I'll have to work for the government. They will have Abe keep a close eye on my work. I won't be able to continue for long. I'm hiding all my viruses at Truheckler's mansion."

"You must have faith. It can't be over yet. My faith is hardly shaken. You must rattle it as Truheckler and his kind had. It came close and it still hangs over us. And Minh and his kind as well, a neo-Marxism in the new world arises in a new form. But you, Conrad, what you do is revolutionary. It takes but one person. You will come even closer yet."

"No, I've lost already."

25

Suicide

On rare occasions, one's consciousness must swell large enough to endure multiple emotions simultaneously and at the same time be singularly pointed to recognize a rarity, be it the birth of something new or the resurrection of prior possibility. Upon opening the door the next day, Conrad experienced this strange mental state, though the emotions themselves had the flimsiness of imaginary substance induced by previous hallucination and privation of reason and were magnified by his own suffering.

"I'm sick, Conrad."

Dia was standing before him, and behind her the afternoon's sunlight hung sedate and wan over the street. Emotions of various kinds surged through him, and the sight of her made things real. He stood still before her, aghast that he could not utter a word.

"I'm sick, Conrad. I don't think I can be on my feet much longer." Her voice seemed trapped in her nose, muffled.

"Oh," he led her in. He took the bag and the cooler from her as she sat down on the couch.

"Can I have something to drink? I have a fever."

"Of course," he said. As he scuttled to the kitchen, he was struck that, since the madness of last night, his fear of germs had vanished. She had cured him. He had no fear of her fever. Strangely detached, he moved about warming a cup of water for her. Perhaps guilt was keeping him detached. He remembered his former state of how he wanted to serve her, only to be near her, but now he saw the person thinking those things not as himself but someone else irretrievably remote. Varied psychic states from the nights when he wandered lost now recurred and battered him with the urgency of choice; what must he assume, happiness compounded with relief, or resentment for having suffered needlessly. But did he suffer needlessly? He wondered; no, because he knew the real suffering had yet to unfold. Holding a cup of warm water, he returned to her.

Dia was leaning back, her eyes closed, her head resting over the back of the sofa, her hands buried between her thighs, seemingly closed in upon herself.

Sitting down next to her, he held out the cup of water. Her eyes opened by a slit; she managed to pull herself up and took hold of the cup. Dark shadows under her cheeks marred the paleness of the face he once saw fearlessness in. An unfamiliar smell of staleness, of dust from a faraway place, of vegetation that grew only in a foreign clime, rose from her jacket, which was stained with dark blotches of dried blood.

"Thank you." She sipped warm water from the cup, then put the empty cup on the coffee table. "What happened to your face?"

"Nothing important." He didn't want to tell her about his encounter with Hucks. "A little incident, that's all."

"I'm sorry I didn't call you to let you know I was leaving. I know they monitor the phone. And it all happened so fast. Anyway you'd better put it away. It's in the cooler. The Black Chicken's thighbone. You don't even know the trouble I went through to get it. In the mountains of Sa Pa. There was this insane Hmong woman, she squirted blood all over me." Her voice was subdued, drifting off as she closed her eyes. "Getting it through customs was scary but they didn't find it. I guess I was lucky."

The pieces seemed to have been preconfigured, and now fully seeing his part in it made his heart drop squarely into his gut. "When was this?" He seemed to whisper.

"What?"

"You said . . . the Hmong woman . . ."

"Oh, that. The day before." Head still resting on the sofa, she turned slightly toward him. "You don't think she got me infected with the Black Chicken virus, do you?"

He hesitated. "You have a fever?"

"It started just a few hours ago. It's not so bad. But my body aches badly."

"Hmm."

"Don't worry," Dia said. "It's probably just a cold. I was pretty beaten up before I left. I already felt nauseous on the flight there. Beside, I'll get over it, right? It's just a cold. Hah." The soft utterance at the end of her breath, a slight giggle of reassurance shined so well with the upturn of her cheeks, suddenly delineated a barren desert separating her and him, behind both a torrent of life for the moment was damped up, and in turn made them aware of a sad awkwardness.

"Right. It's just a cold." He made his voice sound authoritative. After all was he not a professor of virology, of these little primitive things he had known all his professional life and had manipulated and made to order, instructing them when to replicate and when to cease? Feeling more in control, he would act now to prevent the worst case. "I will give you Tamiflu. It's an antiviral. You'll come out of it. Don't worry."

"Whatever you say, darling," she murmured.

She smiled fully now, a smile that was detached and suspended in the air between them, at once jesting and pitying as if an itinerant ghost from across the universe had assumed it to witness something magnificent and tragic. Then she brought her hand up to touch his face, and then he felt himself collapsing over her, his face next to hers, her breath in his ear saying, "I missed you." The hardness of the street under his feet, distant city lights receding, all under the cold air descending, moved through his mind now and dragged back with them how he had been without her. She went on: "I missed you the whole time. I wished you were there with me in Sa Pa. It was beautiful but really sad in the winter. I wished you were there, we'd have enjoyed it. Maybe we can go together. They say it's better in the summer. You should see the rice paddies. They dug up the mountain to make them. They must have been at it for thousands of years. The Hmong and the Dzai, oh there are many different people. They wear different dresses and head scarves, that's how you tell them apart. And the Black Chicken, its skin is more like bluish than black." Immobile between his arms, her frame felt not so much light as fleeting, and he squeezed her a little tighter, taking her in. She turned and kissed him on the cheek, and pushing him away, she said, "Darling, this is the closest that we can be for now. I don't want to give you what I have, whatever it is." Leaning back he nodded. "Let me sleep a little. I'll just close my eyes a little bit."

Into the bedroom, where the blanket lay crumpled and his dirty clothes were scattered about, he descended, swiftly picking up towels, tidying up, making the bed. He wanted to bring her the extra blanket, but then a well of preciousness tugged at him, compelling him back to the sofa where he stood and looked down at her. Her hand twisted acutely under her chin, in her beautiful face reposed a profound peace, like a photograph. An exultation in her image rose up in him as he stood over her, and a force sanctifying and forbidding somehow hovered about her. He kneeled down. As he knelt next to her, he inserted his arms under her knees and her shoulder, and lifted her lightly. Partly stirring, partly acknowledging, with eyes still closed she purred an "Oh," and smiled. He placed her in bed, pulled off her clothes, and tugged the blanket up to her neck, and feeling the heat in her skin, he brought her an aspirin and Tamiflu.

The obligatory chicken soup, aspirin every four hours, vitamin C, and plenty of fluid—he tabulated the essentials as he retreated quietly from the house. With the cooler in hand, he jumped in the car and sped to his lab.

Hours later, under darkness he returned to the house, feeling once again logical as if a vexing need that had consumed him for days before had suddenly been sated. Entering the bedroom, he heard her soft breathing, and with the light coming in from the living room he could make out her features. Almost gliding toward the bed, his feet tread lightly, silently, and when he was next to her, a cotton tip already in his hand was extended into her nose and twirled. She jerked away slightly and opened her eyes, but the cotton stick was already hidden behind him.

"How do you feel?" he said.

"A little better," she uttered softly. "How long did I sleep?"

"A few hours."

She closed her eyes and dug her head into the soft pillow. He stood looking over her for a moment longer, and as he went out, he took out a plastic bag from his pocket and put the swab inside.

From the bubbles popping over the surface of the chicken soup and the steam rising, Conrad, who has been standing over the pan and cursing it silently to boil, turned off the fire and decanted a portion of it into a bowl. Balancing the hot bowl in one hand, he rushed back to the bedroom. Now he turned on the bright light, and he could see her eyes immobile under her eyelids, so she must be very deep in sleep. He put the bowl on the nightstand and sat down next to her. Caressing her face lightly as he called her name, he finally succeeded in getting her to sit up. Then spoonful of soup came urgently from his cooling breath into her parted lips, one spoon after another, stoking her swallowing that was reflexive and continuous, as if in the urgency he was stuffing a goose, until she growled and shook her head. Enough then. Water with vitamin C and Tamiflu followed, and some spilled over the corners of her mouth and dripped down her neck. Not to forget the aspirin, he put a pill in her mouth and watched her neck move as it descended.

At last he fled the house. Thinking of the virus, he was awed that it had existed in this world since before man, awed by the callous planning of Minh the Marxist who left nothing to chance, but, most of all, by the conscious part that was himself interlocking with it all. The hours he had spent earlier dissecting the Black Chicken's thighbone resulted in an indisputable conclusion that it was useless. It had always been Diaphany, her body, that had served as the means to bring back the virus. A chill shook him as he could see the old Hmong woman spraying her with blood.

"THIS IS THE BLACK CHICKEN VIRUS," CONRAD SAID TO DMITRI as he entered the laboratory. He handed over the plastic bag. "Fresh live virus."

"Professor, you were right. Thighbone is no good. Too degraded. Apoptosis. Everything is mush," Dmitri said. He held the plastic bag with the cotton tip close to his eyes to examine it. "Where you get this? Fresh blood on it."

"Never mind that. You'd better culture this one yourself." Conrad knew he must yield to Dmitri's expert hands and his ways around the lab.

"Anything professor says."

Like an expectant child, he scuttled about behind Dmitri and peeked over his shoulder. They worked through the night. Their motions were tense against sleeplessness and propelled and suspended by a knowledge of a devastating triumph. At times in a huddle, their heads crowded over a plate, or a broth of Hela cells in which the Black Chicken virus would multiply.

"In a few days, professor will have all he ever needs. No thing more to do. We wait now."

"We must work fast, Dmitri. They may come at any moment. Abe will know what we're doing."

In early dawn when sleeplessness rattled his mind with a static buzz, Conrad returned home, and only then did he remember that Dia was in his bed. He went into the bedroom, made her drink more water and take the medicines, then he lay down on the sofa and immediately slept.

Days were no longer days but only lighted segments interposed by darkness which was not nights but rather the hours without light, and none mattered to Conrad who slept in short, dreamless intervals while waiting. In between, there was the chicken soup and later chili beans, the constant water with vitamin C, an aspirin every four hours, and Tamiflu. All the while Dia had been breathing softly, an unshakable rhythm of rising and falling of her chest that Conrad could discern as he checked her frequently when he had a peculiar panic that she had died. Her hand under her chin, propping her face up into a statuesque profile, and her body twisting with arms and legs thrown in varied positions, in sleep she seemed to dance still. Every now and then he remembered that Dia needed to evacuate, and after straightening her limbs, pulling her, and finally carrying her off, he deposited her over the toilet seat and stood in front of her as a pillar against which leaned the dreaming head. "Pee, Dia," he commanded and was surprised that she responded with the sound of fluid dripping and the sounds other bodily byproducts made. Sometimes the fever peaked vividly red on her cheeks, an ember in the flesh that drew his gaze and strangely reminded him of the vastness of the universe and of nowhere else he'd rather be.

Time then was not so much measured by the tick of the second hand as marked off by erratic intervals of growing the Black Chicken virus, seeing Dmitri working, and racing back to Dia and expecting her sitting up and waiting for him. Time itself was muddled in his mind by conception and juggling of all viral shapes and DNA together to become a new form, a novel virus. On the third day, Dia's persisting somnolence and fever hit him suddenly that something was wrong. Conrad called in the doctor.

The doctor came right away. Soon, his car stopped in front of the house and the doctor again weighed down by a heavy leather bag moved quickly across the driveway into the front door.

"How long?" the doctor said, dispensing with any sort of greeting.

"Three days," Conrad said. "Through there, in the bedroom."

The doctor marched into the bedroom and directed Conrad to open the curtains. Then with a swift fling of his arm, he threw the covers off Dia's body, which was stripped down to her panties and bra. She was lying on her side, legs curled with knees up into her chest and arms bent and withdrawn, curves of exquisite proportion some wondrous substance had filled to make a breathing creature. The beauty of her face and body momentarily challenged the doctor's professional demeanor; he halted briefly and threw a glance at Conrad, congratulating and sympathizing.

"Why didn't you call me the moment she came back?"

"I've been giving her antiviral. I was hoping she'd come out of it on her own."

"A bit of wishful thinking? Straighten her up," the doctor commanded.

Conrad pulled her legs, and now Dia lay flat on her back.

The doctor patted her red cheeks, trying to wake her, but she only purred softly and turned away. With the stethoscope over the heart, then over the lungs, and finally the abdomen, he listened and counted the beats, the breaths, and the bowels sounds.

"Doctor, I know enough to keep her hydrated," Conrad said.

"How."

"Her urine. She seems to make enough. It's clear enough."

"Good. And the fever."

The doctor put a thermometer into her ear.

"Aspirin, every four hours. She cools down but it came right back."

The thermometer beeped and flashed: 103° F.

"For three days, you haven't slept much then."

"No. But not all because of her. There is the Black Chicken virus."

"Oh, yes, that," the doctor nodded with resignation. He felt her abdomen. "What else? Is she still infectious?"

"I assume so, but with this virus, you need direct fluid exposure," Conrad said, and seeing the doctor's hands over Dia's abdomen, he added, "I've been feeding her chicken soup. She even had bowel movements."

"Chicken soup, ha," the doctor chuckled. "That's not characteristic of you, Conrad. The waste, the bacteria, that's one of your phobias, is it not? How did you manage?"

"Somehow I no longer fear them." Conrad felt strangely at ease at the mention of germs. She has cured me, she has really cured me, he wanted to say.

An abrupt concentration tensed in the doctor's forehead as he palpated her abdomen with both hands, and the tensing instantaneously switched to his eyes as they pierced at Conrad.

"She's pregnant," the doctor hollered but immediately restrained himself so as to nullify any hint of accusation. "We must admit her to the hospital. Right away. I'm sorry for your situation, but Conrad, you've gone all in."

26

Watchful Watching

A tall, bronze cross that had oxidized to a deep green perched on the high roof of Saint Mary Hospital. With a stone façade, the six–story building occupied a city block. Diaphany was admitted to the Intensive Care Isolation Unit, and, while she was being worked on, Conrad filled out the paperwork. Naturally, he felt a deep responsibility for her, and on the admission form, he listed himself as the emergency contact, the next of kin, and importantly the responsible party for the finances.

By the time Conrad was allowed to see her, the IV line had penetrated her veins, the IV fluid had perfused her system, and the EKG machine had recorded the slightest twitches of her heart.

"She's stable for now," the doctor spoke to Conrad from behind a blue face mask. A blue plastic gown covered him completely to his knee. His hands were in brown plastic gloves. Lifting his eyes from the chart, he glanced at Conrad. "I had to put her in isolation. We can't let the virus escape into the general population."

"Yes, I agree," Conrad answered automatically as if finishing the same thought. "That would defeat the purpose."

"I'm correcting some deficiencies in her electrolytes. I'll need to get an MRI of her brain, and if there is no contraindication, I'll perform a spinal tap."

"Spinal tap?"

"Yes, to see if she has meningitis, or encephalitis. The reason for her condition," the doctor replied.

Awkward in the plastic gown and mask, Conrad approached the bed with his gloved hands intertwined, and observed Dia. Behind the double doors of the isolation unit, a sterility marked by a smell of isopropyl alcohol was being continuously maintained by a powerful suctioning through a vent in the ceiling. Despite tubes entering her arms, electrodes on her skins, and the beeping and whirling of machines keeping vigil over her, a most natural position of an arm raised and bent and of head slightly turned had assumed her body so that anyone who happened to observe her might have the impression that in fact none of this was real, but that they were only a part of her dream.

"She will be all right?" Conrad mumbled.

"For now," the doctor said. "She served her purpose, did she not? I'll do my best to see her through."

A profound depth, it seemed to Conrad, was accreting one molecule at a time and opening up to another dimension in her womb. He knew that one could explain it all away as much as one liked, how the sperm found the egg, the chromosomes joined into a whole, or how the genes were expressed, yet a mystery remained locked inside the double helix twisting round and round, descending or ascending like a staircase into the unknown.

"You should go home and rest," the doctor said. "There is no more you can do here. Go back to work. The trick is to keep yourself busy."

Conrad raised his eyes from Dia's abdomen, looked up and wondered how long the doctor had been watching him.

"How long?" Conrad asked.

"The pregnancy? About six weeks according to the size of the uterus."

Yes, that sounded about right. Conrad tried to formulate his next action, taking the maturity of the fetus into consideration.

CONRAD EXITED THROUGH THE DOUBLE DOORS WHERE HE DIS-carded into a trash bin the mask, the gloves, the protective gown. Then he passed through hallways filled with the anxious voices of relatives of sick patients and the bustling of nurses and doctors, just thinking. Outside, the sky was clear and bright, yet the air was cold. An occasional blast of cold air rushed over him. He sat down on a bench nearby, closed his eyes, and put his face toward the sun. Soon a tender warmth soothed his face, and behind his closed eyelids he saw a pure red, not only the color of blood but the beginning of life. He remembered his father and the many study sessions of mathematics, geometry, and literature during which his father had chastised him for his laziness, or mental arrogance. In the end, however, his father always took him on his lap and hugged him tightly and whispered words of comfort. That was before Conrad turned twelve years old. And there were the customary walks through Old Town Pasadena on Sunday afternoons after church. His mother would disappear into stores now and then, and it was during these walks, in public places that Conrad had often felt the need to run up to his father to hold his hand.

A child, his child, as he had been once, would soon come into the world. His memory was now enlaced with an imagining in which he became his father and upon his lap this child would one day sit. Conrad could almost feel the child in an embrace and smell the milky scent of a baby. The rambunctious rebellion he once felt toward his own father suddenly morphed into a sweet nostalgia he now felt strongly only because from this moment on he himself had been irreversibly altered and forced behind his father's eyes. At once he understood the worry behind each of his father's chastisements yielding to a show of affection. Such was the burden of a father, Conrad chuckled, requiring one to become one to know one.

He jumped up abruptly from the bench and walked away quickly as if fleeing from the next logical step, but a cold gust was there to greet him, blowing over him a shearing melancholy. Bracing himself he pushed against the cold, kept on going, thinking on still. Everything would be fine, he reassured himself; even so he knew that in truth it was probability that governed them all, that a game of chance had been written into the atoms, and that he would sooner accept the dictate of pure mathematical probability than the working of some mysterious laws of karmic apportionment of which he had no hope of understanding and less of ever changing. "It's the Godevil," he whispered to himself as he hurried away from the hospital, from Dia, and from the uncertain outcome of chance, and to his lab where he was sure he could reign over uncertainty.

OVER THE NEXT FEW DAYS DIA COULD NO LONGER BE AROUSED and sank progressively deeper into a state which the doctor refrained from calling a coma, since she could move about on her own, though her movements were limited to the twisting and turning that interrupted the ghastly stillness of her pose.

The doctor came in each morning to check her, and on the seventh day he deemed her no longer capable of infecting others and stable enough to be moved out of isolation. Each morning the doctor would find Conrad there waiting for him, watching him. More pronounced tensing around the doctor's eyes and slight shaking of his head when he reviewed the chart informed Conrad that the prognosis was bad.

"What do you think, doctor?" Conrad asked him on the morning of the seventh day.

The doctor turned to him and looked at him vacantly, as if caught in some immense deliberation in which Conrad's question appeared frivolous.

"It's the most unusual case," the doctor replied after composing himself. "I don't know what to make of it. The specialists are just as stumped. But there have been no changes. The EEG still shows the brain rhythm of one who is in REM sleep. No new onset of fever. The blood tests have normalized. The heart is still strong, her lungs sound good. She is getting enough nutrition for both mother and child through the IV."

The answer silenced him, for he began to think she could still wake up. He became cognizant once again of the sounds of quiet breathing and machines humming and the smell of staleness rising from the bed.

In the corner of the room was a chair to which Conrad has consigned himself each day to keep out of the nurses' way, to make himself inconspicuous. Perhaps to convince himself that there was hope for a different outcome, he kept vigil over Dia. Now he sat in the chair and waited. Presently, a nurse came in and moved around the bed in one swift movement, checking Dia's vitals, and changing the IV fluid bag.

"How are you today, professor?" the nurse asked.

"I'm fine, thank you," Conrad replied.

"That's a beautiful vase of flowers." The nurse looked at a vase of flower in the corner. "What kind of flower are they? I've not seen them before."

"Peruvian lilacs. She likes the color."

"Oh, how sweet," the nurse smiled approvingly.

The nurse's steady hands seemed to perform her tasks as if from rote memory. She nodded at Conrad with sympathy as she left the room, taking stock of his pensiveness, his presence that had become as constant as the chair and that attested to either a great love or a great guilt, she knew not which.

"You don't have to be here all the time," the doctor said as he, too, headed for the door. "Things don't change when you're here. Things don't change when you're away. Isn't it better to concentrate on your work? At least make her part count, make use of the Black Chicken virus."

"Her part? She had no part in it," he said as though to absolve her of all future guilt.

"Oh, you're wrong. Her part is as providential as yours, to be sure. Whether she decided as much as you did to take part in this affair, it's hard to tell. You did it to prove a thesis, she did it with a higher purpose."

"What purpose?"

"For love, of course."

"Then I must save her."

"How?"

"Perhaps her brain needs a boost of energy, a reboot so to speak. If I can infuse it with a surge of energy, it might reawaken."

"How?"

"An engineered rabies virus."

"A rabies virus would naturally infect the nervous system,

I see. Then you will somehow send in packages of energy in these viruses so that they can recharge her brain. Yes?"

"Something like that."

"What about the child?"

"It's a risk. That's why I've been holding off," Conrad said, and his mind suddenly swirled from the realization of what was at stake.

The doctor saw the change in his face and said, "Let's hope we won't need it. Let's hold off for a little while. There is still time."

"But not too many days, I'm afraid."

With that Conrad turned and left, perhaps not wanting to show the depth of his despair.

A FEW DAYS LATER, CONRAD BROUGHT A VIAL OF RABIES VIRUS, which had been engineered to give Dia's brain a boost, the last hope to bring her back. And with his mind laid in order and his emotions checked, he stood next to the hospital bed, leaned over the railing, and looked straight at Dia, whose face was turned away from him. He had been talking to her each day since her admission, finding it natural to overcome his initial skepticism of whether Dia could actually hear what he was saying and also quickly dismissing any notion of melodrama in the act. Somehow he knew that he must talk to her amid the muddle of guilt, and that he must carry on this one–way conversation until the very end, and this time was probably the last. He wanted to say goodbye just in case. He said, "Good morning Dia . . . How was the night? No, it couldn't have been good to be here. It was bad for me too. I thought you'd be happy to hear, Dia. The Black Chicken virus. It really brought every-thing together. Parts from all the other viruses came together so precisely. Who would have thought it could be so quick, so easy? When I first thought of making a new virus, I thought it would take years. It's as if they were already there, made ready for assembling. I'm growing the new virus now. I think it has everything, high infectivity rate, high mortality, three weeks' incubation. I named it the Cain virus, hah . . . There is a slight chance I could be wrong . . . Maybe in a couple of weeks, it will be ready for you know . . . this grand experiment . . . Dmitri and I have worked almost continuously. You remember him. What a character, hey. Hmm, and Weed, you know the government agent, he hasn't come back at all. But I'm sure he'll be back soon. People like him, they'll never leave us alone. We're prepared for him . . . and Abe. Of course you remember him. He came by asking for you before you went to Sa Pa. I'm sure he will start the process . . . to expel me from the university. Don't worry. It doesn't matter. We've accomplished what we need." His head dropped and rested over his arms. Dia stirred, her whole body turned toward him, and her face with eyes closed seemed to want to talk to him. Conrad straightened. With the back of his hand, he caressed her cheek as a perverse freedom rippled through the air and seemed to beckon him but then he abruptly withdrew his hand. "I'm sorry but I had to look through your phone. Dmitri unlocked it. It's the only way to contact your mother to let her know you're here. And thank you for curing me of my fears."

In all his life, he had never spoken to anyone as much as he had spoken during these days to her, to a sleeping body, or to an unconsciousness, while holding onto hope of not talking just to himself, of words escaping through a crack of the unknown to reach her. He counted himself fortunate that this hope was not too big; hope too for the little being inside her was for the moment squeezed in and tempered by a gravitational pull of a brooding reality because otherwise it would explode and incinerate even him in the end when nothingness must be faced. He went back to the chair in the corner.

Then there was a knock on the door.

"Come in," Conrad said.

The door swung along its arch slowly and then stopped. Conrad sitting in the corner could not see the person standing at the entrance, and raised his eyes expectantly. For a while no one entered. A void was there at the entrance and prolonged and demarcated off finally by a gasp of horror followed by a figure in a blue jean, a gray sweater, and a young, cherubic face that had recently weathered hardship with darkened shadows beneath the eyes. A shriek followed the gasp, and then came a rueful sobbing as the figure wafted into the room and halted at the side of the bed. Without knowing what to do, her hands groped one another as if one hand was preventing the other from reaching out to Dia's body, as if fear of the unknown was extinguishing compassion until they seemed to have no choice but to reach up to her own face and wipe away the tears.

"Hi," she said; her voice cracked as she looked at Conrad. "How did this happen?" She looked back at Dia. "Ooooh, Dia baby. Can you hear me? Dia."

"She's in a coma." Conrad rose and came up next to her.

"I'm sorry to be like this. But I can't help it," she said. "I'm Martha. Martha Washington. We used to dance together. You must be the professor. Dia told me about you. She was really into you."

"I remembered seeing you on stage with Dia. You were great together."

"Thanks." She took a tissue from her purse, and dabbed her eyes. "Do you know why she is like this?"

"She was infected with a virus," he said as matter–of–factly. "The doctor thinks she has a peculiar form of encephalitis. Somehow, the infection caused the Reticular Activating System to malfunction." But he saw her confusion, and added, "It's making her lose consciousness."

"Oh . . . Dia. Do you think she'll . . . I do hope she'll recover," she said between sniffles.

They stood side by side now, looking over Dia lying in the bed that had been padded along the sides with cushions. Over her was a white blanket from under which an IV line ran to a bag of fluid hanging from a pole. A wire ran to a monitor hanging from the ceiling, showing her heart rhythm.

"How did you know to find her here?" Conrad said after a while.

"Oh, it was her mother. She called me. She was asking me if I knew you. You know, I told her you're a nice guy. Dia was, like, really into you. But now she got sick. It's really weird, you know, 'cause some of the other girls at the club also got really sick too. And Hucks, do you know who he is? Hucks died." A loud cry started from her throat but was instantly smothered so that she seemed to yelp weakly. "It's really horrible. It's like a really nasty bug has been going around."

"Oh," Conrad uttered and remembered his face being pummeled by Hucks's hard fists, and of the dark alley and the vial of viruses that he had splashed over Hucks. He turned to her and couldn't help fixing his eyes on her. "How did that happen? Please go on."

"No, that was it. It was a bug. 'Cause some of the other girls got sick too, you know."

"You see, I'm a virologist. I study viruses and bugs like the one you mention so it might help me understand more. Perhaps to prevent future outbreaks."

"Do you think you can help Dia?"

"Perhaps. The more information I have, the better I can understand this bug. We never know where it will lead," Conrad lied; what he truly wanted to know was how Hucks had died.

"Yeah, okay. But there is not much to tell."

"You said some other girls, I assume the other dancers, also got the bug. How did this happen?"

"Well. okay. We went to a party at Hucks's house, me and some of the girls from the clubs. There were other men there. And they had drugs and started to do some pretty weird stuff. You know a group thing."

"I understand."

"Yeah, like that's how it got passed around. It was weird 'cause I heard that they never left the house for two days straight. The girls didn't come to work so Hank, he's the owner of the Cabaret, went to Hucks's house and they found them. I heard that Hucks and the older guys died. I guess it was too much for them. That's all I know."

It was the West Nile virus that he'd engineered and unleashed upon Hucks, Conrad felt a relief of revenge. Hucks must have infected the others as well. At least now Hucks would never be a problem again.

"You mentioned that you went to this party too," Conrad said. "May I ask how it is that you didn't get infected?"

"Oh. Like I got spooked. I must have had an omen, you know, so I just left," Marty said calmly. "I'm leaving. I'm going back to Virginia."

"I wish you the best."

"Will you call me sometimes?" she said, and as if mustering all of herself, she reached out and held Dia's hand. "Will you let me know how she's doing? She was the only one who was truly good to me. I see that now. Do you think you can save her?"

"I will try."

Martha gave him a sympathetic smile and left.

Conrad turned back to Dia, stayed silent. After a prolonged while, he finally said, "I love you, Dia."

Then he injected a vial of engineered rabies virus into Dia's carotid artery.

27

No Bad Deed Goes Unrewarded

Early the next day, Conrad went to the office of the university's president. He had been summoned for an urgent but unspecified meeting. Holding the crumbled note in his hand, Conrad mounted the stairs to the stately office while feeling displaced out of his recent routine and irked that he could not go to Dia. Like all other official buildings, this one had been built with a Roman veneer with tall columns and grand arches. Inside, the high dome of the ceiling with its multicolored mural of Wisdom-personified seemed to hover over the heads of all those who entered. He walked down a long corridor to get to the secretary's desk. Everything was familiar to him; he had been here many times before during the lawsuit against Abe F. and the subsequent arbitration meetings. Conrad remembered how he had been filled with a sophomoric 'righteous indignation' and an irrepressible haste for justice to be done the first time he came through this corridor, but in the end he had been stymied, taught a lesson in power play, and muzzled by the very system to which he had looked for justice. Now he approached the secretary with a cool face as he already knew what the meeting would be about; he could already see Abe's taut face feigning concerned sympathy as they announced the case against him. After receiving the summons, Conrad had quickly decided that he would not stand to be condescended upon, that he would take it into his hands and announce his departure in a month's time during which the Cain virus would have been fully grown and harvested and all the necessary work for the grand experiment finished. So with a triumphant radiance on his face, he stood over the secretary.

"Oh, professor," the secretary rose to come around the desk. "They're expecting you. Please come in." She led him to a big double door and let him in.

Inside the office which seemed as expansive as his entire laboratory, book shelves covered one wall, and a window made up the entire rear wall of the room. The president of the university sat behind a shiny wooden desk. Her eyes looked on with amusement, and her crisp, tailored suit seemed stiff and mechanical as if it were an exoskeleton supporting not only her innards but her head with its neat curls. As the first black female president, she had made history, and the look of pride seemed permanently etched on her face. The sight of the room surprised Conrad because there were only two people waiting for him, the president and a complete stranger, an old man with a white fringe around his bald pate and a face distorted by a morbid, growling smirk.

"Professor, it's a pleasure to meet you again." The president rose and extended her hand.

"Hello Madame President," Conrad said coldly as he shook hand.

"This is Mr. Rick V.," the president said and indicated the man.

Rick V. rose and extended his hand to Conrad; he said, "Good morning."

The situation was not what Conrad expected, and he wanted to blurt out his resignation, and then storm out to get the full pleasure of it, but something had changed, so he stayed quiet and waited.

"Thank you for coming this morning," the president began officially. "A situation has developed and we appreciate your cooperation first in being so prompt with this meeting and second for your assistance in any future development. We hope we can count on your expertise."

"What's this about?" Conrad said, trying hard to suppress the desire for an outburst.

"If I may," Rick said. "I'm from the Home and Country Department and we believe there is terrorist plot afoot to harm innocent Americans. I believe you have met Agent Weed who has been conducting an investigation into a terrorist situation. Agent Weed was following a lead."

As he heard the mention of Weed, Conrad shifted uncomfortably his weight in the chair and averted his eyes.

Rick went on, "So Agent Weed was acting on information provided to him by Abe F. who was the Chairman of the Department of Immunology and Microbiology. Your department to be more precise. Can you confirm that you met agent Weed?"

As though suddenly shaken out of silence, Conrad stirred and said, "Well, yes..ah..ah. Yes, you mean the Texan man. He did come by the lab. What did he say?"

"That he was. A Texan. He never got around to filing a report."

"Oh," Conrad uttered. He leaned forward. "So what do you need from me? Why don't just ask him to complete a report?"

"Huh, huh," Rick chuckled. "We're a very powerful governmental agency but I'm afraid we can't resurrect the dead. Agent Weed died a few days ago. The circumstances were questionable and irregular as far as I can see."

"Oh," Conrad uttered again and forced himself to say, "I'm . . . I'm sorry for your loss."

"Thank you," Rick said. "Agent Weed was sometimes too jovial, at times even bumbling, but he was my front man. Anyhow as I said the circumstances surrounding the death were irregular. There were other deaths as well. A well known Hollywood talent agent by the name of Joel S. and of course Abe F., your chairman, a certain Mr. Hucks of dubious reputation, and several other questionable characters whom I won't mention. They were apparently involved an intoxicated orgy."

"Did you say Abe died? Did you say orgy?" Conrad asked. His eyes were wide open and he starred at Rick and then noticed how Rick seemed to not so much speak but growl with only the left side of his lips opening and closing.

"Yes, I did. They were discovered nude, intoxicated, and dead," Rick said coldly. "Frankly this is an embarrassment for the Home and Country Department and for the government in general. Of course, this news will never see the light of day. You can imagine the outrage if the public ever finds out that the government, Hollywood, and a common thug were in bed together. Well, they'll never know. We have made sure of that. What concerned us is that there are a couple of survivors of this orgy who have gotten very sick. It seems to be a biological agent of some sort. We want to make sure that this is not a case of biological terrorism and that it was a natural coincidence. A natural outbreak of some sort. Can we count on your assistance?"

"Why do you think it's terrorism?" Conrad said.

"There was also another outbreak at a police station not too far away. I reserve judgment until proven otherwise. It could be a coincidence. That's why we need your expertise."

"That's incredible. Abe is dead, along with your agent Weed." As Conrad tried hard to suppress his glee, in his mind the steps of Hucks' infection spreading to the others during the orgy were clear enough. Martha Washington had told him about the orgy but he had no idea that Weed and Abe were also involved. He said, "What do you want me to do?"

"We'd like you to study the specimens, find out exactly what it is. We need to be certain that it's not an artificial biological agent. A terrorism event."

"Why me? There are others in the department who can study this just as well." Conrad feigned indifference, but he counted his luck that he had been chosen to study his very own creation.

"Though your work has declined over the last couple of years, the president has advised that you are still the best in the department. And professor, we always reward our friends. Since the chairman position is now open, it's yours if you're cooperative. Isn't that right, Madame President?"

The president nodded.

"Well, my small laboratory is very busy at the moment," Conrad said. "It's at full capacity. If I'm to take on more work, I'm going to need a lot more funding."

"Money is no object. The Home and Country Department has a direct line to the Central Bank. You will receive immediate funding. And you can take over Abe's laboratory, effective immediately," Rick said.

"I'll do my best," Conrad said coolly.

"One last thing," Rick growled approvingly. "Whatever you should find will have to remain strictly confidential. You will not publish any of it. Consider it a State Secret."

"Oh, of course," Conrad replied, feeling pleased that his engineered virus would be a secret forever and that he could misdirect them as he pleased, knowing full well that none of this would matter if he were to release the Cain virus.

Then they all stood and shook hands. Conrad left hurriedly,

running back to Dia, and in his mind he was already speaking to her, telling her the news and this strange machination that must be the working of the Godevil.

23

Of Godevil, of Man

The machination of the Godevil, Conrad could not tell Dia.

That Dia's being was sinking deeper into something unalterable each second she remained in her condition, which Conrad could only witness, at first dominated his mind, then captured him wholly, and to his amazement rendered him completely helpless. It delivered him wholly altered in mind and spirit to a bleak place so as to become a beholder of all things dying. But each second being a unit of time was only artificial and in this bleak place could be divisible into a multitude of smaller units approaching an infinity in which Conrad could behold moments of death similarly approaching an uncountable number. So each day as he stood over her, what he beheld was multiplied by an infinitude of different moments, as if each was endured by a different person. Each bodily movement that Dia made now and then reawakened a hope that was echoed somewhere very far away by cries of newborn, joyous sounds of parents, and a bright and anxious future, a hope that became a moment of extinguishing just as instantly as the stillness of her body inevitably followed. A wretched sorrow wrecked him and left him fighting to suppress an outburst of sobs. And despite the bouquets of Peruvian lilies next to the bed, a bleakness fell over the hospital room that seemed to hold Conrad captive, where at most he could only take a few paces and where he spent more and more time as if waiting for that unspeakable moment.

Two nurses had been tending to Dia's needs. The morning nurse was stout and performed her tasks heavily while breathing loudly; the night nurse walked lightly while being meticulous. They gave Dia a sponge bath every other day and instructed Conrad to turn Dia from side to side if she didn't move by herself, to prevent decubitus ulceration. A special airbed had been brought in after the first week. And changing the IV fluid bag, taking vitals, emptying her urine, feeding her through a tube that ran through her nose to her stomach, adjusting the various electrodes and attachments to Dia's body, had become routine. The nurses seemed to waltz through the room, busying their hands, and afterward leaving behind only pity in the air already dense with such. Then there were mentions from the good doctor, even only in passing, of the need to place a gastric tube for better feeding, of a possibility for a tracheostomy tube if her breathing should ever deteriorate, and of a consideration for a nursing home, or even a hospice. But above all, the flimsiest probability of the child surviving to full term in a comatose mother defied calculation, being akin to a miracle, and as such the good doctor counseled Conrad on being realistic and objective given his scientific background.

Dia's body, having gained fluid and fat and lost the sharp edge of her chin struck Conrad with a visceral burning he'd never before felt as if he was given new sight. Her beauty, delineated in her lines and curves, had been lost some days ago and now remained only in his memory. A human beauty that was imbued with consciousness embodied in its nature tragedy, and as he stood over her, he could see the missed opportunities that such beauty seemed to promise, and the regrets as the days wore on, leaving only bitterness. He went back to his chair in the corner, dropped into it, and in doing so descended to the very bottom. He looked at his watch to see that the night was ripe. His mind reeled in a depressive fatigue mixed with a paradoxical vigil that it seemed to break away from his control and parade in scenes that he did not want to see, like a vaudeville show with deformed freaks being forced on stage.

He saw the Cain virus, all the places where it would spread and all the different people it would infect. It would certain go back to Sa Pa like a transformed prodigal son only to decimate the villagers, to India and China with their teeming masses, and to old Europe. Leaning his head back against the wall, Conrad closed his eyes. Mental fatigue tightened around his remaining awareness as he lost himself farther into something approaching a nightmare. Death to them all had been his pledge, to destroy that which the Godevil had parodied into life and in doing so to prove his will. In the fuzziness of the reverie and with his mind transmigrating as a ghostly harbinger, circling the globe, whether in the slumps of Calcutta, the high–rises of Shanghai, or the plains of Russia, the hospital room was replicated again and again with the same air dense of pity, the whiff of decay, the bleakness, the same body, the same dying multiplied by a multitude of humanity. That human death was no horror but a process, just as Cain the virus a process, a volcano or an asteroid also a process, became the logic of destruction. But is this true?

Now in the chair still drifting farther into somnolence and following the Cain virus on its journey, he turned on his side, crossed his arms, and bent his head, bounding up within his chest a cocoon from which escaped a distorted, paroxysmal cry of pain and grief. Pain that he had ignored up to now must be suffered. All was lost, she was gone forever, he seemed to submit. Intense pain at the edge of an expanding fire of grief, tearing him up and numbing as it percolated outward, was perceived mostly acutely by his mind trapped in a sort of transition from the concrete world to something unknown. Grief accompanies truth, he yielded to it. Bounded up within all the atoms in the universe, truth simply is. The conundrum remained unbreakable, unsolvable, and reduced his logic and Cain itself to frivolousness, for his grief merely became theirs. Then the fire of grief was scorched with anger, and he would not relent, he must defy it for having taken her. Swiftly returning to his journey to bring ruin to the masses of humanity and thus to the Godevil, he diluted his pain with the moans of the sick and the grieving that were too horrendous to bear, but amid the sea of devastation a meek gargling somehow found a way as it always had since time immemorial and came through as a voice. The voice looped simultaneously from outside and inside of his being, magnifying the horror the virus would wreak on the world and the one true horror of his own realization that any man was capable of such. Then the gargling voice came to him loudly, as though disguised because its true nature was too hallowed for his ears: Sleep and know.

Conrad fell asleep and dreamed of Cain.

On the third night, once the last light vanished from over the wheat stalks, Cain called out, 'Come forth Bearer of Light, Giver of Knowledge, Punisher of Evil.'

Quickening with a terrifying suddenness, a blackest grain of space in front of him enveloped him in a cocoon while at the same time as fierce flaming eyes blinded him. Cain tried to squeeze his eyes shut but found he had no eyes, instead he was now as he had been the night before, a floating awareness. And inside his being fear ignited as fiercely as the flaming eyes, threatening to incinerate him. But he held steady and was reassured that he would not be destroyed as he heard the voice.

'What doth thou seek?'

'Give me knowledge. Knowledge of the Lord God's purpose. Why hath he made heaven and earth, and Adam and Eve?'

'That I hath entered a pact not to reveal,' the voice said solemnly. 'I will show thee how the cosmos was made, and past and future that thou might find the Lord's purpose for thyself.'

The flaming eyes then were emulsified into speckles of shining dust, which were blown by an invisible wind and spread out in all directions through which Cain moved. Distant clouds of swirling dust, as he came near, sparkled with innumerable lights. As he came nearer still, he was astounded that they were but stars, the same as his beloved stars that he had gazed upon and charted. Closer still, he saw them as giant balls of flames.

'Is that thy home? The burning flames?' Cain asked.

'Yea and elsewhere,' the voice said. 'They are as thy sun. They are everywhere throughout the cosmos. They give light and warmth and life on the outward, and yet inside them are infernos where the wicked shall burn in boiling waste. Behold, the cosmos were made according to unalterable laws. And there is light but also darkness. And darkness shall exist, for without darkness there is no light. Behold the infinity of the cosmos and yet thou, Cain, exist and thou art in it and yet apart from it.'

Everywhere his curiosity beckoned him he could go with the ease of his thoughts. Wondrous objects of myriad different colors, some too bright and too blinding, others the blackest of all, spinning worlds around stars, and swirling dust expanding into vastness, Cain saw all as he traveled.

Then arose a blue sphere. An irresistible curiosity drew him closer, he hurried there. He saw that it was unlike any other worlds, for on its dark side there were lights webbing over the surface.

'Come hither. See thy descendants.'

'My descendants,' Cain cried out with joy and swooped down onto its surface. Though plants of various kinds and rivers and mountains looked familiar enough, there were also enormous structures with sharp spikes jutting into the sky and the air had an acrid odor. From a tower high above the doleful peals of bells rang across the land. 'To what place hast thou brought me?'

'Tis the earth, thy home in the future. Behold the cathedrals thy descendants have built.'

'For what purpose?'

'To worship the Lord God.'

'Ah, then all is good.'

'Behold their industry and cunning,' the voice said and took Cain whizzing through time and space to see all the people of the world.

Cain saw roads spreading across the land, factories rising from the earth, and cities sprawling toward the rivers. At night everything was lit up magnificently.

'Ah then all is good. Then 'tis is the purpose of the Lord God,' Cain said. Joy and pride overcame him as he gazed upon the surface of the earth his descendants had conquered. Then a melody sang sweetly and softly as though an angel was praising the glory of the Lord God, and stirred his soul. 'What wondrous sound?'

'Your descendants. Tis their music.'

'Music. As sweet as when the angels sang.'

'But more sublime. Thus the angels weep.'

Suddenly, Cain saw a flash of light in front of him and immediately heard a terrible boom louder than thunder, and many more flashes and booms followed and buildings collapsed.

'What doth happen?' Cain yelled in horror.

'Come thither and see for thyself.'

Now amid the ruins, Cain saw people dying, infants crying, and survivors beseeching a silent God.

'Come thither. There is more to see.'

Over a field Cain saw two groups of men shouting and rushing toward each other. He watched with amazement as they held contraptions that could kill at a thousand paces. Many fell and bled. And when they were at arm's length they stabbed and hacked one another with knives. And the blood saturated the air and soaked the earth.

'Oh, tell what it is?' Cain yelled with all his might.

'Tis called war. Deceived, thy descendants fight and kill for trinkets and false idols.'

'To what purpose?' Cain wanted to run between them, to put his hands on them and tell them that as brothers they ought to love each other. But the killing continued.

'There is more to see.'

All was dark now, but a low chorus of human moaning pervaded the air in which an awful stench thickened.

'Tis a place for rotting corpses?' Cain asked.

'Nay, tis a slum, a dwelling place for thy descendants, deceived and stripped bare.'

Now Cain saw as clearly as under a scorching sun broken men and women huddling in huts made of tin and mud, with sewage running along them, and toddlers tumbling barefoot through the sewage. Then he saw another mass of the suffering horde and yet another all over earth as his mind wanted to see more and more, fighting himself to confirm and at the same time repudiate certainty. His thoughts transported him through space and time until Cain howled toward heaven, 'How my descendants suffer.' And the howl sent wingbeats fluttering noisily across the wheat field. Still crying, Cain jumped up only to see the sun rising over the horizon.

Cain pushed himself up and looked, through tear–filled eyes, across the vast wheat field that would soon be ready for harvest. The early sunlight gleamed red over the wheat stalks heavy with kernels. Had it been but a dream? No, he answered himself; he'd witnessed a future truth of which he was as certain as the forbidden fruit and Garden of Eden and the voice of the Lord God from the sky. Almost unconsciously now, into the wheat field his legs wandered, while inside him the killing and suffering hordes amplified his anguish, and from his soul waves of excruciating pain pulsated outward, benumbing his flesh. He collapsed on the ground, moaning weakly, with his tears dropping onto the wheat.

What to do? From the friction of his unflappable will intervening between his soul and his flesh, an idea escaped obliquely like a flint, and Cain rose to the baas of the sheep from the far side of the hill. To it he ran as the idea became clear and more solid and finally undeniable, for it was but a simple calculation.

Cain saw his brother herding the sheep, leading them toward dawn. The morning fragrance of the grass rose with the light, and the moisture from the morning dew wet his toes.

'Abel, my beloved brother,' Cain called out. His voice crackled hoarsely.

'Cain, my brother. What brought thou at early dawn?' Abel said and rushed to embrace his brother.

'Abel, my beloved brother,' Cain said as he embraced Abel. He spoke softly next Abel's ear, 'I saw a terrible future. Years hence our descendants, how they suffered, Brother.'

'Suffer how?'

'Deceived and stripped bare. Hungry and sick. Worse than the animals to be slaughtered,' Cain said breathlessly. 'At least thou love thy sheep.'

'The earth is plentiful. How do they go hungry? Worry not, my brother, the Lord God shall provide,' Abel said as he pounded his staff on the ground and looked after his flock, which continued to move toward the early sun.

'Tis the truth, my brother. Thou must believe and do as I ask, as I shall do.' Cain's voice suddenly became stern, a finality having been concluded beyond all questioning as to what he must now do.

'What dost thou ask of me?' Abel asked.

'Hath I not loved thou and cared for thou all thy life?'

'Yea, brother. Thou art kind.'

'Hast I not shown thee the ways of rearing and herding sheep be that tis easier to earn a livelihood as a shepherd than a farmer? Twas my right to choose as first born and yet I let thou be a shepherd and go the easy way.'

'Yea, brother, thou art wise and generous.'

'Hath I not let thee take Zillah as thy wife though she is fairer and more lovely, though twas my right to choose as first born.'

'Yea, brother. Thou art noble.'

'Hath I not let thee shine before the Lord God with thy offering of three sheep? I could offer my yield of fruits and wheat and nuts, indeed too much abundance for a hundred men to carry, a hundred times more than all thou have. Instead I offered but one basket and suffered the Lord God's ill favor.'

'Yea, brother. Thou art love.'

'Then do as I bid thee. Swear onto me that never shall thou and Zillah bear children as forever will I and Adah shall do the same.'

'The Lord God hath commanded us to go forth and multiply.'

'To no purpose but killing and suffering, my beloved brother. Thou must obey me. Future was made certain when Adam partook the forbidden fruit.'

'Nay, Brother. Thou must not disobey the Lord

God as Father hath done,' Abel said as sincerely as the round eyes on his youthful face.

'Thou must heed me, Brother. I have seen how deceived, they suffer and kill.'

'Tis a dream, brother. A dream.'

Turning away from the Abel, upon whose youthful face innocence masked incomprehension, Cain fell upon his knees. His arms, as he suddenly brought them before his eyes, appeared to him not as the muscles of a man but as voluble vines woven into useful appendages extending into something resembling not fingers but powerful roots and reminded him of the care and the singularity of purpose with which he had tended to the plants. Now he shoved his hands into the dirt as though trying to bury his sorrow deep into the earth and perhaps to gain strength for what he must do. An ounce of blood today thus prevents an ocean of blood tomorrow, Cain felt his will strong and vigorous, a will that was bolstered by sorrow and magnified by love. Though with his hands in the earth, he gathered no comfort.

'Beloved brother. Tis a dream that will pass,' Abel said as he stood behind Cain and put his hand on his shoulder. Then after a moment, Abel said, 'Beloved brother, I must tend to my flock. I must take leave of thee.'

Cain heard his brother's staff thudding on the ground as Abel moved after his flock.

'Abel. Of them all, I love thee the most,' Cain uttered.

'Yea. And I thee,' Abel answered.

Cain suddenly remembered the red eyes' warning,

'Therefore taketh care to protect thy head at all time, or else thy mortal life itself is in danger.'

Then the act came, too fast. Cain picked up the stone before him and sprung up and struck. Blood flowed from Abel's head as his innocent eyes gazed at Cain, questioning. Cain sat down next to his brother, clasped his hand, and said, 'Enter heaven and leave behind all earthly sorrows. Know that I love thee more than life.' Cain saw in Abel's eyes a comprehension of that awful knowledge as he breathed his last. That love, known without knowing hate and despair, shined in a false light now came clear to Cain so that his love for Abel, made glorious and vast by his hate for their fateful future and despair for their suffering, burst from his chest and transformed his will. Never could he imagine the vastness of that love that was many times more than his heart could now bear. He looked to the sky and howled. Never could he now strike down Adam and Eve, and Zillah and Adah, and at last himself to put an end that fateful, hate–filled future.

He kneeled and wept until Abel's body grew cold. Then he wandered aimlessly, following an idea, chasing the end of himself.

'Where is Abel thy brother?' the voice from behind the sun said.

'I know where he lies. Am I not my brother's keeper?' Cain answered.

'What hast thou done? The voice of thy brother's blood cried onto me from the ground.'

'I hast done what I thought must be done. Not of hate but of love,' Cain said, and knelt before the sun

and dropped his head low. 'Do away with me. My suffering is greater than I can bear.'

'The voice behind the sun said. 'I see thy soul and
will. Thy soul is still pure from love suffered. The
Bearer of Light shall not strike thee. Rise and go east.
And build a city and multiply.'

'How can I build a city? It is beyond my strength.'

'Have faith, for faith is but love exalted."

'Praise to thee, Lord. But what of them? What do
they think of me?'

'Fear not. Let them burn the olive trees, erect tall
walls, claim righteousness and covenant where there
is none. Let them bleed for silver. But for thee, matter
shall yield their secrets, for thy descendants truth
shall shed its light. Upon thee I set a mark. Only thou
shall know my purpose. And thy descendants who-
ever bear the mark of Cain shall know of me.'

THE HALLOWED VOICE RANG DISTORTEDLY IN HIS EARS AS
grief and anguish peaked. Who are you? Are you the Godevil?
Please return her to me, Conrad pleaded. Sharp through his
ears, a shriek chastised him and shook him from his dream
state. He jumped up to the monitors beeping and nurses rushing about the room. With utter amazement, he stole upon the
bed and heard the gargling noises from Dia's throat as she
yanked the feeding tube from her nose and the IV line from
her arm. Her eyes glared wildly, and her arms pushed off the
nurses and their reassuring words.

"Dia. Darling, it's me," Conrad said to her.

Her eyes turned quickly to him, catching his voice.

A Great Good

Three years had passed since Diaphany awakened from the coma, and on this particular day, they were at the beach, the very spot where they had encountered each other for the first time. Sunlight began at the edge of space and descended toward earth as if to clarify the still air, and the ripples of the ocean waves spoke of the vast oceans being cradled within the folds of the earth and not the tempestuous rivalry between water and land.

"You're great because you're good."

Diaphany had said that to Conrad, something she had remembered from a book. "Of course you could make the Cain virus. Only you could. It destroys but you're good. And that's the paradox," she had said to him at different times since then, when he told her the true design of his quest.

"Ha, yes, you don't say," Conrad said as he had often said before. Still he didn't know if it had been the engineered rabies virus that had brought Diaphany back to him or if her resurrection had been granted by the Godevil. On the soft, warm sand, he lay at her feet, and the tips of his fingers explored her shapely feet, that had left imprints on the sand three years ago and led him to her.

"How does it feel to have such power in your hand?" Dia said.

"Odd. I'm just a man and if I choose to unleash the Cain virus, even the King of the World couldn't escape."

"Yes, the incredible power in the hand of one."

On this beautiful summer day with its calm, they had returned to this stretch of beach to mark the end of one strange journey and to begin the next. They had decided to move to Sa Pa. The decision came casually enough, out of a talk that they couldn't remember afterward who had started the whole thing, a reply to a why–not. When examined closely in the following days, the decision appeared as if it had been the result of a great and meticulous deliberation, a perfect antidote that at the moment of its realization shed light on their increasingly comfortable existence. So they sold all their possessions, including the house, and with much sadness the old Mustang, and Conrad had resigned the chairmanship of the department. They had bid farewell to Dmitri who had hugged them both. Truheckler had sobbed sweetly. And Minh had bellowed an ironic, joyous laugh and offered to use his contacts to arrange all their papers. The decision however seemed as a matter of course to the doctor to whom everything that was touched would be forever changed.

What will we do when we get there? A question had no doubt been simultaneously conceived of, when they had stopped amid packing and raised their eyes toward each other, but inevitably between them a smile blossomed, reassuring them that whatever awaited them in Sa Pa would be exactly what they needed. An aura of a rustic pilgrimage that had been growing in both of them as the day approached seemed to become as real as the mountains, the rice paddies yellowing under the summer sun, and the Black Chicken that lived there.

"You don't regret giving up your career?" Diaphany said after a while.

"I'll go wherever you lead me. We'll go and live in the mountains, where we can't understand their languages but only other things."

Then childish giggles came from behind him as his son came running from the water's edge and jumped on his back and tugged on his hair. The boy jumped up and down on his back as though riding a horse. Conrad laughed too.

With the child heavy on his shoulder, he leaned down to kiss Dia's feet, while looking up at the old scars on her thigh entwining seamlessly with stretch marks from the pregnancy into an arabesque of life and the unknown, outside of which all was empty.

THE END